# THE

# PAINTER

*Silver Linings Mysteries Book 4*

*A Regency Romance*

# by Mary Kingswood

Published by Sutors Publishing

Copyright © 2020 Mary Kingswood

Cover design by: Shayne Rutherford of Darkmoon Graphics



Version 3

Author's note:

this book is written using historic British terminology, so *saloon* instead of *salon*, *chaperon* instead of *chaperone* and so on. I follow Jane Austen's example and refer to a group of sisters as the Miss Wintertons.

# The Painter: Silver Linings Mysteries Book 4

**About this book:** *The sinking of the* Brig Minerva *results in many deaths, while for others, the future is suddenly brighter. But it's not always easy to leave the past behind…*

*Felicia Oakes is the illegitimate daughter of… well, someone or other. A pirate, perhaps, or a spy, or a royal prince… who knows? Her vivid imagination conjures a myriad possibilities, all more exciting than her position as governess to two motherless children. But when their father is drowned aboard the* Brig Minerva, *Felicia must take them to their new guardian in the North of England, where her life is about to be turned upside down.*

*The Earl of Finlassan has turned his back on the world to pursue his art, and the prospective guardianship of two young girls horrifies him. He soon finds that it's not his wards who unsettle his life, it's their governess, who is irritatingly impertinent with a distractingly mischievous smile. Gradually he finds himself drawn out of seclusion by his new muse. But when danger strikes, they will have to uncover the past before they can look to the future.*

*This is a complete story with a HEA. Book 4 of a 6 book series. A traditional Regency romance, drawing room rather than bedroom.*

**Isn't that what's-his-name?** Regular readers will know that characters from previous books occasionally pop up. None actually appear in this one, but there are mentions of Sir James and Lady Godney, from *The Widow*, and the Narfields, from *The Apothecary*. There is also a mention of one who dates right back to *The Daughters of Allamont Hall*. The Earl of Strathmorran lives in Scotland, at Glenbrindle Castle in the mythical county of Morranshire. His heir, Lord Kilbraith, a cousin to the Allamont sisters, made a romantic appearance in *Dulcie*, and turned up again in *Lord Humphrey*. Congratulations to anyone who spotted this reference.

# The Painter: Silver Linings Mysteries Book 4

**About the Silver Linings Mysteries series***:* John Milton coined the phrase 'silver lining' in *Comus: A Mask Presented at Ludlow Castle,* 1634

> *Was I deceived, or did a sable cloud*
>
> *Turn forth her silver lining on the night?*
>
> *I did not err; there does a sable cloud*
>
> *Turn forth her silver lining on the night,*
>
> *And casts a gleam over this tufted grove.*

Ever since then, the term *'silver lining'* has become synonymous with the unexpected benefits arising from disaster. The sinking of the *Brig Minerva* results in many deaths, but for others, the future is suddenly brighter. But it's not always easy to leave the past behind...

**Book 0: The Clerk:** the sinking of the *Minerva* offers a young man a new life *(a novella, free to mailing list subscribers).*

**Book 1: The Widow:** the wife of the *Minerva's* captain is free from his cruelty, but can she learn to trust again?

**Book 2: The Lacemaker:** three sisters inherit a country cottage, but the locals are surprisingly interested in them.

**Book 3: The Apothecary:** a long-forgotten suitor returns, now a rich man, but is he all he seems?

**Book 4: The Painter:** two children are left to the care of a reclusive man.

**Book 5: The Orphan:** a wilful heiress is determined to choose a notorious rake as her guardian.

**Book 6: The Duke:** the heir to the dukedom is reluctant to step into his dead brother's shoes and accept his arranged marriage.

Want to be the first to hear about new releases? Sign up for my mailing list at marykingswood.co.uk.

# Table of Contents

# The Painter: Silver Linings Mysteries Book 4

# The Warborough Family

Hi-res version available at marykingswood.co.uk.

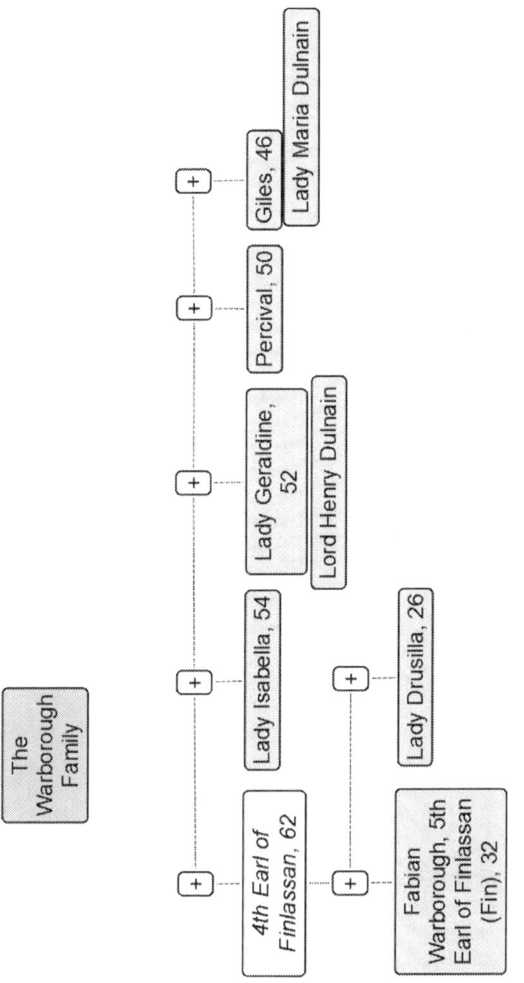

# The Buckley and Dulnain Families

Hi-res version available at marykingswood.co.uk.

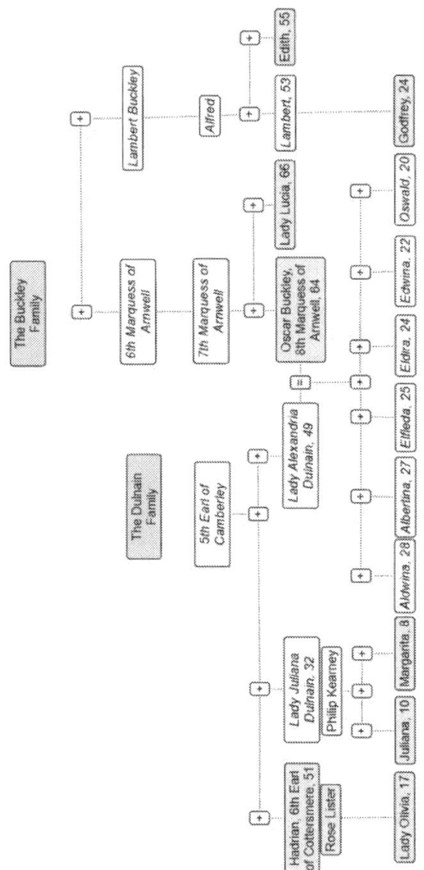

# Prologue: Miss Latimer's Academy

FOUR YEARS EARLIER

Felicia gazed at her work with a critical eye. The faces… yes, she thought she had contrived them rather well, all things considered. And the trees… she had always been good at trees and flowers and curvaceous smears of colour. But the cottages! How was it that simple straight lines gave her so much trouble? The honeysuckle growing around the door was as realistic as any she had drawn, but the poor cottage itself looked as if a puff of wind would see it off. The walls were crooked, the window frames askew and the chimney pots tilting. The smoke— yes, the smoke needed something.

She reached for a stick of the palest grey, and blended it into the drifting cloud emerging from the chimney. Then some darker grey, a little white, and just a touch of black, smudging the colours together with her thumb so that they mingled and merged. Another stroke of white just there… Smoke and clouds were so satisfactory with pastels. It was hard to go wrong, in truth. But walls…

There was no sound, but she became aware of someone behind her. Miss Gertrude, of course. No one else had quite such an uncanny ability to sneak up noiselessly behind a person. No, that was unfair, for she had no intention of sneaking. It was just her way.

Felicia reached for a cloth to wipe her hands, and turned with a smile. "Miss Gertrude? Have you an errand for me?"

"You're wanted in the Principal's room."

"At once? Then I shall wash the dust off my hands."

"Nasty, messy stuff, those pastel sticks," Miss Gertrude said with a sniff. "I can't see why you don't stick to watercolours like a proper lady."

"Perhaps because I am not a proper lady," Felicia said, as she poured water from the ewer into a basin. "I am only… oh, a pirate's daughter, I think, abandoned at port in my cradle when he had to escape the Excise men in rather a hurry. He will come back for me one day. My mother was a Persian princess he captured, whose father offered a fortune for her safe return, but my father had fallen in love with her and married her by then. I expect she died of grief when I was left behind. There! I am a trifle cleaner, I believe."

"You and your stories," Miss Gertrude said sourly, turning to stalk away. "Pirates and Persian princesses! Ha!"

Felicia chuckled at her receding back, and ran lightly after her, down a floor to the main teaching rooms. The Latimer Academy for Young Ladies was a respected institution, where girls from twelve to eighteen could learn the feminine arts of French or Italian, music and singing, the management of household accounts, sewing, dancing and deportment, and a little history and knowledge of the world as an aid to conversation, but not so much as to deter potential husbands. Heaven forfend that they should be turned into blue-stockings! After which, they would be fired off into society and expected to make good, or at least respectable, marriages and bring honour upon their families. Felicia sincerely pitied them.

On the ground floor was the dancing room, where the rather fraught dancing master was attempting to instil gracefulness into a small group who seemed determined to bump into each other and then collapse into giggles, while Miss Mason banged away determinedly on the pianoforte. Felicia smiled, and executed a few steps of the cotillion as she passed through the hall in Miss Gertrude's wake, her skirts flaring around her as she twirled. Oh, to dance and lose herself in the music! It was a long, long ten days until the next assembly, and she had her gown and hair ornaments already planned. And this time, she was determined, Jane would dance every set and enjoy herself. She was coming along so well, and in another few months, her shyness would be almost unnoticeable in company.

Across the hall were the domestic offices, where Miss Latimer had her study. Unusually, she was not seated at her desk when Felicia entered. Instead, she stood at the window gazing out into Bugle Street, one of Southampton's most salubrious thoroughfares.

"Miss Oakes is here, sister," Miss Gertrude said. She never called Felicia anything else, conveying her distaste for her by means of rigid formality.

"Ah, Felicia. Do sit down." Miss Latimer settled into her seat behind the desk and Miss Gertrude took up her usual position, standing a little behind her sister, hands clasped before her, an expression of displeasure on her face, as if she had trodden in something unsavoury. The two sisters were as unlike as could be, Miss Latimer as round and soft as a floured dumpling, and Miss Gertrude as thin and sharp as a spear.

Felicia took the chair in front of the desk, and waited expectantly.

"I have had…" Miss Latimer began, then halted with uncharacteristic hesitancy.

"Yes?" Felicia said.

"A letter," Miss Latimer went on, more strongly, picking up a paper that lay on the desk. "A proposal, if you like. A gentleman wishes to engage a governess for his two daughters."

"A *governess!*" Felicia burst out. "I am hardly qualified—" A shiver passed down her spine, but whether of fear or anticipation was more than she could determine. A governess lived the most miserable life on earth, neither gentry nor servant but abused by all, and yet… to leave Southampton, perhaps, and see a little of the world beyond… that would be something!

"Hear me out," Miss Latimer said. "It is… a most unusual case. He is a married man, but he took a mistress who gave him two children, and he seems to have cared greatly for them. They have been well provided for, at all events. The mistress has recently died, and now he wishes to engage a governess for his natural daughters. And here is the interesting part, Felicia. He insists that the governess must be an artist, and her primary role is to nurture the creative talents of the children. His mistress was a talented painter, it seems, and he hopes to see that ability transferred to her offspring. You can see why our thoughts turned at once to you."

"Does he know that I am only eighteen?"

"Oh yes, and that does not weigh with him. He believes you may be suitable, despite your youth."

"But I have neither the aptitude nor the desire to be a governess. I am perfectly content here with you until I reach my majority, and I had always supposed you to be satisfied with my accomplishments here."

"Oh, indeed! Very satisfied, dear Felicia! We do not wish you to leave, no, no, no! Not in the least. But... there is just the tiniest problem. Mr and Mrs Pollard."

"Have they complained about the instruction I provide Jane? Her drawing is coming on apace, and I still have hopes of improvement in watercolours, too."

"It is not that," Miss Latimer said hastily. "It is... oh, Felicia, you are too friendly with Jane, and that is the truth of the matter."

"Who could not be friendly towards her, so sweet as she is!" Felicia said with some heat. "She is the most charming girl."

"Of course," Miss Latimer said. "No one doubts your sincerity or your good intentions, and Jane has come on tremendously under your tutelage, as I have tried to explain to Mr and Mrs Pollard. But they have heard rumours of your attendance at the assemblies, and they are concerned. Jane was seen dancing with an *apprentice*. Mrs Pollard is rather upset."

"He was a ship owner's clerk, and perfectly respectable," Felicia said sharply. "He was even shyer than Jane, and it had taken him half the evening to gather his courage sufficiently to ask for an introduction. You would hardly have wished her to snub him. Why, he would have been crushed! And it was so good for her, since she had to exert herself to make all the conversation."

"But hardly a suitable person for her to be acquainted with," Miss Gertrude said reprovingly.

"Miss Mason was chaperoning us, and she made no objection," Felicia retorted. "Besides, if Jane must dance only with persons her mother regards as suitable, she will not dance at all. It is better for her to overcome her shyness here in our quiet provincial backwater than in the full glare of the London season, and that strategy was agreed with the Pollards from the outset."

"Oh yes, but you are so lively and so *pretty*, Felicia, that Jane cannot show to advantage. And… and…" Miss Latimer hung her head shamefacedly, then, with a long intake of breath, she went on, "There is your lack of *connections*."

"You mean that I am a bastard and an orphan?" she said mischievously, setting Miss Latimer twittering in distress. Felicia was amused, for she had long since ceased to regard her ancestry with dismay. "The Pollards may be only an inch away from trade, but they are more respectable than I am, certainly."

"They are very wealthy, and Mrs Pollard, at least, has some excellent connections. They have *ambitions* for Jane. In fact, it is their cherished hope that she might make an impression on the Marquess of Beckhampton when she is out."

"Beckhampton? Wait, is that the heir to the Duke of Falconbury? That will never fly! I cannot see retiring little Jane ever wanting to marry a duke, even supposing she should meet him."

"What she wants is neither here nor there," Miss Gertrude said abruptly. "It's for her parents to say whom she marries, a great heiress like her, and they are acquainted with the duke, so it's perfectly possible, whatever you may say about it, Miss Oakes."

"Well, if she likes him and he is worthy of her, I wish them both joy, I am sure," Felicia said. "But what is that to do with me? You want me to give up accompanying Jane to the assemblies, I gather."

Miss Latimer flushed bright red. "I rather fear it is more complicated than that, my dear. Mr and Mrs Pollard are hinting that they will remove Jane from our care, and as you know—"

"Yes, yes, all the extras, and it is so good for your reputation."

"That is why this proposal from Mr Kearney is so fortuitous. For him, your… your lack of connections is no obstacle, but a positive benefit."

"Oh certainly," Felicia cried, "for who better to educate two bastards than another bastard." She chuckled merrily.

"Felicia!" Miss Latimer cried distressfully.

"I beg your pardon — I could not resist."

"You do not *know* that you are a… a natural daughter, after all."

"I know nothing," Felicia said sourly. "It is a reasonable deduction, though, for why send away a legitimate child? Never mind. Where is this position as governess?"

"At Itchen, just across the river," Miss Latimer said, latching eagerly onto the happier topic. "Near enough that we might see you sometimes. It will not be for ever, as they will be going to school as soon as they are old enough and will have no need of a governess. Will you at least consider it? Mr Kearney will be here again on Thursday, so you may speak to him about the position then."

"Of course I will consider it," Felicia said gently, and was rewarded by seeing Miss Latimer's clouded face lighten a little. "I do not wish to be the means whereby you lose your most profitable pupil."

"We do not wish to lose you, either," Miss Latimer said, "but you do see how it is, I am sure."

"Oh yes. Either I go or Jane goes. That is perfectly clear." Miss Latimer protested, but Felicia only laughed. "Do not distress yourself. It is only three years before I come into my inheritance, after all, so why should I not while away that time as a governess?"

"There! I knew you would see the bright side," Miss Latimer said happily.

~~~~~

Philip Kearney was a handsome man, dressed in a casually expensive style with no great pretensions to fashion, and all in black, with crepe on his hat. He was perhaps forty, with a little grey beginning to show in his hair, but with none of the signs of over-indulgence so common in men of that age. There was an easy charm to his manner which would make him something of a danger to susceptible women. He was an architect, he told Felicia when they met in Miss Latimer's office under the hawk-like eyes of Miss Gertrude, and his work required him to travel here and there, but he had his main office in Liverpool.
~~~~~

"That is where my wife lives," he said. "Since it was her money and connections that established my career, I still keep a base there, but my heart has long been here in Southampton, in the Itchen village cottage." He paused for a moment, his grief obvious. After a moment, he composed himself and went on, "You know of my great loss. My beloved Juliana was a woman below notice in the eyes of the world, but to me she was everything. Now that we are separated in this life, our two little girls fall to my sole care. Miss Oakes, I do not expect you to love my daughters, for that responsibility lies with me, and a welcome one it is. My only requirement is for them to receive a little learning, and an encouragement to develop whatever of artistic talent they may have inherited. Their mother was a painter of great ability, and I would not see her daughters denied their chance to follow her example."

"What age are your daughters, sir?"

"Juliana is six and Margarita is four. Their mother had already begun teaching them to draw before her tragic death, and now that the Lord Chancellor has confirmed my guardianship, I wish them to continue that training as soon as possible. Miss Latimer tells me you have some considerable talent with pen and brush yourself."

"I make no claim to any superior accomplishment," Felicia said. "I have a degree of competence, which I strive constantly to improve, but that is all I would say of myself. I have some little experience of imparting my modest knowledge of the skills required, but if your daughters have truly inherited their mother's talents, they will surely require the aid of a master to reach their greatest potential."

"Such instruction as they require will be given them when they are old enough, but for now they need only the essentials, and Miss Latimer believes you eminently suited to such teaching. May I see some of your work, such as you deem fit for public scrutiny?"

With Miss Gertrude following them closely with her usual glower, Felicia led him to the studio on the upper floor. Three moon-faced girls whispering over their easels turned curious eyes on them, before being chased out by a glare from Miss Gertrude. Felicia showed Mr Kearney her sketchbooks and the several completed works awaiting framing, but his gaze soon fell on her half-completed cottage.

"Pastels? An interesting choice. Do you prefer such a medium to watercolours or oils?"

"I do. Watercolours are my bread and butter, naturally, since that is what the parents mostly want their daughters to learn, but for my own pieces I often choose pastels."

"May I ask why?"

"The intensity of the colours, the ease of blending and over-layering, the many ways a stick may be used to create different effects. On its side, I can cover the paper rapidly to build a base, then use the ends in different ways to add detail. And I love using my fingers to soften and merge the colours."

"There is nothing in oils here."

"I rarely paint in oils. I find it... complicated."

He laughed. "True enough! You have some talent, that is clear, but there is something amiss with the cottage in this picture."

"I am incapable of drawing straight lines," she said.

"It is fortunate, then, that you are not an architect," he said, his face softening into a wry amusement. "Buildings are *my* bread and butter, Miss Oakes, and with those I can achieve a likeness. Trees, too, although not with such panache as you. But people? No, that is beyond my limited talents. I like you, Miss Oakes. The position is yours, if you are so minded. One hundred pounds a year, plus board and whatever equipment you need for your teaching."

"That is generous. To reside in Itchen, I take it. And will you be in residence also, Mr Kearney?"

"Occasionally, as my work permits, but the household comprises a housekeeper, cook, housemaid, two nursemaids and a manservant, so you need not fear for your reputation."

His smile was so full of charming good-humour that she found it impossible to take offence. Besides, she preferred such plain speaking. It was best to get everything laid out in clear sight, with no room for misunderstandings.

"I have no reputation to fear for, being only the abandoned bastard of nobody knows whom."

He laughed, but said, "Everyone has a reputation, Miss Oakes, even abandoned bastards, and your father may yet be found. Why, you might even be the daughter of the Prince of Wales."

"Heaven forfend! More likely a coal merchant's get, I should say."

"Whoever he is, he should not have left you unprotected. The world is unforgiving towards those born out of wedlock, and those responsible have a duty to provide for all their children, whether legitimate or not," he said in severe tones.

"I honour you for such sentiments," Felicia said. "However, I must correct one misapprehension. My father, whomsoever he may be, did indeed make provision for me. It was not his fault that the protector he chose died when I was ten."

"Would your protector have known who your father was?"

"Very likely, but she never dropped so much as a hint to me, and never will now. All is not lost, however, for when I am one and twenty I shall inherit the small cottage she owned, and my trustees will permit me to see all her personal papers. Then perhaps I shall find the answer, and will know whether I am the daughter of a coal merchant or the Prince of Wales."

# 1: Summer Cottage (March)

FOUR YEARS LATER

MARCH

"Oh, great Heavens! The new duke is dead!" Felicia cried, laying down the newspaper on the breakfast table in shock.

Agnes set down the pot of tea she was in the process of pouring. "The new duke? Not the Duke of Falconbury!"

"The very same. *'DUKE OF FALCONBURY LOST AT SEA'*, it says here. *'It is with the utmost sorrow, a sentiment which the entire nation must share, that we report on the tragic loss of the* Brig Minerva, *on a voyage—"*

Agnes snatched the newspaper from Felicia's hands, scanning it avidly. Felicia made no protest, recognising Agnes' superior claim to it at such a moment. The housekeeper was a sober and hard-working woman who ordinarily eschewed all gossip and speculation, but her one weakness was the nobility. Her favoured reading material was found in the society pages of any newspaper and journal she could find, and when those had been read the requisite three times, she found solace in a well-thumbed copy of the Peerage.

"How dreadful! Listen to this! *'The tragic loss of the* Brig Minerva*, on a voyage from Dublin bound for Southampton, which has foundered on the rocks of the treacherous southern Cornish Coast some miles to the west of Trehowick. The cause of this disaster…'* Well, we do not much care about the cause. Hmm… hmm… Ah, here we are. *'One of those believed to be counted amongst the dead is His Grace the Most Noble the Seventh Duke of Falconbury, a young man returning from foreign parts to assume the heavy mantle of his responsibilities after the great sorrow of his father's death only six months ago. His Grace was sojourning in the New World, in the country that now calls itself the United States of America, when news of his father's demise reached him. Immediately His Grace set aside his own sorrow to travel by any means possible back to his native land to comfort his family and take his place amongst the highest in the land. This journey, it seems, has now been cut short. His Grace having never married and therefore leaving no heir, the great responsibility of the ducal coronet now falls to his noble brother. Our hearts and prayers go out to His Grace in this dark hour, and all the Litherholm family.'* Dear me. Deary, deary me."

"Is he *our* duke?" Juliana said.

"Our local duke? Yes, indeed," Agnes said. "The very same who lives at Valmont. His poor brother! To lose the Sixth Duke so short a time ago, and now this. They were twins, you know. Not alike in looks, or in character either, by all accounts, but as close as ever brothers could be. Such a tragedy for the family!"

"And especially the ladies," Felicia said. "They would have been barely out of mourning for the old duke, and now they are straight back into blacks again. Such a dispiriting colour, black. A lady always looks ill in it."

"Tush, Felicia!" Agnes said. "You're too frivolous sometimes. The mourning period is no time for any lady to care about her appearance."

"A lady always cares about her appearance," Felicia said. "Why else spend such vast sums on it? Forty guineas for that bonnet in Miss Tucker's window. Wicked! All these grand folk you revere so much feel more affection for their bonnets than their children. They never see their own offspring, and would be hard put to recognise them if they bumped into them in the garden."

"Felicia! Whatever your own feelings regarding our great nobles, you should instil the proper level of deference in the girls. Take no notice, either of you. Felicia does not mean it."

The two gazed at her, round-eyed, Margarita solemn, Juliana with a slight twinkle that recognised Felicia's teasing tone. Yet it was true that she had no great respect for the nobility, since most of them were of a dissolute and idle disposition, and served no useful function that she could discern.

Not being inclined to argue the point, however, she said only, "It hardly matters, since they will never meet anyone of rank. They are not nearly rich enough, and thank goodness for it. We are all better off escaping the notice of those far above us. Here we are in our little corner of Hampshire, with nothing at all to trouble us beyond a headline in a newspaper. Come, girls, if you have eaten your fill, shall we leave Mrs Markham to savour the sinking of the *Brig Minerva* in peace and begin our lessons?"

Agnes smiled, and lifted the newspaper a little closer, the better to enjoy the tragic news.

~~~~~
~~~~~

*'To Miss J. Pollard, Laura Place, Bath. My dear Jane, Have you seen the latest word? The poor new Duke of Falconbury is now residing at the bottom of the English Channel. How strange to think that if you had married him four years ago, as your mama intended, you would now be a dowager duchess at the extraordinary age of one and twenty. I should not like to be a duchess, I think, but a dowager duchess — now that is something that would appeal to my odd sense of humour. One could have a great deal of amusement floating through society, receiving the deference of all and causing a great deal of trouble for all the servants yet without any of the bother of a husband. Yes, that appeals to me very much, so if ever you hear of a very elderly duke in need of a wife for his few remaining years on earth, be sure to send for me at once. Is Bath very dull now that Mr T. and Captain R. have left? I have always believed that Bath is very dull at all times, but there, you are such an open-hearted soul that you find enjoyment everywhere, even in Bath. When do you remove to Dorsetshire? Do let me know how you go on. Yours in affection, Felicia Oakes.'*

~~~~~

Later that day, Felicia, Juliana and Margarita were returning from their daily walk, cheeks aglow in the frosty winter air. They had been down to the shores of the River Itchen. In the summer they would have taken their sketch books, but even at this lifeless season there was much pleasure to be had in watching the sturdy little ferry ploughing back and forth, and the distant sails of the Southampton ships. Margarita, who had a morbid interest in dead things, had collected a bundle of desiccated stems, their brown leaves rattling, to draw later, and Juliana triumphantly carried an intact bottle, washed ashore from some passing boat.
~~~~~

"Look, there is Mr Pierce," Juliana cried, pointing at the arriving ferry.

"Is it?" Felicia said, startled, for the attorney seldom ventured far from his office on French Street.

"See how he leans upon his cane," Juliana said. "And that limp — no other has such a limp."

"It certainly does look like Mr Pierce," Felicia conceded. "He must have business on this side of the river, but nothing to do with us, I am sure. Come along, now. If we hurry, there will be time to arrange those twigs ready to be immortalised in paint tomorrow."

But Mr Pierce walked steadily, if lopsidedly, towards them and they met at the gate of Summer Cottage.

"Ah, Miss Oakes," he said, but his eyes were on Juliana and Margarita. He stopped, his face working as if wrestling with some inner emotion. "Miss Kearney. Miss Margarita. Good day to you all."

Felicia watched the two girls make their curtsies, even as she made her own. Yes, there was an increasing gracefulness in their deportment that must please their father. They were growing up very well, and would be elegant young women in a few years time.

"Are you come to see us?" Felicia said.

"Indeed, or rather — I must talk to *you*, Miss Oakes."

That was a surprise. A frisson of alarm shivered through her. "Then pray come inside, sir."

Handing the children into the care of Ellen and Mary, the nursemaids, she led Mr Pierce into Mr Kearney's study. With the shutters closed and no fire lit, it was a dark, unwelcoming room, with just a hint of dust and neglect in the air. Hastily she threw back the shutters to let in low, slanting beams from the winter sun, and lit the fire.

"Shall we sit here?" she said, indicating the comfortable chairs set either side of the hearth. "This will be the warmest place. May I offer you some refreshment, sir?"

"That would be most welcome. Most welcome indeed. It is still cold out, and not the least hint of spring in the air."

He agreed to some Canary, but would accept nothing to eat, which was just as well, for all the morning's cakes had been consumed at breakfast. She unlocked the tantalus and poured a glass for him, which he sipped from nervously and then placed carefully on a low table. Felicia perched on the edge of her chair and waited for Mr Pierce to impart his bad news. She had formed no clear idea of what he might say, but that it would be bad was certain. His very agitation proclaimed it so, yet his first words took her by surprise.

"Have you seen this in the newspapers?"

He drew forth a small cutting from a Southampton newspaper, and she recognised the substance of it at once. "The Duke of Falconbury is drowned off Cornwall. I am very sorry for it, I am sure, but what is it to us?"

He ran a finger inside his cravat, as if it were too tight. Then, slowly, as if reluctantly, he pulled from his pocket a folded paper. "I received this two… no, three weeks since," he said, handing it to her.

A letter. She recognised Mr Kearney's handwriting from the direction. "You wish me to read this?"

Wordlessly he nodded. She unfolded it and read, *'Sir, My business here is concluded for the moment, so I return to S. in a few days. I am being greatly entertained at Kilrannan House, where the earl is attempting to impress the Duke of Falconbury, to no avail, for His Grace remains steadfastly unimpressed by minor Irish nobility. I plan to stay as long as His Grace, so will take passage with him on the* Brig Minerva, *which will—'*

Felicia cried out in distress. "Mr Kearney was aboard the *Brig Minerva?*"

He had pulled out a handkerchief, and was polishing his spectacles vigorously. "So it would appear. In which case—"

For a moment, Felicia felt as if she could not breathe. "He is dead, then."

"I am awaiting *confirmation* of it, but it is believed so, yes. He was not amongst the few *survivors* so we must prepare for the *worst*. Indeed we must. The bodies are... forgive me for speaking so bluntly, Miss Oakes, but it is *necessary*. Most necessary that you know all."

She had made some little sound of distress, but she nodded and gestured to him to continue.

"The... the *mortal remains* of the poor unfortunates are presently being recovered, and once Mr Kearney's... um... um... have been identified, he will be *transported* to his last resting place."

"Liverpool," she said. "To his wife. Widow, I suppose."

"Correct," he said, with a little more briskness. "And then his will may be read *formally*, but on that head I may reassure you at once. I have written to Mr Kearney's solicitor in Liverpool and he has been *most* helpful. He tells me that Mr Kearney made *ample* provision for his daughters. Indeed, they will have *excellent* fortunes."

"Poor things," she said softly. "Excellent fortunes are no substitute for a mama and papa. They are orphans now. Whatever will happen to them? Will they be able to stay on here? The cottage is leased, so—"

"There is a *guardian* appointed," Mr Pierce said hastily. "It will be for him to say where they live, naturally, but I expect he will want to have them a little *nearer* to his home. More conveniently *situated*, you understand, for their better *instruction* and *guidance*. Yes, I am sure he will want them to live with him in Derbyshire."

"Derbyshire!" Felicia exclaimed. "Such a great distance from all that they know. Surely—"

"They will be better off there," he said firmly. "A *vast* deal better off, Miss Oakes. Indeed, they could not have wished for better protection. They will never be able to move in the *highest* society, given their um... unfortunate origins, but on the *fringes*... Yes, indeed. They will be very well placed to make *splendid* matches, I make no doubt. Not the least doubt in the world. What a fine thing! A most *fortuitous* circumstance. Such a fine *opportunity* for them."

"I imagine they would rather have their father than any number of opportunities," she said acidly. "Nor can I imagine that Derbyshire is any more likely to provide them than Hampshire."

"Now there you are *quite* wrong," he said smugly. "Their guardian moves in the most *superior* society."

"Who is this paragon?"

"Why, none other than the Earl of Finlassan."

"*The Earl of Finlassan!* I never heard Mr Kearney mention such a person. He mingled with noblemen all the time, but only in the course of his work. I am surprised that he knew one well enough to appoint him as guardian to his daughters."

"Indeed, indeed. There is just as much *surprise* in Liverpool, I assure you. Neither the widow nor the solicitor were *aware* that Mr Kearney was even *acquainted* with the earl. But so it is. I have written to his lordship to apprise him of the *duty* laid upon him by his friend, but have not yet been *honoured* with a reply."

"So what must we do?" Felicia said.

"We wait," Mr Pierce said, polishing his spectacles again. Then he noticed his glass of Canary with a start of surprise, and reached for it with a pleased smile. After a sip or two, he went on, "We must await *official* word of the Miss Kearneys' inheritance to arrive from Liverpool, and we must also await *instructions* from Lord Finlassan. That will give you a little time to *prepare* the young ladies for this very great *change* in their lives." He gazed at Felicia over the top of his spectacles. "You will perhaps take this *opportunity* to relinquish your employment? After all, Miss Oakes, you are of age now, your inheritance is in your own *hands*. That is a very *snug* little house you own. Very snug indeed. You will be very *cosy* there, I make no doubt."

"Oh yes, very cosy," Felicia said bleakly. Her childhood memories of Boscobel Cottage were grim ones — tiny rooms, smoking chimneys, draughty windows and the unremitting labour of growing vegetables and raising chickens and pigs. She had been constantly cold, hungry and grimed with mud. Summer Cottage was very much more to her liking, provided as it was with a staff of six and enough money for all the necessities of life, and a few luxuries, too.

She had made just one visit to Boscobel Cottage since then. When she came of age, her trustees had permitted her to look through Miss Armiger's papers to see if they contained any hints as to Felicia's origins. What a disappointment that had been! Laundry lists, translations from Greek, bills from the apothecary — but not a single personal letter or mention of Felicia anywhere. Nothing at all to suggest where she had come from, or why she had been given into the care of a woman who was not her mother. That was the only fact Miss Armiger had given her, that she was not Felicia's mother. It was not very helpful, and now she would never know who she was.

Later that evening, when the two girls had gone to bed, Agnes looked up the Earl of Finlassan in the Peerage. "Fabian Warborough," she said. "The Fifth Earl of Finlassan. Came into his honours twelve years ago. He will be… hmm, two and thirty. Unmarried, according to this, although it's not the latest edition. One sister, the Lady Drusilla, who must be six and twenty, also unwed. No other surviving issue. Principal residence Hawkewood Hall, Derbyshire. Shall I look that up in Paterson?" Without waiting for Felicia's reply, she ran out of the drawing room to fetch the book from her room. It was almost as well read as her Peerage, and just as familiar, for she found the relevant page at once. "Here we are. *'Hawkewood Hall, residence of the Right Honourable the Earl of Finlassan. A magnificent mansion, constructed of fine stone in the form of a centre and two side wings, the west face enhanced with a recently added portico with Doric columns. The principal apartments are of noble proportions; they are fitted up with great elegance and are adorned with an excellent collection of paintings by the first masters. The ballroom more particularly requires notice, it being an extremely splendid apartment, furnished in the most chaste yet expensive style, with a very handsome ceiling.'* Well, that sounds grand, doesn't it? A ballroom! Juliana will like that!"

Chaste yet expensive? Curious, but still, a ballroom… Felicia sighed at the thought. A proper ballroom and private balls… oh, how glorious that would be! Her mind was filled with music and swirling silk, the ladies graceful, the gentlemen athletic, and on all sides the nodding feathers of the chaperons' turbans as they gossiped and plotted and hoped for good matches for their charges. And the room, so eloquently described as an *'extremely splendid apartment'*, would be considerably larger than the assembly rooms at the Dolphin. She could scarcely imagine it, or the number of couples required to fill such a space, and she would be at their head, in a silk gown with a spangled net over-tunic, dancing with… an émigré, perhaps. A handsome Frenchman, the last of his line, who had barely escaped the troubles with his life and the shirt on his back. His hair would be very dark, almost black, and curling into his neck…

Agnes was not driven into raptures by the description of the ballroom, however, so she read on. *"'The house is situated on a low eminence with another, somewhat larger, hill to the west, the lower slopes clothed with fine woods and the upper, topped by an elegant temple, affording a magnificent prospect in all directions. It would be impossible to overstate the beauty of the surrounding countryside, which encompasses all the majestic wildness of that fair county, the charming valley of the River Shotter and a portion of the even more extensive parklands of Shotterbourne, residence of the Most Honourable the Marquess of Arnwell.'* Goodness! A marquess next door!"

That sent her off on another chase through the Peerage, but Felicia was not much interested in all these lords and their ladies, especially when she was unlikely to meet any of them or dance in their ballrooms, however handsome their ceilings or chaste but expensive their furnishings. It would be Juliana and Margarita who would dance there, and enjoy the magnificent prospect of majestic wilderness.

She could not decide whether she most envied or pitied them when they discovered their fate.

~~~~~

Margarita was the most clearly distressed. Juliana, always the more rational of the two, saw the advantages of the earl's patronage at once, even while she grieved for her father. She reasoned that he had been a friend of her father, and must therefore be an amiable gentleman who would take very good care of them. Margarita saw only the desolation of leaving the familiar.

"It will be a great adventure," Felicia said to them. "Just think, you will have a new life in a new home with a great many new friends. Not every young lady is so fortunate."

"It's a pity there's no countess," Agnes said to Felicia one evening. "Girls need a mother to raise them properly for society."

"The earl has a sister," she said. "I daresay he has aunts and cousins, too. I wish he would send word of how the girls are to travel to Derbyshire, though. I have written twice now, and Mr Pierce has written several times, yet there has been no answer. We cannot stay here indefinitely, for the rent is due on Lady Day, and it would be wasteful to pay for another year when they have another home awaiting them."
~~~~~

"Perhaps he is elsewhere?" Agnes said tentatively. "If he's from home, then he can't be expected to answer letters."

"He never leaves Hawkewood Hall, seemingly," Felicia said. "He is something of a recluse, according to Mr Pierce's acquaintance in London, so he is certainly there, but refusing to respond. There is no help for it — I shall have to take them to Derbyshire myself. I shall write again tomorrow, informing him of the plan, and we shall leave on Monday next. I shall have to take Ellen and Mary, and it will be a great help to have Temple with us. You, Eliza and Lilian can close up the house here, and then you may stay at Boscobel Cottage until you have decided what you wish to do next."

"You're very kind," Agnes said. "We shall make ourselves useful there, you may be sure. Then, when the girls are settled and you are able to return, we shall have all ready for you in your new home. I expect we'll all have to find new situations, in time. Mr Kearney was very generous in leaving each of us five hundred pounds, and I've a bit put by as well, but I don't think it's enough to live on. Besides, I'd not want to be idle."

"Truly? Being idle is glorious, Mrs Markham. I adore being idle, and I can scarcely contemplate returning to a life planting potatoes."

"You're not idle, Miss Oakes! Look at all you do with the girls — giving them their lessons and taking them on long walks and showing them how to be little ladies. Why, you never stop!"

"That is just books and talking, not work, and there is plenty of time for my own occupations." She sighed. "But that will all be at an end once I have delivered Juliana and Margarita to Lord Finlassan, and it must be soon. Oh, why does he not answer my letters? It is too bad of him, indeed it is. One more letter, and then they must be gone to the north, reply or no."

But no letter came from the earl. The following Monday, therefore, Felicia squeezed into a post-chaise with her two charges and the maids, with Temple sitting outside amongst the luggage, and set off for Derbyshire.

# 2: A Post-Chaise And Four (April)

APRIL

The journey was shockingly expensive. Felicia had never laid out so much money in her life, but Mr Pierce had insisted that the wards of Lord Finlassan should travel in a post-chaise and four, with their governess, both nursemaids and a manservant, as was appropriate for persons of such standing in society. Since he was a trustee for the girls' fortunes and had authorised the expenditure, it was not her place to question the matter, but even so she was consumed with guilt every time they changed horses or sought accommodation for the night, and she was obliged to hand over yet another collection of coins for Temple to dispense to the greedy palms of ostlers, tap boys, chamber maids and the Lord only knew who else.

Guilt or no, though, she was determined to enjoy the journey. Their mourning clothes, the size of their entourage and the name of Lord Finlassan ensured that they were attended to everywhere with great efficiency and a pleasing degree of deference. The inns Mr Pierce had recommended provided comfortable beds and good food served in private parlours. It was a mode of travel to which she could easily grow accustomed. She would be returning on the common stage in a far less pleasant manner, so she would savour her last little taste of luxury.

When she returned south, it would be to Boscobel Cottage, to pigs and potatoes and not a neighbour within five miles. Why had Miss Armiger chosen such a remote spot to settle? She had asked once or twice, but Miss Armiger would never answer. As to why it rained when the wind was westerly but not from the east, or why the Battle of Hastings was lost, or why slavery was a bad idea — on these subjects she could discourse at length and with fervour, but as to who Felicia's parents were or where they had gone or why Felicia was required to live at Boscobel Cottage, those questions had been rewarded with pursed lips and disapproving looks and silence.

The travellers passed through London on the second day, and by their fourth night had reached Loughborough, weary but glad to be nearing their destination. Juliana had entertained herself by watching the ever-changing view from the chaise windows, especially the perpetual drama of passing towns. Margarita was inclined to be tearful until Felicia had thought to supply her with a sketchbook and pencils. The nursemaids had demonstrated an extraordinary ability to sleep whenever no duty called them. Felicia herself idled away quiet moments by imagining the delights of that splendid ballroom, the portico on the west face — what exactly was a portico? — and the intriguing temple on the hill.

And then there was the girls' guardian — what would he be like? An earl should be fair, she decided. Fair of face, blue-eyed and with hair the colour of sun-bleached corn. He would dress in the height of fashion, and his reclusiveness was merely a ploy. In fact, he spent most of his time cunningly disguised as… a naval captain… no, that was too obvious. A merchant of some kind, selling stockings. Did anyone travel about selling stockings? Hmm… jewellery of some kind, then. Snuff boxes… yes, that was better. He travelled to and from France pretending to trade in snuff boxes, when in truth he was a spy for the Government. A hero, in fact. Definitely a hero.

The final day of their journey took them through Derby and beyond. The postilions knew the way to Hawkewood Hall, and so, a little after noon, they drew up at a pair of elaborate ironwork gates, each ornamented with a coat of arms, with a metal lion prowling far above on a decorative arch. The gates were closed, but a woman in an apron and a loosely tied shawl, her sleeves rolled up as if she were about the laundry, wandered out to see to them. Temple spent some minutes talking to her, during which time the shakes of her head became increasingly vehement, and at last, with a final gesture of seeming defiance, she turned and went back into the gate house. Moments later, swathed in a cloak, she disappeared into woods to one side of the drive.

"She's going to find her husband, although she's not sure where he is," Temple reported. "She has instructions not to open the gates except to family members."

"The girls *are* family," Felicia said. "They are his lordship's wards."

"But not expected," Temple said. "She knows nothing about no wards. His lordship is definitely here, though — she told me that much. Just like we heard, he never goes nowhere. Maybe we could leave a note to tell him we're here, and then go back to that last inn we passed? Don't you think? Wait for him in the warm."

"Write another note for him to ignore? No, the girls have the right to be admitted, whatever the Mistress of the Gates may think. We will wait."

Temple nodded rather disconsolately, pulling his greatcoat more tightly around him. Wrapped up in rugs inside the chaise, and with a hot brick to her feet, Felicia had scarcely noticed the biting easterly wind, but she saw now that Temple looked perished.

"This is ridiculous. Let down the steps, Temple."

She descended from the carriage, and walked towards the great iron gates. Despite their massive size, there was no lock on them, only a large ring handle on each side. Impulsively, Felicia turned one. With a metallic creak, it moved and the latch lifted. A hard push, and the gate shifted and opened, the hinges protesting loudly. No one else emerged from the gate house to challenge them. To his credit, Temple did not hesitate. Within moments both gates were open, and the chaise rolled through.

For some time the road was blanketed by dense woodland, but abruptly they broke into the open and the occupants of the chaise all cried out in wonder at the sight before them. There was the house on its low hill, and the description in Agnes's book had not nearly done it justice.

"It is enormous!" Juliana whispered, awed.

"So beautiful!" Margarita said.

Felicia could hardly catch her breath. Nothing in her life had prepared her for the grandeur of the earl's home. As the chaise rolled to a halt, the steps were let down and they all tumbled out in wonder. The others chattered excitedly, but Felicia could only gaze speechlessly at the elegant stonework, the endless rows of windows, and the massive front doors, the many steps leading up to them each flanked by a pair of stone urns, increasing in size with each step.

"Now what, Miss Oakes?" Temple said.

She had no idea. In novels, when the heroine arrived at the Gothic castle, the doors opened at once and a troop of footmen emerged to attend to the luggage, and the wicked lord was there to receive her. These doors remained firmly closed, and there were no footmen and no lord, wicked or otherwise.

But he was inside. Somewhere in those scores of apartments of noble proportions the earl was... doing what? If he truly was wicked, then perhaps he was somewhere in the basement torturing a hapless tenant farmer who was a week late with his rent. Or in his bedroom stealing the virtue of one of the housemaids. She was not at all sure how one tortured a victim, or stole a maid's virtue, either, but it was certainly something a wicked earl would know. But perhaps he led a blameless life, and was even now writing a sermon in his own hand for his chaplain to declaim from the pulpit on Sunday next.

She sighed. Making up stories was amusing, but got one nowhere. Picking up her skirts, she climbed the many wide, stone steps to the entrance, Temple trailing in her wake. There was a giant lion's-head knocker, so she lifted it once and let it fall with an echoing thump, then twice more. For good measure, she pulled vigorously on the bell as well.

For an age she stood on the top step, the chill air gradually seeping through her heavy woollen cloak, then her gown, then through all her undergarments until she felt as if even her bones were turning to ice. Beside her, Temple stamped his feet, his arms tucked under his armpits for warmth. It was hard to believe it was April and the leaves already showing on some of the trees.

There was a sound of bolts being drawn — many, many bolts — and the door opened a crack. The supercilious face of a man of middle years peered out at them. "Yes?"

It was not a promising beginning. Felicia reviewed her options rapidly. If they were truly not expected, despite the many letters, then there would be explanations to be made and she would have to present to the earl all the papers she had brought with her to demonstrate the legality of his guardianship. That could hardly be done on the doorstep, yet if she merely requested a meeting with the earl, they might be left standing out in the cold while he was fetched, or this haughty individual might deny them admittance altogether. What to do? She settled on brazenness.

"Ah, at last!" she cried, marching straight up to the door and pushing it open. The butler, or whatever he might be, was too much taken aback to defend his master's territory, and in an instant she was inside, stepping neatly past the sour-faced fellow and into the hall.

Where she stopped, jaw dropping in amazement. It was a cavern several stories high, the arched ceiling with its delicate fans of plasterwork supported by massive marble pillars. The floor was a mosaic of muted marble colours in a pattern of octagons. Around the walls, niches held statues of near-naked women with artful drapery. A staircase without visible support wound delicately upwards from a circular ante-chamber. It was exquisite, and Felicia's fingers itched to capture such beauty in paint.

"No… wait, you can't come marching in here like this," the butler said, his tone so outraged that Felicia almost laughed.

When she turned, she saw that Temple, the two girls and the nursemaids had all followed her inside, and were staring around, open-mouthed.

Two younger men had appeared, presumably footmen. The butler's scowl lightened with the arrival of reinforcements and he turned to Ellen and Mary, who were nearest to him. "Out!" he said sharply, and with scared glances they scuttled back through the open door. The butler turned next to Juliana and Margarita.

This was not going well. It was time to be brazen again. She would be… a dowager duchess, accustomed to instant obedience. Yes, that should do the trick. "Where is Lord Finlassan?" she said loudly, in a manner that she hoped would brook no argument, although she quaked to her boots. "Fetch him to me at once!"

It worked. The butler and footmen straightened automatically. "His lordship is not to be disturbed," the butler said, his tone more conciliatory.

"He must be disturbed," she said. Was her manner regal enough? Or would he see straight through her veneer of hauteur to the cowering governess inside? "Tell him that Miss Oakes and the Miss Kearneys are arrived. You two!" She turned to the footmen watching interestedly. "Bring in our boxes."

The footmen lounged towards the door, but this was an impertinence too far for the butler. "You will do no such thing! Madam, I have no idea who you are but you will leave at once. Make an appointment and—"

"I have an appointment!" she cried desperately, and it was true. At least, she had written to tell the earl of their plans, which was almost the same thing. "His lordship is expecting us!" And that part was probably not true, but he *ought* to be expecting them. If only the wretched man had bothered to read his letters!

But the butler had made up his mind. "Throw them out," he said to the footmen.

"No, you must listen!" Felicia cried. "Let me speak to the earl first!"

It was no good. The footmen marched purposely across the hall towards Juliana and Margarita, who promptly ran away, ducking behind pillars and dodging this way and that to evade capture. Temple raised his fists, quite prepared to defend his womenfolk, while the butler barked out instructions and even deigned to chase after Margarita himself. Then, realising the futility of trying to catch an agile child of eight, he stopped and turned towards an easier target.

The moment he grabbed Felicia's arm, she let out a piercing shriek. He pulled, she screamed and full-scale pandemonium broke out. Into this bedlam, a loud voice echoed down from above.

"What the *devil* is going on?"

The butler, the footmen and even Temple, who recognised the voice of authority when he heard it, froze and bowed deeply to the figure standing at the top of the stairs. Juliana and Margarita skittered out of the door to safety. Felicia was too angry to be deferential, even though it was clear that the newcomer was none other than the earl himself.

Stepping forward, she said coldly, "Are you Lord Finlassan?"

"What if I am? Who the devil are you and what are you doing here?"

His face was thunderous, and even in the midst of her rage, she grieved for the loss of the fair nobleman of her imagination. This man was as far from her flattering image as could be. He was tall, but also thin and pale, like a sapling grown lanky in shade. His hair was dark and tousled, and he was, to her eyes, only half dressed, as if he had just that moment risen from his bed. He wore no boots, waistcoat or coat, and not even a cravat, his sole concession to modesty being his breeches and a loosely-worn shirt. He looked nearer to the wicked earl than the saintly.

This was no time to be craven. She reminded herself that she had every right to be there, so she lifted her chin and said, "I am Miss Oakes, governess to the Miss Kearneys, and I have brought them to you." When he looked blank, she added, "Your wards."

"Nonsense! I have no wards," he said gruffly, although he descended a stair or two.

"Indeed you do, my lord. Mr Kearney named you in his will as their guardian." A horrid thought assailed her. "You are aware, I take it, that Mr Kearney is dead? I am very sorry if this news distresses you."

"Why should it, since I know no one by the name of Kearney, alive or dead?" Three more stairs.

Her mouth flapped open in bewilderment. "You did not know him? Then why did he appoint you as guardian?"

"Your question must be rhetorical, since I cannot possibly answer it. You had best be on your way, madam. Whether you have fallen into some unaccountable error, or your purpose is a darker one, you have no business here. Bagnall, escort this person to the door."

Felicia was bewildered. It could *not* be a mistake, it could not! It was in the will, she had the papers to prove it! "You are Fabian Warborough, the Fifth Earl of Finlassan?"

His scowl darkened, as if he would have liked to deny it, but he nodded curtly.

"Then you are named in the will of Mr Philip Kearney of Liverpool as guardian to his two daughters. I can show you all the documents."

"Why the devil would any man undertake such an unfathomable act? To my knowledge, I have never met this Kearney fellow in my life, let alone been on such terms with him that he would entrust his daughters to me. Daughters! What am I supposed to do with them? It is quite impossible for me to undertake such a burden. Whatever was their father thinking? It is the foulest kind of cruelty to inflict them upon me. Such an imposition! "

"It is a greater cruelty to two orphans to refuse them shelter. Are you expecting sympathy, my lord? Forgive me but I reserve *my* sympathy for Juliana and Margarita who are left without... without... My lord?"

He had gone so white that she wondered if he were about to swoon. His appearance was already delicate, but now he looked positively ill.

Rushing down the last few stairs, he said hoarsely, "Juliana? Margarita? What was their mother's name?"

"She was a Juliana, too."

He uttered a low growl deep in his throat. "And this Kearney fellow? Was he an architect?"

"He was! So you *do* know him?"

"Never knew his name. Never wanted to. My father always called him *'that architect fellow'* and the epithet stuck. Oh God! Then she is dead! When? When did she die?"

"Their mother? Four years ago."

He let out a long, slow breath like a sigh. "Where are they?"

Striding to the door, the footmen sprang forwards to pull the doors open for him, and out he went in his shirt and bare feet, leaping unheeding down the steps. "Juliana! Margarita!" he cried and they turned towards him. "Come here!"

Watching the little group from the top of the steps, Felicia held her breath. She heard the disappointment in his voice as he said, "I suppose you must take after your father. You — which one are you? Juliana... you have your mother's eyes, and her chin, perhaps, but that is all."

"You knew our mother?" Juliana said.

He gave a laugh then, but it was not a pleasant sound, more a bark of anger. "Knew her? Oh yes, most certainly I knew her. I almost married her... *would* have married her, but for one minor detail. She jilted me three days before the wedding to run away with your father."

# 3: Hawkewood Hall

Fin dressed mechanically, hurling clothes on with careless haste, while Matthews wrung his hands and made little mewing noises of distress. One would think the valet would be used to his starts by now.

Juliana's daughters! It was extraordinary! And now she was dead, and that last tiny spark of hope that would never consent to be extinguished was gone for ever. She was dead and he would never see her again.

The woman was already in the sitting room when he arrived, gazing at the pictures on the walls. Woman… girl… she could not be much more than twenty or so. Without the old-fashioned cloak, she looked respectable, if nothing more. The gown was plain — not dowdy, but serviceable rather than fashionable. Appropriate for a governess. What was her name? Oats? Oakes, that was it. Miss Oakes, governess, destined for a life of dull servitude spiralling into poverty and ill health.

"Tell me about her," he said, as he came into the room. "Was she happy with that architect fellow?"

She raised an eyebrow, but answered composedly, "Mrs Kearney? The servants said so, but I never knew her myself. She died before I went as governess to the girls."

"Mrs Kearney? Did she marry him, then?"

"No, he had a wife in Liverpool, but she always called herself that, seemingly. No one knew her right name."

"Dulnain," he said softly. "She was the Lady Juliana Margarita Dulnain."

Both eyebrows shot up. "*Lady* Juliana? From a nobleman's family, then?"

"The youngest daughter of the Fifth Earl of Cottersmere."

"Well! Agnes will be excited to hear that." She gestured towards the wall. "I recognise Mrs Kearney's hand in some of these paintings. Her style was quite distinctive, and her work was all over the cottage. Every wall was covered with them. You only have a few of hers... these two and that one over there. Whose are the rest?"

"Mine."

"Oh, you are a painter too?"

"I am. Have you brought her paintings with you?"

"Her sketchbooks, and a few small portraits of the girls which were small enough to be packed in the travel boxes. The rest are in the care of Mr Kearney's solicitor in Southampton."

"Southampton! Why the devil did the fellow have a solicitor in Southampton? Oh — was that where she lived? This cottage was in Southampton, was it? How odd. You have had quite a journey of it, then."

"Oh, yes!" she said, and her face lit up with sudden mischief. "Five days on the road, and although we travelled in some comfort, coaching inns are not the most restful places in the world. I do not understand why the mail coach must come through at such an unholy hour, and make such a racket about it. I shall be glad for a couple of nights of peaceful sleep before I set off for home again."

"Home again? What do you mean? You are the governess, are you not?"

"Indeed I am, but it was only ever intended to be a temporary situation, just until the girls were old enough to go to school. But that will be for you to decide now, and if you choose to keep them here with you, no doubt you will want a proper governess, who is fluent in several languages, can play the harp and sing at the same time, and is capable of setting three stitches in a straight line, which is more than I can do. Straight lines are the bane of my existence, my lord."

"Why were you chosen, then, if you are so woefully inadequate in the ways of governessing?" he said, bemused by a woman who admitted defeat on the matter of straight lines.

"Because I have some modest skill in art, my lord, and Mr Kearney wished the girls to have the opportunity to practise, so that they might discover if they have inherited their mother's talent. And also because I am a bastard, too, just like Juliana and Margarita."

She smiled at him disarmingly, but he was so disconcerted that he found himself with nothing at all to say.

~~~~~
~~~~~

Drusilla and Giles arrived the next morning before breakfast. Even though he had not sent for them, he had known they would come. It was astonishing how quickly news flew the two miles to the village.

"Juliana's daughters! Is it really possible, Fin?" Drusilla said.

"Why should it be so strange?" Giles said. "It is a not unexpected consequence of the arrangement into which she had entered."

"Certainly, but to appoint *Fin* as their guardian, of all people! It is too eccentric for words."

"The architect could hardly expect his wife to take care of them, could he?" Giles said.

"No, but he must have relations or friends or *anyone* closer than Fin."

"I daresay they would not have them. He knew Fin would never reject Juliana's offspring."

"How could he possibly know that?" Drusilla said.

Fin let them rattle on without interruption, for it was too much trouble to attempt to discuss any matter rationally with them. They would have it their own way, and nothing he said made a difference. Drusilla was his only sister, and a more managing female would be hard to imagine. It was no surprise that no man had ever succeeded in taming her. She had driven Fin to distraction when she was at home, so as soon as she had attained her majority, he had made her a generous allowance and banished her from Hawkewood. She had settled nearby, and spent her days assisting Uncle Giles at the rectory and he was very welcome to her. He seemed not to mind her ways, for he was cut from the same sort of cloth himself.

While they talked together, Fin pondered the best way to bring Juliana's paintings home from Southampton. A devilish long way, and who could he trust to do the work and ensure they travelled safely? And how many were there? The woman had said they were on every wall of the cottage, but then it might be a very small cottage. Or a large one. He would have to go himself, he supposed.

"Shall we see them?" Drusilla said, rousing Fin from his abstraction.

"See them?"

"These girls. Your wards. They are in the nursery, I take it. It will be a good opportunity to interview this governess to make sure she is suitable."

"Suitable?"

"Must you repeat everything I say, Fin? Of course we must ensure she is suitable — check her references, and so forth. These matters must be done properly, you know."

By *'we must…'* he knew she meant *'I must…'.* Well, let her interview the woman, if she wanted. It was a matter of no interest to Fin. "She says she will not stay," he said.

"Nonsense! Of course she will stay, for where else will she go? No governess likes to look for a new position, and we cannot give her a reference yet, since we know nothing of her. I shall talk to her, if you are not minded for it. Come along, Fin."

Meekly, he went. He had not been into the day nursery since he had gone to Eton at the age of twelve, but as soon as he opened the door the familiar smells of chalk dust and musty books took him straight back to childhood. Two footmen were scurrying about with small desks and chairs, piles of books and boxes of wooden toys. A pair of housemaids were folding away Holland covers. The air was thick with dust. One of the girls was riding the rocking horse, while an anxious Bagnall hovered, hands outspread to forestall disaster. Where was the other child? There she was beside the governess, gazing out of the window, and to Fin's amusement they were holding pencils to judge perspective. He went straight to them.

"What are you planning to draw?" he said to the girl.

She pointed out of the window. "The temple on the hill."

"Ah. Interesting. Why that particular view?"

"Because it is mysterious."

"You may not think so once you have examined it more closely," Fin said gravely.

"Miss Oakes said we may not visit it until we have drawn it. We will draw what we can see from the window, then we will draw what we think it is like up close. We are to use our imaginations, for Miss Oakes says half of all art is imagination. Then we may go there and draw it again, but closer. Miss Oakes says that there is a fine prospect from every window and we must draw them all."

"Miss Oakes likes landscapes, does she?"

"We do still life as well. I like that better, but Miss Oakes says we will never improve our landscapes and portraits if we do not practise. We do silhouettes, too, but those are hard! Miss Oakes is very good at taking likenesses of people. She drew Temple, and Mrs Markham said it was more lifelike than the real Temple." She frowned, and added, "I think she must have been joking, for no painting could be *more* lifelike than the original, could it?"

"Not more lifelike, no, but a portrait may capture some aspect of the person that is hard to see in reality. Art is vision as well as seeing."

She frowned even more, but the older child — Juliana! — who had descended from the rocking horse, said, "That is true, for you must remember Miss Oakes' picture of Mrs Markham, Margarita. Mrs Temple wept when she saw it and said it captured all the tragedy of her life."

For the first time, Fin felt a twinge of interest in Miss Oakes, whose portraits could capture the tragedy of a woman's life. He was aware abruptly of the silence in the room. Drusilla and the portrait-painting Miss Oakes had vanished, presumably for the one to be interrogated by the other as to suitability, but Giles and the servants were staring at him with undisguised curiosity.

He grunted, not at all pleased to be caught out in a lengthy conversation with mere children. Turning on his heel, he said to Giles, "I shall be in my sitting room."

It seemed a long time before Drusilla and Giles joined him there, whispering together as they entered the room, then turning to him with false smiles on their faces. At least, Drusilla's was false. Giles looked amused. That was not a good omen, for it meant Drusilla was about to harangue him. There was nothing Giles enjoyed more than Drusilla haranguing her hapless brother.

"She will not do," were Drusilla's opening words. "She has no qualifications at all, so far as I can see. No references, either. I cannot imagine why anyone considered her suitable as a governess. She was only the art teacher, you know. No languages, apart from a little French. She can add and subtract, but not much more than that. Her knowledge of history—"

Giles burst out laughing. "Take no notice of her, Fin. The real reason why she dislikes Miss Oakes has nothing to do with her competence or otherwise in arithmetic. She is too pretty, that is the long and the short of it."

"Too pretty?" Fin said. "What the devil does that mean? Too pretty for what?"

"To be under your roof," Giles chortled. "Drusilla thinks the chit might end up as a countess."

"Good God! That is downright insulting," Fin protested. "After Juliana, am I likely to fall for some dab of a governess, pretty or otherwise?"

"Oh, never tell me you had not noticed how pretty she is," Drusilla said.

"Well, I had not," Fin said. "I cannot say that I noticed her at all. She shouted at me a great deal, that is all I remember of her. Lord, Drusilla, you must think me a great idiot if you imagine me susceptible to such a girl."

"All men are idiots where women are concerned," Drusilla retorted. "But that is not all my objection to her, Giles, and you know it. She is not even *respectable.*"

"Good Lord, Drusilla, will you speak straight?" Fin said in exasperation. "She looked respectable enough to me. What the devil is the matter with her?"

"She is a bastard," Giles said, still chuckling. "A bastard to teach the bastards. Now do not bridle up at me, Fin, because it is true enough. Those girls may be your wards, but they are not *legitimate*, there is no getting away from it."

"That is neither here nor there," Drusilla protested. "Fin's protection will allow the children to take their place in society at some level, but the governess is in far worse case, for she does not even know who her parents may be. She is entirely unsuitable to be in the household of an earl, Fin. You must give *some* consideration to your position, my dear."

"What the devil does it matter?" Fin said irritably, with an indifferent lift of one shoulder. "She told me herself she was a bastard, and obviously the children are, but I cannot see what difference it makes. Still, if you feel her to be improper in some way, then let her go. She wants to go, in any event."

"She never said so," Drusilla said, with an elegant lifting of the eyebrows.

"I daresay you gave her no opportunity," Giles said.

"Well, that is a bit rich!" Drusilla cried. "Here she is in the home of a *peer of the realm*, and she prefers to go back to some hovel in Southport or wherever it was."

"Southampton," Fin said.

"*Southampton!*" Giles cried. "No *wonder* she wants to go home, for is it not paradise on earth?"

"Now look what you have done, Fin!" Drusilla said in disgust. "You have set him off again! Giles, Southampton is undoubtedly as vile and pestilential as any other of our sea ports. Just because you spent a year of marital bliss there before your wife died does not make it paradise for the other poor souls who live there. Fin, you must settle this business of the governess at once, for the manservant who accompanied the children is to depart on Monday, and she may travel with him. The nursery maids will do, for now, but the governess must go."

"Very well. Let her be brought in."

While they waited, Giles, still chuckling to himself, poured Madeira for them all. Drusilla refused hers, but Fin accepted one resignedly. When Drusilla was in this sort of mood, which she almost always was, it was not worth fighting her, and a glass of something in the hand was a great comfort. She would soon be gone, he consoled himself, and the house would be his again. The two children would be safely tucked away in the nursery and would not disturb him.

The governess arrived, and for the first time Fin assessed her properly. She was pretty enough, he conceded, although nothing to compare with Juliana, naturally, and the gown, although sober and perfectly appropriate for her station, yet had a touch of flair about the sleeves and bodice. She curtsied demurely, but when she lifted her head, she looked straight at him. He liked such directness, better by far than timidity or excessive deference.

"Miss Oakes—" Drusilla began, but Fin lifted a disapproving hand.

"I shall deal with this, thank you, sister. Miss Oakes, you wish to leave Hawkewood Hall, I understand."

"Oh no, my lord, not at all."

He was taken aback, but there was a decided twinkle in her eye.

"But you told me—"

"That I *should* go home, yes, but I do not *wish* to leave Hawkewood Hall. Indeed, I must be a very odd creature not to enjoy the luxuries of your house, my lord. I have never been surrounded by such comforts in my life before! The softest bed, with silk hangings around it, my own maid, a fire in my room — both my rooms, for I have my own sitting room, and we were served salmon in the nursery yesterday." She sighed heavily. "I am very fond of salmon. And the glories of your house are such a spur to my imagination. It is very clear to me now that my father must have been an earl, at the very least, so much at home do I feel here. Walking about these glorious rooms, as to the manner born, I feel very much that I must be Lady Felicia. It will be a wrench to surrender such delights, I assure you. However, I know you will want a proper governess for Juliana and Margarita. I am sure you will have no trouble securing a candidate with the most excellent qualifications."

There was such a mischievous look on her face! She was teasing him, the insolent chit. But she was right — if she left he would need to find a replacement. That aspect of the matter had not occurred to him. "Oh… I suppose we will have to look for someone." He looked helplessly at Drusilla.

"I have it in hand," she said smugly. "Miss Claypole will be here first thing on Monday morning."

"Miss Claypole? I thought she must surely be dead by now."

Drusilla gave a tinkling little laugh. "Dead? By no means! She has a great many years of service yet within her, I am certain. She has been very helpful at the rectory teaching the village children."

"Then she may stay there, for she is not coming *here*."

"But Fin—"

"*No!* Good God, Drusilla, she made my life a misery when she was governess here. Discipline! That was all she cared about, discipline and rules and being punctual. I would not inflict her strictness on those poor girls for the world."

"As a temporary measure?"

"Not for five minutes. Miss Oakes — I beg your pardon, *Lady Felicia* — how would you like to enjoy salmon and a soft bed for a while longer? I will pay you twice your previous salary, and feed you fish or game every day, if you will only preserve me from Miss Claypole."

"I am very much obliged to you, Lord Finlassan," she said, curtsying with demurely downcast eyes. "I should be delighted to accept your very generous offer." Then, with a sideways glance at Drusilla, she added, "Until such time as an acceptable replacement is engaged."

Giles laughed, but Drusilla pursed her lips and gave a grunt that might have been annoyance or grudging acceptance, Fin could not tell and did not much care. He seldom minded Drusilla's high-handedness, preferring it to the exertion of arguing with her, but this time she had taken a step too far. Every man had his limits and Miss Claypole was his.

When the governess raised her eyes again, they were brim full of amusement, and Fin found himself laughing out loud at her effrontery. She was no shrinking miss, that much was certain.

After that, Giles began questioning her about Southampton and there was no more sense to be got from anyone, so Fin crept back to his studio in relief.

# 4: The Painter

Felicia walked about in a dream. Every room in the house revealed some exquisite extravagance — a window of painted glass, an intricately carved stone hearth, statuary and portraits or a painted ceiling. Even the furnishings were beautiful. Not that she saw many rooms, for most had their doors closed, but here and there one would be ajar and then she would peep at the wonders within and imagine herself living here. Lady Felicia! And there would have to be a lord to tenderly escort her in to dinner, and partner her for the opening dance of the grand balls they would no doubt have. Not Lord Finlassan, of course, for he was far too surly and cross to be the hero of her imagination. Felicia's hero would be smiling and handsome and very charming.

Juliana and Margarita were overwhelmed by the splendours in which they now found themselves. The size of the house, the number of servants and the sheer scale of everything, even nursery meals, were sources of amazement to them. Lady Drusilla spent two hours assessing their wardrobes, pronouncing them entirely inadequate and making lists of all that they would now need.

"I shall order some bolts of material and arrange for the Miss Trimms to make up the garments." She looked Felicia up and down assessingly. *"You* will need something more suitable, also, if you are to be here for some time. Do you have an evening gown? Half dress, that is, for you will hardly need a ball gown here."

Lady Drusilla had none of her brother's countenance, being rather long-faced and plain, but Felicia liked her straightforward nature. One knew exactly where one stood with such a person, for she always spoke the absolute truth. Felicia could only agree with her assessment.

"I do indeed have evening dress. You think that his lordship may wish me to bring his wards to the drawing room after dinner?"

She gave a bark of laughter. "He would never think of such a thing! On Sundays, however, it is the custom of the Warboroughs that the children of the house dine with the family. There is a service in the chapel at three, then dinner at five. Naturally, you will be there to supervise your charges and ensure that they remain silent unless spoken to. Mr Warborough and I will be there as well as Finlassan, so there is nothing improper in it. I need not remind you, I am sure, that you must not put yourself forward. Your position here is only temporary, Miss Oakes, so do not get any ideas above your station. I shall see that you are given a good reference for your next employer. It might even be within my power to find you a new place."

"You need not concern yourself with that, my lady," Felicia said. "I have a house of my own to go back to and an independent income. I shall not need to look for another position."

Lady Drusilla's eyebrows rose so high, they merged with the curls of hair framing her face. "An *independent income!* Whatever kind of a governess are you, to have your own house and an independent income?"

"A very fortunate one," Felicia said, chuckling. "Whoever my father was, he was no pauper."

"But not an earl, I suspect," she said in severe tones.

"Very likely so, but a girl may dream, may she not?"

"Not in this house," Lady Drusilla said sourly, "and definitely not of my brother."

Felicia only laughed. It was typical of the nobility, she thought, to presume that every lowborn young woman had an eye towards an elevation in rank. The earl was handsome enough, she conceded, if one admired a brooding countenance, a short temper and a distinct lack of manners. She adored his house, but as for the owner of so much magnificence, she hoped only to avoid him as much as possible.

Sunday was delightful. Having no lessons and kept indoors by persistent rain, Felicia persuaded the housekeeper to show them around the public rooms. Mrs Shayne knew little of the architecture or decorations of the house, but, having been born on the estate, and in service since the age of ten, she was a wellspring of anecdotes about the Warborough family. Her memories stretched back to the Third Earl, the present earl's grandfather, who sounded like a rackety sort of character, to Felicia's ears. There were duels and gambling and *'women of terrible bad character'*, as the housekeeper put it with a sniff, glancing at the two children. Mistresses, Felicia guessed, with a sudden pang of realisation that one day someone would have to explain to Juliana and Margarita that their mother, too, was of *'terrible bad character'*.

Of the present Lord Finlassan, Mrs Shayne could not mention him without adding *'poor man'*.

"Is he so much to be pitied?" Felicia could not resist asking.

"Oh, indeed, Miss Oakes. Such a tragic life he has led." Glancing hastily at the two girls to be sure they could not overhear, she whispered, "Jilted three days before his wedding, poor man. Soured him against all society, it has, and here he stays, with only his painting to console him."

"But surely that was years ago." Felicia looked at Juliana and did some sums in her head. "Eleven years ago, at least."

"Thirteen. Indeed, but he was so in love with her, there was never anything like it. So delightful to see him happy, and oh, what a lovely pair they were! So affectionate together… ah, but she was a deceitful little minx. Never cared nothing for him at all, for all her smiles and blushes. Artful creature! Cut his lordship to the quick, she did, and he has never recovered, poor man. Let us hope her daughters have a better disposition."

Felicia had gained a very different image of the Lady Juliana Dulnain from the servants at Summer Cottage, but there was no sense in arguing the point. "Her daughters are very good-natured," was all she said. "I am sure his lordship will not have any cause to regret his guardianship."

"It's to be hoped not," she said with a sniff. "Although what's to become of them, the poor lambs…"

She left the thought unfinished, but it was not Felicia's problem. She would miss them abominably, for they had been her life for four years now, but she had always known she would have to let them go eventually. Her task had been to place the girls in the charge of their guardian, and, that done, their future was for Lord Finlassan to determine. And Lady Drusilla, she admitted. Probably in a year or two they would be sent away to school, to be trained to become superior governesses or to move on the fringes of society, where their noble guardian's rank might outweigh their unfortunate origins. Would they remember their first governess? Probably not, but she would remember them long after she had left Hawkewood Hall.

Mrs Shayne led them through one elegant saloon after another, and each a different shape, a different style, but all beautiful. And so many textures! Felicia ran her fingers over cool marble, rough stone, polished mahogany, delicately traced silverware, soft silk and velvet hangings and intricately carved wood, savouring each one, and itching to draw them all, to capture some ephemeral element of the awe she felt in such surroundings.

They entered another room, the housekeeper throwing open the door with the words, "This is the library."

There was the earl, sitting at a desk with a book open, taking notes. He looked up in surprise, his pen dripping ink.

"Beg pardon, my lord," Mrs Shayne said, rather flustered. "I thought you would be in your sitting room just now, or I should never—"

"Mama!" cried Juliana, running forward.

There over the fireplace was a huge portrait of a woman, just her head and shoulders, and several times larger than life. Without Juliana's words, Felicia would have assumed it to be of the earl's mother, perhaps, or some other relation. The other portraits in the room, and there were many of them, were all of older people, mostly men in their peerage robes, wearing the voluminous wigs of the previous century. That the earl should keep a painting of the woman who had jilted him in such dreary company struck her as odd.

"Come, Miss Juliana!" Mrs Shayne said sharply. "We must not disturb his lordship."

The earl had looked up, glowering, as they entered, but his expression softened at the eagerness in Juliana's face. "No, let them look at it. Is it like, do you think?"

"Yes, very. I like the way her mouth is painted. That is exactly how she smiled when she was trying not to laugh."

Felicia looked more closely. She had been a beauty, there was no doubt about it, with rich curls framing a heart-shaped face, the full mouth made for laughter and perhaps for kissing, too. Yet there was something in the eyes that spoke of sorrow... or was that just her fancy? Or perhaps the knowledge of how her life had ended, as a mistress and mother to two natural daughters, when she could have been a countess.

While the two girls gazed up at their mother, Felicia took in the rest of the room. Although not large, the library was sufficiently high-ceilinged to accommodate two levels of book cases, with small tables or desks in alcoves for the convenience of readers, leaving the mosaic floor mostly clear. Only one object seemed out of place, a large wooden box, filled to overflowing with unopened letters.

"Why do you do that?" the earl said, looking straight at Felicia. Such blue eyes, and the gaze so intense! Yet she felt no hostility in it, only curiosity.

"Do what, my lord?"

"Touch the chair back that way. Stroking it."

"I like the feel of it, my lord. The carving of the wood and the slipperiness of the upholstery."

"Slippery? Is it?" He strode across the room and ran long, slender fingers over the padded back of the chair. "Hmm. Interesting. And the carving…" He closed his eyes, allowing his hands to tell him of it. "There is a slight irregularity just here."

"And a flaw in the wood lower down," she said, touching the place.

"How observant you are," he said. "You see with your hands."

"My art master at Miss Latimer's Academy taught me to use every sense," she said, "although I confess it is more difficult to make use of the sense of smell when capturing a scene in paint."

"Scents… aromas… are more subtle," he said. "Sometimes, when I want to paint the summer I have roses brought from the hot houses. Or lilies… that always evokes summer sunshine for me. In the middle of winter, I have dried lavender scattered about."

She shuddered suddenly, assailed by memories. "Lavender would not work for me. Pies, though… the pie seller always makes me think of autumn. Such a wonderful aroma! And chestnuts roasting."

"Chestnuts… yes! Very true," he said, laughing. Then, abruptly, he said, "What else do you notice about this room?"

"The letters," she said at once, gesturing at the overflowing box. "Do you never open your mail, Lord Finlassan?"

"Never," he said. "Why should I do so, when such missives bring me only unwanted invitations to evening parties or balls, or complaints from my tenants? Uncle Giles goes through everything from time to time to deal with it all."

"If you had read your letters, my lord," Felicia said crisply, "you would have known about your wards and the household would have been prepared for their arrival."

He lifted one shoulder in obvious indifference. "Has there been any deficiency in that regard? No? Then it would have made no difference. Letters are too much of a distraction, Miss Oakes." Abruptly, his face changed, as if he were suddenly aware of his housekeeper and the two children who were watching him in silence. His habitual glower returned. "You may go now."

They went, leaving him to his scowling contemplation of his letter, but Felicia was left with a lingering memory of a quite different man hidden away behind the testy exterior.

~~~~~

*'To Miss J. Pollard, High Farley, Dorsetshire. My dear Jane, You cannot conceive the luxury with which I am now surrounded. Hawkewood Hall is magnificent and I have been persuaded, with how much becoming reluctance you may imagine, to remain as governess until someone more suitable is engaged. May it be many weeks! Ellen and Mary are to stay on with the girls. I did think Ellen would regret the loss of Peter Kennett, but I suspect she will find acceptable consolation in the vast array of footmen here. The earl is very rich and as yet unwed so would satisfy your mama's requirements admirably, except that he never stirs from home so you are unlikely ever to meet him. He is also very cross and ill-tempered, and not at all likely to make a conformable husband. On*
~~~~~

*Sunday, after the briefest service imaginable in the chapel here, the girls and I were instructed by the earl's sister to present ourselves, suitably attired, for family dinner. 'What are you doing here?' said the earl, on seeing us. 'Go away!' Meekly, we went, only to be berated by the sister and instantly dragged back to the drawing room, where the two of them argued over us as if we were cattle at market. In the end we were grudgingly permitted to eat with His Mightiness, who said not a word throughout. We did not care, for there were two full courses, with three joints, plentiful fish and game, and such an array of pastries and jellies and sweetmeats that we were as stuffed as the veal. We have not ventured outside much on account of the rain. Have you had rain in Dorsetshire, too? Or perhaps it is only Derbyshire that is about to float away. When next I write, you will be in London no doubt, enjoying the delights of the town and the attentions of all your admirers. Do tell me all about it, and of any new fashions you observe, for I am quite prepared to have Mary rework all my sleeves again if you command me so. Yours in affection, Felicia Oakes.'*

~~~~~

Felicia woke, as she always did, to the sound of the chamber maid remaking the fire. The girl went about the business as quietly as she could, but there was no hiding the metallic chink of the fire irons, or the rattle of coal, and such sounds were so unfamiliar that Felicia could not sleep through them. On previous days, she had been so tired from the journey that she had rolled over and returned to sleep, only waking again when her hot water arrived. Oh, such pampered luxury! She would miss it excessively when she had to leave. Today, however, further sleep eluded her, and when the maid had crept out of the room, Felicia slipped out of bed and wrapped herself in her old woollen shawl.
~~~~~

The clock on the mantel — a clock in her room! Heavens! — showed that it was not yet six, although the morning light filtered through the shutters. Throwing them open, she was struck by the low angle of the sunlight at this hour, and was driven to seek out some of the principal rooms and admire them in a new light. She had seen the drawing room at noon and by candlelight, but she was sure it would look quite different this morning. Silently, she crept out onto the corridor and down the stairs.

The drawing room was full of housemaids straightening and dusting and tidying, so she slipped away unseen to the library, her bare feet making no sound as she trod lightly from polished wood to carpet then wood again. The shutters had been opened, and the fire lay ready for lighting, but the room sat in watchful quietness, shafts of sunlight catching the dust motes and making them dance. From there, she went through the open door to the next apartment, all elegant curves and cool silver and gold — was it the White Room? Then to the South Saloon with its big French doors to a terrace where steps curved down to the lawn, an immaculate sea of plush green. Beyond that, another open door to the earl's sitting room. A quick peek told her it was empty, so she ventured in to admire the paintings on the walls, Lady Juliana's all greenery and lush, peaceful gardens, while the earl's were men in full robes in heroic poses, while cherubim flew above them.

After a while, she noticed another door to a room she had not yet seen, a door which had been firmly closed on her previous visits but which now lay temptingly ajar, light pouring through the crack. Silently she tiptoed nearer and peeked inside.

The earl was there, his back to her. Despite the morning light, he was surrounded by candelabra, some still burning, the wax melted into great mounds as if he had been there all night. He was dressed almost as informally as the first time she had seen him, wearing only shirt, breeches and paint-spattered slippers. In his hands he carried a palette and an array of brushes, and he stood before a huge paint-covered canvas, dabbing at it in a frenzy of concentration, adding small dots of colour here and there. It looked random, but she could guess from the quick way he changed brushes from time to time and then continued without pause that he was placing those spots of colour with great precision.

Mesmerised, she drew nearer, her silent feet bringing her pace by careful pace to within a few feet of the canvas. It was filled with stormy swirls of colour, with trees lashed by wind and lightning exploding from the sky. In the centre of it, serenely untouched by the turmoil and backlit by a brighter patch of sky, was the temple on the hill.

From the painting it was a small step to perusal of the painter. She had never seen him like this, so enthralled in his outpouring of creativity that he noticed nothing around him. If the storm of his imagination were to break against the windows at that moment, it would not disturb his absorption. His focus was absolute. She moved nearer, fascinated by the confidence in his quick movements with the brush, by the intensity in his face. His hair, unbrushed and tangled, as if he had repeatedly run his fingers through it, curled about his forehead. His throat, revealed by the open shirt, was long and slender, his skin as pale as a girl's except for a hint of shadow on his unshaven chin. A small dot of blue paint had caught one cheek. The sleeves of his shirt were rolled up to reveal strong forearms. She had never seen a man so exposed before, so masculine and yet so *vulnerable,* and she could not take her eyes off him.

Gradually his movements stilled. He gazed at the painting with a slight frown on his face, assessing it. Was it finished? She could not see any scope for improvement, and perhaps he thought so too, for after many minutes of such contemplation, he let out a soft sigh, and took a step back.

Without turning his head to look at her, he said, "What do you think of it?" His tone was gentler than any she had heard from him before.

"It is magnificent," she said without hesitation.

"I think so too," he said, turning intense blue eyes to her with a sudden smile. "It is the best thing I have ever done, I believe."

That smile! Such warmth, such genuine warmth as she had never seen in him before. Her heart jolted in response with a violence that shocked her to the core. The very air between them seemed charged. She gasped, and took a step back.

He noticed nothing, for he turned back to the painting at once. "It is so rare, to capture precisely what I wished to accomplish. Do you not find it so? How often does one begin with high hopes and the clearest imagery in mind, but the result falls short. Yet not tonight... But I perceive that it is morning already. I must go and clean the paint out of my hair." He laughed, and tossed his palette and brushes onto a table. "And you had best get dressed, too, Miss Oakes." Another quick laugh, he kicked off his painting slippers and then he was gone.

Felicia stood rooted to the spot, too shaken to move. What had just happened? One moment she had been watching a painter engaged in his art, and the next... he had smiled at her, and then...

Such madness. She could not, *would not* fall in love with Lord Finlassan. That way led only to heartbreak.

She spun on her heel and ran swiftly back to her room.

# 5: Settling In (May)

It was fortunate for Felicia's peace of mind that she saw nothing of Lord Finlassan for several days. She quickly re-established the schoolroom routine for Juliana and Margarita, which consisted of a great many long walks through the manicured grounds of the Hall, together with hours of art work each day, with very little of other subjects. They read a page or two of Shakespeare every day, and, finding a child's history book on the nursery shelves, read a chapter on wet days. It was rather out of date, ending with the Union with Scotland, but Felicia could not see that much of importance could have happened in the hundred years since, apart from the wars with France, and why should anyone want to know more about that?

Lady Drusilla came once or twice, tutted over the lack of music, needlework and languages, and went away again, promising to write to all her society acquaintances for recommendations for a proficient governess. Felicia was now rather torn about the prospect of leaving Hawkewood Hall. Its beauties lifted her spirits and its luxury brought her satisfaction of a more basic kind, but its owner preyed on her mind rather. When she walked about the house now and created her romantic little stories in her head, the broodingly handsome earl featured more often than she would like. Try as she might to relegate him to some dusty corner of her mind, he would keep intruding on her imagination, his shirt unfastened and his blue eyes alight as he smiled at her...

Such madness. There was nothing to hope for there.

On one point, Lady Drusilla moved with great swiftness. Within a few days of their arrival, she had visited a warehouse in Derby to procure lengths of suitable fabrics for the wards of an earl, and arranged with the Miss Trimms in Church Compton for the making up of the items. Felicia was given instructions on when and how to present herself and her charges for measuring and fitting. In their walks about the grounds they had not yet ventured to the village, so there was some excitement at the outing. Since it was little more than a mile away by the most direct path, they eschewed the use of the carriage and walked along an avenue of rough-barked elms to a small gate.

The Miss Trimms lived on the far side of the village, where the church, rectory, coaching inn and smithy sprawled around three sides of a large square. On the fourth side stood a pair of massive stone gateposts, but the gates hung askew and beyond them the drive was choked with weeds. The fine avenue of oaks showed gaps here and there, and what might once have been lawn was as high-grown and brown as a cornfield. Felicia stopped, fascinated by so much extravagant decay.

The girls stared in open curiosity. "Who lives there?" Juliana said.

Her high voice was overheard by two passing women. "That's Shotterbourne, miss, where the Marquess of Arnwell lives," one of them said, stopping to smile at the girls.

"Why is it all ruined? Is the marquess very poor?"

The women laughed. "Not he! But he lost his whole family in a fire years back and went mad from the grief. Now he don't care about nothing. Turned off the gardeners and gamekeepers and most of the indoor servants, too. He lives in a couple of rooms and never goes nowhere, not even to church."

"Maybe he has a chapel of his own, like our guardian does," Juliana said brightly.

The women looked at her with renewed interest. "Ah, so you are Lord Finlassan's wards. We heard there were two young ladies staying at the hall... with their governess." Their eyes fell on Felicia, and they executed little curtsies. "Beg pardon for not realising who you were, madam."

"Why, how should you, indeed?" she said, laughing. "But you will get used to us coming and going, I dare say. We are on our way to the Miss Trimms, but I am not sure which cottage it might be. We were told to look for the black and white cottage with the brown door, but that seems to describe half the houses within sight."

The women laughed, too. "Oh, it's just across the square — that one with the low hedge all round it, next to the inn."

Felicia thanked them, which brought another outbreak of curtsies, and they walked on round the square, past the fine Norman church, the rectory next door and then the smithy, where they stopped for some time to watch a horse being shod. A smith may not be a man of education, but there was much to admire in the strength and deftness of his arms as he pursued his trade, Felicia found, storing images in her mind to be set to paper at a later date.

They had just, with some reluctance, turned away from this interesting spectacle and were passing the arch of the coaching inn when a fashionably dressed gentleman came striding out from the inn yard, almost barrelling into them. He jumped back, sweeping off his hat in apology, but then he caught sight of Felicia and started.

"Lady Olivia? This is a surprise!"

Felicia smiled at his error. "You are mistaken, sir. To my regret, I am not Lady Olivia... or Lady anything."

He bowed with an elegance that Felicia could not but admire. He had the sort of features that would be called handsome by most observers, having a pleasing regularity combined with an open, genial countenance. His manners, too, were beyond reproach, as his first words proved.

"I do beg your pardon, madam! Forgive my ineptitude. Just at first I thought I saw a likeness... but now it is clear to me that I was quite wrong. If you are inclined to be censorious for my foolishness, however, please be assured that the Lady Olivia Dulnain is regarded as a diamond of the first water, a great beauty and much admired by society. I can only beg you to take that into account before you condemn me utterly."

Dulnain... was she then some relation to Lady Juliana? Margarita was still distracted by the smith and had not heard the name, but Juliana jumped and seemed about to speak. Cautiously, Felicia laid a restraining hand on her shoulder.

"Such mistakes are easily made and therefore easily forgiven, sir," she said to the stranger, whereupon he repeated his apology in the fairest terms, and bowed again. Felicia curtsied and they moved on. As soon as they were out of earshot, she said to Juliana in a low voice, "It is better not to mention your mother's family to strangers. It is for Lord Finlassan to explain you to the world in whatever manner he deems fit."

"But Lady Olivia must be related to us!"

"If so, it would be for the family to acknowledge the relationship, should they wish to do so. You must make no claim yourself."

They had reached the seamstresses' cottage by this point, so the conversation ended, and for two hours their heads were filled with gowns and pelisses and spencers and chemises and all manner of other excitements. Felicia was enchanted by the muslins and cambrics and printed cottons and merino wools supplied to make up her own garments, and although the colours were drably suitable for her station as a governess, still the finished items would be finer than anything she had previously worn. With such pleasant thoughts to beguile the walk home, nothing more was said on the subject of Lady Olivia Dulnain, but Felicia made up her mind to write to Agnes, who would be sure to know all about the Dulnain family.

~~~~~

The Lady Drusilla found some excuse to visit the nursery almost every day. She had not, as yet, found a governess to replace Felicia, for her requirements were many and the very best candidates, she explained, were already employed. However, as a temporary measure she had engaged a French tutor, a dancing master, an instructor on the pianoforte and a singing master, and had herself engaged to instruct Juliana and Margarita in the arts of embroidery, the netting of purses and tapestry. Ponies had been obtained, and the head groom was to teach them to ride.
~~~~~

"You may continue to teach them painting and drawing," she said to Felicia, "but I do not care for all these bowls of fruit and shrivelled-up leaves. Watercolours of the finest prospects about the estate, suitable for framing, and the painting of fire screens, that is what they must produce. A young lady must be able to display her accomplishments, and these *horrid* collections of dead objects are not of the least use."

Felicia curtsied and said that yes, of course she would direct her charges' efforts in the required directions, although she wondered just what difference it would make in the end. Would the girls ever be able to take their place in their guardian's level of society, where a facility in French was expected? It seemed likely that they would be looking for husbands from amongst the outer circles of society — the cits and nabobs and half-pay officers who would be happy to take them for their fortunes and the tenuous connection to Lord Finlassan. Would such people care about painted screens or the singing of Italian airs? She could not say, but it was not for her to question her orders.

The influx of tutors meant that Felicia had more time to herself, whole hours when the girls were otherwise engaged and she could pursue her own interests. As often as not, this meant taking her easel to some interesting point about the house and attempting to capture the exquisite beauties which so enchanted her. She was in the Pillared Saloon one day when she became aware that she was not alone. Someone was standing behind her, watching her work, and she knew, although she could not say how, that it was the earl.

For a long time he watched in silence, but then he said, "You spoke the truth when you declared straight lines to be the bane of your existence. Yet here you are painting a room encircled with pillars."

That made her laugh out loud. "Indeed! Yet I know not how to remedy the deficiency."

"You have captured the marble magnificently," he said, drawing nearer. "The statue of Vesta is perfect. But those pillars...! Yet I believe the problem is that you define the edges too precisely. I think the effect you desire could be achieved a different way. It would be enough merely to suggest the edges by applying light and shade. May I show you?"

His hand hovered over her box of colours, then he selected two sticks and began to draw with quick, decisive strokes. At once the pillar was transformed, the wavering outline replaced by subtle shading that merely insinuated the shape.

"Oh, that is clever!" she cried.

He fished in the box again, and applied some stippling to the new colour, to match the rest of the pillar. Then he stood back to admire his efforts. "It is a long time since I tried pastels, but the effects are interesting. May I attempt something with the fireplace?"

When she assented, he chose several more sticks and began dotting colour with quick, firm movements. As with his own painting, his concentration was absolute. Felicia was mesmerised by his face, the way his brows lowered as he focused, the slightly open mouth, his lips warmly blood-red in his pale face, the way his hair curled over his shirt points. She felt oddly disconnected, light-headed, like a dandelion seed floating free from its mooring, drifting into the sky and driven here and there by the wind. What was the matter with her?

He turned his blue eyes on her, and it was as if she were drowning, swirling away from her safe world into uncharted waters.

"This is good," he said, and then, when she was already clinging to sanity by a thread, he smiled.

He smiled, and her heart melted.

Felicia hardly knew how she got through the rest of the day. Somehow, inexplicably, the hours passed and no one commented on her air of distraction. But when she was able to retreat to her own room at last, she found herself shedding hot tears of frustration. All her tranquillity was shattered by a pair of blue eyes and a smile! How foolish — how unutterably *stupid* to fall in love with such a man, who was as far above her as the moon. Even if he loved her in return, there could be no question of marriage, not between an earl and the natural child of no one knows whom. Even if she were, as she had joked, the daughter of the Prince of Wales, there could be no question of it.

Was this how it had been for Lady Juliana Dulnain? Betrothed to the earl, but then falling in love with her architect... and she had chosen love over her position in society. Could Felicia do that? If the earl spoke words of love to her and begged her, would she become his mistress? Would that be enough for her? In all truth, she could not say. All she knew was that she must leave Hawkewood Hall as soon as she could, for her own peace of mind. Once away from Lord Finlassan, she could recover her equanimity.

~~~~~

MAY
~~~~~

Juliana and Margarita now had a very densely-packed rota of lessons. A steady succession of tutors arrived each day in gigs and dog-carts and, in one case, an extremely stylish curricle, whisking the girls away to dance or play or conjugate irregular verbs, as required. Juliana thrived under such a regime, but her sister blossomed only with a pencil or paintbrush in her hand, or on the now much-curtailed walks around the garden. Even these walks were less interesting to her than at Itchen, for the Hawkewood gardens were cosseted and pampered and trimmed to the point that not a single stray leaf or flower petal disturbed the purity of the velvety lawns and smooth flowerbeds. The shrubs were shaped to perfect balls or tapered towers, and the flowers grew in regimented squares like a chess board. There was little there of the wildness that fired Margarita's artistic imagination.

With so little call for her services as governess, Felicia began to fear that her new freedom would give her too much opportunity to brood about a certain lord with vivid blue eyes. She seldom saw him, but one day he burst into the schoolroom.

"Hmpf. There you are," he said, glowering at Felicia, as if she had been hiding from him. "I have been thinking about Juliana's paintings, and how they might be got here. Is there anyone you would trust to pack them up and arrange for transportation?"

"There is a frame maker in Southampton who is accustomed to packing and moving valuable art. You wish everything to be brought here? Then perhaps Mr Pierce, Mr Kearney's attorney, would make the arrangements. He has the care of the paintings now. Shall I give you his direction so that you may write to him?"

He hesitated. "Such letters are tedious to write."

"Then may I compose the letter for you?" she said, trying not to laugh at his discomfiture. "You need only sign it."

"Hmpf. That might be acceptable."

It took her no more than half an hour to compose the letter, and three days to find the earl in a suitable frame of mind to sign it. He was either in his studio and not to be disturbed, Bagnall informed her, or he was sleeping and not to be disturbed, or he had gone out for a walk and could not be found at all. But one evening Bagnall fetched her from the schoolroom, where she was taking supper with the children.

The earl was in his own quarters, eating his dinner from a tray, a book propped open in front of him. In a corner, Matthews, his valet, waited silently.

"Bagnall tells me I must sign this wretched letter of yours, Miss Oakes," he said with a rueful smile.

"It is your letter, my lord."

"Very well. Matthews, bring the writing box over here and fix me a pen."

It took some minutes for the pen to be made to his satisfaction, but then the letter was signed with a flourish, sanded and handed back to her.

"Are you not going to read it?"

"I trust you, Miss Oakes. Now go away, all of you. I want some peace and quiet."

"It needs to be sealed," Felicia said, without moving.

"Good Lord, girl, you can seal it yourself, surely? Use a wafer or some such."

"It is an official letter conducting business in your name, my lord. It needs to be sealed with your own seal."

"The devil it does! I have no idea where my seal is. In the library, I daresay." With a melodramatic sigh, he rose from the table. "I can see there is to be no peace at all until this is done. Come, then, Miss Oakes. To the library!"

It took the four of them, Felicia, the earl, Bagnall and Matthews, the best part of an hour to rifle through every drawer and cupboard in the room, before Bagnall uttered a triumphant cry. Then there was sealing wax to be found and melted, but at last it was done. The earl scrawled *'Finlassan'* and his address across the back, sanded it and handed her the letter.

"It says who it is from inside," she said. "Do you need to write your name on the outside as well? I have never done so."

His eyes registered something that could only be amusement, although he did not smile. "I have franked it, Miss Oakes. A letter franked by a peer or a Member of Parliament is conveyed free of charge."

"Oh. Thank you, my lord." Her eyes strayed to the box of letters in the middle of the room, so full now that a few missives had spilt over the edge onto the mosaic floor.

"Your gaze reproaches me, Miss Oakes," he said, but there was amusement in his voice. "I choose neither to read nor to write letters, and Uncle Giles is too busy with his own affairs to attend to mine, seemingly."

"Should you like me to look through them?" she said. "I could at least sort them into categories for Mr Warborough to examine. I daresay many of them are invitations to card parties last December or some such, and may safely be burned."

"It is an onerous task to inflict on one who already has many other duties."

"Now that your wards have so many other teachers, my days are long. It would please me to remove that eyesore from this room."

He gazed around, as if seeing the room for the first time. "You are quite right. It is an affront to the symmetry of the room. Bagnall, have the box removed to… let me see, is the billiard table still covered over?"

"It is, my lord."

"Very well, take it to the billiard room. You will have plenty of space there, Miss Oakes."

Such interactions with the earl were survivable, she found, so long as he did not smile at her. She could cope admirably with his curtness, but his smile would be devastating.

Meanwhile, Lady Drusilla had devised a scheme which also absorbed some of Felicia's spare hours. Her ladyship had decided, in her brook-no-argument way, that the girls needed to be taught the care of an animal. Since the head groom at Hawkewood resolutely refused to allow them into the stables, she bestowed upon them a puppy from a recent litter at the rectory. The creature was at least trained to behave itself indoors, but it needed prodigious amounts of exercise each day, and as the girls' hours were filled, it fell to Felicia's lot to walk the pup each morning and afternoon.

"His name is Hercules," Lady Drusilla told them.

"Hercules?" Felicia said, eyebrows lifting. "That is not a very dog-like name."

"But it is the one he answers to," she said.

There was one advantage to walking with a bundle of boundless energy, which was that she explored corners of the park not previously seen. Beyond the formal gardens and lawns and well-regulated shrubberies, she found interesting expanses of tussocky moorland, outcrops of rock, meandering natural streams and pools, and several acres of woodland. These were still peppered with neat paths and convenient seats, but felt somehow less regimented. It was pleasant to unleash the dog and allow him to race about as he wished, while Felicia followed sedately on the path.

One day Hercules ran on ahead, tongue lolling and ears flapping, and then, perhaps detecting an intriguing scent, shot off at an angle from the path into dense woodland.

"Hercules! Come back!" Felicia called futilely, for despite Lady Drusilla's assertion, the pup never responded to his name.

He disappeared, only a loud rustling in the undergrowth suggesting his route. With a sigh, Felicia plunged after him, glad that she was not wearing one of her stylish new gowns, as she picked her way through brambles and skirted a boggy patch. She soon came upon a narrow path, perhaps a deer track, and a flash of Hercules' rump in the distance told her that he had turned onto it. She followed, catching glimpses of her quarry far ahead, and hearing his excited yaps occasionally.

After some time, the trees opened out and there ahead of her was a high wall, built of the natural stone of the area, all shapes and sizes piled expertly together to make a boundary.

Beyond the wall were more trees, and one of them had fallen directly onto the wall, causing it to collapse at that point. Hercules was sniffing enthusiastically around the heap of stones.

"Hercules, come here now, boy," Felicia said, producing the leather leash. "Time to return to the house."

The dog turned mournful eyes on her, tail wagging. Then, with one great leap, he was atop the pile of stones and over into the trees beyond, vanishing from sight.

"Oh, Hercules, you fiend!" Felicia muttered.

But there was no help for it. Holding up her skirts in one hand, she clambered gingerly onto the hill of stones, up and over, and into the mysterious grounds beyond.

# 6: Shotterbourne

Felicia had no trouble following Hercules, for he crashed about in the trees like a herd of swine. The same deer track reappeared on this side of the wall, so she kept to its easier passage until, quite abruptly, the trees ended and she emerged into the open.

She knew at once where she was, for the rank, waist-high grass and wildly overgrown shrubs dotted here and there told her that it must be Shotterbourne, the adjoining estate, and home to the reclusive Marquess of Arnwell. The deer track led on up a rise, and Hercules' eagerly waving tail led the way. She followed, and since the dog darted here and there as interesting odours attracted him, she made as good progress as he did.

Cresting the rise, the land opened out and there below her was the house, or rather, mansion. It was larger even than Hawkewood Hall, a block of golden stone with neatly pointed roofs and a pillared entrance — a portico, she now knew — with four matching wings, one at each corner. It had an austere beauty, the embodiment of perfect symmetry, except for one thing — one of the wings was a burnt-out shell, only four blackened walls remaining. The village women had mentioned a fire which had claimed the marquess's entire family, and seeing the devastation it had wrought, she could well believe it. If they had all been in that one wing, perhaps fast asleep in their beds, when the fire had taken hold… She shivered. Even their great wealth and noble rank had not saved them. Everyone was equally vulnerable to disaster — fire or accident or illness, or the sinking of the ship which had taken Mr Kearney's life. So much tragedy. For the marquess, it seemed there was no comfort left in the world, but for Juliana and Margarita perhaps there was the chance of a better life under Lord Finlassan's patronage than in Southampton.

Hercules was out of sight, but she heard him barking not far ahead. He rarely barked except at other humans or when chasing the stable cats, and she hurried on in case he was getting into mischief. Around some high bushes was a pillared marble pavilion adorned with statuary, and for an instant she was confused, mistaking it for the temple on the hill at Hawkewood. But then she saw her error, for although this one was similar, it was smaller and rather more elegant, with the same simplicity that characterised the house below.

She could not see Hercules, but as she drew near enough to see inside the pavilion, she realised he was inside, sitting wagging his tail furiously at the feet of an elderly man who was stroking him.

"I beg your pardon, sir," she said rushing up. "He ran away from me, but if I might fasten a leash around his neck, I will take him away and disturb your solitude no longer."

"That would be a pity," he said. "He is a friendly fellow, and I have not seen a dog since my last pointer died. Will you not sit with me awhile, since he seems to enjoy my company as much as I enjoy his?"

"You are very kind to say so," she said. She had no hesitation in sitting down beside him on the cushioned marble bench, for he seemed not at all grand or hostile. His clothes were of good quality, although sadly out of date, but unlike so many men of his age he wore no wig, for he had a full head of white hair. She gazed out with interest from the pavilion, which had been sited to give a fine prospect over the house and what might once have been pleasure grounds, but were now as wild and weed-infested as the rest of the estate.

"What is his name?" the man said, rubbing the dog's ears so that he closed his eyes in bliss.

"Hercules."

He laughed, and it was pleasant amidst so much decay to hear merriment. "A strange name for a dog!"

"So I thought, too! But all the rectory dogs have such names — Vulcan and Apollo and Flora and Neptune."

"Do they, now. How curious. Roman gods."

"Are they? I did not know. Forgive me, sir, but I am not sure to whom I am speaking."

With a smile, he said, "Who do you think I am?"

She thought, if she were applying the rules of common sense, that he might well be the marquess himself, but the village women had said he had gone mad with grief, and this man seemed perfectly sane to Felicia. Besides, he was not at all high in the instep, and it would be embarrassing to call him *'my lord'* and then discover he was merely a very grand butler or steward. But her sense of mischief bubbled up in response to such an inviting question.

"Why, I do believe you are an Italian count, driven from your home by the machinations of your jealous younger brother. Here in the heart of Derbyshire you may hide incognito until the time is right for you to return to your native land to claim your rightful heritage."

He laughed out loud, and said, "Very well, then. Let me be *il Conte di Niente.* And how, pray, am I to claim my heritage?"

"You will challenge him to a duel, naturally, and because he is cowardly he will run away rather than face you."

"No," he said thoughtfully. "I will force him to face me and then I will kill him, in vengeance for all that he has taken from me."

There was something intense in his tone and she knew not how to answer him. But almost at once he went on in a lighter manner, "But what of you? You are more than a walker of dogs, I think. Do you have a secret identity, too?"

"Of course! I am… a princess, the secret heir to the throne of… oh, a small principality in Europe, which I am not at liberty to disclose to you…"

"Aha! You are the *Prinzessin von Nichts.*"

"I am! Whatever that means. And my country has been at war with its wicked neighbours, who wish to annex it and take control of our great wealth, and so I have been sent away to safety in England, where I masquerade as a humble governess."

"Until you can be married to a great lord who will bring his army to crush your enemies in revenge for all your suffering," he said, with satisfaction.

"Vengeance again?" she said hesitantly, wondering if perhaps he was indeed mad.

"*'Vengeance is in my heart, death in my hand, Blood and revenge are hammering in my head'*," he said, his voice resonating in a way that sent shivers down her spine. "Shakespeare covers all eventualities, and I am patient." Then, with a sigh, he added, "But I daresay if one achieves it in the end, it is less sweet than imagination makes it."

He fell into silence, and Felicia could find no words to lighten the darkness that lay in the air between them. What could anyone say to a man who talked so calmly of waiting to claim his revenge? She no longer doubted that he was the marquess, and in a man who had lost his entire family to fire, perhaps such thoughts were understandable. Not excusable, for whatever evils had been inflicted on him, no man should take it upon himself to mete out punishment purely for revenge. Even so, she could acknowledge the grief that prompted them, and appreciate to some degree why he no longer cared about his estate. That was a kind of madness, certainly.

Such a horror, to be swept up in a tragedy of that magnitude. What must it be like to have your family around you, and then to lose them all at once? But she had never had a family of her own, nor lived with one, and her imagination could not encompass it. A father and mother and their children, grumbling sometimes, squabbling occasionally, but loving and being loved in return — what must that be like? She had known only Miss Armiger's sternness, and the kindly but distant care of the Miss Latimers. Since then, she had been a paid employee, observing the families, living amongst them but as an outsider. Families were a mystery to her.

But when the dog whined, she was brought back from her musings. "I must get back," she said, in alarm. "I shall be missed." Quickly she tied the leash around Hercules' neck.

She rose, and the man rose too, bowing to her with the greatest civility. It was only then, when she faced him directly, that she saw the other side of his face and the terrible destruction there. Nor was it just his face, for his arm on that side hung limply, the hand closely covered by a glove.

"Oh, whatever happened to you?" she cried out before she could stop herself.

"I was burned in a fire," he said, his tone bleak.

"The fire that killed your family," she said, and he nodded.

"They tell me I was the fortunate one — I survived." He could not hide the bitterness in his voice. "But let me tell you, there is nothing of good fortune in my life, not any longer."

Felicia's heart was wrung by the pain in his face. "But there could be," she said quietly. "Even if you have no family left to you, you might still be of value to society — to your tenants and neighbours, and to your country. You have a seat in the House of Lords, after all, and could do some good in the world."

"Ah, you have some romantic notion of nobility, I dare say."

"No, only of the resilience of the human spirit. You are not the first man to be plunged into tragedy, my lord, nor will you be the last. I have no family, either, but I do not allow that to drag me down into misery. There is so much of good in the world, of happiness and joyfulness, of friendship and good company... and of *beauty!* You have all of this..." She waved a hand over the wildness of the gardens and the house, still majestic despite the ruination of one wing. "...and it could be made wondrous again. The house could be made good, and the gardens restored to order, and would you not feel better if it were so?"

"*No,*" he said, with such violence that she involuntarily took a step back. More moderately, he went on, "Let the place rot, for all I care. There is no *feeling better*, not for me. But you are right in what you say of friendship and good company. I have enjoyed your company today, and Hercules' also. Will you come to see me again? I am here most afternoons."

She hesitated. Making a friend of a marquess was not something that a person in her position would normally contemplate, but he seemed lonely and unhappy, and the dog brought him some pleasure.

"I should be happy to," she said. "At least... if I can. My time is not my own."

He chuckled. "You are still assuming the rôle of governess, then."

That made her laugh. "Farewell, my lord Count."

"*Bis wir uns wieder treffen, Prinzessin.*"

~~~~~

*'To Miss J. Pollard, Charles Street, Mayfair. My dear Jane, So glad you have arrived safely in London, but disappointed to hear that your mama is not pleased with the house she has taken. I am sure the smoking chimneys are not so bad as she thinks, for is not smoke a preservative, as with kippers? Besides, you will not need fires for much longer. As for the cook, if she is so temperamental, it is better to be rid of her at once and get a steadier person. Just think if she had taken umbrage in the middle of the season — the*
~~~~~

*inconvenience! If the mould will not come out of your gowns (have you tried boiled fig leaves? Most efficacious), you will just have to buy new ones. You see, there is always a benefit to such disasters. I am still at Hawkewood Hall and cannot see the possibility of an early release from my so-pleasant servitude, for every prospective governess falls short of Lady D's requirements. On another matter, you could not be more wrong! I do not know what I have said to give rise to your most unwarranted conjectures, but be assured that you are far out, for Lord F barely knows I exist. I have not mentioned him because I so rarely see him. He secludes himself in his studio and rarely emerges, and we do not even see him in the chapel on Sundays, since we have formed the habit of walking to Church Compton for Morning Service, where at least we get a few psalms and a sermon. But if I see little of the earl, I have formed an even nobler acquaintance in the Marquess of Arnwell, our even more reclusive neighbour. He is a sad and lonely old man, to make friends of a governess and a half-trained puppy, but he seems to enjoy my company as I enjoy his. We pretend that we are exiles, he an Italian Count and I a German Princess, and in such disguise we may speak of all manner of things. I have hopes of drawing him out of his self-imposed cage and back into the world before too long. Yours in affection, Felicia Oakes.'*

<div align="center">~~~~~</div>

Fin was restless. After the burst of creativity which had produced, for once, a painting he could be proud of, he had fallen back into his usual lethargy. He had prepared a new canvas, but no subject occurred to him. Remembering the governess's representation of the Pillared Saloon, and the way she had brought the fire to life, he had filled several sheets with sketches of flames. Two days had been spent in blending a certain shade of red that he thought might do, only to be discarded as unsatisfactory. The new canvas remained reproachfully blank.

One morning, as he was making his way to his studio to begin another day of fretful inactivity, he heard excited voices emerging from the South Saloon. He discovered his two wards and the governess standing by the big windows, all frantically engaged with sketchbooks and charcoal, drawing hastily in broad sweeps across the paper, only to discard the sheet and almost immediately begin another. The floor was littered with their attempts.

"What the devil are you doing?"

"We are drawing the clouds!" Margarita cried, her little face alight with enthusiasm. "They go by so quickly that we must draw as fast as we can to capture each fleeting configuration."

Outside the windows, the wind bent the trees into dancing life and the clouds scudded overhead like great waves breaking and reforming almost instantly. A quick glance at the many sheets on the floor showed him some half-decent attempts to capture the movement. His fingers itched to improve on them.

"May I try?"

The two sisters laughed merrily, and the governess said, "Of course, my lord. Spare sketchbooks are on that table there. Charcoals in the box here. But you must draw as quick as you can — no stopping to perfect each line."

Smiling, he agreed to it. This was more fun than agonising over exact shades of carmine! For a while, caught up in their enthusiasm, he sketched, discarded, sketched again. It was liberating, he found, to draw without a critical eye, to simply sweep a few bold lines across the paper, and then begin again. As he worked, his outlines became even simpler and yet he felt he was capturing something of the essence of each cloud, not just the shape but the movement, the swiftness of the change and the tempestuous wind that drove them.

The room was silent. Only the governess remained, quietly scooping up the many drawings on the floor.

"Where did they go?" he said, surprised.

"It was time for their riding lesson," she said, looking up at him with an impish smile. Such a pretty face, with its wide eyes and generous mouth, a few stray curls escaping from their confinement. As she turned back to gathering the drawings, one long curl lay on the nape of her neck, mesmerising him. She had nothing of Juliana's serene beauty, but there was a liveliness to her that he rather liked, now that he had grown accustomed to it.

"I had not noticed them go," he said.

She laughed. "So I observed. I envy you that, my lord."

"What do you envy?"

"Your ability to concentrate so fiercely that the world disappears, if only for a few minutes. It is an admirable trait."

"Is it? All I know is that it has kept me sane these past years. If I had not been able to lose myself in my painting I should have had no reason to live." For a moment, all the bleakness of his loss swept over him once more. No Juliana, no close family life such as he had once dreamt of, no happiness.

"There is always a reason to live," she said, sharply. "However desperate a situation, there is always good to be found in it, and the hope of better days." Then, in softer tones, she said, "It was thirteen years ago, my lord."

For a moment her effrontery took his breath away. What right had *she* to criticise him? But something in her eyes — sympathy, perhaps — touched him. She was right. It was self-indulgent of him to talk so, when he was, in many ways, so fortunate. He had lost Juliana, but he had his health and the comfort of wealth, and his life could be so much worse.

"Do you hope for better days, Miss Oakes?"

Instantly her face was alive with merriment. "*These* are my better days, my lord! When I go home, as I soon must, I shall miss this place abominably."

"The food?" he said, smiling at her.

"Oh yes! The sugarplums! The syllabub! The partridge and pheasant and woodcock! And I shall not be sketching clouds so extensively when I must pay for all my own paper, you may be sure."

"When you leave, you may take a box of paper with you. Several boxes. But you will not be poor, I think. You have a house, and some money of your own, I understand."

"True, but who knows how well I shall manage on it? I have never lived alone." Her expressive face was bleak and his heart was unexpectedly touched.

"I do not think your fate is to live out your days alone, Miss Oakes."

For some unaccountable reason, she blushed a fiery red, muttered something unintelligible and fled the room.

# 7: The Heir

*'It is not your fate to live alone.'*

Felicia paced up and down the schoolroom until her emotions were under better control. He meant nothing by it, she knew that. It was no more than pity from an employer towards his employee, a kindly piece of encouragement to lift her spirits. He did not mean that she would ever share her life with *him*, how could he? It would be too insulting for words if he were to offer her *carte blanche*, and anything more formal was utterly out of the question. No, he was merely paying her a casual compliment — *'I am sure you will marry one day'*. And perhaps she would. It may be that in time she would grow sick of loneliness and the misery of unrequited love, and find herself a gentle young farmer to wed. Or, more optimistically, she might forget the enigmatic but enticing earl altogether and fall in love with someone more suitable. Someone of her own rank, whatever that might be.

A tap on the door made her jump. When it opened, and the earl's apologetic face appeared, she almost wept. Why oh why could he not leave her alone?

He coughed. "So sorry to disturb you once more, but... um... you left these behind." He held out a sheaf of cloud drawings, then quickly pushed them onto the nearest table.

"Oh... thank you." If only she could stop blushing! She was not a green girl of seventeen any longer, and it was humiliating. Clearly it embarrassed him, for he rubbed one hand on his breeches and chewed his lip worriedly. Could she tell him to go away? Would it be insufferably rude?

"Miss Oakes..." A long pause, then, in a great rush, he went on, "Pray forgive me for distressing you. It was unintentional. May I... may I mention your cloud sketches? I hope you do not mind, but I looked through them and you have a great facility with charcoal. Your drawings have a simplicity to them which yet is more effective than any of mine. You see here... and this one here... and this one is mine..."

He laid them out in a line, and then hurriedly stood back so that she could draw near to examine them.

She hardly knew how to respond. What did he want of her? Was this merely a discussion of art or was there more to his words and manner than she could divine? So she stood uncertainly, willing her rosy cheeks to subdue and torn between wishing he would go and hoping he would stay.

"You need not fear me," he said gently.

"Oh no! I do not... not at all!"

"I would never do anything you would dislike, but I should very much like us to be friends, Miss Oakes. In my whole life, I have never met anyone else to whom I might talk about my art, except Juliana and now you. That is all I ask of you, nothing more... to be able to share ideas with someone who *understands*. Even when the new governess arrives, I should like you to stay on here and eat as many sugarplums as you wish and… and paint alongside me. My studio is at your disposal. Will you consider the idea? Please?"

How could she possibly refuse him? Her head told her that this was a terrible idea that would lead her in very short order to desolation and years of misery. Her heart answered without hesitation.

"I should be very honoured, my lord."

"Fin… all my friends call me Fin."

"Thank you, Fin." And she could not stop an absurdly wide smile from spreading across her foolish, lovesick face.

~~~~~

Felicia had her own space in the earl's studio, which was a glorious room with a high, painted ceiling, a huge bow window at one end and more windows on two sides, with blinds which could be raised or lowered to adjust the light to suit. A silent footman came at regular intervals to wipe up spilt paint, clean brushes, pestles and mortars, and replace paint-spattered aprons and cloths with immaculate fresh ones. A cabinet was filled with every kind of paper imaginable. Another contained pencils, brushes, knives and trowels, and more bottles of pigment and oil than she had ever seen outside of a shop. When she set up her own modest easel, the earl immediately offered her a much larger one. Even without the thrill of the earl's company, she could scarcely believe her good fortune.

With so many tutors and instructors to attend to Juliana and Margarita, her duties as governess were now reduced to no more
~~~~~

than two or three hours of each day. By handing Hercules over to a willing footman each morning, she was able to devote several hours before breakfast to her own experiments in oil painting, under the expert eye of Lord Finlassan. Or Fin, as she must learn to call him.

If she had harboured the slightest illusion of an attachment on his part, his method of instruction would have instantly disabused her of the notion. His teaching consisted of showing her how to mix the oils, telling her blithely to *'have a go, and you will soon get into the way of it'* and then criticising every single aspect of her efforts in the most uncompromising fashion. Her oils were too thick, too thin, too oily or not oily enough. Her brush strokes were too hesitant or too bold, her colours were all wrong and her palette management was execrable. Had she been more sensitive, he would have reduced her to tears several times a day. It was fortunate indeed that she had the kind of spirits which were amused by such scoldings, and many a time she would laugh in his face, and say that, yes, it was a dreadful execution and should she burn it at once? Whereupon he would contrive to find some small degree of merit in the curl of a leaf or the colour of the sky.

At church, she finally met the legendary Miss Claypole, former governess and terrifier of the young Fin, finding her to be, as she had suspected, a formidable person, her hair iron-grey beneath a stern cap, but whose eyes twinkled appreciatively when told of the earl's horror of her return to Hawkewood Hall.

"He always wanted to be painting or drawing or mooning about over twigs and rosebuds and other such nonsense," she said, "whereas I was duty bound to inflict upon him poetry and arithmetic and history and an awareness of the world. Naturally we fell out a dozen times a day. But I always won, Miss Oakes. *That is what rankles with him now, I'll wager.*"

Felicia laughed and thought very likely she was right.

One day, after a visit to the small shop in the village, she fell in with Lady Drusilla who was leaving the rectory.

"Come back with me for tea, Miss Oakes," she said, in the exact tone that was so effective with servants and her brother, so that Felicia instantly agreed to it. Not that she objected to the idea, for she was curious as to where Lady Drusilla lived. That it was somewhere in the village she was aware, and yet she already knew the occupants of all the houses of substance. Somehow she could not imagine her ladyship living in one of the many small cottages that lined the road.

To Felicia's surprise, they passed right through the village and turned in at the main gates of Hawkewood Hall. Almost at once, however, they turned aside onto one of the lesser roads leading through the woodlands that covered this part of the grounds. Before long the trees opened up, and there was the prettiest house Felicia had ever seen. It was a very modern building of substantial size, and the modest growth of the formal gardens with which it was surrounded suggested that it was no more than a few years old. On the southern side, lawns sloped away to a delightful pair of lakes where swans floated serenely, and a heron sat on the margins.

"How lovely!" Felicia cried.

"Do you think so? The style is a little too plain for my taste, but it has been much admired. Do come in."

A footman admitted them, and after depositing bonnets and gloves, they went through to a charming sitting room overlooking the lake, where Felicia was introduced to Lady Mabel Warborough, a very elderly lady who presumably acted as chaperon and companion to Lady Drusilla. Since she was asleep when they arrived and fell back into a doze as soon as the introductions had been completed, it was not to be supposed that she exerted much constraint on Lady Drusilla's activities.

"I had no idea this house was here," Felicia said, turning round and round to admire the clean lines and delicate embellishments. "It is the dower house, I presume?"

Lady Drusilla gave a bark of laughter. "I suppose it will fulfil that rôle admirably in the future, but… do you truly not know what this is?"

"I have not the least idea."

"This is the house that was built for Fin and Juliana, before their marriage. There was a very old house here where the gamekeeper used to live, but Papa knocked it down before it fell down. Then, when Fin's marriage was arranged, he engaged an architect to build a suitable home for the heir."

She paused, head tilted to one side, as Felicia worked it out.

"Oh… an *architect!* Mr Kearney designed this."

"And built it, too, and when it was done, he took his fee and the prospective bride as well. Poor Fin! He could never bear to look at the place, so it sat here, unwanted and unloved, hidden in its trees, until I was banished from the Hall." She chortled merrily. "The arrangement suits us both very well, I can tell you. I keep out of Fin's way… well, most of the time. Sunday chapel and dinner, that is all, and the occasional family emergency. And when there are visitors who would otherwise stay at the Hall, I can accommodate them here, you see, and Fin is not bothered with them in the slightest."

"Do you not think he *should* be bothered with them?" Felicia said cautiously. "That is to say, is it not his duty as head of the family—"

She laughed even more at that. "Do not talk to him of duty, I beg you! The only time he quarrels with me — proper raging quarrels — is when I dare to mention his duty. Of course it is his duty! His duty to take his seat in the Lords, his duty to keep a watchful eye on the rest of the family, his duty to marry... but he will have none of it."

"He is as bad as the Marquess of Arnwell," Felicia said crossly. "I have no patience with them, these men who wallow in misery."

Lady Drusilla raised an elegant eyebrow. "You speak your opinion forcefully, but since you know Fin only a little and the marquess not at all, it would be best to keep silent on the subject. Ah, here is one of my guests now. Do come in, Godfrey, for Miss Oakes is just leaving, I am sure."

Felicia rose obediently to her feet, even though the promised tea, which she had hoped would be accompanied by cake, had not yet appeared. When she turned to the door, she received a surprise, for the man who stood there, immaculately clad in fashionable attire, was none other than the man who had mistaken her for Lady Olivia Dulnain.

He started as he recognised her. "Why, it is the mysterious stranger of the Shotter Arms! What a delightful surprise. Drusilla, pray introduce me at once, for I must know who it is that I so carelessly accosted that day."

"Oh, you know Miss Oakes, do you? Governess to Fin's wards, Godfrey." A hesitation, then with obvious reluctance, she went on, "This is Mr Buckley, heir to the Marquess of Arnwell."

He made her a florid bow, far greater than her rank required. Although she was astonished to learn his identity, Felicia managed to make him a suitable curtsy, but her head was swimming with questions, the principal of which was — why was he staying with Lady Drusilla when he had the right to stay at Shotterbourne with the marquess? But it was not a question she could ask.

"Such a pleasure, madam. I trust you have taken no hurt from our brief encounter. Drusilla, I must tell you that Miss Oakes was almost bowled over by my intemperate departure from the inn yard, yet not a word of censure escaped her lips. You are quite well, Miss Oakes? I did not cause you any injury?"

"No, indeed, sir, none in the world."

"I am very glad to hear it. But you are not rushing away, I sincerely hope? You will stay for a little while, so that I may further my acquaintance with you. So many times since that day I have wondered who you might be, and what sequence of events brings you to this little corner of England, for all my diligent enquiries about the village told me only what I might guess for myself — that you are governess to Finlassan's wards. Do, pray, resume your seat, Miss Oakes, and tell me all about yourself, for I am quite determined to have my curiosity satisfied."

Felicia looked at Lady Drusilla, but she gave the slightest shrug and gestured towards the chair. The footman arrived just then with the tea tray, and although there were no cakes, there were macaroons and biscuits, so Felicia sat and drank her tea when it was offered and ate as many macaroons as she could before Lady Drusilla surreptitiously directed the footman to move the plate out of her reach.

Between bites, she answered the questions tumbling out of Mr Buckley as best she could. Where she was born was a mystery, but she told him all that she knew or had been told of the move to Boscobel Cottage at the age of three, the death of her protector when she was ten and her consequent removal to Miss Latimer's Academy, and her time at Itchen. He listened with a flattering degree of interest, and whenever she made some gentle enquiry of him in return, he turned it aside and reverted to his own questions.

When she felt obliged to leave, Lady Drusilla rose with alacrity, saying, "So soon? But if you must go, we will not detain you further."

But Mr Buckley jumped to his feet too. "Allow me to escort you to the Hall, Miss Oakes, so that I may enjoy your company for a few minutes more."

She could hardly refuse, but it was embarrassing to be the object of such pointed attention from a future marquess. Nothing could be less appropriate, and she could not imagine what more he might wish to know. In the event the walk was a pleasant one along a path lined by towering shrubs smothered in huge pink blooms. The questions were banished as he entertained her with a succession of amusing tales of Lady Drusilla, whom he had known since they were both children, and for whom he harboured an obvious affection. She had been a shy and touchingly inept debutante, Felicia discovered, brought out by a pair of aunts and struggling through several seasons before surrendering with relief to spinsterhood.

"She has been a great help to Giles Warborough and to the parish ever since," he said. "Finlassan found her too interfering, but to his credit he set her up very comfortably with the house and a generous allowance. How do you get along with Finlassan? He is a strange fellow."

"A little unusual, perhaps," she said cautiously. "He values his solitude."

"Ha! He is a recluse, not to put too fine a point on it. He and Arnwell are a fine pair, are they not? Such shining examples of the peerage, locking themselves away in their great houses, and the world may go hang itself, for all they care. At least Finlassan keeps his estate in good heart, which is more than Arnwell does for Shotterbourne," he added. "It grieves me more than I can say to watch it dwindling to nothing under his management. I talk to the steward about it, and he is in despair, poor fellow. Every year there is some other tenant farm abandoned for lack of improvements from the landlord. All the woods and coppices untended, the game birds gone for want of a little care, the trout lake silted up and most of the house under holland covers, and I can do nothing about it for he will not even see me."

He fell into morose silence. Felicia could think of no sensible response, so they walked on without speaking until they were within sight of the Hall, where he bade her a graceful farewell and hoped he would see her again soon.

Felicia was thoughtful as she made her way to the schoolroom to see if Juliana and Margarita had returned from their riding lesson. Finding them engaged in their studies with the history tutor, she changed into stouter boots and collected Hercules for a long walk.

She did not know quite what to make of Mr Godfrey Buckley. He seemed a personable young man, and she could not but sympathise with his position as heir to Shotterbourne, excluded from all communication with the marquess and watching the estate deteriorate before his eyes. Yet she was puzzled by his interest in her. What could he mean by it? She was a person of no family and no fortune. Not knowing what lay behind it, she had taken care to tell him of the cottage and modest independence that awaited her in Southampton, in case he thought her desperate enough to consider becoming a man's mistress. Yet his interest had not waned at that point. It was a mystery, but perhaps he would be gone soon and she need puzzle over him no more.

Hercules needed no persuasion on the walk, for he knew well where they were going. He bounded ahead of her, occasionally diving off in this direction or that, as smells or insects or the occasional fast-disappearing rabbit enticed him, but always he returned to their usual path to the fallen tree and the collapsed wall. Then he was up and over, and into the delights of the Shotterbourne wilderness. Felicia followed more circumspectly, for once she had torn one of her new gowns on a stray branch from the tree. Now she clambered inelegantly but slowly over the stones, and made her way out of the trees, then over the hill to the little pavilion.

On some days, the marquess was not there, but he left a little note tucked into the conveniently splayed fingers of one of the statues. *'Wretched physician'*, one note had said, and another read, *'Too much rain about for my stupid lungs'*. But today the sun was shining and there he was, seated in his usual spot. Beside him on the bench were the treats he had taken to providing — a decanter of Madeira and two glasses, and a box of cakes, lemon today. On the floor lay the hamper lugged up from the house by some unseen footman.

"Good day to you, Princess," he called, with a cheerful wave of his good hand, before returning to his attentions to Hercules. "The sun is shining at last! I thought this rain would never let up."

She could not recall more than one day of rain, but to the marquess, rain loomed large in his mind since it kept him indoors. She smiled inwardly at the thought that Fin was the exact opposite — he seldom left the house and so he never noticed the weather.

They talked about nothing very much for a while — the dog, the new bonnet she wore, the tasteless beef he had been served for dinner the day before — but she could not for long stay silent on the subject uppermost in her mind.

"I made a new acquaintance today — Mr Godfrey Buckley."

The effect was startling. His face darkened and his fingers clenched so tightly in Hercules' fur that the pup whined. "That wastrel! He is a scoundrel, a villainous rogue like his wicked father and uncle before him! You must have nothing to do with him, Princess, you hear me? Cut him dead, and never speak to him again, or—"

"Or what?" she said, genuinely wondering.

"You will have to choose. His friendship or mine, for you cannot have both."

# 8: An Invitation

Felicia was shocked at the vehemence of the marquess's response, and towards his own heir! It was inexplicable. "Whatever did he do, that you hate him so much?" she cried.

The marquess took a long draught of Madeira, visibly controlling his anger, although his hands shook. "It was not Godfrey, but his father and uncle who set themselves against me, in fact, against the whole family. Shall I tell you of it? I think I must, for when you know how far that branch of the Buckleys will go to attain their ends… well, perhaps you will understand, and treat him with the utter contempt that such a worm deserves."

He drained his glass and set it down on the bench beside him, folding his arms. When he spoke, his voice was almost calm. "When my father died, more than twenty years ago now, the inheritance fell to me. The title, the entailed estates and a great deal more. But I had no brothers, and at that time, no sons, either. Five daughters, but no heir. No uncles or first cousins, no great-uncles… it was necessary to go all the way back to my great-grandfather to find a younger brother with a surviving line. My heir presumptive was Lambert Buckley, Godfrey's father." He spoke the name with some effort, and the hands clenched again.

"What must Lambert do, but put in his own claim for the title! He had found some minor irregularity in my parents' marriage that he claimed put the legality of the marriage into question. It was nonsense of course, and the greatest insult imaginable to my mother. It destroyed her, all that legal uproar, and the uncertainty of it. Within a year of Father's death, she was gone too, and all Buckley's fault. It was as good as murder, and so I told him. He killed her, as surely as if he had taken a sword and thrust it into her heart. She could not stand the pain of all the questions, the finger-pointing and the innuendo. There was not a word of truth in any of it, yet people always like to believe the worst of others, do they not? *'No smoke without fire'* they say, winking knowingly to each other. It was despicable, what Lambert did."

He seemed inclined to keep to this vein for some time, so Felicia said hastily, "But it was all settled in your favour in the end, clearly."

"Of course it was! There was never any doubt in *my* mind, but they spun things out as long as they could. It took two years to settle the matter, and Buckley was almost bankrupted in the process by the high-and-mighty lawyers he engaged, so *some* good came out of it. I forbade Lambert the house from the day the claim went in, the worthless traitor. And by the time it was settled I had my son, so they had nothing to look forward to. But then—"

He stopped with something like a sob, covering his face with his good hand.

"The fire?" she said gently, and he could only nod. "Your son was killed, and now Godfrey Buckley, the son of your enemy, will inherit after you, so you are making sure that his inheritance is a ruin." Again he nodded. "Vengeance," she said.

"*Yes!*" he said with a sudden fierceness, so that she started and instinctively leaned away from him. "Lambert took his miserable self out of the mortal sphere two years ago, but his son lives on, and I will not rest until the estate is worthless to him. There is a limit to how much I can do," he went on, brows lowering. "The title is his, no matter what, and the Shotterbourne holdings are entailed, so he will get those, but their value is far less than it was, and whatever could be, has been transferred elsewhere."

"And you never thought to remarry, and get another son?" she asked quietly.

"Ah, if only I could have done so, but after the fire… no, there is no possibility. I did think…" He laughed gently. "It would have amused me to marry and allow my wife to get herself a son elsewhere, for as long as I acknowledge the child, he is mine in law. Yet I could not. It was beneath my dignity to resort to such underhand tactics."

Felicia was astonished at such extraordinarily twisted logic — too underhanded to make a pragmatic marriage, yet it was acceptable to destroy the estate? She could not comprehend the depth of hatred that would drive such actions. She looked at her hands, resting in her lap, and pondered the question. No, she could not blame him for hating Godfrey Buckley's father, but Godfrey himself?

"When did you last see Godfrey Buckley? For he may have changed greatly since—"

"I have never seen him, and never will." His chin jutted forward defiantly.

"Having met Mr Buckley myself," she said hesitantly, "I found him to be a personable man, very gentlemanly. He is genuinely distressed by the ruination of his inheritance. He comes here to talk to your steward about it."

"Aye, so Hamlett tells me. I do not mind him knowing all that I have done. Let him be distressed! It is nothing to the distress my poor mother felt at his father's actions."

"But he is *not* his father," Felicia said, with a little heat. "He cannot be blamed for the actions of another, undertaken when he must have been no more than a babe in arms. He may feel all the wrong of his father's actions, and wish to heal the breach between the two branches of the family, and if he is to inherit—"

"Oh yes, he wants to heal the breach! Of course he does, for he hopes I will reverse all the changes I have made, and allow him to inherit the full value of all my holdings. But I will not. Everything entailed is worthless now, and the unentailed properties and investments will go elsewhere. I have a natural daughter living somewhere in the south — Plymouth or Portsmouth or some such place. She will have everything else, and Buckley will get *nothing* except the title and the monstrous encumbrance of Shotterbourne, and the longer I live, the more of an encumbrance it becomes. I plan to live for a very long time, Princess, and the only condition which will cause me to retreat from my present path is if Buckley dies before me."

"You are implacable, then?"

"I am, and if you care anything for me, you will cease all acquaintance with Buckley at once."

Felicia rose to her feet, brushing a stray crumb of lemon cake from her gown. "I *do* care for you, Lord Arnwell, very much. Even in the short time I have known you, I have grown to enjoy your company, and to appreciate the man of good sense and principle hidden beneath the gruff exterior. The village people say you are quite mad, but you are too rational for that. I am deeply sorry for the ills that have befallen you, but what you do here is *wrong*. So far as I know, Mr Godfrey Buckley has offered you neither insult nor injury, and I will not be a party to injustice. I regret to say that I cannot come here again."

The marquess jumped to his feet too, his face blazing with anger. "You would choose that vile specimen of humanity over me, then?"

"I choose Christian forgiveness and compassion over bitterness, my lord. Good day to you. Come, Hercules."

She turned her back on the marquess and strode away.

~~~~~

*'Miss Felicia Oakes, Hawkewood Hall, Church Compton, Derbyshire. My very dear Miss Oakes, I have indeed information on the Lady Olivia Dulnain, for as you so correctly surmised, she is in my Peerage. In fact in my <u>new</u> Peerage, bought with a little of Mr Kearney's very generous bequest. So kind of him to remember all of us servants, but then I have always said that he was a true gentleman, despite his somewhat unorthodox profession. To the point — the new Peerage informs me that Lady Olivia is the eldest daughter of Hadrian Dulnain, who is newly elevated to the Peerage as the Sixth Earl of Cottersmere. Such an interesting connection, for of course he is the brother of <u>our</u> Dulnain, the Lady Juliana, so is uncle to our own dear Juliana and Margarita, and Lady Olivia is their cousin! There is another connection also, for Lord Cottersmere is also brother to the Lady Alexandria Dulnain, wife to Oscar*
~~~~~

*Buckley, the Eighth Marquess of Arnwell. There are six children listed, and such interesting names! Aldwina, Albertina, Elfleda, Eldira, Edwina and Oswald, the last the only boy. But how tragic to hear that they all died, and the youngest only a babe of a year old. A dreadful event, but not mentioned in my Peerage. I wonder why? We are very happy here at Boscobel Cottage, and the window in the scullery has been mended, so you need have no further concerns on the question of our safety. Jimmy would like to raise a pig, if that would not be disagreeable to you? There is a pen which may be made good with a very little work, if so. The chickens are laying well already, and we shall have an excellent crop of beans this year, despite the lateness of sowing. We are very content here and you need not feel you have to rush home on our account. Yours in friendship, Agnes Markham.'*

~~~~~

Felicia was unhappy with her breach with the marquess. He was a lonely man, who had become increasingly friendly and open with each day that had passed. She knew he had no visitors, for she had asked the Miss Trimms. Their cottage lay directly opposite the gates to Shotterbourne, and they sat in the window of their tiny parlour day after day as they stitched away, every movement of carriage or wagon or walker passing through the village square noted by them with interest. Not a stray dog or a horse for shoeing came or went without them knowing of it, and they told her that the marquess had no callers, apart from his physician, his steward and his lawyer.

Yet Felicia could not regret her actions. What the marquess was doing was utterly abhorrent to her, and she could not condone it. Her conscience forbade it. She understood his grief and despair, but bitterness and retribution was not the answer. If he
~~~~~

would not turn from that path, then she could not continue the acquaintance, no matter how much sorrow she felt at the loss of his friendship.

And at the back of her mind was a thought she tried to suppress, but could not — the marquess had a natural daughter somewhere in the south of England. *'Plymouth or Portsmouth or some such place.'* Or Southampton, her heart whispered? Was it possible? Oh, how she longed for it to be true, to have a *family* for the first time, to know where she belonged. It was incredibly unlikely, she knew that, for surely the marquess would know her name if it were so, but... stranger things happened in the world, did they not? And she had felt such an affinity for him, something more than mere friendship. Yet she dared not allow herself to hope, and tried to put the prospect out of her mind.

Her thoughts were soon turned in a different direction. Lady Drusilla came one morning very early, summoning Felicia from the studio to the entrance hall, where she paced about, her anger not concealed.

"What did you say to him, that is what I should like to know. For there must have been some... enticement. He would scarcely have noticed you otherwise."

"I am sorry if I have offended you in some way," Felicia said, surprised but not unsettled. "However, I am at a loss to understand you."

"Oh, that is the attitude you intend to take, is it? Complete innocence... as if you have not determined to set your cap at him from the first."

"I assure you I have not set my cap at anyone," Felicia said. "If you mean the earl—"

*"The earl!"* Her face registered incredulity, fading swiftly into suspicion. "You would not—"

"Of course not!" Felicia said, stung into a hasty response. "He is as far above me as the moon!" Yet she could not suppress a blush, even as she spoke the words.

"Hmm..." Lady Drusilla narrowed her eyes, perhaps not entirely convinced, but she decided not to pursue the point. "I refer to Godfrey Buckley, as if you could possibly mistake my meaning! You must have said *something* to him on that cosy walk back through the park."

"Oh... Mr Buckley... I cannot think... Oh yes, he told me how you hated the season in London, my lady, and how useful you now are to Mr Giles Warborough and the parish. Nothing else was talked of, I promise you."

"Hmph. Well, whatever was said, he wishes to further his acquaintance with you, so you will come to Compton House for dinner on Wednesday next. You may wear the blue spotted muslin. We eat at six, and I shall have a turbot which must not be spoilt, so be there promptly by half past five."

Felicia opened her mouth to object, realised there was no possible way to escape the engagement without giving offence and closed it again with a snap. A respectful curtsy signalled her acquiescence.

"Hmph," Lady Drusilla said again. "Miss Oakes, you are not a fool, so I will speak plain. Godfrey is an amusing rattle, but he will be a marquess in the fullness of time, and must marry according to his anticipated rank in society. Expect nothing from him and you will not be disappointed, for he will not look for a wife from the governess class, you may be sure. Above all, do not be drawn in by him, not if you place any value on your reputation. Even the lightest flirtation could be damaging. Do I make myself clear?"

"I understand you perfectly," Felicia said. "You need not have any fears on my account, or on his. Mr Buckley is a very agreeable man, but I know my station in life, I hope, and have no desire to attach myself to *any* man, least of all one of his ilk. He is quite safe from me."

*And I am safe from him*, she could have added. Her heart had already been bestowed, and no other man, be he ever so agreeable and amusing a rattle, could win her affection.

When she returned to the studio, she was so unsettled that she could not take up her brush again immediately. She retreated to one of the comfortable window seats in the bay window at the far end of the room, where she gazed out at the regimented pleasure grounds with their straight paths and square beds, not a leaf out of place.

"What the devil are you doing?"

She jumped, and instinctively blushed, but she had grown so used to Fin's irascible manner that she no longer regarded it. "Thinking."

"Hmm. Never a good idea," he said, which made her laugh. He plumped himself down on the other end of the window seat, feet up. So close! "Are you quite well?"

"Perfectly well, merely puzzled. I have been invited to dine at Compton House, at the express request of Mr Godfrey Buckley." She was having troubling breathing, so her voice sounded odd in her ears.

"Buckley? What the devil does he want with you?"

"Exactly the question I ask myself, although couched in more decorous terms," she said, her lips twitching in amusement.

He gave a bark of laughter. "A just reproof, Miss Oakes. I apologise for my intemperate language." The laughter quickly faded into a frown. "As for Buckley, I was not aware that you were at all acquainted with him."

"I have met him precisely twice, once when he almost knocked me over outside the Shotter Arms and mistook me for the Lady Olivia Dulnain, and once at Lady Drusilla's house over a cup of tea, after which he accompanied me the quarter mile back to the Hall."

The frown deepened. "Lady Olivia!"

"The eldest daughter of Lord Cottersmere and a great beauty, I am given to understand, so I suppose I should be flattered."

"Juliana's niece," he said thoughtfully. "There is much beauty in that family, it is true. Her older sister Alexandria was a very handsome woman." Felicia struggled to place Alexandria. Was she the one who had married Lord Arnwell and died in the fire? She rather thought she was. Fin went on, "I have never seen Olivia, but I see no resemblance between you and either Alexandria or Juliana. Do you have any connection with the family? Is it possible that your father was a Dulnain? You have been left well provided for, after all, so he must have been a man of wealth."

"I have not the least idea who my father is," she said. "Or my mother, either. The only person who might have known was Miss Armiger, who looked after me when I was a child, but she told me nothing except that she was *not* my mother. She died when I was ten."

"And she left no clue? No papers? No letters from anyone who might have been related to you?"

"Nothing," Felicia said sadly. "When she died and I was sent to Miss Latimer's Academy, the cottage in which we had lived was let to the curate for a peppercorn rent. All Miss Armiger's things were locked away in her room, and I was not allowed to look through them until I was of age. The attorney and clergyman who were my guardians and trustees felt there might be letters containing things I should not know about until I was an adult. But when I was finally allowed to examine them, there was nothing — no letters at all, no documents, no journal that might have given me some clue. So I am none the wiser, my lord, and I do not imagine I will ever discover the truth now."

# 9: Dinner At Compton House (June)

Felicia looked forward to dinner at Compton House with keen anticipation. She could not expect the society to be congenial, but at least Fin would not be there to unsettle her nerves, and she was determined not to be embarrassed at finding herself in such elevated company. Having been invited, she would behave as was proper for her station, initiating no conversation but responding to any overtures. With luck, the food would be plentiful, and she need not restrain herself from enjoying all that was on offer. She had been hungry enough in the past to make her heartily grateful for a well-provisioned table.

It was a long time since she had dressed for an evening engagement. As a parlour boarder at the Miss Latimers', she had accompanied them to evenings with friends, and there had been the assemblies, too, but once established at Summer Cottage, there had been no more such occasions. The Itchen residents had not been unkind, and the servants had had their friends, but for Felicia, and presumably for Lady Juliana before her, there had been no invitations.

At least she did not have to consider what to wear. Lady Drusilla had decreed the blue muslin and so the blue muslin it would be. Some scraps of matching ribbon would decorate her hair and shoes, and Mary hastily stitched a reticule. As for jewellery, she had none, apart from the small silver cross the Miss Latimers had given her on the occasion of her confirmation. That, therefore, would be her only adornment.

That morning, she was reading to Juliana and Margarita in the schoolroom when the door opened, and Fin's head appeared. All three of them, as well as Ellen, who was sewing in the corner, rose and curtsied to him.

"Miss Oakes, at what hour would you like the carriage ordered for you?"

"The carriage! We do not need the carriage today, my lord."

"You are to dine out this evening, are you not?"

"Oh… oh, I see. Yes, but… but there is no need… I can walk, my lord. It is not far, and the weather is settled."

"Nonsense. Drusilla dines at six and you will want to be there by a quarter to the hour, so—"

"Half past, my lord. I am instructed to present myself at Compton House at half past five precisely, or else the turbot will be spoilt, and that would be a great tragedy."

His lips flickered into a sudden smile, and Felicia's heart executed a somersault. Lord, if he would only refrain from smiling!

"Carriage at a quarter past five, then, and no argument." So saying, he whisked out of the room again, leaving Felicia thoroughly discomposed.

But that was not the only surprise that day, for when Felicia descended to the hall in her finery, she found the earl there before her, pocket watch in hand, and he too was dressed for the evening. She had never seen him formally dressed before, for on Sundays after chapel he had never bothered to change for dinner. Now, however, he wore silk knee breeches, stockings and pumps, with a deep blue coat and a cream waistcoat embellished with gold thread. He looked magnificent, and Felicia could not quite catch her breath.

"You keep to time, at least," he said in his usual brusque manner. "The carriage is on its way round. Miss Oakes, are you quite well? You look a trifle pale."

"Pale? Well? No… I mean, yes… perfect… perfectly well, sir. My lord."

He chuckled at her confusion, and she hoped he did not suspect the reason for it. "You do not look it. No need to be nervous, you know. You will not be expected to entertain the company with exceptional wit or erudition. Ah, here is the carriage now."

She could not take her eyes off him. As she gazed at him, the perfection was not merely in the unusual clothing, but in the form beneath. He was not a sportsman, broad of frame and with the muscles of a smith, but his height was imposing, and the well-fitting coat and breeches emphasised his slender waist and shapely legs. In such a setting, beneath the towering pillars and the soaring ceiling, standing amidst the splendours of Hawkewood Hall, he was the embodiment of nobility, and it was crushing to realise just how far above her he was — in rank, in wealth, in education, in every possible measure. Except perhaps in civility. *'Not be expected to entertain the company with wit or erudition'*, indeed! In manners, at least, she could count herself his equal if not his superior.

Somehow she got herself past the impassive butler and footmen and out of the door, although her legs were trembling. The earl himself handed her into the carriage. In a moment of pure terror, she thought he would get in beside her, and she could not imagine how she would cope with such proximity. Instead, he waited until she had arranged her skirts and then said, "I shall walk down. Tell Drusilla there will be one more for dinner."

She was too flummoxed to do more than nod her head, and before she knew it, the door was shut, the signal had been given and she was rolling slowly down the drive. One more for dinner? He planned to attend, then, and he had not given his sister warning of his intentions.  Yes, he was very definitely lacking in manners.

It took some time to reach the front door of Compton House. The grounds of Hawkewood Hall were criss-crossed by a spider's web of small footpaths but there were fewer carriage drives, so the route was circuitous and by the time the door was opened and the steps let down for her, Felicia had had plenty of time to compose her thoughts.

"Lord Finlassan will be joining the company for dinner," she said to the more senior of the footman attending her, as she mounted the steps to the entrance hall.

"Lord Finlassan? For dinner, madam?" he said, in a strangled voice, and his junior gasped audibly.

"I am afraid so," she said, trying not to laugh at his horror as she unfastened her cloak. Handing it to the junior footman, she said to him, "Better go and alert the kitchen, and I shall myself inform Lady Drusilla of the delight in store."

There was no need, however, for the man himself arrived at that moment, smiling benignly at them. "Good evening. Laver, I believe? Is everyone in the drawing room?"

The poor footman uttered another gargling sound, but he led the way with as much dignity as he could muster.

Felicia was enchanted, having never seen the earl in this mood before. His manner was light, almost playful, and she could have sworn that he winked at her as they followed the footman.

"What the devil are you doing?" she whispered.

For an instant, his eyes widened in shock at her language, then he burst into laughter. "Annoying my sister," he hissed back, and this time he definitely winked.

Laver threw open the door to the drawing room. "Lord Finlassan, milady," he said, forgetting to announce Felicia altogether.

"Fin?" Lady Drusilla said. She had been deep in some light-hearted conversation with Mr Giles Warborough and a dumpy middle-aged woman, but the smile faded from her face as she saw her brother, and took in his attire. "Whatever are you about?"

"The turbot, sister, that is what I am about. I am excessively fond of turbot."

"Fin, you cannot simply turn up unannounced for dinner."

"Why ever not? You turn up unannounced at the Hall frequently, so why may I not return the compliment? I am sure you can squeeze another cover around the table."

"You *never* dine out!"

"Tonight I do."

"But the numbers are perfectly balanced."

"Well, then Giles may take himself home. He can eat here any day of the week, I daresay."

There was a long, tense silence. Then Lady Drusilla said, "Laver, lay another place for dinner."

"Yes, milady."

"Wait… I must speak to Hampton. Giles, do the honours, will you?" So saying, she bustled out of the room, the hapless Laver trailing in her wake.

Giles whisked Fin away to be introduced around the room, and Felicia found herself abandoned on the threshold. She did not mind, gazing unembarrassed around her. She recognised Miss Claypole talking to an elderly man, and Lady Mabel half asleep in her chair. From the other side of the room two ladies of middle years, rather overwhelmed by jewellery, eyed Felicia and whispered behind their fans.

It was Mr Godfrey Buckley who crossed the room to greet her with a smile and a graceful bow. "Miss Oakes! How delightful to see you again. The room is brighter already for your presence. The footmen seem to have disappeared, so may I assist you to a glass of sherry?"

She declined it, and he offered her a dish of bon-bons instead, which was far more to her taste.

"Lady Drusilla always provides every comfort to her guests," he murmured, as she helped herself to a second one.

"Have you often been staying here?" Felicia said.

"Once or twice a year, in my fruitless attempts to see Lord Arnwell," he said, in a good-humoured tone. "Nor does he respond to my letters. I should dearly love to get to know him a little, and perhaps demonstrate to him that I am not entirely a good-for-nothing fellow. It is my great hope, if the time comes that I inherit—"

"If?" she said in surprise.

"The future is always uncertain, Miss Oakes. I make no assumptions. If it should come to pass, however, I would wish to be worthy of the honoured title he now bears, and it would be beneficial for me to learn from his experience and example. I must soon be looking for a wife, too, and should be glad of his advice on the subject. As head of the family, he may have strong opinions on the subject, and I should not like to go against his wishes."

"Your feelings do you credit, sir," she said. He sketched a small bow of acknowledgement, and she went on, "Yet it is hard to see what may be done about it. If he will not meet you or correspond with you, then you must conclude that he has no interest in whom you marry."

"Indeed, and his actions must also reduce my prospects of marrying well."

Felicia could not help laughing at his glum face. "Hardly so! The heir to a marquessate may marry as high as he chooses, surely? You need only go to London and let it be known that you are considering marriage, and the daughters of the nobility will be scrambling for your favour."

"No daughter of the nobility will be of the least use unless she brings with her a large dowry. My own fortune is small, and unlikely to be enriched by Shotterbourne."

"There must be many such," Felicia said with a smile. "Come, I will not have you downhearted, Mr Buckley, for tonight we have bon-bons in abundance, and later there will be turbot to enjoy."

Lady Drusilla returned just then. "Oh! Miss Oakes! Well," she said, startled, as if she had forgotten that she had herself invited Felicia. "Do come and meet everyone."

There were two middle-aged couples who had driven out from Derby for the occasion, and Felicia was intrigued to discover that the dumpy lady was Godfrey Buckley's aunt, Miss Edith Buckley. She was drably dressed, a nondescript woman but with sharp eyes and an astute glance that seemed to quickly appraise Felicia.

"It is a pleasure to meet you at last, Miss Oakes," she said, her voice almost as deep as a man's. "Godfrey has talked about you a great deal, and I confess to some curiosity to know more of you."

"There is little enough to know," Felicia said, politely, although wondering greatly at such interest in one so lowly. "My ignoble history is no secret, after all, nor has my life been so interesting as to be worthy of retelling."

"No one has a life so dull as to be unworthy of retelling," she said. "Even we women who toil in the service of others have our stirring moments, those times when we become heroines in our own lives. Is it not so, Godfrey? For me, such opportunities are in the past, but for you, Miss Oakes, there may yet be a time when you step forward to take your place at the front of the stage."

Felicia laughed and shook her head. "Only in my imagination, Miss Buckley. It amuses me to pretend that I was born to this kind of life, that I am some kind of noblewoman entitled to be here. But the truth is that I am trying not to step on my fine new gown or drop my reticule, and before too long I shall return to my rustic cottage in Hampshire and spend the rest of my life growing potatoes. No heroine, just another spinster struggling to survive."

Miss Buckley looked ready to contest the point vigorously, but Felicia was spared any further discussion on her history by the return of Laver to announce dinner. To her surprise, when they began to settle themselves in the dining room, she found herself seated between nephew and aunt.

On the other side of the table, a brief skirmish between Fin and Lady Drusilla was resolved decisively in the earl's favour.

"Do sit there beside Miss Claypole, Fin," Lady Drusilla said, with a bright smile, gesturing at the last remaining chair.

Fin assessed the seating arrangements, then smiled blandly. "How remiss of you, Drusilla, to place Mr and Mrs Denham together, for they may dine thus on any day of the week. For tonight, they must be separated. Denham, may I invite you to enjoy Miss Claypole's company, while I entertain the charming Mrs Denham?"

And Lady Drusilla could not well object to it. Felicia dared not catch the earl's eye in case he winked at her again, for if so she would not be able to suppress her laughter. She enjoyed the moment all the same. Fin was so much fun in this mood! If only he was always this way.

The table was laden with a vast array of appetising food, and Mr Godfrey was assiduous in obtaining everything that Felicia had a mind to try. Once her plate was full to overflowing with tasty morsels, he began to talk to her about Hampshire, and readily responded to her questions about his own home in Lincolnshire.

"Farndyke is a beautiful old house," he said, with a fond smile. "The estate is not large, not so large as it was in my great-grandfather's day, when it first came into the family, but I have begun some improvements in farming methods which I hope will increase yields and thereby benefit my tenants greatly."

"Such an outcome must be very pleasing for you, especially as the rents may be increased also," she said, smiling.

He laughed at that. "Very true! Every landlord must have an eye to his own income as well as that of his farmers. Any gains must apply to both sides or else there is discontent. I hope I may describe myself as a good landlord, Miss Oakes, one who takes account of the needs of his tenants as well as his own."

There was an earnestness and sincerity in his manner which she could only approve. She could fault neither his principles nor the expression of them.

After a while, Mr Buckley turned to converse with Lady Drusilla, and Felicia took the opportunity to talk to Miss Edith Buckley.

"I confess, Miss Buckley, that I was unaware of your existence before this evening. Do you live at Farndyke also?"

"Not since I was a girl. My home is at Shotterbourne," she replied in her gruff way.

Shotterbourne! Felicia could not hide her astonishment.

Miss Buckley smiled. "I understand your surprise, for the quarrel between our families is well known, so how can this be?

The answer is that I am companion to Lord Arnwell's sister, the Lady Lucia, an arrangement which predates the quarrel. Lady Lucia is not well at times, and I know how to calm her when she is agitated. It would distress her were I to leave, so there I stay, making myself useful."

"He has a sister? Goodness! So many new names for me to learn. Do tell me about Lady Lucia. Is she older or younger than his lordship?"

"Two years older, never married and so has always lived at Shotterbourne. She is a very sweet lady, such a darling, and with such an unsullied approach to life. So many women of her age and position become jaded by life, but Lucia still enjoys simple pleasures. Why, she is already planning the celebrations for her birthday next month."

"Is she? How charming!"

"Is it not?" Miss Buckley said. "For myself, I have reached an age when a birthday is not something I care to mark with any degree of pleasure, although perhaps when one is born in December, one may be forgiven the omission. There are few activities more enticing at such a time than huddling near the fire with a shawl. Do you celebrate your birthday, Miss Oakes? I hope you have a more fortuitous season in which to do so."

"When I was at school, there was always a special cake made for anyone who had a birthday. Happily, that meant that there was cake at least once a week. I am very fond of cake."

"And were you permitted to enjoy your cake as part of a picnic? Such excursions make the day more special, I feel."

"Sometimes, for those whose birthday fell in the summer."

"And yours did not?"

"No. The weather is too uncertain for such activities in March."

"Oh, March! My mother's birthday was in March. Poor Mama! How she hated acknowledging that she had been born on the Ides of March. The fifteenth, you know. *'Beware the Ides of March!'* Shakespeare. I hope your birthday is on a more felicitous date, Miss Oakes?"

It was a peculiar subject to be discussing, but Miss Buckley made her words seem like a direct enquiry so Felicia could not well refuse to answer. "Mine is on the thirteenth."

After that, Miss Buckley's attention was diverted by a dish of stewed peas, and Felicia turned back to her plate with relief, her only amusement being Mr Godfrey's attempts to entertain Lady Drusilla with a string of anecdotes, which usually began, *'Once when I was in Somersetshire, the marquess said to me...'* or *'There was an occasion when I was staying with Lord Bentley...'.* Since he could hardly be saying such things to impress the sister of an earl, she supposed them to be true, but it made him seem like a gadabout. But perhaps all well-to-do young men were adventurers of that nature, hopping from place to place as opportunity arose and never settling anywhere.

The second course succeeded the first, with the turbot in pride of place, and after that the third course arrived, by which time even Felicia's appetite was flagging. This course provided the most entertaining moment of the evening. A huge *epergne* was brought in, filled with an array of fruit, and placed in the centre of the table.

"Whatever is that monstrosity?" Fin said, his voice echoing loudly from behind the display of strawberries, cherries, apricots and a single rather small pineapple. "Laver, remove it."

"Really, Fin!" Lady Drusilla protested, while Mr Giles Warborough smothered a laugh with his napkin. "We must have fruit!"

"Take it away! Put the fruit in bowls or some such. Heavens, Drusilla, how can you bear to have such a thing in the house, never mind in the centre of the table? Your guests are no doubt too polite to express their disgust at your lack of taste."

"It is solid silver, and a wedding present to Mother and Father. You gave it to me when I moved here."

"Impossible. I would never have given you anything so hideous."

"Well… you told me to take anything I wanted."

"But why would you want *that*?"

He clicked his fingers imperiously, and the two footmen gently lifted the *epergne* off the table. They would have set it down on a sideboard, but it was still within Fin's vision and at a gesture from him, they took it out of the room altogether.

"That is much better," he said, sitting back on his chair with a sigh. "If you must have such a thing, I shall buy you one a little better suited to its surroundings. No room of this elegance should be despoiled by such an abomination."

There was a sudden hush around the room.

"You approve, then?" Lady Drusilla said. "You like the house?"

Fin's face shadowed a little. "Yes," he said curtly.

"Then will you come again?" she said, with touching eagerness. "I know I was a touch cross with you for descending upon me without warning, but it is a pleasure to have you in my house at last, Fin. Do tell me it will not be the last time."

"If you invite me. Perhaps. If I feel like it. Are you going to hold on to those sugared almonds all evening, Uncle Giles? Pass them down the table, will you?"

Felicia let out her breath with a whoosh. She had not realised that Fin had never even entered Compton House before, his hatred of the architect who had stolen his betrothed being too great to be readily overcome. In thirteen years, he had not set foot over the threshold. Yet tonight, he had done so and he liked what he saw. How could he not? The house was beautiful! And he was right about the *epergne*, which was indeed a monstrosity.

When she looked across the table at him, he was watching her, his expression solemn.

"Sugared almond, Miss Oakes?" He pushed the dish right across the table.

"Thank you, my lord."

As she popped one into her mouth, she could not help wondering why a man who had not set foot inside his sister's house before should suddenly decide to do so. It was a mystery.

# 10: A Painting Expedition

The evening seemed interminable. While the gentlemen enjoyed their port and, judging from the raucous laughter, told each other ribald jokes, the ladies withdrew to the drawing room, where Felicia savoured the respite from the inexplicable attentions of the Buckleys and the distraction of Fin in his evening splendour. The five ladies sat on one side of the room and the two governesses on the other. Felicia would not call Miss Claypole a friend, but she was grateful for her company. They both produced items of embroidery from their reticules and if conversation lagged, their stitchery at least kept their hands busy.

As soon as the gentlemen re-joined them, Mr Godfrey Buckley made straight for Felicia's side. Since Miss Claypole had been drawn away to help hand round the tea things, Felicia was left alone with him. It was her only opportunity to confront him.

"I am very curious as to your motives, Mr Buckley," she said boldly, lifting her chin and looking him in the eye. "What, I wonder, can the heir to the Marquess of Arnwell find of interest in a humble governess?"

He laughed easily. "May I suggest that you examine your looking glass tonight. You might find an answer there."

He smiled, eyes twinkling in amusement, but Felicia was not fooled. In the circles in which he moved, he must be surrounded by diamonds of the first water to whom she could never compare. She could only suppose that he was merely amusing himself with a flirtation.

The end of the evening was a muddle, for somehow the two couples from Derby were waiting in the hall for their carriages at the same time as Felicia. Then all three carriages arrived at once and there was a great confusion of farewells on the steps. Felicia was hard put to it to escape from Mr Godfrey Buckley, and eventually Fin hustled her into the carriage, climbed in himself and the door was slammed shut.

The darkness was her greatest saviour. She could barely make out his face, so she was fairly sure he could not see her flaming cheeks. For a moment they sat in silence, the carriage unmoving, as they waited for the other vehicles to move off.

Then he said, "Did you enjoy the turbot, Miss Oakes?" She could hear the smile as he spoke.

"Oh yes," she squeaked, her voice not quite under control. "It was delicious. Everything was delicious."

"Except the *epergne*," he said, and this time she knew he was frowning. "I know a silversmith who might undertake a commission for something a little more pleasing to the eye." A long pause, then he went on in much the same tone, "Buckley has asked my permission to take my wards to Ashbourne for the day on Friday. There is a very fine medieval church there with some interesting monuments and a splendid spire. He thought the girls may care to paint it. You would accompany them, naturally, with Miss Claypole for propriety. He will borrow Drusilla's barouche for the purpose, and provide a parlour at the Green Man for refreshments. What do you think?"

"It… it sounds like an agreeable excursion," she said cautiously. "The change of scenery would do them good, and a church always provides many possibilities for interesting subjects."

"That is what I thought, also. I agreed to it, subject to your approval. In fact, I might join you. I have not been to Ashbourne for years."

"There will not be room in the barouche for so many," she said in alarm. A whole day in his company! That would be disastrous for her heart.

"Buckley and I will ride," he said. Another, longer, pause. "Over the port, your likeness to Lady Olivia Dulnain was discussed. It is curious, yet I see no resemblance to any other Dulnain. Nor does a connection there seem likely. Very devout, the whole family, and to be frank, I cannot see any of them producing a base-born child. Hadrian's wife, though… she is a Lister, and a more rackety family would be hard to find. Sir Royston Lister, the present baronet, could well be your father, and thus your resemblance to Lady Olivia would come from her mother's family, not her father's. Their estate is in Hampshire or Surrey or one of those southern counties, so depositing you at Southampton would fit. But if so, there is nothing to hope for from the family, for they would never acknowledge you publicly. They tidy up their messes, but they never admit to them publicly."

That made sense. A wealthy family, a little wild, packing off their 'messes', as he called her, to the care of Miss Armiger, with enough money to sustain them and nothing to connect them to the family and thereby sully their public reputation. Yes, it was logical, and yet a little disappointing, too, if she could never get to know her father. And what of her mother? If her father was a gentleman who had seduced a chambermaid or the steward's daughter, then why was Felicia not left to her mother's care?

No, there was more to her story than a rakish baronet, and a tiny corner of her heart still hoped that she might be the natural daughter of the marquess. Even estranged from him as she now was, and recognising all his eccentricities, at least she had known him for a little while and seen that beneath the bitter exterior was a kind heart which allowed him to befriend a humble governess and a half-grown dog.

~~~~~

Fin rather looked forward to the expedition to Ashbourne. There was the fun of deciding on the necessary equipment for their art, and the exact numbers and styles of easels, paper, chairs, brushes and so forth to be taken. Then there was the finding of a box in which all this might conveniently be conveyed and the fruits of their labours returned safely. Miss Oakes, he discovered, approached the day from another angle altogether. She looked up Ashbourne in all the guidebooks the library offered, and the route to be taken in Carey's Itinerary, so that the girls would be prepared for the sights. She even extracted from the back of a schoolroom cupboard a painting of the church executed with more enthusiasm than competence by his twelve-year-old self.

"I have no memory of painting this," he said, gazing at it in astonishment. "Not one of my better efforts, I think. It is best returned to the dark place whence it came."
~~~~~

"Oh no, for although it is clearly the work of a child, it contains many hints of the talent to come. These trees are very well done. I shall pin it to the wall to inspire us."

He was absurdly pleased with the compliment.

Friday morning saw them gather in the hall awaiting the arrival of the barouche. Fin's horse was already being walked about outside by the groom. Juliana and Margarita were arrayed in matching gowns and bonnets, and their governess… he could not deny that Miss Oakes looked surprisingly fetching. Her gown and spencer were sober enough, and her bonnet unadorned by more than the ribbon fastened under her chin, but somehow the way the bonnet framed her face and those mischievous eyes only emphasised the dimples beside her mouth. Such a shapely mouth, curved like a cupid's bow. Very kissable lips, which would no doubt enchant the impoverished vicar or well-to-do burgher it was her destiny to marry. Surely she would marry one day, for it would be a waste for so pretty a girl to fade into untouched spinsterhood.

The sounds of flying gravel announced a rider approaching at some speed. With an economical movement of one hand, Bagnall directed Robert to attend to the arrival. He returned almost at once, to confer with the butler. A silver salver was fetched, a letter placed upon it and Bagnall crossed the hall to the little group, and bowed to Fin.

"A letter for Miss Oakes, my lord. From Shotterbourne. The groom is awaiting a reply."

"Well, give it to Miss Oakes, then, man. No use telling me about it."

"Very good, my lord."

With another bow, the butler turned to Miss Oakes, bowed again and held out the salver. Calmly she took the letter and opened it, for all the world as if she received such missives every day.

Fin understood Bagnall's scruples. Miss Oakes was a single woman and an employee in the house who should not be receiving letters from a gentleman, as the hand clearly showed the writer to be. For himself, he cared nothing for that — let her have an admirer if she would, she deserved it — but he was very curious as to who her mysterious correspondent might be, and how she had come to know anyone from Shotterbourne. At church, perhaps? He was well aware that she had begun to attend Morning Service at St Miriam's, where the Shotterbourne servants attended. Yet somehow the thought disappointed him. He had not known Miss Oakes for long, but he had grown to respect her and hoped she would do rather better for herself than an under-footman or groom.

The rattle of the barouche was heard from outside, and moments later Drusilla bustled into the hall.

"Ah, there you are, Fin. I have decided to come in Miss Claypole's stead, for I know Godfrey's ways. He will ply her with wine at the inn, whereupon she will sleep the afternoon away leaving poor Miss Oakes unchaperoned and exposed to all Godfrey's wheedling ways. *I* shall not fall asleep, you may be sure. But why is there a Shotterbourne groom outside?"

"He brought a letter for Miss Oakes."

"A letter? For Miss Oakes? From whom? Man or woman?"

Fin's lips quirked at the indignation on her face. As Miss Oakes was standing a little apart, engrossed in reading the second sheet of her letter — two sheets! An ardent admirer, then — he replied in a low voice, "A man, I believe."

Drusilla's cluck of outrage echoed around the hall. "Miss Oakes? Are you *betrothed?*"

"Hmm?" She looked up in surprise. "No, indeed. Why—? Oh, the letter! No, it is from Lord Arnwell, that is all."

Fin almost burst out laughing. She was so self-possessed, it was extraordinary. *'Lord Arnwell, that is all',* indeed! Such insouciance was quite admirable.

Drusilla's eyes almost popped out of her head. *"Lord Arnwell!* How could you possibly *know* him, still less be on corresponding terms with him? The poor man is quite insane and never leaves his house."

"He does not, but Hercules — the dog, you know — got over the wall into the Shotterbourne grounds and I was obliged to follow him, and so we came upon the marquess there. We met him many times, until I fell out with him last week. You will excuse me, I am sure, but I must write a note in reply. I shall not be above five minutes."

Fin ardently wished he had his sketchbook in his hand to capture the look of astonishment on Drusilla's face. Yet it would not be of the slightest use, for he could not do it justice. Such a priceless expression! Not only did Miss Oakes know Arnwell — *'We met him many times!'* Astonishing woman! — but she had actually fallen out with him. A governess falling out with a marquess! It was deliciously amusing, but all his curiosity was aroused. What subject could arise between them to cause a falling out?

Buckley came in, to encounter the full force of Drusilla's outrage.

"She is acquainted with Arnwell?" he said in bewilderment. "Yet she never said a word."

Miss Oakes returned and handed her letter to Bagnall to be conveyed to the Shotterbourne groom.

Drusilla turned on her at once. "What did he say? What was the quarrel? Are you to see him again? Is he as mad as people say?" Her tone was sharp with disapproval. A governess on friendly terms with a marquess upset all her ideas of social order, and distressed her beyond measure.

With a dimpled smile, Miss Oakes said, "He seems sane enough to me, if a trifle eccentric. We quarrelled about his lordship's treatment of Mr Godfrey Buckley. I believe it to be quite wrong to banish his heir from his presence and wilfully to destroy his inheritance, and all because of something Mr Buckley's father did. It is ungenerous and unchristian, and so I told Lord Arnwell, and thus am banished in my turn."

Buckley made her a florid bow. "I am greatly obliged to you, Miss Oakes, for speaking on my behalf. It is gratifying that our brief acquaintanceship should affect you so powerfully as to risk the wrath of so great a man. I commend your courage, madam."

She looked startled. "Pray do not feel any obligation, Mr Buckley. My objections were more in the general than the particular. I should have said exactly the same had I never met you, as anyone would, I am sure. For any man to treat his heir so is contemptible. My acquaintance with you was only instrumental in raising the subject with his lordship, which revealed to me the full extent of his malice. I could not stay a moment longer once that was known to me."

He bowed, looking not at all displeased.

"But what did the letter say?" Drusilla said impatiently.

Fin watched as Miss Oakes hesitated then turned her clear eyes on him. "Lord Finlassan is my employer and therefore has the right to read my correspondence if he wishes. Do you so wish, my lord?"

"Certainly not. You are of age, and may correspond with whomever you please, Miss Oakes. Let us not keep the horses standing any longer, shall we? Ladies? Buckley?"

"By all means," Buckley said smoothly. "May I, Miss Oakes?" As he offered her his arm, he looked as smug as a mouse-filled cat.

As their procession got underway, Fin discovered that there were advantages in conveying the ladies in an open carriage. After overnight rain, the roads were not at all dusty, so riding behind the barouche gave him a good view of the occupants. In the rear-facing seats, the two girls whispered together excitedly, their heads bobbing this way and that to catch sight of every interesting feature. In the forward-facing seats, Drusilla's expensive bonnet nodded constantly as she rattled away to Miss Oakes, maintaining the conversation almost single-handedly.

As for Miss Oakes, her head remained still, but the long strings of her straw bonnet danced in the breeze. Those ribbons enchanted him with their gay delight in their freedom. They were as free as their owner, doing the job they were required to do but with a lively independence. He had never known a governess quite like Miss Oakes, whose humiliating background should make her the most subservient mouse, yet she was far from it. Buckley had spoken of her courage, and that was true, but her manner held more than courage. There was a natural dignity to her deportment. She was perfectly self-assured in any company, just as if she had every right to be there. One could take her to London or any of the fashionable watering places and, to those who knew nothing of her history, she would pass muster anywhere as a lady.

Ashbourne was much the same sleepy little town he remembered, nestling amidst rolling hills with the River Dove shimmering through them. They left the barouche and horses at the Green Man, where the best parlour had been reserved for their use all day, and then made directly for St Oswald's Church, two men from the inn lumbering in their wake with the box of painting equipment.

"The inside first," Drusilla said. "There are some fine monuments to be seen."

"It would be better to begin our paintings at once," Fin said. "The monuments may be viewed when a convenient break occurs."

"We have been looking forward to seeing the Boothby monument," Miss Oakes said. "May we look at it while you choose a prospect and have the easels set up, my lord?"

"The Boothby monument," he said thoughtfully. "I had forgotten that. By all means let us look at it."

The beauty of it took his breath away, as always. How many times had he seen the sleeping girl, carved in cold marble yet so lifelike, and yet every time he was moved almost to tears by it. The two girls gazed at it in awe, and Miss Oakes walked slowly around it, the better to admire the sculptor's art, while Drusilla, never moved by anything, intoned the history of it, names and dates and facts, and translated the inscription.

"So sad," Juliana said softly.

"So beautiful," breathed Margarita.

"Indeed it is very sad, but then children die all the time," Drusilla said briskly. "Heaven knows what her parents paid for this, and yet it did not change anything. It is unhealthy to grieve to excess. One mourns and then moves on with one's life." She cast Fin a fulminating glance as she spoke.

"You have no soul, Drusilla," he said, and stalked outside to set up the easels.

# 11: St Oswald's Church

For a while, all was peaceful. A spot in the churchyard was settled on, the easels put in place and the painting got underway. Buckley generously took Drusilla away to the far side of the church, whence their voices drifted back occasionally but did not trouble him. Drusilla had a good heart, Fin reminded himself, even if her manner was abrasive sometimes. At least, he found her manner abrasive. She was easier to take when Giles was with her, for then they talked to each other and needed no attention from him.

After a while, Drusilla ceased to exist. The governess, the girls, the occasional wagon or horseman passing on the road... they all disappeared. There was only the church before him, and the image of it appearing minute by minute on the paper before him. His hand chose brushes, dipped them, carried the colour to the paper, dabbed and swept and dotted and blended, but his mind was on shapes and outlines and tones and shadows. Shadows were difficult, yet he thought he had captured them well, for once.

A clock struck the hour, bringing him back to himself. The girls' easels were abandoned. Only Miss Oakes remained.

"Where did everyone go?" Fin said.

She gave him her mischievous smile. "They left some time ago. Juliana and Margarita were hungry, so Lady Drusilla and Mr Buckley have taken them to the inn for some food."

He saw now that Miss Oakes had moved her easel so that she faced a little away from the church. He frowned.

"What the— I mean, what are you painting?"

"Come and see," she said, looking slightly conscious.

When he saw her work, he raised his eyebrows, bemused. Her subject was not the church but the grouped artists, the two girls chattering together and Fin himself—

"Do I truly look like that?"

She nodded, blushing.

"Now, why are you embarrassed?" he said. "The execution is good, but I look so... so scowling and black-humoured."

"No, no! Intense, that is all," she cried. "When you paint, your concentration is absolute. I wish I could do that."

"Do not wish it, Miss Oakes. It is not an ability I would wish on anyone, for it arises from... circumstances I try to forget by shutting out the world."

"You mean Lady Juliana," she said matter-of-factly. "Lady Drusilla said that you brought her here when you were betrothed. She thought that was why you ran out of the church earlier."

He had to catch his breath before he could reply to such plain speaking. "Not... not for that reason, no." A long pause, but he composed himself and went on, "I *did* bring her here... Ashbourne... Dovedale. Ah, Dovedale! Juliana... Juliana loved Dovedale more than anywhere else in the world, and the whole of the Dove River. Up in the hills, that was where she was happiest. We went there often to paint, side by side, as I hoped we would for the rest of our lives. I brought her to St Oswald's only once, and she looked at the Boothby monument and told me that one day we would have children of our own just as beautiful."

He fell silent, and after a moment Miss Oakes said to him, "Those are good memories to have. You need not fear them."

"The bad memories are the ones I fear," he said, his voice sounding harsh in his ears. "Two days later I went away to London and she stayed here to supervise the decoration of our house with the architect. I never saw her again. She left me a letter, that was all. The bad memories far outweigh the good."

"It is better to have memories, good or bad, than to have none at all, and at least you have had the great joy of loving and being loved in return, even if her affection for you did not last."

"Oh, she never loved me," he said, and he could not suppress the bitterness in his tone. "It was an arranged marriage, did you not know that? I thought the servants might have told you the whole story."

"I do not gossip with the servants," she said with dignity.

"Of course you do not. I beg your pardon, Miss Oakes."

"Nevertheless, I should be glad to hear the whole story, if you are willing to share it. I have found that a painful past may be alleviated somewhat by speaking of it openly."

He could not resist a wide smile at that. "It is impossible to believe that your cheerful demeanour hides a painful past, Miss Oakes."

A shadow crossed her face, but she said nothing, and he did not like to pry. He hesitated. For thirteen years he had spoken to no one about Juliana. Drusilla and Giles, separately and together, had tried to persuade him to talk about her, but he never had, hiding himself away in his studio and shutting out the world utterly.

Yet this strange governess was different. She had arrived in his life as the storm he had painted that night, sweeping away his solitude and dragging him into the real world again. She was his muse, perhaps, inspiring him to new artistic endeavours, but she also felt like a friend. More so than Drusilla or Giles, that much was certain.

For reasons he could not articulate, he wanted to tell her everything. So he dragged his painting stool nearer to hers and began.

"It all arose after we fell out with Lord Arnwell after the fire," he said. "He would have nothing to do with us, but when the Dulnains—"

"Wait — *you* fell out with Lord Arnwell? The Warboroughs, not the Buckleys?"

"Correct. You did not know that? I see I must go right back to the beginning. The three families — the Warboroughs, the Buckleys and the Dulnains — have been connected for a long time, the Warboroughs and Buckleys as neighbours, and when Arnwell married Alexandria Dulnain, he drew that family into the friendship also. My Aunt Isabella and Uncle Giles both married Dulnains, albeit distant cousins."

"Aunt Isabella," she murmured. "I have not heard of her before. Aunt Isabella and Uncle Giles."

"There is Aunt Geraldine, too. She and Aunt Isabella had the joy of bringing out Drusilla." He laughed. "Poor Drusilla! How she hated all that business — the gowns, the balls, the stammering young men whose only interest was her rank and dowry, and mostly the dowry, it had to be said. She was very unhappy. I cannot find it in me to blame her for giving it all up, but the aunts still reproach themselves for what they see as their failure to secure her a husband. And then there is Uncle Percival…"

He stopped, suddenly reluctant, but Miss Oakes' great dark eyes were fixed on him, so with an effort he continued. "Uncle Percival was Arnwell's secretary. By the time of the fire, he had been with him for about ten years, had steered him through the difficulties of claiming the title and dealing with Lambert Buckley's rival claim — you know about that? Good. Arnwell depended utterly on Percival, and there was never the slightest trouble between them. But then… then came the night of the fire. It was to be a huge celebration. The battle for the marquessate had been won, and the succession was secure at last, for there was a son, Oswald, born that year after five daughters. Cause for rejoicing indeed. So for Lady Arnwell's thirtieth birthday, there was a grand dinner and then a ball at Shotterbourne, with fireworks at midnight and every imaginable delight. Everyone was there — all the Dulnains, all the Buckleys, except Lambert and his brother, of course. Giles was back from Southampton and ordained by then, so he was there. And Percival was there, too."

He paused, pondering. So long ago! Nineteen years, and he had been only a boy of thirteen, having to listen enviously to the talk of the preparations, and watching his parents and Uncle Percival go off in the carriage that night. Later, he had gone up to the attics, found a window with a view towards Shotterbourne, and watched the spectacle of the fireworks lighting up the sky. Not long afterwards, the carriage had brought his parents home again. Not Percival, though. He had stayed on to help in the card rooms and the supper room, and to do his duty by the wallflowers.

Fin had crept away to bed at that point, and when he awoke the next morning, the sky was full of smoke…

Taking a deep breath, he went on, "The ball was a great success, everyone agreed. By four or five in the morning, most of the guests had departed and the family had gone to bed. Just a few determined card players still huddled around the table, for there was money to be won. It was Percival who raised the alarm — fire in the family wing. Arnwell and the remaining guests and servants ran there but the whole wing was alight, the central stairwell carrying the flames and smoke to the upper floors. Arnwell ran up the service stairs to try to reach his wife, but the fire was too fierce. He pressed on, too distraught to see the futility of it and it almost consumed him, but the butler and a footman dragged him out, half dead. Well, you have seen him, you know to what lengths he went to reach his wife. His efforts were in vain. She was gone and all the children, too, and several of the servants — the nursery maids, the governess, the Negro boy who slept on the landing. And Percival was gone, too."

"In the fire?" she said, but he could see from her face that she suspected the truth.

He shook his head. "That was what everyone thought at first, that he had tried to help and himself been consumed by the fire. No bodies were ever recovered, for the fire was too fierce. The roof collapsed, and the ruins burned for days, leaving nothing but ash, and Arnwell was too distraught to permit anyone to dig around for remains. Poor fellow! They say that the grief has sent him quite mad, and no reasoned argument can reach him, so all stays just as it was. No one could say for sure who had died, but anyone missing was presumed dead, Percival among them. He was accounted a hero. But then…"

Again he stopped. So long since he had talked of these matters! And to speak so dispassionately, as if it had happened to some other family, to different people altogether, as if it were not *his* family, *his* uncle who had betrayed everyone.

"Then?" she prompted, sympathy in her face.

"Then it was discovered that twenty thousand pounds had been taken from the safe."

"Oh! And that was Percival?"

"He was the only person, apart from the marquess himself, who had a key. Arnwell was very ill after the fire, but once he recovered somewhat from his injuries, the lawyers needed some documents from the safe and the loss was discovered. Only Percival could have taken the money, and it must have happened *during* or after the fire because that room had never been unattended since earlier that day, when the ladies' jewels for the evening were removed from it. The money had been there at that time, and servants and guests had been in the room ever since — until the fire."

"So while everyone was frantically fighting the fire, Percival crept in and stole the money when the safe was left unattended."

"That is what everyone believed — or worse! Perhaps he had even started the fire himself, that it was no accident. Most people supposed it was merely a theft gone wrong, that the fire was meant to be a small distraction that got out of hand."

"It seems… such an unlikely thing for a man to do," Miss Oakes said thoughtfully. "Percival had a good position, a trusted position, which no doubt paid well enough."

"Very generously, and Arnwell rewarded him well for his efforts to secure the title. He had an allowance from Father, too."

"So why would he want to steal?"

"That is exactly how Father reasoned, too," Fin said. "He said that Percival was too honourable, too loyal to Arnwell's family and his own ever to do such a thing, and he must have died in the fire."

"Then how did he account for the missing money?"

"Ah, that is the question, is it not? *Someone* stole that money, and if not Percival, then who was it? And how did he get hold of the key?"

She frowned, pondering the question seriously. "It makes no sense either way. There is no reason for him to steal money in the first place, and even if he had planned such a scheme, starting a fire in the family wing is madness. Where did he keep the key? I could imagine a situation where he might throw aside his coat in the urgency of the moment, and someone might find it and take advantage."

"That would be an ingenious solution, except that the key was kept on a chain around his neck. No, you cannot make Percival an honest man, Miss Oakes. Even if the fire was accidental, he took advantage of it to steal. And then he must have run away to live like a lord somewhere he is not known. Abroad, most likely. It is a shameful episode in our history. But then—"

A voice hailed them and he jumped. He had been so engrossed in his story that he had forgotten everything else. The present had receded, and only the past, the dark and miserable past, remained. Buckley's voice jolted him back to where he was, sitting on a low stool in the St Oswald's churchyard.

"Ahoy there, Finlassan! Miss Oakes! Are you coming back to the inn? They have laid out a good spread for us."

"Not yet!" Miss Oakes hissed in an undertone. "I must know how it ends."

"We will be there directly, Buckley," Fin called. "Go back and we will join you in a few minutes."

Buckley's eyes shifted from him to Miss Oakes' upturned face, then back again, but he said nothing, merely turning with a wave and disappearing again.

"Do go on," she breathed.

Her absorption in his family's troubles made him smile at her. Oddly, she blushed, but he chose not to comment on it and embarrass her further. No doubt she felt her interest was improper, but he found her wide-eyed attention enjoyable. How many years was it since he had basked in the riveted attention of a beautiful young woman? Not since Juliana...

He cleared his throat, and continued, "Several years after the fire, the Fifth Earl of Cottersmere died and Hadrian Dulnain assumed the title. Hadrian is a good man, and he wanted very much to bring about a reconciliation. Even though his own sister had died in the fire, he never blamed anyone, not even Percival. So, a marriage was arranged between Hadrian's younger sister, Juliana, and me."

It surprised him how calm he was. The single most devastating time of his life, and yet he could recount the events of those days lucidly, dispassionately. But now he had come to Juliana, and that would be the greatest test of his fortitude. Could he speak of her without an upwelling of grief? Could he speak of her at all? Yet he must try.

"We were just nineteen years of age, Miss Oakes. Too young, perhaps, but my marriage was considered a matter of urgency, for after me, Percival was the next in line, if he still lived, or Giles if he did not, but there was no way to be sure. Uncertainty in the succession is the very devil, so I was to marry and produce an heir. I resigned myself to a marriage of duty, but then..."

"Then you met her!" she said breathlessly.

"I did! Oh, it was not just her beauty, although she was extraordinary in that regard, but her nature was the purest, most open and generous I have ever known. So open... I had no resistance to her, none at all. Within days, I was deep in love, beyond the reach of reason or sense. She was an angel, who carried me aloft to the clouds with her, and I was lost to the commonplace world. And when she betrayed me—"

He stopped, aware that his hands were clenched painfully tight. Consciously, he loosed them, breathed, calmed himself. The governess watched him in avid silence, her lips parted, her eyes huge in her pale face.

"When she left me," he said, his voice ragged, "I retreated within myself. I could see no one, go nowhere, do nothing. I painted, Miss Oakes. That was the only solace I could find. When I painted, the hurt receded and I could forget for a while. So I painted. My mother died, and then my father, and I did all that was needful. Uncle Giles and Drusilla told me what I must do, and I did it. And afterwards, I went back into my studio and I painted.

And I waited, frozen in time, unable to move forwards. I waited for her, because surely she would think better of it. Surely the power of my love could reach her wherever she was, and she would understand and regret what she had lost and return to me. But she never did. She chose absolute ruin above me."

"She chose a man she adored rather than a loveless marriage," Miss Oakes said softly. "Can you imagine how she felt? Suppose, loving Juliana, you had been faced with marriage to another, a woman for whom you felt nothing — could you have borne it?"

The idea was so shocking that for an instant his mind was empty of all but outrage. Marry another, feeling as he did? Impossible! And in that moment, he understood for the first time the agonising choice facing Juliana.

"What would our marriage have been like?" he mused. "If we had married, when she was in love with her architect... she would have been desperately unhappy. Nothing I could have done would have made her otherwise. Was she happy with him?"

"Blissfully," Miss Oakes said. "I never knew her, but the servants told me so and her paintings... you will see when they arrive. There was so much joy in them. Mr Kearney was devastated by her death. He never set aside his black coats."

He let out a long breath. "Then she made the right choice," he said, and smiled.

# 12: The Muse

Fin was quietly pleased with himself after this conversation with Miss Oakes. Not only had she induced him to talk more about himself than he had done for years, but she had also brought him to the realisation that he could not have made Juliana happy. No degree of adoration on his side could ever have compensated her for the loss of the object of her own affection. She had loved her architect so well that she had given up the world for him, borne him two children and lived with him in great joy for a number of years. He could not wish her life to be otherwise, except that she had been able to marry Kearney, and fate had denied her that comfort.

That night he was inspired to paint again, the same view as before but this time with a gentler aspect, the trees immobile, the temple lit from behind by a fiery sun. When dawn came creeping through the shutters, he began to look for Miss Oakes, for usually she would be in the studio for an hour or two before breakfast, but today she did not come. That was a disappointment. She was his muse, his inspiration, and he had hoped the new work would receive her approbation.

He sent for a tray of food and ate standing up, gazing at the painting, trying to find room for improvement but somehow unable to see what needed to be done next. Where was Miss Oakes?

The door opened and he turned in pleasure, but it was only Drusilla and Giles. He sighed in disappointment.

"What are you doing eating in here?" Drusilla said, bustling in and tiptoeing around the rough sheet he spread to protect the floor from splashes of paint. "How uncivilised you are getting, Fin. No one would take you for a peer of the realm."

"He is an earl," Giles said. "He may do as he pleases, and it pleases him to eat cold meat standing up."

"Well, he should not. It is undignified."

"In his own house, a man may be as undignified as he chooses. One cannot be always on parade for the world."

"But Fin is *never* on parade for the world. He hides away in here like some kind of hermit. If he would..."

He ignored them, his thoughts already turning back to his painting. A little more gold around that tree... and the grass was not quite right. Something lighter, perhaps, and—

"*Fin!* You are not even listening to me!"

If she would only say something worth listening to, perhaps he would. "What do you want, Drusilla?"

"Godfrey wants to take the governess on an outing to Derby. I have told him I will not be a party to his little schemes to bed the girl, but he will not listen to me. He says it is for *you* to approve or otherwise, so you will just have to refuse your permission."

"I see no reason why the girl should not go if she wishes," Giles said. "Let her enjoy herself."

"A *governess* enjoying herself?" Drusilla said in outraged tones.

Giles laughed. "Two governesses, since Miss Claypole is also invited along as chaperon. Why ever not? It must be a miserable life, being at the beck and call of two children all day."

"She is hardly ever with them now, so Fin pays her *two hundred pounds a year* to paint and walk the dog."

"Is that what he wants?" Fin said, frowning.

"What who wants?" Drusilla said.

"Buckley. You said he wants to bed Miss Oakes. Is that true?"

"Well, he is not going to *marry* her, is he?" she screeched. "Really, Fin, what else does a man want when he pays attention to someone of her station?"

"It seems to me that a man who is trying to seduce a young woman does not arrange for her to dine with the nobility, introduce her to his aunt or ensure she is fully chaperoned at all times. If that is his objective, it is a devilish queer way to go about it."

Drusilla opened her mouth, then closed it again with a snap.

"He has a point," Giles said. "Dashed odd thing to do. He would be making secret assignations if his intentions were less than honourable."

"I refuse to believe he has marriage in mind," she said, but with less conviction.

"Perhaps you should enquire as to his intentions," Giles said, with a grin.

"Whatever his intentions, Miss Oakes may have her day in Derby if she wishes," Fin said.

"What about her lessons with the girls?" Drusilla said.

Fin shrugged. "I will teach them that day. She only has them for drawing and painting now, so I should be able to manage that. Or they may have a day off. And she is worth every penny of two hundred pounds a year to me, whether she teaches them or not."

Giles laughed, but Drusilla was too shocked to say more than a horrified, *"Fin!"*

"She is my muse," he said, gesturing to the painting. "She inspires me. You cannot conceive how glorious it is to have someone to *share* my art with, someone who understands, who listens and makes suggestions, someone to teach me and to be taught. She is learning to paint in oils and I have rediscovered the possibilities of pastels. We are both finding new depths of imagination within us. I do not expect you to understand this, Drusilla, but Miss Oakes is invaluable to me."

"Then you should put more effort into deterring Godfrey," she said snappishly. "If she marries him, he will whisk her away to Farndyke and you will not see your muse above twice a year."

"He may want to marry her, but I doubt she wants to marry him," he said with a shrug. "She has more sense. Was there anything else? For I have a painting to finish."

"And your breakfast," said Giles, chuckling, as Drusilla left in high dudgeon and he followed her out.

After they had gone, Fin chewed thoughtfully on a piece of bread, examining the painting. Then he added a few dabs of colour here and there… some jonquil and daffodil here, a little spring green there. Dissatisfied, he set aside his palette and brushes and kicked off his paint-spattered slippers. Too impatient to ring the bell, he padded barefoot down the hall to the Pillared Saloon and through to the entrance hall, where a footman always stood.

"Where is Miss Oakes today?"

Before the footman could do more than open his mouth in surprise, Bagnall materialised from the North Anteroom. "You will find Miss Oakes in the billiard room, my lord."

"The billiard room? What the devil—?" He remembered the box of letters. Through the North Anteroom and then into the billiard room. He never went to that part of the house, for it was too near the dangerous ground of the ballroom, and he could not remember the last time he had been in there. The furniture was still shrouded in holland covers, but the shutters were open and the wooden cover protecting the billiard table itself was almost invisible beneath the heaps of papers spread out across it. Miss Oakes herself— devil take it, he could not keep thinking of her as Miss Oakes!

"What is your name? Your Christian name."

She looked up at him with a face full of mischief. Setting down the letter she was reading, she turned, dipped him a respectful curtsy and murmured, "Good morning to you too, my lord. I trust you are well this fine day?"

"What the—? Oh." Her effrontery made him smile. "You are reproaching me for my abrupt entrance, I suppose?"

"It is customary to make a civil greeting on first meeting an acquaintance for the day." An acquaintance? Was that how she saw him? "Then one might enquire into the general wellbeing of the acquaintance before progressing to sundry remarks upon the weather."

Laughter bubbled up inside him. Such playfulness, and she was not in the least shy or timid with him. He liked that in her! Without a word he turned, strode out of the room and closed the door behind him. Then he knocked and entered the room once more.

Bowing, he said, "Good morning, Miss Oakes. How are you today?"

Her face brimming with merriment, she curtsied. "Good morning, my lord. I am well, I thank you. I trust you are in good health yourself?"

"Perfectly, I thank you. It is— Hmm, I have no notion what sort of day it is." Crossing to the window and glancing out, he went on, "It is a fine day, although I fear there may be rain later."

The laughter spilt out of her, and she put one hand to her mouth to hide it. Such a charming gesture! He had the urge to draw it… to draw her. Were his skills up to the challenge? People… he had never been able to draw people. But she could. She had painted his two wards, capturing their innocent young faces to perfection. And she had painted him, too, scowling… no, she had said he looked intense.

"What was it you wanted? Oh, my name. Felicia, my lord."

Felicia. "From Felix, I suppose. Happy. It suits you, for you are always happy, are you not?"

"I try always to see the best in any situation," she said, but he thought there was something darker behind her words. "Was that all, my lord?"

He tried to remember why he had sought her out but could not. Waving a hand at the heaps of papers on the table, he said, "Are you making progress?"

"Indeed I am. Everything will be arranged in the most orderly fashion before long, ready for Mr Warborough's attention. I have found my own letters here, you see, and those from Mr Pierce, to advise you of your great good fortune in acquiring two wards of whom you have never heard and with whom you are entirely unconnected. There is also a more recent letter from Mr Pierce to say that he has received your instructions regarding the paintings. And also…" She hesitated, and picked up one of the letters from the top of a pile. "There is a letter from Lord Cottersmere regarding Juliana and Margarita, offering them a home if you should find the charge too onerous, to be raised alongside his own daughters. He is their uncle, after all. He sounds a kindly man."

"Hadrian is the best of fellows. His father excised Juliana from the family when she ran off with Kearney. Her name was struck from the Bible and she was never to be mentioned again. But Hadrian has forgiveness and reconciliation in his soul, so his offer does not surprise me. He was very fond of Juliana, although she was so much younger than he was."

"Shall you send the girls to him?"

"Good God, why should I? The charge is mine, and I do not shirk it."

"It would be good for them to know their cousins. They have no other kin, after all, and if Lord Cottersmere acknowledges them—"

"He may acknowledge them if he pleases, but they stay in this house." She flushed, and he realised his tone had been harsher than he intended. "I beg your pardon," he said gruffly. "I did not mean to rebuke you for your thoughts. When the girls are older, they may visit Hadrian sometimes."

"Or perhaps he and his family might also visit here?" she said, looking up at him with twinkling eyes. She was teasing him!

"Perhaps," he said, smiling. "Perhaps one day I might not mind having my solitude imposed upon by a rabble of guests. One day far in the future."

"Or you might impose upon the solitude of others," she said, with an answering smile. "For here are invitations enough. Lord This, Lady So-and-so, Sir Something-or-other, the occasional plain Mr or Mrs. You might have hunted in any of ten counties last winter if you had been so minded, or attended any number of horse racing events, or displays of fireworks, or lectures on the use of Argand lamps in the home — gas is much more efficient than candles, apparently, despite sounding alarmingly dangerous — oh and balloon ascensions! You might have observed several  of those, and how you could resist such an attraction is beyond my understanding. It would make a grand subject for a painting."

"Are you reading everything? That must be tedious indeed."

"I must read each missive in order to know which pile to place it upon, and some of them are dull indeed. Lawyers have a very dry style, I find. Nor is there anything of a personal and scandalous nature to liven the chore. However, there is one that must be from a spy, for I feel sure it is in code, so little sense does it make."

"My father and his cronies used to communicate in code," he said. "Government business. It is hard to imagine that anyone would write to me in such a manner, however."

"True enough. I daresay it is no more than an eccentric hand. Perhaps Mr Warborough can make it out. But the invitations are amusing. What is a Venetian breakfast? It sounds delicious, but whatever would one wear to such an event? One feels that it must be a rather grand occasion, so an ordinary morning dress would not do. Yet one would not wish to be dressed too fine, and be an object of ridicule."

"I deal with such questions by never attending anything," he said.

"Oh, but you should!" she cried. "You should mingle with your neighbours and attend Parliament, at the very least."

"Do you presume to tell me what I *should* do?" he said, but he could not be angry with her, not when her eyes gleamed with amusement. Even when she scolded him, she did it in a light-hearted, teasing way. Not like Drusilla's hectoring!

"If I can presume to tell a marquess what he should do, I shall not hesitate for a mere earl," she said.

He burst out laughing. "Miss Oakes, you are refreshingly original. Have you healed the breach between yourself and Arnwell?"

"Not yet," she said, her face suddenly serious. "I fear I shall not be forgiven. He wrote me a very conciliatory letter asking me to resume my visits, but I have told him that if he wishes to see me, he will find me at St Miriam's for Morning Service. That is another *should*, my lord. He should attend church regularly, and so I told him."

"Do you think I should attend church, too?"

She frowned. "At least you permit Mr Warborough to hold a service in the chapel here, but…"

"It is perfunctory, is it not? Giles comes here for his dinner, and twenty minutes of mumbled prayer is a small penance to pay for a seat at my table. Is he more conscientious in his own church?"

"He preaches a proper sermon, if that is what you mean, as well as the full measure of the office. He does not write his own sermons and as often as not he leaves it to his excellent curate, but a man may still be a dutiful incumbent despite that. I greatly prefer the service at St Miriam's, and I meet some of the local people, too." After a small hesitation, she added mischievously, "That would not be an attraction for you, I daresay."

"But you think I should, do you not, Miss Oakes? I should mingle with my neighbours."

"You should get to know them, certainly. There is much good that may be done by the principal landowner in a parish, if he is so minded, to assist with disputes, to help the poor and to advance the careers of the worthy. It is your duty, I believe."

He grunted in annoyance. "My duty! You will be telling me I should marry, next."

"I hardly need to tell you that, because you must be aware of it," she said quietly, then, her humour bubbling up again, "I am quite certain that Lady Drusilla has pointed it out to you."

He gave a bark of laughter. "True enough."

"We all have our duties, my lord. Yours are pleasant ones — to set an example to your neighbours, to add your voice to the government of the country and to find yourself a congenial wife. Mine are to do as I am told."

"Yet your duties are not unpleasant, I think, Miss Oakes? Boring, sometimes, but not unpleasant. And I must leave you to be bored by my letters." He had turned for the door when he remembered why he was there. "Where were you this morning? I expected you in the studio as usual. I wanted your opinion on a new work."

"I was out for my daily walk."

"Why so early? Do you not usually take your exercise later in the day?" She tipped her head on one side, a quizzical expression on her face. Perhaps she was right, so he went on quickly, "I beg your pardon. It is no concern of mine."

"I have found," she said slowly, "that if I walk at my usual time, I am inclined to encounter Mr Godfrey Buckley also walking about the grounds."

"And his company is disagreeable to you?"

"Not at all. He is a very pleasant man, but I do not feel it proper for me to stroll about the grounds with him as if I were someone worthy of his notice. It is kind in him to be attentive to a mere governess but it is better not to encourage him."

Fin considered whether to say more. His own opinion was that Buckley's intentions were not dishonourable, but even so, his object might be no more than a pleasant flirtation to while away his sojourn in Derbyshire. It would be wrong to raise hopes that might easily be dashed.

Cautiously, he said, "Better for whom? Is your aim to prevent him from making an unfortunate alliance, or to protect your own reputation? Or your heart?"

She chuckled. "My heart is in no danger, and I have no reputation to protect. I am a bastard, after all, the lowest of the low. But since nothing can come from an association with Mr Buckley, I prefer to meet with him as little as possible."

That was very much as he had supposed. And yet… "Supposing there were the possibility… would you be tempted?"

"Not in the slightest."

So very decisive! "No? If a future marquess were to offer you marriage, you would turn him down?" For some odd reason she blushed furiously, and he was immediately contrite. "Yet again I must beg your forgiveness, Miss Oakes. My questions are intrusive. You have no need to answer them, or to explain yourself to me. Whatever your views on Mr Buckley, however, I fear you are destined to be an object of his attentions for some time yet. He wishes to take you on an outing to Derby."

"With Juliana and Margarita?"

"I believe not. With Miss Claypole."

"Oh dear. I wish he would not! And yet I should dearly love to see Derby. There are many fine churches there, so I hear."

"The same might be said of any town in England. They all have many fine churches with carved medieval rood screens, some Roman antiquities and two or three coaching inns. Every village has a church, too, where a monument of note may be viewed beneath a Norman tower, and there is a manor house nearby where Good Queen Bess once slept. That woman was never at home. However, Derby is a fine place, so by all means go if you wish, Miss Oakes. Should you like me to accompany you, in order to defend you from the unwanted attentions of Godfrey Buckley?"

She blushed again, even more deeply, and murmured something incoherent. Seeing that he had embarrassed her again, although he could not quite see why, he made some non-committal noises and left her to her letters.

# 13: Morning Service At St Miriam's

Felicia was discomposed by this conversation with Fin. In truth, his presence always discomposed her, but when they worked together in the studio or met around the dinner table on Sundays she could produce some semblance of ease in his company. The neutral subject of art or the presence of others enabled her to act in what she hoped was a convincingly natural fashion.

She was all too aware, however, of the growing intimacy between them. His confidences in the churchyard at St Oswald's were flattering, and she could sense that he was beginning to regard her as a friend. Nothing more than that, obviously, for it was clear that his heart still belonged to Juliana, but increasingly he turned to Felicia. Their conversation that day had been more intimate than she liked. Yet how difficult it was to maintain the proper distance from him, and remember that he was merely her employer for a short time.

Gazing at the piles of papers laid out on the table, she sighed. The box was not yet empty, for although much of Fin's correspondence was dull stuff, to do with the estate or impenetrable legal matters, there was so much that set her imagination flying. The distant relations reporting betrothals or births or celebrations. Naval or army promotions, ordinations, a scientific expedition to China, inheritances. Houses bought and sold, journeys to the Continent, moves to Bath or London. A few deaths. An election as a Member of Parliament. People's lives recorded in small measures. So fascinating.

The unintelligible letter caught her eye again. She picked it up and squinted at it, but it still made no sense. Perhaps if she were to examine it in better light? But even carrying it to the window was no help. It still looked like a jumble of meaningless letters. Each letter was clear to read, but combined into no words that she could make out.

Perhaps it was indeed some sort of code? If she transcribed it onto fresh paper, she might be able to disentangle the meaning. For ten minutes she worked at it, diligently copying every letter exactly as she saw it, then stuffed the copy into her reticule to be worked on in her room. It would be a good project to fill an evening after the girls had retired to the night nursery, and if she could finally make sense of it, that would bring her some satisfaction and chase away the niggle of annoyance. She so disliked mysteries! There was no way to solve the mystery of her own origins, but here at least was a small mystery that might be amenable to unravelling.

As always when she was unsettled, she wandered through the echoing saloons, the vast and beautiful public rooms of Hawkewood Hall. At the southern end of the house, where lay the studio, Fin's private sitting room and the library, there were fires, and sunshine and signs of life — books open, a bowl of walnuts or vase of flowers, a discarded plate or glass. Here at the northern end, however, the rooms were cold and empty, the curtains tightly drawn and shutters closed.

From the billiard room, she walked through the gloomy half-light of the card room, its tables folded away, the sideboards shrouded. She imagined it as it must have been, the guests intent on their games, the sudden bursts of noise at a good play or an unlucky throw of the dice. There would be silent footmen moving about with wine, and another figure moving here and there, helping the jollity along, would be the master of the house — Fin's father, the image in her mind taken from his portrait of old age hanging in the library.

From there, she stole through the high doors into the East Conservatory. After tripping over a chair on her first venture there, she had left a shutter ajar to provide some light. Now she moved swiftly over the dusty tiled floor, her light feet making no sound, and threw open the double doors beyond.

And there it was. The ballroom, that *'extremely splendid apartment, furnished in the most chaste yet expensive style, with a very handsome ceiling.'* Moving down the room, she flung open one shutter after another, until the room was flooded with light. There were no holland covers here, no shroud for the chandeliers. The sconces were neatly filled with fresh candles, the side tables bore trays of upturned glasses. If there had ever been carpets laid, they had been rolled up and taken away, the polished wooden floor left ready for the dancers. On the balcony, the music stands for the orchestra could be seen. Chairs lined the sides of the room, awaiting the silk-clad forms of the noble guests.

But there had been no guests. The planned ball, to celebrate the marriage of the heir to the Earl of Finlassan to the daughter of the Earl of Cottersmere, had never taken place. Juliana had run away with her architect, and the ballroom had been closed up, untouched, abandoned just as it was. No footman had gone in to put away the crystal glasses or cover the furniture. No housemaid had waved her feather duster. Long cobwebs dangled from every protrusion and the floor was thick with dust.

It was a sad place, and yet, seeing it thus exposed, not shrouded like the other rooms, it was easier to picture the splendour of a ball. If she closed her eyes, she could imagine it all, could hear the music, could watch the couples moving to its rhythm. The ladies' gowns swirled, their jewels flashed, their arms moved in elegant poses. The gentlemen leapt and twirled, their feet skipping energetically. Felicia twirled, too, taking her place in the imaginary set, her feet moving, her arms outstretched, her skirts swirling about her legs.

But it was not just dancers. Around the fringes of the room, the matrons watched, together with a few young men too shy or lethargic to dance. Young ladies without a partner looked on eagerly, hoping for better fortune in the next set. One or two couples would be slipping out onto the terrace for a private assignation. Everywhere there would be meaningful glances, polite disdain, gushing deference, hopeful mamas and evasive suitors. All human life existed in a ballroom, as much at this polished level of society as at the rougher assemblies in Southampton.

She had to paint it, this scene so vivid in her mind. She would begin at once.

~~~~~

*'To Miss J. Pollard, Charles Street, Mayfair. My dear Jane, I am very sorry the son of the baronet failed to come up to scratch. Are you much disappointed? You sound cheerful, but you must be a little*
~~~~~

*downhearted. He sounded a most amiable man, and I daresay you would have ceased to notice the squint after a very short time. Every man has some affliction and better a squint than weakness of character. As you see, I am still in Derbyshire and not likely to return south very soon. Lady D is still dithering over the new governess, and Lord F insists I stay so that he has a fellow painter in the house. You need not be concerned about Boscobel Cottage, for Mrs M and the T's have very kindly agreed to stay on there to take care of it for me. They are raising a pig and growing vegetables, and Mr T has asked if he might undertake some small improvements, such as painting and minor repairs to the wainscoting and shutters. It is very good of them, when they might be looking about for a new employer. I hope your new cook is an improvement on the three previous ones, and that the card party goes well. Have you decided where you will go when the season ends? Yours in affection, Felicia Oakes.'*

~~~~~

On Sunday, Felicia walked to St Miriam's Church with Juliana and Margarita and the two nursery maids, Ellen and Mary. Some of the servants preferred the brief chapel service, but for most, the church was an opportunity to meet friends and exchange what news a small village and two great houses might afford. The two girls chattered together, and a few paces behind the two maids did likewise, but Felicia was subdued. She was beginning to realise that, for her own peace of mind, she ought to leave Hawkewood Hall, yet how could she? The girls still needed her, and now it seemed that the earl needed her too. What on earth would she do with herself at Boscobel Cottage?

The walk lifted her spirits, however. The Derbyshire air was so clear and fresh, and the summer greens all around her — so many
~~~~~

greens! — could not fail in their effect. She could not be downhearted when there was such beauty all around her.

Her spirits sank again as they reached the village and joined the streams of people entering through the lych gate, for the first person she saw, loitering as if awaiting her arrival, was Mr Godfrey Buckley. He smiled widely as he saw her, and moved at once in her direction. With a sigh, she accepted the inevitable.

"Mr Buckley," she said as she rose from her curtsy. "Good day to you."

"Good morning, Miss Oakes! Good morning! No need to enquire how you are for I can see that you are in the very bloom of health. Such roses in your cheeks! I have never seen you in greater beauty."

She gave a little bow to acknowledge the compliment, but felt no inclination to respond to such arrant nonsense.

"I wonder, Miss Oakes, if I might venture to make a small proposal to you. I have it in mind to go to Derby, to look about the shops and so forth, and it struck me that it might be an enjoyable expedition for a lady such as yourself. It would be of no interest to your charges, I daresay but I have it in mind to… have it in mind… Good God!"

Felicia followed his frozen gaze to see a carriage drawing up outside the lych gate, one she had not seen before. The coachman and his junior wore full livery, and two footmen stood behind, and if she had had the least doubt of the importance of the arrival, the coat of arms on the door underlined it. Even as she murmured, "Who is it?" to Mr Buckley, she knew the answer.

The carriage stopped, the footmen jumped down, opened the door and let down the steps. The Marquess of Arnwell descended. Turning, he offered his arm to an elderly lady, her hair as white as his beneath her cap and old-fashioned broad-brimmed hat. With a wide grin, looking up at him coquettishly, she took his arm and they began the walk through the lych gate and up the path to the church. A second lady of middle years emerged from the carriage, drably dressed, whom Felicia recognised as Miss Edith Buckley. She briskly smoothed down her skirts and set off after the marquess.

The assembled parishioners watched in astonished silence, dropping into deep curtsies or low bows as the little procession passed by. At the church door, Mr Warborough issued some terse instructions to the verger, and then raced down the path to greet the newcomers with several bows, and a great many deferential words of welcome. Since the marquess did not slow down his progress, the clergyman was obliged to walk backwards in front of his noble parishioner all the way to the church steps.

"Is that him?" Mr Buckley whispered, as the group disappeared into the church.

"Do you not recognise him? Yes, that is the marquess."

"Never expected to see him alive," he said breathlessly. "Yet I am heartily glad of it. I cannot imagine he would acknowledge me — how could he, when we have never even been introduced? — but I am delighted to have seen him. A fine figure of a man, despite the disfigurement. Such an upstanding carriage! Such dignity! And yet, not overweening, not proud. I see nothing of conceit in his bearing. I hope I shall look half so well at his age, indeed. And that must be the Lady Lucia Buckley, Lord Arnwell's sister. She is said to be deranged in the head with the sudden rages of a child. She must have been quite a beauty in her day. Did you see her complexion? So clear, and hardly a wrinkle, yet she is older than—Ah, we are going in."

They separated inside the church, he to join Lady Drusilla and Lady Mabel in their pew, and Felicia, rather relieved to have escaped him at last, to join Juliana and Margarita in the Hall's rather grander pew. There she found that the other richly appointed pew, directly opposite, was now filled by the faces of the Shotterbourne family. The marquess gave her the tiniest nod of acknowledgement before turning his attention to his Prayer Book.

The outer doors were closed with a solid clunk, and Mr Warborough stood before the congregation in his vestments.

"*I acknowledge my transgressions, and my sin is ever before me. Psalm 51:3*," he began, as he always did. "Dearly beloved brethren, the Scripture moveth us in sundry places to acknowledge and confess our manifold sins and wickedness; and that we should not dissemble..."

The door creaked and he broke off, his face a picture of astonishment. Booted feet thumped down the aisle in the silence that fell, then the Hall pew door opened and Fin sat down beside Felicia, slamming the pew door closed again.

"Carry on, Uncle," he said loudly. A ripple of laughter passed through the church.

Mr Warborough cleared his throat. "Manifold sins and wickedness," he said with emphasis, glaring at Fin. "And that we should not dissemble nor cloak them before the face of Almighty God our heavenly Father; but confess them with a humble, lowly, penitent, and obedient heart; to the end that we may obtain forgiveness of the same..."

Felicia gripped her Prayer Book tightly and gazed down determinedly at its pages. She would not laugh, she would not! Oh, but it was so tempting. On her other side, Margarita leaned forwards to gaze at Fin and when she caught his eye, she beamed at him and waggled her fingers. Felicia tapped the Prayer Book in the girl's lap pointedly, and she dutifully turned her eyes towards it, but the grin remained.

Now Felicia had the distraction of Fin sitting beside her, almost touching her. If she looked up to watch Mr Warborough, she was aware of Fin's folded arms and every tiny wrinkle in the cloth of his coat. If she dutifully concentrated on her Prayer Book, she could see his legs, closely wrapped in pantaloons. His nearness made her agitated and restless, yet she dared not move in case she accidentally brushed against him. She sat rigid, scarcely daring to breathe, through the interminable service. How she wished she had not come! Her efforts to avoid the earl at the brief service in the chapel now seemed to have put her in a much worse position.

She must leave Derbyshire at once! Yet all the same objections rose to her mind. The girls needed her... she must stay until they were settled with a new governess... and her painting... yes, her painting of the ballroom. She could see it so vividly in her mind's eye, and could not leave until it had been completed to her satisfaction. The rest of the service passed her by, as she focused her mind on the details of dancers and musicians and candles. Ah, the candles! That would be an interesting challenge.

At the end of the service, the marquess and his party left first, followed by Fin, Felicia and the two girls, with Lady Drusilla scuttling along behind them.

"What are you *doing?*" she hissed at Fin, grabbing his arm.

"Attending Morning Service, like the good Christian I am," he said blandly. "Would you rather I stayed at home?"

"Well… it is good to see you showing yourself a little," Lady Drusilla admitted. "One might wonder why you chose today for your return to church." She cast a quick glance at Felicia, but they had reached the church door by then and she was distracted by the sight of the marquess standing just a short distance away, watching them. "But that is an even more remarkable return. Miss Oakes, were you aware that he would be here?"

"Not in the least, my lady, although I hoped my letter would induce him to attend."

"Induce him? How?"

"Lord Arnwell asked to see me, so I told him that I might be found at Morning Service. Excuse me, my lady, I believe his lordship wishes to speak to me."

Felicia was aware of the stares as she walked towards the marquess and made her curtsy.

"Well, madam, here I am," he said, lifting his chin defiantly. "Are you satisfied? Will you now resume your visits to the Sanctuary?"

"The Sanctuary! I never knew its name. Certainly I will come, if I can. It is not always possible for me to escape."

His lips quirked into an approximation of a smile. "Are you caged? Or merely hedged about by the whims of others?"

"Neither, my lord, but I must not neglect my duties to my charges."

"Who are your charges?"

"Lord Finlassan's wards, the Miss Kearneys. I am their governess, for the moment. Not a very good one, so I am to be replaced as soon as Lady Drusilla can find a suitable person."

"Hmm. So you truly are a governess. I thought that was no more than one of your little stories, Princess. I heard about Finlassan's wards... the Miss Kearneys. Juliana's children. Where is he? Finlassan! A word with you."

Fin ambled over and made his bow. "Arnwell."

"These wards of yours, Juliana's girls — are you taking good care of them? My nieces, after all."

Fin bridled. "Naturally I am, although it is hardly a concern of yours. The Dulnains wanted nothing to do with Juliana."

"I am not a Dulnain," the marquess said stiffly, drawing himself up a little, the better to look Fin in the eye. Fin was unusually tall, but the marquess was almost his equal in height. "Juliana was my wife's sister, and I never bore her the least grudge. Let me know the girls' names and I will leave them something in my will. Daresay they will not have to wait too long for it, either. Princess, who is that fine buck eyeing you up? You were talking to him before the service, too. He looks eager to speak to you. Something between you, is there? Are you planning to leave governessing behind?"

"Not at all, my lord, and that fine buck is your heir, Mr Godfrey Buckley. He is a guest of the Lady Drusilla Warborough." Some mischief in Felicia led her to say innocently, "Should you like me to introduce him to you?"

The marquess's intake of breath was audible and his brows lowered in anger. She thought for a moment that he might explode. Then he said, "Hmpf. I suppose you will tell me that I ought to meet the fellow." She said nothing, smiling encouragingly. "Oh, very well, very well, but I warn you, if he is a toad-eater, he can take himself off again at once. I want no Spanish coin from him. Bring him over and let me see if he is any better than his despicable father, for he could not be worse." Then, with a bark of laughter, he went on, "Whatever are you doing to me, Princess? If this goes on, you will turn me into a righteous and upright Christian, and then where will we be?"

"She has that effect on people," Fin murmured. "But I believe we both have a long way to go yet, Arnwell, so do not give way to despair."

The marquess's rumble of laughter echoed around the churchyard.

Mr Buckley was brought across and introduced to the marquess, and said everything that was proper. He was respectful and deferential, and Felicia detected no Spanish coin in his well-phrased expressions of pleasure at making Lord Arnwell's acquaintance at last, and his hopes for better relations between them in the future.

As Felicia walked home, with the girls ahead of her, the maids behind and Fin agitatingly close to her side, she wondered at all that the day had brought and hoped that the rapprochement between all parties could be maintained.

# 14: Dinner At Shotterbourne

Three days of relentless rain kept Felicia and the girls indoors, and the soggy task of walking the dog twice a day and bathing him after each outing was delegated to an unlucky footman. Several of the new tutors were deterred by the weather, too, leaving Felicia to fill the gaps. She was struggling with the globes one morning when Fin swept into the schoolroom.

"That dancing fellow is not coming, nor the Frenchman. Lily-livered idiots to be deterred by a drop of water. Come down to the studio and do some drawing. You, too," he added to Mary, who was sewing in a corner.

"Me, milord?"

"That is what I said. You are to be our subject. Today's lesson is portraiture."

They sat in a line, all four of them, sketchbooks on their knees, while Mary placidly sewed. Felicia would have preferred charcoal, but Fin insisted on pencils. Then they drew.

After an hour or so, Felicia said, "Are you going to see how we are getting on, my lord? Or will you wait until we are finished before you examine our efforts?"

"Oh, am I supposed to instruct the girls? Is that what you do when you teach them?"

"Sometimes, if it is a new technique, or they will ask if they need advice. But this is your lesson, not mine."

"If it were yours, what would you do?"

"I would say, *'How are you getting on?'* to them."

"Hmm. How are you two getting on?"

"Fine," Margarita said at once, but Juliana sighed.

"This is *hard*," she said. "I cannot get the eyes right."

At once he was out of his chair, kneeling beside her, examining the drawing and making suggestions. Felicia was delighted to see such attention from him. What could be more proper than for a guardian to devote time to his wards, and place his knowledge and experience at their disposal? How advantageous for them to learn from him, rather than from a succession of tutors and masters, no matter how expert. And perhaps, in time, when he had grown accustomed to their presence in the house, he would become a father to them, and his wife a mother.

His wife. For he must marry, in time. That was his duty, after all, and the same imperative that had driven him towards an arranged marriage with Juliana was still there. His heir was Percival, yet there was no knowing whether he were alive or dead.

"See how Miss Oakes has managed it," Fin said. "The eyes, the lips, the bloom on Mary's cheeks — yet she is most economical with the lines of her pencil."

"I could never do that," Juliana said sorrowfully. "It is Mary to the life! That way she is looking down so demurely, yet she looks as if she is full of merriment."

"Perhaps you will never quite have Miss Oakes' ability to capture the essence of a sitter," he said gravely. "Her talent is quite special. Yet with practice you will improve, as Miss Oakes has practised and worked on her artistry."

He gazed at Felicia over the top of Juliana's head, and smiled so warmly that she blushed crimson.

"Now we have embarrassed her," he said. "That will never do. Back to your sketchbooks, young ladies."

Felicia was left mortified by her own want of self-control. If only he would not smile at her! When he talked to her, his manner was so brusque that she could answer him calmly, as if he were no more than a common acquaintance. But when he smiled, her insides melted, her brain became an incoherent muddle and her cheeks flamed with colour like a schoolroom miss. He thought she was embarrassed by the compliment, but it was his attention that betrayed her — the intensity in those blue eyes, and the approval in his expression.

Such moments hardened her resolve. Fin must marry and produce an heir, and Felicia must leave the Hall for good. But not yet. Not until her painting of the ballroom was completed.

~~~~~

*'My dear Princess, This miserable weather confines me to the house and my wretched physician forbids me to venture outdoors again until all risk of dampness in the air is eradicated. Since the summer may be over before that happy event, would you do an old*
~~~~~

*man the kindness of dining with him tomorrow night? My sister will be here, and I shall invite the Warborough rabble as well, so you need not suffer the confinement of my company alone. At this point, I hear your voice quite clearly, whispering in my ear. What about your heir, it says. I think you must be my conscience, Princess, sent to torment me to some semblance of charity towards my undeserving kin. So I shall invite him also, and endeavour to like him, for your sake. I dine at six. Do not fail me. Arnwell.'*

~~~~~

Despite a flurry of letters between them, the stolid groom riding back and forth uncomplainingly, Felicia's efforts to convince the marquess of her unsuitability as a dining companion were in vain. He told her in no uncertain terms that if he did her the honour of inviting her, no question regarding suitability could arise. He reserved the right, he said, to choose his own dining companions. Since it would be unspeakably uncivil to refuse, she once again donned her blue spotted muslin, fastened the small silver cross around her neck and made her way to the hall to await the carriage. She hoped she looked composed, but inside she was melting. A whole evening with Fin in all the splendour of his evening dress! She was terrified that she would disgrace herself.

She sat in agitated silence in the carriage, every nerve aflame, as Fin sat opposite her. Happily, he chose silence. They drove the short distance to Compton House, where they collected Lady Drusilla and Godfrey Buckley, but not Lady Mabel, who deemed herself too old to venture from home in the evening. Then they splashed through the puddles in the village to gather up Giles Warborough from the rectory. This was a terrifying moment for Felicia. With five in the carriage, the three gentlemen, being larger than the ladies, could not all squeeze onto the rear-facing seat.
~~~~~

Would Felicia be forced to suffer Fin sitting so close that their legs and arms were touching? She determined that she would walk the remaining distance rather than endure such torture. To her vast relief, Mr Buckley gallantly surrendered his seat to Mr Warborough and climbed up beside the coachman. It took the full length of Shotterbourne's drive, some two miles in all, before Felicia's palpitations steadied and she felt capable of presenting a calm demeanour.

Shotterbourne was probably not much larger than Hawkewood Hall, but its design, of a central block with an additional wing protruding at each corner, gave it a frontage even more imposing. To one side was the blackened shell of the family wing. Only portions of the walls and the central chimney stack remained, everything else burned to nothing. Unchecked ivy grew rampant over one wall, and through the empty windows bushes and small trees could be seen growing where once there had been sitting rooms and bedrooms. Felicia averted her eyes.

Inside was the same array of marble floors, massive pillars and statuary as at the Hall, but the colours were darker and heavier, and every room was solidly square. Felicia was struck as never before by the ingenious architect of the Hall, who had introduced curves everywhere. There were circular rooms and ovals and bay windows, and even when a room was rectangular, there would be curvaceous finials and ceilings and decorative touches. At Shotterbourne there was nothing but squareness.

The marquess was in the great hall with its spectacular pillars to greet them and lead them up the magnificent staircase to the saloon. Felicia could hardly believe she was in such a place and as a guest, not a servant. She tried to keep herself at the back of the group, walking carefully, for the steps were polished marble, but she found that no matter how slowly she ascended — one step, a long pause, then another — she had Fin on one side and Mr Buckley on the other, keeping pace with her. Mr Buckley maintained a stream of comments to divert her. Fin said nothing at all.

In the saloon, Lady Lucia and Miss Buckley waited. Lady Lucia wore a dainty muslin gown that would have looked enchanting were she a girl of seventeen, rather than a woman of more than sixty years. As Mr Buckley and Felicia were introduced to her, she simpered at them and shifted her gaze coyly, for all the world as if she were flirting.

Miss Buckley wore drab brown, looking more like a governess than Felicia. She greeted Felicia cordially, asking her with apparent interest about her home in Southampton. She was not much interested in the Miss Latimers or Summer Cottage, but she was very curious about Boscobel Cottage.

"This Miss Armiger — what sort of age would she be?"

"No one knew," Felicia said. "She never told anyone her age. She would have been above forty when she died."

It was a peculiar conversation, and Miss Buckley showed signs of continuing in this vein for some time, except that Mr Buckley intervened smoothly. "Lady Lucia needs you, I believe, Aunt."

Lady Lucia was looking about her vaguely. "My fan! Where is my fan? Ah, Edith, have you seen my fan? I am certain I had it a moment ago."

"It is on your wrist, Lucia. We tied it on so that it would not go astray, remember? Here it is."

Mr Buckley gently steered Felicia towards the windows. "Aunt Edith is a dreadful rattle," he said in a low voice. "Who can blame her, when she is cooped up here day after day. Naturally she delights in company, but she becomes so excited by it that she talks a great deal of nonsense. There now, is that not a fine view? The famous Shotterbourne portico. It is not as wide as the one at Hawkewood, but taller, I believe."

"You are very knowledgeable for a man who has never been here before."

"I may look up the family seat in the guide books, may I not? Aunt Edith talks of it, naturally, and I have a painting of it at home, too, but nothing quite prepares one for so much… so much…"

She could not resist such an opening. "Ostentatious display? Flaunting of wealth? Vainglorious flamboyance?"

For an instant, she feared she had stepped beyond the limits of propriety, but he merely smiled good-humouredly. "Grandeur. That was the word I sought. Do you despise such magnificence, Miss Oakes?"

She was not obliged to answer, for the dinner was ready and they were summoned. There was no lesser word appropriate, for the butler was every bit as haughty as the marquess, and somewhat more so than the earl, lounging at his ease with one arm on the mantel. They combined into their processional couples and again Felicia fell back in order to take her expected place at the rear, and again she was thwarted, for Mr Giles Warborough offered her his arm. They progressed at a stately pace along the gallery above the hall to reach the dining room, which was more modest than she had expected, the table being only large enough to seat twenty or so.

They sat four each side in the middle of its length, and to Felicia's embarrassment, she was seated between Lord Arnwell and Mr Warborough, with Fin directly opposite her. For a while there was little conversation, as the marquess carved with great skill, despite his damaged hand, and dishes were passed here and there. Once the soup had been removed and the first hunger assuaged, the company began at last to talk.

Mr Warborough set the conversation in motion with some comment about the Midsummer Fair, which threw Lady Lucia into a torrent of delighted chatter. She greatly enjoyed such festivities, it seemed, and talked happily of such occasions in the past, although the May Day celebration was her favourite. She loved to dance around the may pole, she told them, her face alight with excitement. Felicia watched her enthusiasm with a smile. She was so childlike, her mind not at all formed beyond that of a girl of perhaps ten or twelve, and yet one could not but like her. Even the marquess's stern features softened when he looked at her.

After a while, the more general conversation splintered into smaller groups. Her companions being both engaged elsewhere, Felicia was left to her own thoughts. When that palled, she turned her gaze onto the room, which was less overpowering than the pillared entrance hall but still imposing.

"How do you like my house of ostentatious display, Princess?" the marquess murmured into her ear.

"You heard that, did you? It is very beautiful, my lord, but I should not like to live here."

"It is fortunate, then, that you are not obliged to."

"Indeed," she said. "Fortunate for me that I have my own snug little cottage to live in."

"Hmm. Shotterbourne is not snug, I grant you, but then snugness would quite defeat the purpose. Such houses are not designed for comfort, Princess, but to impress. It is not so much wealth that is flaunted here, but power. Anyone who walks through the rooms of Shotterbourne sees the authority of the nobility of this country of ours. Here in these great halls in the shires of England, this is where laws are born and the great minds of the government plan our glorious future. They are built to impress, for that is their purpose. England is strong, they proclaim. England is beautiful and rich and cultured and *immovable*. Here we have been for a thousand years and here we will be a thousand years from now. Do you not see all this here?"

"I see the beauty, certainly. No one could be unmoved by such magnificence. But so much cold marble and stone! So much emptiness! I do not see any laws being born here."

Lady Lucia must have heard only a part of this, for she clapped her hands delightedly.

"Oh, how true! The house is so empty now. How charming Shotterbourne was when the children played here. Aldwina and Albertina loved to gallop about in the great hall on their hobby horses, with little Elfleda running after them. So pretty they were, and so happy. The whole house echoed to their laughter. They used to play hide and seek behind the pillars just as we did as children, do you remember, Oscar?"

"I remember," the marquess said in a low growl. His good hand was clenched so tight on the arm of his chair that the knuckles were white.

The atmosphere was so charged that Felicia could scarcely breathe. She was shaking with fear.

Fin cleared his throat. "Those are *good* memories, Arnwell. At least you have good memories to look back on."

The shock of hearing her own words repeated almost undid Felicia. Was she about to swoon? She would not — *could* not!

Once more Lady Lucia came to her rescue. "Oh yes, such good memories! Such wonderful memories. Edith, do you remember when..." And off she went into some tale from her own past. Mr Godfrey Buckley gallantly joined in, and then Miss Edith Buckley, and the conversation became general again.

Felicia felt it safe to take a breath. Then another. Only the marquess's hand gripping the chair gave a sign that he had not yet recovered. She laid her hand on his.

"I am so sorry," she murmured.

He frowned, then turned his head towards her, his expression vague, as if he had forgotten who she was. "Nineteen years... nineteen years. Lord, how the years fly by. The girls would all be married by now, I daresay. Perhaps not Edwina. Ha! The youngest always stays at home, and better so in her case. Such a mischievous child, always up to some rig or other, but such a charming little tease. You would have got on famously with her, Princess, being a charming little tease yourself."

On her other side, Mr Giles Warborough coughed and spluttered. When all heads turned towards him, he said hastily, "Beg pardon. A mouthful of claret went awry." He coughed again, napkin to mouth. "So sorry. Pray ignore me. Ah, thank you, Edith, some water would —" Another burst of coughing cut him short.

"Wasting my good claret," the marquess muttered. "It should be left to those of us who appreciate it. If you have finished choking, Warborough, might we have the next course brought in?"

Felicia could only be grateful to Mr Warborough's timely intervention for drawing the marquess back from his melancholy.

The rest of the meal passed without incident, perhaps because Lord Arnwell devoted his attention to Lady Drusilla on his other side, and Felicia became the target of Mr Warborough's notice. He talked to her, as he did whenever they met, of Summer Cottage, where he had lived briefly with his adored wife, who had died in childbed within a year of the marriage. He had at first been astonished at the coincidence that Lady Juliana and her children had lived in the very same place, until Felicia had pointed out that he spoke rapturously to everyone of the delights of Southampton. It was hardly surprising, therefore, that when Juliana had needed a place to hide she had been drawn there, and finding the very cottage available for lease, had taken it at once.

Today, however, he passed quickly over Summer Cottage, and said, "But tell me of *your* cottage, Miss Oakes."

"Must I? For it was a dreary place, not at all as pleasant as Summer Cottage."

"You lived there with your guardian, I understand?"

"Miss Armiger was not my guardian, nor any kin of mine. She would never tell me how it was that she was left to raise me, and it was a great puzzle to me, for she never much liked me, nor I her. She was not unkind, but everything must be just as she said, and there was always so much to be done in the kitchen garden."

"Had you no servants?"

"None. There was a maid when I was very small, but she left and then there was no one except the two of us to do all the work."

"How very eccentric of her!" he said, his forehead creasing. "Yet when she died, you were well provided for, as I understand it. She was not a poor woman. She must have had quite a good sum by her, to enable her to buy the cottage and to leave you a good independence. How much would she have brought with her, do you suppose? It must have been several thousand pounds."

Felicia hardly knew how to reply to such an odd question. "I have not the least idea," she said, bewildered. "My attorney might know, but I do not."

"Would your attorney be Bradon? That was who I used when I lived there."

"Mine is Mr Pierce."

"Ah. That would be on... um, French Street?"

"The High Street."

"Hmm, I do not know him," Mr Warborough said. "He must have been after my time there. But you must have been very young when you travelled to Southampton."

"I was three when we first moved to the cottage, but as to travelling, I cannot say where I was before that, for I have no memory of anything before Boscobel Cottage and Miss Armiger never told me."

"Boscobel Cottage," he said, with a strange burst of laughter. "Boscobel... the woods where King Charles hid himself, is it not? He hid in an oak tree." He laughed again. "Such a curious name for a cottage. What an interesting history you have, Miss Oakes." And he laughed again.

It was such a peculiar conversation that she was relieved when, after some gentle hints from Miss Buckley, Lady Lucia rose to lead the ladies back to the saloon.

# 15: A Paid Employee

Felicia could not complain of the dullness of her evening at Shotterbourne. Indeed, it was so far from dull that she was heartily glad to see it end, after an hour trapped with the ladies and a further hour or more trapped at the card table with Mr Buckley, Miss Buckley and Mr Warborough, with some unexplained tension between the men. Then there was the supper tray to be endured before — finally! — the carriage was sent for and they could proceed home.

Home! How easily she had fallen into viewing Hawkewood Hall as home. Yet it felt so, despite the scale of the place and its magnificence. She felt small and insignificant there, and especially so when she saw the portraits of Warborough ancestors glaring down forbiddingly at her encroaching self. Yet the beauty all around her raised her spirits, and in some odd way she felt comfortable there, in a way she never quite had at Summer Cottage and certainly never had at Boscobel Cottage.

And there was Fin, of course, but she would not think about that.

When the carriage decanted them at the front door, she entered as hastily as was consistent with decorum and would have made straight for the stairs, but Fin said, "Will you take a brandy with me?"

Oh, this was dangerous! To be alone with him at night would not be good for her state of mind at the best of times, but after such an evening, when she was so unnerved by all that had been said... Those peculiar conversations with Miss Edith Buckley and Mr Giles Warborough. The unwanted attentions of Mr Godfrey Buckley. The very odd Lady Lucia. And the marquess — he was believed to be mad, yet she could see little sign of it. Eccentric, perhaps, in keeping the burnt-out family wing just as it was, and letting the estate fall into ruin, but he was rational enough in conversation. She felt as if she had swum out of her depth amongst such people, the water threatening at any moment to close over her head and throw her into panic. With such emotions roiling in her breast, there was a real danger that she might throw herself into Fin's arms, and that was unlikely to end well.

While she dithered, Fin went on, "I have a new painting upon which I should like your opinion."

A painting. A discussion of art. That would be manageable.

She followed him through the echoing rooms to the south saloon, and then to his private sitting room, where he poured a generous measure of brandy for each of them. Then next door to the studio.

"I have told Giles to deal with all those letters you have sorted out," he said, as he went around lighting one candelabrum after another, with utter disregard for the price of candles. "He will be here tomorrow. My lawyer will be here next week, so he can deal with any legal business, and Hamlett will take care of anything to do with the estate. You will not need to spend any more time over the matter, so you can get back to your painting. You have not been near your easel for days."

"I have a work in mind," she said.

"Good. When you start on it, you will be able to proceed quickly. Now, here is my latest effort. What do you think?"

There was no time to explain that her painting of the ballroom was already underway, for he whisked away a cover to reveal his painting. It was a pair to the one he had been engaged on when she had first seen him at work, a view of the temple surrounded by trees, with light behind it — sunset, presumably.

"Where is the other one?" she said. "I should like to compare the two side by side."

He obligingly set it up on another easel, and Felicia prowled back and forth between them.

"Well?"

"There was so much anger in this first one," she said. "Such a violent storm. This new one is much calmer. You were happier when you painted it, I think."

"Anger? Happiness? What does that have to say to anything? What of the composition? What of the brush strokes, the colours, the trees, the perspective, the light? Do you not see the improvement in the second one? Is there not a much stronger contrast between the light of the temple and the darkness beneath the trees?" His voice was a growl, like a dog.

She laughed. "Oh, do you want me to praise you? I shall not. You know your own ability well enough without any flattery from me. But tell me, why have you surrounded the temple with trees? You have done so in both paintings, yet there are none in reality."

His anger deflated at once. "There used to be. When I was a boy, the temple was a mysterious and secret place, hidden away in its trees, quite invisible. No one ever went there, except for me. Whenever I could escape from Miss Claypole, which was not often enough, that was where I ran to. I kept my drawing things there, and I could spend hours hidden away in perfect happiness, surviving on a couple of apples from the orchard. But then I was sent away to school, and when I came home after the first term, the trees had gone, and the temple was there for all the world to see, visible from miles around. I have never been back since."

"Why were the trees cut down?"

"I have no idea, and my father was not a man of whom one asked questions. *'Because I say so'* was his habitual response."

"The steward might know, and if you do not like the temple to be so exposed, why then, replant the trees. Hide it away again."

He gave a grunt that might have been laughter. "I suppose I could. Do you truly see anger in this one? Perhaps I was angry at the time. My quiet life had been disrupted by your arrival, and I was very cross about it. Maybe that shows in the painting." He gazed at it thoughtfully. "Not cross, exactly... agitated... upset. The girls revived all sorts of memories — good *and* bad — and I did not like being assaulted by such distressing remembrances. But now..." He turned to the more recent painting. "I have come to terms with it. It pleases me to have something of Juliana's here, some legacy of her to cherish. Although, it is an odd thing that I no longer see any resemblance in the children. At first, I could see it, sometimes, a little glimpse of her, but now... now it is gone. It is as though she is slipping away from me."

Felicia tactfully remained silent, but she wondered greatly at a man who was still so attached to a woman who had never cared for him, had left him thirteen years ago and had been dead for four. Although, to be fair, he had not known that. She had simply vanished from his life, never to be seen again, and she could understand the frustration in that. It was the not knowing that clawed at one's insides, like a canker.

"Perhaps I should paint a whole sequence," he went on. "One for each season, perhaps. Winter would be interesting, with the bare trees. Yes, that would work... the black boughs of the trees silhouetted like lace against the pale, rain-washed sky, the temple starkly exposed. And in autumn, the rain lashing down, and the colours... oh, the colours! Reds, oranges, golds, yellows, browns and still some hints of green... so many colours... I shall need more powder, I believe. Oil... I have plenty of oil... "

He mused on in this vein, but Felicia hardly heard him. Her thoughts drifted to the events at Shotterbourne that evening. Not the upsetting memories for the marquess — not really her fault that Lady Lucia had misheard her words — but to Edith Buckley and Giles Warborough and their odd interest in Boscobel Cottage and Miss Armiger. She supposed they were just being polite, but such questions raised memories she would rather forget.

She remembered something Edith Buckley had said at their first meeting, about being a heroine in her own life. For all her platitudes, Felicia could never see herself as any sort of heroine. *'There may yet be a time when you step forward to take your place at the front of the stage'*, she had said. Felicia should not even be on the stage, let alone at the front of it! She was nobody, yet here she was mingling with all these great people as if she were one of them, and Mr Buckley paying her attention as if— As if what? What was driving him? Was he—?

"You are not even listening to me!" Fin said.

It was too much. "It is two in the morning and I am exhausted," she snapped. "I would rather like to go to bed."

"Well, why the devil… why on earth did you not say so?"

"Because I am a paid employee, my lord, and must do as you bid me."

He looked dumbstruck, as if this thought had never occurred to him. "Then I bid you go to bed, Miss Oakes. Footman! *Footman!* Ah, Neil, light Miss Oakes to her room. Good night, Miss Oakes."

Silently she curtsied, then followed the footman's candelabrum through dark rooms, up the stairs and along a corridor. He carefully lit the candle sitting on a table outside her room, bowed and made his way steadily back down the corridor, the flickering light of the candles making the shadows dance. She entered her room, shut the door, leaned against it in relief. The day was over at last, and she could sleep. Undressing with all speed, she scrambled into bed, blew out the candle and curled up into a ball.

Perversely, sleep eluded her, despite her tiredness. Her mind was wide awake, filling her head with dreams… but no longer were her fantasies of her father as a pirate or a prince or a spy. Now she saw only herself skipping through the enchanting rooms of the Hall as its mistress, a countess, a loving and happy wife. And there was Fin, smiling at her, holding her, telling her how much he loved her, that she had driven Juliana from his mind, that he had never known true love until now, Fin touching her, kissing her...

She buried her head in the pillow and wept until the thin shards of dawn crept through the shutters, and exhaustion caught up with her.

~~~~~

Fin swirled his brandy in the glass. Long after Felicia had left him, he sat on, stretched out on the window seat — her window seat, as he had come to think of it, for she so often sat here. But not lately, and that was puzzling. Why had she not been in the studio for several days?

Then there was this odd friendship of hers with Lord Arnwell. He was a man of impeccable lineage, educated, cultured, powerful. She was a half-educated governess and the natural daughter of somebody or other. He owned half a county, and pieces of half a dozen more. She owned a small cottage where she planned to grow potatoes. He was old, scarred and bitter. She was young, vibrant, pretty... Well, maybe that part of the attraction was not so surprising after all. An old man reminded of his youth by a pretty face.

Perhaps Godfrey Buckley's interest in her was equally explicable — a young man used to the ways of the *ton*, intrigued by a woman who had no time for such niceties. There was something so refreshingly different about her. She had no idea how to behave in public, and her pertness bordered on incivility, yet Fin liked her straightforwardness. She said exactly what she thought! Despite her protest that she was merely a paid employee, she was like no servant he had ever known. But then, she lived without fear of dismissal. If he were to turn her off, she would go
~~~~~

serenely back to Hampshire and grow potatoes. The very thought made him smile. She was not made to grub in the dirt like a peasant!

Buckley may even have marriage in mind. He had proposed a toast to their host — unexceptional although significant on account of the differences between them. He had used the opportunity to make a very elegant little speech expressing his delight at the invitation, his hope for further progress towards reconciliation and his intention to do everything in his power to promote it, and to ensure that Lord Arnwell never regretted his generosity. Arnwell had responded with a non-committal grunt, but Fin had thought he was pleased by the words and the obvious sincerity behind them. Buckley had said he would be contemplating marriage in the not-too-distant future, and hoped Arnwell would advise him. That had led to some lively discussion as to the attributes required of a bride! Eventually Arnwell had said, "Make sure to marry where your heart lies. That is the only way to ensure a happy family life."

That was remarkably sensible advice from a man who was reputed to be quite insane. He was eccentric, of course, in keeping the burnt-out family wing untouched and letting the estate fall into ruin, but there had been nothing of insanity in his behaviour that evening. His dress, his conversation, the meal he provided were all unexceptional. It was an odd household, with the childlike sister and the drab Buckley woman, and that was perhaps more peculiar than anything, for Arnwell's hatred of the Buckleys was legendary, yet there Edith Buckley sat at the heart of his family.

But if Arnwell was an impenetrable mystery, Felicia was not. He smiled as he thought of the way she had self-effacingly held back from the others as they moved from room to room, always trying to be the last. Yet even in the simple muslin gown that Drusilla no doubt considered suitable attire for a governess, she lit up the room as none of the other ladies could. Lady Lucia had a certain aged charm, but Edith Buckley looked the nonentity she was and Drusilla — he sighed. He was fond of his sister, and she was his closest kin, but she always looked as if she disapproved of everything and everyone she saw. She was never pleased, whereas Felicia was always pleased. She enjoyed her food, she enjoyed the company most of the time, and she had even looked as if she were enjoying whist with Giles and the two Buckleys, inconceivable as that seemed. Felicia! Never was anyone more aptly named, for she was always happy.

With such pleasant thoughts, Fin sat on in the window seat, drinking brandy and considering Felicia's many charms until the first light of dawn drove him to his bed.

~~~~~

He woke to the same thoughts. Felicia! He would ask her directly what she thought of Giles and his impertinent questions. He jumped out of bed, scrambled into his clothes and hastened to the studio. She was not there, nor was her easel. Now that he considered the matter, the easel had disappeared some days ago. She was painting somewhere, some view that had caught her eye, perhaps from a window or out in the grounds somewhere. The temple? It could be. It had always fascinated her. Well, he would not tease her about it. If she wanted to paint in secret, so be it, and she would show him the results when she was ready.

He rang for a breakfast tray to be brought to him.

"Certainly, my lord."
~~~~~

"Oh, and Mr Warborough will be here later to deal with the correspondence, so make sure the billiard room is warm enough, and refreshments laid out."

"The billiard room is already adequately warm, my lord. Miss Oakes is at work there, so I took the liberty of lighting the fire, given the present spell of cool weather."

"She is, is she? Bring my tray to me there, and a tray for Miss Oakes, too."

She was sitting at the covered billiard table, heaps of unopened letters in front of her.

"I thought you had finished all this paper-shuffling," he said.

"Almost," she said, looking up with her mischievous smile. "There are always more letters, you know. The box may be empty, but more come in every day. Who is Lady Darwin? She writes to you a great deal."

"Some distant relation, I believe. I cannot imagine why she bothers to write to me."

"Can you not? If I tell you that she has a daughter called Alicia who is... now where is it? Ah, here we are. *'Most agreeably accomplished now. Her tapestry work is exquisite and her Italian airs are so much admired, nothing could be like it. Such a pretty, good-humoured girl, everybody says so. We shall be visiting friends in Derby next month and would so like to see dear Hawkewood again and know how you are going on.'* Could you hazard a guess as to why she writes so much? Are you not tempted by the exquisite tapestry work?"

He laughed, but before he could reply the breakfast trays arrived and then Giles, and the talk was all of letters and business.

"The London lawyers in this pile," Felicia said, "the Derby attorney here and the Nottingham one here. This is estate business, as best I can tell. These are all invitations whose dates have passed. This is family news, but I have compiled a list of births, deaths and unfortunate mishaps to save his lordship the bother of actually reading any letters. There are three proposals of marriage—"

"What!" Fin cried. "Surely not?"

"Couched in more decorous terms, naturally. A felicitous alliance… matter of mutual interest to our families… that sort of thing. Oh, and this one I cannot make out at all, so I hope you have more luck with it, Mr Warborough. Is it in code or just badly written?"

Giles seemed oddly flustered. "Oh… well now… hardly likely… just written very ill, I daresay…" He picked it up and scanned it briefly before cramming it into a waistcoat pocket. "I daresay it is just a mistake… nothing meaningful. I will do what I can with it. So these are to do with the estate? I shall see that Wistman gets them. Well, you have been most industrious, Miss Oakes. Most industrious indeed, has she not, Fin? However, I do not think it necessary for us to trouble you with this task again. I can manage perfectly well myself."

She curtsied deeply. "I beg your pardon for my interference, but I was asked to undertake the work by Lord Finlassan and must do as I am bid," she said demurely, but her eyes were twinkling.

"Oh, indeed!" Giles cried. "No censure implied. Not interference, but… you have more important duties… would not for the world take you away from your responsibilities to the little girls."

"She is teasing you, Giles," Fin said, amused.

"Oh. Oh, I see." But he was puzzled, Fin could see. He was as bad as Drusilla for preferring his world to be well-ordered, with everyone in their right place, and a teasing governess was too far out of kilter for him to understand. "But never mind, Miss Oakes," he went on brightly. "I daresay you will be returning to the delights of Hampshire soon, and will be far, far away from these troublesome letters."

"That is for Miss Oakes to decide," Fin said curtly.

"Of course, of course. Merely thought… assumed… no intention of… Really, Fin, you are very snappish today."

"He is always snappish," Felicia said. "Shall I leave you to be snapped at without my interference, Mr Warborough? After all, I have more important duties to attend to."

And with a neat curtsy she departed, taking her breakfast tray with her, leaving Giles spluttering in outrage and Fin laughing at her impertinence.

# 16: A Day In Derby

A day was settled upon for the outing to Derby, and although the party had grown to encompass Fin, Drusilla and Giles as well as Felicia and Miss Claypole, Fin thought that all concerned would regard it as an improvement. Felicia would surely be happy to have some additional chaperonage to protect her from the smooth-talking Buckley, and his attentions towards her would look less particular in a larger grouping. Naturally, with Drusilla involved, there was some dispute as to the best equipage for their transportation, and whether the Bell or the King's Head was the superior inn, but Buckley gave way gracefully on all points, which was always the best way with Drusilla.

On the day there was steady rain, so the barouche was abandoned for a closed carriage to convey the three ladies and Giles. Rather than ride, however, Buckley insisted on taking his curricle.

"The rain is not so great, and we shall be more comfortable than on horseback," he said cheerfully.

Fin doubted it, but was not prepared to argue the point, although he hardly relished an hour of such close company with

Buckley. In the event, however, he found him an amusing companion and reassuringly competent with the reins, so the time passed pleasantly enough despite the dampness. While the ladies explored the shops with Giles in attendance, Fin and Buckley dried off in a private parlour and refreshed themselves with a glass or two of Madeira.

"That was not so bad, now was it?" Buckley said cheerily, standing with his back to the fire to dry his buckskins.

"Apart from being soaked to the skin, not bad at all."

Buckley only laughed. "I daresay you can squeeze in with the ladies for the journey home, but for myself I would sooner be in the fresh air, even when it is rather fresher — and wetter — than I might prefer. This is a very cosy room, is it not? I have not been here before, having always used the Bell, but it is very well appointed, and the Madeira is not at all bad. All in all, I believe this was an excellent idea of mine."

"Excellent indeed if you had wished to accompany the ladies to the shops, yet here you sit."

"They will get on better without me," he said, not at all discomfited.

"Yet I do not quite see what you achieve by your excellent idea. If your object is Miss Oakes—"

"I have no object, apart from providing the ladies with a little pleasure," Buckley said quickly. "The life of a governess is an uncomfortable one in general, and although both Miss Oakes and Miss Claypole are treated kindly, still they are in an awkward position, neither servant nor family. It must be a lonely life, and who would not wish to bring a little gaiety into it?"

Fin said nothing. The sentiments were admirable, and he saw nothing of insincerity in Buckley, yet he could not shake the unsettling feeling that there was more to his interest in Felicia than benevolence towards a governess.

Buckley swirled the wine in his glass, and went on, "I will not conceal from you that I should like to get to know Miss Oakes a little better, but her wellbeing is always uppermost in my mind." Then, with sudden fierceness, he added, "She has nothing to fear from me, nothing at all."

"I am happy to hear it," Fin said, rather startled. To move his thoughts into happier channels, he said, "Is she really so like Lady Olivia?"

Buckley's face lit up. "Oh yes! Indeed there is a marked resemblance, very marked. It is not so obvious now that I know Miss Oakes, for she has not Olivia's fine figure or the delicacy of her complexion, and no one can match Olivia for beauty — she is quite incomparable — but about the face, in the eyes and the smile, they might easily be taken for sisters. It is an extraordinary coincidence."

"Coincidence? Is it? Miss Oakes has not the smallest idea who her parents might be, so is it not possible that there is a family connection? That she may have Dulnain blood? Or Lister, perhaps?"

"Lister!" He seemed startled at the idea.

"Surely you must have wondered?" Fin said. "The Dulnains are too strait-laced to produce a bastard, but the Listers—"

"Sir Royston, perhaps? So that she would be a cousin to Olivia... it might indeed be so. Yes, Finlassan, I do believe you have hit upon the very solution to the mystery." He chuckled. "Sir Royston Lister! It must be so, I am quite sure of it. But perhaps we should not mention it to the lady. It would never do for word to get about. Lister is not the man to take kindly to such talk."

Fin grunted noncommittally, since he had already mentioned it to the lady. It had not occurred to him that Felicia would take it further, or that Lister might cut up rough at finding one of his by-blows turning up in his life. He must speak to her about that.

The waiter came in just then to take their orders for refreshments, and Buckley left with him to talk to the cook, and to ensure the horses had taken no harm from their wetting. Fin was left alone to wonder just why Buckley had never considered the possibility that Lister had fathered Felicia. It seemed such an obvious answer, yet it had never occurred to him. It was very odd.

~~~~~

Felicia had had a wonderful morning. Derby was not much bigger than Southampton, but the shops were new and different, and she had received her first salary at Midsummer, so her purse was full. Fifty pounds! The coins weighed down her reticule. At Miss Latimer's she had never been permitted more than ten pounds a year for her own use, and at Summer Cottage most of her salary had been put straight into the bank on Mr Pierce's advice. Here she was beyond the reach of Mr Pierce or the bank, and Fin's attorney had come out from Derby with a bag full of money to pay all the servants, and had put fifty pounds into her hand, and now she was determined to spend some of it.

Within an hour, she had acquired a mountain of packages and lightened her purse considerably. When the little group returned to the King's Head, and Mr Buckley had asked if she had
~~~~~

enjoyed herself, she had only to point to the array of purchases in Mr Warborough's arms. Yes, she had enjoyed herself enormously, even if her companions had not. Miss Claypole had bought one bottle of Atkinson's curling fluid and a square of ambrosial soap. Lady Drusilla had bought nothing, and wore a disapproving frown.

After a very substantial meal, with both hot and cold dishes, Miss Claypole settled down for a nap, a glass of Madeira at her side, while the rest of the party looked around the Church of All Saints. Felicia found herself beside Mr Warborough as she gazed about the interior of the building.

"Do you like it?" he said.

"It is very beautiful," she said. "Elegant and modern. This feels more like a house than a place of worship. A church should not be modern, one feels. There should be ancient timbers and medieval stonework and a crypt with rats."

"Ah! A traditionalist," he said, with an avuncular smile. "I like a modern church, myself. Less risk of breaking one's neck on uneven flagstones, being flattened by a dislodged gargoyle or wading to the pulpit every time it rains."

That made her laugh. "I take your point. I think the others are leaving. Shall we hurry and catch up with them?"

"One moment, if you please, Miss Oakes."

She had already taken some steps in pursuit of the rest of the party, now approaching the door while they still lingered near the beautiful wrought-iron screen, but she turned back to him with a smile.

"Miss Oakes," he began, his lips twisting as if unsure of his next words. "As your rector, I hope I am not presuming too far, but

I am a trifle concerned by Mr Godfrey's rather marked attentions towards you. Has he given you any indication as to the purpose of his interest? Some reason for it?"

"Must there be a reason other than gentlemanly civility towards a humble governess?"

"In many men, that would be so, but in a Buckley… one never knows. Drusilla likes him but her judgement is suspect where personable young men are concerned. A little flattery goes a long way with her. Has Buckley… at least, it is not for me to enquire into such a personal matter, but I do hope he has not made you any *improper* proposals?"

"He has not made me any proposals, improper or otherwise," she said easily. "Nor do I expect him to do so."

"Ah." Oddly, she had the feeling that he was relieved by her words.

She went on, "He knows I am not in the sort of financial position that would make any improper offer acceptable to me, and obviously he is not going to make me a marchioness."

"Of course. The inheritance from your governess," he said musingly.

"I suppose she was my governess, in a way," Felicia said. "She was certainly strict about lessons, and very knowledgeable. She could have been a governess, if she had not been burdened with caring for me."

"And you will have a good income? Enough to live upon?"

Had anyone else asked her such a question, she would have turned it aside with a noncommittal answer, but there was something so reassuring about a clergyman, and Mr Warborough epitomised the type — genial, trustworthy and more worldly than some. So she saw no reason not to be open with him. "Five or six hundred pounds a year, according to my trustees."

"So… fourteen or fifteen thousand," he said musingly. "And it will have grown somewhat over the years, no doubt. Some lucky investments, perhaps."

That was too intrusive, even for a clergyman. "I have no idea."

But he chuckled. "A very handsome inheritance, Miss Oakes. I congratulate you, and you will be settled in your little cottage very soon, I make no doubt, and far away from Buckley."

"You do not like him," she said.

"I do not *trust* him," he said. "I speak plainly to you, Miss Oakes, for you are a sensible woman and I would have you be on your guard against him. He is a charming and plausible young man, but do not be taken in by him."

"You need not be concerned about me, Mr Warborough. I am very much on my guard against Mr Buckley and his aunt, and their strange questions."

"Strange questions?" he said, his eyes widening.

"They wanted to know my birthday, can you imagine? I hope they will give me a present next March the thirteenth. Ah, here is Mr Buckley now, come looking for us. We are on our way, sir. Merely detained by the beauties around us."

"I feared you had become lost," Mr Buckley said with his pleasant smile. "Miss Oakes, may I offer you my arm? Mr Warborough, are you quite well?"

"Oh indeed, quite well. Perfectly well."

"You look a little pale," Mr Buckley said.

"No, indeed, I am in the best of health. Let us re-join the others as soon as we may."

They made their way slowly back towards the King's Head, Lady Drusilla haranguing Fin about some imagined offence, while Mr Warborough followed them in his habitual pose, head down, hands behind his back, one hand flapping against the other as if in perpetual agitation. At the back of the group, Mr Buckley walked slowly, commenting jokingly on whatever came within view, to entertain her. But when they had dropped a little behind the others, his voice became more serious.

"Now that the sun is shining," he began, "I wonder whether you would enjoy driving back to Church Compton in the open air. I am sure Lord Finlassan would be glad to surrender his seat to you, and since my groom sits behind, it will be quite proper, I believe. What do you say to the idea?"

While she was reluctant to give him any encouragement in his attentions, the prospect of the curricle and a pleasant view of the surrounding countryside was very tempting. The alternative, the carriage with Mr Warborough and Lady Drusilla gently bickering the whole way, was unappealing.

"What a kind thought! I should like that very much. Thank you!"

"I will arrange it with Finlassan," he said.

Although she doubted the possibility of changing the seating plans without first consulting Lady Drusilla or attracting a great deal of opprobrium upon their heads, somehow he managed it.

When Miss Claypole had been woken from her nap, the carriages had been brought round and all their parcels safely stowed, Felicia found herself being handed into the curricle without a word of protest from her ladyship. It was Mr Warborough who began, "I do not think—" and Fin who hushed him. Then the curricle turned out of the yard and into the main street.

They rattled at a startling pace through the town, Mr Buckley silent with concentration as he threaded his horses between the thronging traffic, and Felicia silent with fear, expecting at any moment to be entangled with another vehicle. But there was no entanglement and they escaped Derby unscathed and set off on the Ashbourne road. Now her fear was quite gone, for all around her were fields and hedges and trees in their summer magnificence, and Felicia laughed with delight to find herself perched so high and with no obstruction to her view in any direction. Apart from the inconvenience of needing to hold tight to her bonnet, she had no fault to find with the curricle.

"You are enjoying yourself, I may presume," Mr Buckley said, throwing her a wide smile.

That reminded her that she was attempting to discourage his advances, yet what could she do? It was so much fun! "Oh, yes! I do believe— Oh! Look there! Is that not a beautiful sight? Oh, such colours! If only I had my paints!"

Two fields away was one that had been ploughed and then left, although whether unneeded for a crop or neglected was impossible to say. It was filled with the pale palette of wild flowers — the delicate blues sand pinks of cornflowers and corn cockles, splashed with the yellow of marigolds and the vibrant red of poppies, all mingled with white yarrow and oxeye daisies.

"It is very lovely," he said. "Ah, look, here is the farm track." With a deft tweak on the reins, his horses turned off the main road and began bumping along the rutted track. "If we can  get close enough, I shall pick some for you to take home to paint."

"How kind you are!"

They drew to a halt beside the field, where only a neat fence separated them from the flowers. Felicia had never seen anything like it, for in Hampshire such flowers had grown only around the fringes of the fields, and were weeded from the crops. The groom held the horses while Mr Buckley lifted Felicia down from the curricle. She was too excited to be made nervous by his hands at her waist.

"There is a stile just a little further along." And within moments he had helped her over, and she was amongst the flowers, touching them, watching the way the gentle breeze rippled across the field in pastel waves.

"Here you are." Mr Buckley pushed a bundle of flowers into her arms. "Ah, how well you look, so adorned, Miss Oakes. You are just like a bride."

He smiled at her so warmly that her heart sank. She saw her mistake then, in willingly accepting his company for the drive home and allowing him to turn aside off the road. Now she was quite alone with him with only his servant nearby, so she supposed she must suffer the consequences. This would be the true test of his intentions. She thanked him as civilly as she could, but with a sick feeling in her stomach.

At first, Mr Buckley said nothing unsettling, merely asking Felicia to identify this flower or that, picking armfuls of blooms and wondering how easy it would be for an artist to capture the delicate beauty of the field. Then he spent some time contriving to tie them into bundles with grass stems and, when that did not serve, with his handkerchief. When that was done he started on some rambling tale of a garden in Hertfordshire belonging to an old friend of his, and Felicia began to suspect he was nervous. Yet why? He habitually conducted himself with such aplomb, no matter the circumstances, that his unaccustomed agitation made her nervous too.

"Mr Buckley," she said tentatively, "I believe we have enough flowers now. Shall we continue our journey? If we are missing when the others arrive—"

"Of course, of course," he said quickly. "But then… Miss Oakes, I—" He stopped, his breathing rapid and his expression uncertain.

If she had been at all attached to him, or perhaps if she had any ambitions to be a marchioness in the fullness of time, she would have waited and given him the time to order his thoughts and make whatever proposal was in his mind. But she had no wish to listen to any proposal of his, mistress and wife being equally unacceptable to her. So she said, "We should not dally, Mr Buckley. My two charges will be wondering what has become of me."

He let out a heavy breath. "You are quite right, as always, Miss Oakes. Pleasant as this spot is, I have detained you here too long. Let me assist you over the stile." He climbed nimbly over first, laid down the bundles of flowers, then set his hands at her waist and swung her to the ground. In a low voice, he said, "You are delightfully distracting company, Miss Oakes, and it is so very tempting to linger here, but I must not keep you from your responsibilities. It would not be right." Then, more firmly, "Indeed, it would be quite wrong."

Only then did he release her. Within moments she was aloft in the curricle, the flowers handed into the inscrutable charge of the groom. Mr Buckley deftly turned the vehicle and they set off to re-join the road. For some minutes he was silent, but then he laughed suddenly. "What a charming day we have all had, would you not agree, Miss Oakes? Was it not a perfectly agreeable day, in every respect?"

"Indeed it was, sir. I have not the least fault to find with any aspect of it."

He laughed again, and regaled her with amusing tales of his fashionable London friends all the way back to Hawkewood Hall.

# 17: Flowers And Friendship (July)

JULY

Felicia hoped that she had now done enough to deter Mr Buckley from any further pursuit of her, and this seemed to be the case. For the two following days, she walked Hercules at her usual time yet saw no sign of Mr Buckley, and then came the news, conveyed by no less a messenger than Lady Drusilla herself, that he had returned to his own estate in Lincolnshire.

"I was very much afraid that you would succumb to his charming ways," she said to Felicia with a disparaging sniff, "but it seems that you have better sense."

"Or he has," Felicia said mischievously.

"Oh, I make no doubt he would have caught you in his snare if he could. I hoped that your little jaunt with him the other day would have done the trick, and he would have taken you away with him, but here you still are." Her brows lowered in suspicion. "I hope you are not harbouring ambitions towards my brother, Miss Oakes."

"Certainly not," she said, for it was perfectly true. Yet she could not help blushing hotly, and was unable to meet Lady Drusilla's gaze.

"Do not imagine he has the slightest interest in you," Lady Drusilla said acidly.

There was no point pretending, so Felicia lifted her eyes and said, "He sees me only as a fellow artist, so you need have no concerns on that score, but he increasingly depends upon my advice, and that makes it difficult for me to leave Hawkewood, as I must and would prefer to do. It would be a great deal easier if you were to engage a proper governess for Juliana and Margarita."

"Hmpf. A good point. I have not found any single person who fulfils my requirements in every particular, but there are two who, combined, might do. And then you will leave?"

"I will. It should not be hard to manufacture a crisis in Southampton that requires my immediate return there."

"Then we are agreed," Lady Drusilla said.

Felicia knew perfectly well that leaving Hawkewood Hall was absolutely the correct thing to do. For her own peace of mind, she must go and never return. Yet it was so hard to face the prospect of never seeing Fin again. She would miss Juliana and Margarita, too, who had been her life for four years now, but it was not the same. The ache in her heart whenever she considered leaving, or thought of the empty life that faced her in Hampshire, was all for a man who barely noticed her, except when he wished to talk about art.

Yet however little she relished the prospect, her days at Hawkewood Hall were now limited, and this threw her into something akin to panic. Her painting of the ballroom must be finished! It was the largest work she had ever attempted, and there was so much detail still to be added. She woke early each morning, entirely unable to stay abed when there was so much energy inside her, just waiting to be poured onto the paper. For two or three hours she worked, motionless in front of her easel in the ballroom, only her hands moving, reaching for this stick or that, stroking, blending, layering or delicately dabbing at the paper. Then she wiped her hands and began another colour. And gradually the scene was coming to life in front of her, the musicians playing, the dancers dancing, the onlookers watching and whispering together. Only when Bagnall brought her breakfast tray did she stop, stretch her aching arms and step away from the easel. The rest of each day was merely waiting until she could begin again.

Every afternoon, when the weather permitted, Juliana and Margarita went riding. This was now their favourite activity, and mounted on their own ponies and with two grooms in attendance, they cantered all over the estate, through the adjoining woods, along meandering streams and onto patches of rugged moorland. After the stifling confinement of Itchen and Southampton, they now had half a county to explore, and their rides grew longer and longer. Their enthusiasm reassured Felicia that they would not miss her nearly so much as she would miss them.

This left Felicia free to take the dog out for long walks which inevitably ended at the little pavilion in Shotterbourne. The Sanctuary, the marquess had called it, and so it was. Even when he was not there, which was quite often these days, for his chest bothered him greatly in the damp weather, he arranged for the cake and Madeira to be left there, with a little note explaining his absence. On such days Felicia sat and ate a great deal and drank a little, and thought about the marquess rattling round in his vast house, sad and lonely and not terribly well.

But when he was there, he seemed just as usual, and not sad at all. He called her *Prinzessin* and insisted that she call him *Conte*, and their conversations ranged widely. He had undertaken a grand tour in his youth, so he told her of his travels and how sad it made him to read in the newspapers of all the great changes in the countries he had visited. He talked of Parliament, too, and how proud he had been to take his seat in the House of Lords and participate in the debates there.

"Mind you, London is a rackety place now. I have no time for the Prince of Wales and all his no-good brothers. They, at least, should do their duty by the country. Not a legal son amongst the lot of them! Irresponsible, that is what it is. If I were there now, I should tell them so."

"Why do you not do that?" Felicia said.

"What, go to London? Never!"

"Does your physician forbid you to travel?"

"Ha! He would forbid me to leave my bed in a morning if he could. No exertion, he tells me, in the cause of preserving my lungs and preventing further deterioration. Too much smoke got into them, that is the truth of the matter. I suppose it is a miracle I have lasted as long as I have, for they never expected me to survive the week. But here I still am, and Lambert is gone, for all he was ten years younger. And now there is just Godfrey, but no danger of *him* going anytime soon. He will outlast me, *Prinzessin*, and there is nothing I can do about that."

Felicia did not want to talk about Godfrey Buckley or the marquess's feud, for they would never agree on that matter. She was all too aware that her time in Derbyshire was drawing to a close, and any day might be her last chance to talk to the marquess. She decided, therefore, to be reckless and raise the matter that had buzzed in her brain for some time now.

"My lord—"

"*Conte, Prinzessin.*"

"*Conte,* may I ask you a question, and I know I should not pry but... it is about me, and I cannot bear not to know."

"You may ask me anything," he said. "Of course, I might choose not to answer."

"I understand. *Conte*, you told me once that you have a natural daughter living somewhere in the south, and *I* am somebody's natural daughter, also from a southern county, and I wondered... I thought perhaps... *I* might be your daughter."

"Oh, child, would that it were so," he said, his tone so gentle that Felicia almost wept. "I should give a great deal to have a daughter like you, but to my sorrow you are not mine. She is much older than you, a mistake of my youth. Her name is Diana, and never was a girl less aptly named. No goddess she! Not like you, *Prinzessin.* When I watch you walking through the meadow towards me, you are so light on your feet that you look as if you are floating, or dancing, perhaps. I should love to see you dance! Diana is nothing like that. She was a great lump of a thing when she was a child, and as an adult she was already stout. I have not seen her for years, but she must be about forty now, and fearfully respectable. Her husband is mayor of somewhere or other. She writes to me to tell me of his progress, and the children. They have a score of children."

"A score!" Felicia said, laughing. "Gracious!"

"Oh, maybe not quite so many, but a lot, in any event." He reached with his good hand, and placed it on Felicia's. "I am so sorry, *Prinzessin.* Have you no notion at all who your father might be?"

"None, nor my mother either."

"Were you left to an orphanage, then? Simply abandoned to your fate?"

"Not at all," she said. "That would perhaps concern me less. A milkmaid who found herself with child by the shepherd — she might indeed leave her unwanted offspring with the nearest nunnery or orphanage, but my history is not so commonplace. I was raised by a lady by the name of Fidelia Armiger. She had money of her own, yet we grubbed in the dirt like peasants, and then she died when I was ten, leaving no word of my antecedents. So I know nothing of my history, *Conte*, except that I must be a bastard, for no legitimate child would be abandoned in that way. I amuse myself by inventing my history. Perhaps my father is a prince, or a pirate, or a spy… he could be anyone, I tell myself, even as I know that in truth he was most likely the younger son of minor gentry, whose father paid Miss Armiger to make the problem disappear. It would never do to have such a blemish on the family's reputation, would it?"

"You are bitter, *Prinzessin.* We are both bitter at the hand life has dealt us. We neither of us have the comfort of a loving family about us. It is no wonder that we feel — or perhaps I should say, that *I* feel — such an affinity for you. Yet she gave you no clue, your faithful esquire?" When she looked puzzled, he laughed. "That is what the name means, *Prinzessin.* Fidelia Armiger… faithful esquire, in Latin. Not her real name, I imagine. She was defending you, perhaps, although from what is impossible to say. She told you nothing of your father, not even when she was dying?"

"There was no opportunity," Felicia said sadly. "She died very suddenly in her bed one night. Her heart gave out, without warning. She went to bed that night just as usual, and the next morning… she did not wake up. I did not realise. I thought she was asleep, you see. Well, at ten, one does not think of death, does one? So I did my chores, made breakfast for the two of us, ate my share. Then I did my lessons in the morning, and worked in the kitchen garden in the afternoon. For three days, I did everything according to the timetable laid down for me, and wondered why Miss Armiger did not wake up. But then it was Sunday, and I walked to church. Five miles, all on my own for the first time in my life. *'Where is Miss Armiger?'* they said to me. *'Is she unwell?' 'She is asleep,'* I said. *'She has been asleep for three days.'* So they went to look, and discovered her there and explained to me that she was dead. I never cried for her, not a single tear. There was a will and money and a trust fund for me, and the vicar found me a place at a school in Southampton. But no letter left with the will. No *'Dear Felicia, Here is what you need to know about your parentage.'* Nothing like that. My trustees would not allow me to examine Miss Armiger's personal effects until I was of age, but when I was finally allowed to look, there was no clue. I am nameless, *Conte.* I have no history, no family, no one who cares for me. I am alone."

"Not so," he said softly. "Not alone. Never alone, *Prinzessin*. And nor am I, any longer."

He put his arm about her, and drew her towards him, and she wept on his shoulder and wished with all her heart that he was truly her father, but if that could not be, that she could stay there as his friend for ever. But it was impossible. For all his fine words, she had no place in the life of a marquess. In a very few days, she would have to leave Derbyshire and then she would never see him again. Then she would be, as she had been for her whole life, truly alone.

~~~~~

Fin was full of energy. He could not account for it, but for some reason the lethargy which had afflicted him for years was quite gone. It had first struck him after the outing to Derby. He had not tried to prevent it, or to intervene when Buckley had taken Felicia up in his curricle, for why should she not have her chance of happiness? If Buckley showed himself willing to overlook her murky heritage and treat her honourably, then why should she not marry him, if it pleased her? If there had been the least hint of dishonourable intentions, why then he would have sent the scoundrel packing, but marriage was another matter. She had shown no sign of partiality, but she had never discouraged the fellow, either, so perhaps she would have been tempted.

But off they had gone together, and nothing had come of it. They had taken a detour somewhere, so perhaps they had stopped and had some talk, but when they turned up at Hawkewood just behind the carriage, there had been no awkwardness between them. They had seemed quite at ease, in a friendly sort of way, and then Buckley had gone away and Drusilla had no expectation of his
~~~~~

early return. He was gone, and Felicia seemed unaffected by his departure, and Fin could only be glad of it.

He had begun a new painting of the view from the library, in the style of the Dutch painters, so that most of the scene was indoors but with a view of the outside seen through the garden door. He was rather pleased with the way it was progressing, but he would not show it to Felicia until it was nearing completion. She would approve it, he was sure.

After dining at Shotterbourne, he had felt obliged to call upon the marquess to thank him for his hospitality. His lordship was out walking, he had been told, but he had left his card with a scribbled note on the back, and then, in a fit of virtuous neighbourliness, left cards with three more local acquaintances. Not the ones with marriageable daughters, for he had no wish to be swamped with hopeful young ladies, but those with only sons, or no children at all.

By the time he returned his horse to the stables, he was buoyed by his own conscientiousness, and summoned Wistman, his steward, to discuss replanting the trees around the temple on the hill. He was surprised to discover that the trees had been cut down to please his mother. The temple being a favourite spot with her, when she had grown too ill to go there, Fin's father had caused the trees to be removed so that she could see it from her boudoir. Wistman had agreed enthusiastically to replant.

"I'll get men to work clearing the ground in preparation, so that we may undertake the planting work in the autumn. I wonder, my lord… would you care to ride over to the old mill one day? It wouldn't take a great deal of work to repair the water wheel and we could do our own grinding again, like we used to in your grandfather's day. And I have some improvements in mind over at Fulton…"

"Very well, very well, tomorrow, perhaps. Anything else you wish me to do, Wistman, while you are dragging me away from the house?"

"Only the barn at the upper dale, my lord, and then there are the cottages at—" Fin pulled a face. "Well, well, maybe those can wait a while. I wonder if you plan to do much shooting this year, my lord? If not, Sir Geoffrey Barnet would be happy to have the use of some of your lesser coverts. He likes to have his house full of sporting gentlemen all through the autumn, what with his brothers and nephews and his own sons, and now that his two eldest are married, he has their brothers-in-law as well."

"What, Roger and David are married already? They are younger than I am."

"Indeed, my lord, but Mr Roger Barnet turned thirty last year. He has been married for four or five years, I believe, and has a son of his own already."

"The dev— I mean, does he, indeed? Good grief. I had no idea. I am sadly out of touch."

This conversation spurred him to find Felicia, and ask her if she recalled any such neighbourly news from her reading of the letters. So much had passed him by! Probably Drusilla would have relayed such information to him, if he had ever listened to a word she said. Felicia never came to the studio these days — where was this painting she was engaged on anyway? — so he bethought him of the billiard room. Perhaps she was still sorting letters for him. She was not there, but she had begun several new piles of letters on the table. Idly he picked up one or two. A distant cousin was betrothed, he discovered. And there was an invitation to dinner from Lady Barnet. Perhaps he would even accept, and then he could discuss the shooting arrangements with Sir Geoffrey.

But where was Felicia? Surely she could not be out walking so early in the day? She usually walked the dog at three o'clock or thereabouts. Helplessly he looked around, as if she might be hiding in a corner of the room. Ah, the door to the card room was ajar and there was a dim light beyond. Perhaps she had gone exploring? She was not in the card room, but the door to the East Conservatory stood open and again there was light beyond.

What the devil? Who had gone in there and opened the shutters? And if someone had ventured this far, perhaps he — or she — had dared to go beyond and—

With a growl of displeasure, he flung open the doors to the East Conservatory. No one there. The door to the ballroom was almost closed, but there was a noise beyond, some distant, low sound. Humming... some *devil* was in the ballroom — *in the ballroom!* — and was *humming!* The nerve! The absolute nerve!

He crossed the room in a few strides and threw open the doors so hard that one of them banged against a table. Something broke, with a tinkling sound. Felicia jumped, turned, smiled.

"What the *devil* do you think you are doing in here?"

Her smile vanished. She gazed at him uncertainly, her box of pastels in her hand. Behind her stood an easel with a large painting, but he had no interest in that.

"No one is allowed in here!" he yelled. "This room is *sacred*, do you hear? Sacred! No one comes here, no one. Get out!"

"I... I did not know." Her face was ashen. "I only wanted to—"

"Get out! *Get out!*" He strode towards her and hurled the box from her hands so that it flew across the room and crashed to the floor, scattering sticks of colour everywhere. "GET OUT!"

With a scream, she jumped back into the easel so that it wobbled dangerously, then with a gasp of dismay, picked up her skirts and fled.

She was gone. The only sound in the room was Fin's rasping breath.

# 18: Forgiveness

Felicia flew up the stairs to her room, locked the door and hurled herself onto the bed in a paroxysm of weeping. How could she have known? No one had ever told her that the ballroom was forbidden. Neglected, yes, and out of use, but not *forbidden*. And Bagnall had brought her trays of food, and said nothing. Perhaps he assumed she had permission to be there. She was painting, so naturally he would think that Fin knew all about it. Dear God, what had she done?

After a while, the flood of tears dwindled and then stopped altogether. Felicia was not one to waste time in useless regret. Whenever she had cried as a girl, after a fall, or the time the fox got into the hen house, Miss Armiger had said briskly, "No use crying over it, child. Tears never mended anything." So she had always wiped away her tears quickly and put on a cheerful face. She had been astonished when she had first gone to Miss Latimer's Academy to find the girls so often in tears, calling out for their mamas, and always one of the others would offer a consoling hug. Sometimes Miss Latimer herself would be the comforter. Felicia had mostly given up crying by that time so she seldom needed comfort from anyone, but she had thought how lovely it would be to have a sister or a mama to console one, and enter into one's feelings when one ached with misery.

Now she rose from her bed, washed her face and straightened her rumpled clothing. Then she went to her closet and examined her clothes, deciding what to pack. Her boxes could be sent on to her, but she would need to take a few things for the journey. Four nights on the road for the journey north, but that had been a very different mode of travel. She could hardly afford a post-chaise and four! It would be the mail coach for her, most likely, down to London and then west to Southampton, a far less comfortable affair. She pulled out her portmanteau from under the bed, and began to pack.

She had not been thus engaged for long when there was a scratching at the door, so faint that she was not sure if she heard anything or not. When she opened the door, the maid who attended to her room stood there.

Bobbing a quick curtsy, she said in a rush, "Beg pardon for disturbing you, madam, but I'm to give you this."

Thrusting a small box into her hand, she dashed away.

Felicia shut the door again, and looked in bewilderment at the box. It was of light wood, with the name of a Derby confectioner stamped onto the lid. When she opened it, a folded paper fell out, revealing rows of tiny fruits. There was an orange, a lemon, a strawberry, something could have been a peach or a pear, it was hard to tell. Several she could not identify at all. But when she picked up the orange and gingerly bit into it, it tasted of almond paste. She laughed in delight. Marzipan fruits! How ingenious.

She reached down for the paper that had fallen out.

*'Forgive me. Fabian.'*

His Christian name. He had shared his name with her. Such a proof of intimacy. Fabian. She ate the lemon and something that might have been a cherry, then returned to her packing.

Half an hour later, another scratching at the door revealed the maid again, bearing a plate of cakes. Treacle, her absolute favourite, still warm from the oven. She ate three, one after the other, eyes closed in bliss, before unfolding the note that accompanied them.

*'I should very much like to talk to you, if not inconvenient. Fabian.'*

She was not sure she was ready for that. She ate another treacle cake, then a marzipan strawberry, and then, absentmindedly, another cake. It would be best to pack and then send a footman to procure tickets for the mail coach. Derby… it would run from Derby, but at what hour? Could she leave tonight? She would need to look it up, and that would mean venturing down to the library, and what if he should be there? Could she face him? She decided she could not. She ate one more treacle cake, then determinedly set the plate and the box of marzipan on a high shelf. She changed into her travelling gown and returned to her packing.

The slightest sound from the door. Not a knocking, more a sort of sliding noise. When she looked there was another paper there, pushed through the gap between door and floorboards.

*'Please come out.'*

Nothing else.

Cautiously, she opened the door and peered out. Fin was sitting on the floor just a short distance down the corridor, legs crossed, arms folded, head sunk almost to his chest, the very image of desolation. He jumped up at once.

"Felicia…"

There was so much grief in his face, that she could not bear it. She had disappointed him! So much he had given her, and she had abused his trust. "I am so sorry… I did not realise—"

He held up his hands, as if to ward off a blow. "No, no! Do not you apologise to *me!* It is for me to apologise… I do, I do apologise, I humbly beg your forgiveness, if you can find it in your heart to pardon my fearful lapse of temper. Felicia, may I—"

"Oh please, say no more!" she cried. "It is not right for you to speak so. You are an earl and I am your employee, so why should you not upbraid me when I transgress?"

"You are too generous," he said in a low voice, bowing his head again. "I would not have you afraid of me, as if I were a tyrant. My rages may seem terrifying, but they exhaust themselves in moments and would never turn against *you*. I would never hurt you, Felicia. Do not fear me!"

That surprised her. "Oh, I do not! I was upset because I had done wrong, and—"

"You did nothing wrong!" he cried, crossing the small space between them and sweeping her hand into his, lifting it as if he intended to kiss it. Perhaps thinking better of so intimate a gesture, he released her again and stepped back a little. "Oh God, what must you think of me? Surely I am so sunk in your estimation that recovery is impossible. Can you ever forgive me for frightening you so? What can I do to make things right?"

"My opinion of you is greatly improved already," she said solemnly.

"It is?" He looked disbelieving. How she longed to smooth away the anxious expression on his face, to kiss away his pain. The desire to reach across the small space that separated them was almost overwhelming. To touch him, stroke his face, wrap her arms around him... He would be shocked indeed if she attempted any such thing! He must not know how she felt... he must *never* suspect it.

She hoped her tone was light enough as she answered. "Indeed it is. Treacle cakes will always make me think well of the giver, and as for the marzipan sweets...!"

His lips twisted a little. "The marzipan was Mrs Shayne's... a birthday present for her sister. I was desperate for something, anything, to give you while the cakes were baking. Did you like them?"

She nodded, finding it hard to answer him. He looked so hopeful, like the puppy when he saw her coming with his lead.

He went on eagerly, "I am sorry that so many of your pastels were broken, and the box is damaged, too, but I shall buy you another. A new box, fresh sticks, whatever you want. May such things be obtained in Derby, or should I send to London? I shall do it today."

With a bubble of laughter, she said, "Shall I write the letter for you?"

He did not laugh in return, but some of the tension left his face. "Such a fool you must think me!" He leaned his back against the wall and folded his arms. "I *am* a fool, I admit it. Felicia... will you come with me to the ballroom. I... I should like to go back there, but not alone. Your company would be the greatest help to me."

She nodded, and they walked side by side along the corridor, down the northern staircase and as far as the main doors to the ballroom. There he stopped, hands on hips, his breathing rapid. She waited, and after a moment, he took a deep breath, exhaled slowly and then opened the door.

Felicia followed him into the room, and stood while he gazed all around — at the uncovered chairs, the side tables with their rows of dusty glasses, and the cobwebs dangling from all the sconces.

"What a sad place," he said softly. "Everything in readiness for the nuptial ball, and the only thing lacking was the bride. No wedding, no ball, no celebration. My father found me howling with grief in here, so he ordered the place shut up, to be left untouched until such time as Juliana returned. For we all agreed that sooner or later she would return. It was a momentary madness on her part, and for a certainty she would think better of it. Nothing was to be moved or put away, because that would be to admit that she was gone for good. I had a special licence ready, and surely she would be back before it expired. But Juliana never came back, so this place stayed just as it was. Not long after that, Mama became ill, and then Papa, and they died one after the other, as if they could not bear to be apart, and still this room was shut up, untouched. I was still waiting, you see. Still hoping. Like a hedgehog, I went into hibernation, waiting for a spring that never came."

"There is always a spring," Felicia said. "No matter how desperate the winter may be, it is always followed by spring and warm sunshine and bluebells in the woods. And spring is followed by high summer and poppies in the fields. Then autumn, and hazelnuts and blackberries."

"And then winter and desolation again."

"*Yes!* Everything changes, nothing stays the same, and there is goodness and beauty in every season. Even in the darkest days of winter, there is the promise of the spring to come in the tiny snowdrop flowering in the snow. To pretend that it is always winter, as you have done for thirteen years, and Lord Arnwell for even longer, is to waste your life in regret. Life is to be lived and enjoyed. Look to the future, not the past, for the future is full of hope."

"Is it? What hope is there for Arnwell, with all his family gone?"

"That is no reason to wallow in bitterness!" she cried. "He could have married again and given himself the comfort of female companionship. He could have gathered his remaining family around him. He could have devoted his life to his duties as a peer and landowner. There is much that he could have done of good for his fellow man that would also have assuaged his grief somewhat. Instead, he dwells in such misery that even the company of a boisterous dog and a woman of no family brings him pleasure. It is such a *waste!* And you are no better, hiding away here, going nowhere, seeing no one. Mankind is designed not for hibernation, but for the society of others. It is time to wake up and be joyful again."

"Joyful? How can I ever be joyful again?"

He meant it, too. He truly could not even conceive of the possibility of happiness. She reached out a hand and touched his sleeve, feeling the heat of his arm beneath the linen. "You are *alive!* How can you not see the joy in the world, when it is all around you? When you wake each morning, are you not excited to know what the day will bring? Yesterday, there was a bluebottle in my room, buzzing back and forth between the windows until I freed him. Have you never noticed how beautiful a bluebottle is? Such colours, such flimsy wings, such great eyes! He was fascinating, and I managed to sketch him before he flew away."

He laughed then, and it was a real laugh, not forced. "You see the good in everything, Felicia."

"I see what is there," she said. "And if it is *not* there in the real world, for it cannot be denied that life is sadly deficient sometimes, then my mind is able to create it. In my head, I have a loving father and mother, I have brothers and sisters and a place in the world. I can be a princess, a beloved daughter, a friend of the heart. I can be anything I want in my mind."

"And in your art," he said, moving down the room to where the painting still stood on its easel, the floor around it sprinkled with dust of many colours where the pastel sticks had broken. "Here you are dancing," he said, pointing at a figure in the painting. "That is you, is it not? And I am here, too, although hopping more elegantly than I ever did in reality, I believe. And this... this is Juliana." His voice softened. "I can see Drusilla, too, and Giles, and this is Lord Arnwell, whose visage is miraculously free of scars. He looks like such a kindly old man, by your hand."

"So he is, beneath the hardened bitterness," she said quietly. "The man who adored his wife and children, the man who was *happy*, is still there, buried deep inside. If he would only turn his face to the sun, he would learn to be happy again. Indeed, I think he is already learning it. As you could, also. If you would only open your eyes to the world again, you would find it a wonderful place."

"And how should I do that, o wise one?"

"You mock me, but you know it is true. You should go to London. Take your seat in Parliament again, find yourself a wife, raise children who will make you smile."

"I do not mock you," he said earnestly. "You *are* wise — wiser than I am, certainly. I... I want to smile again, to be happy, and I will open my eyes to the world, as you put it. Indeed, I have already begun. I have ordered the trees replanted around the temple, and I am minded to accept an invitation to dinner from Sir Geoffrey and Lady Barnet."

"That is excellent progress!" she cried.

"But no wife... not yet. One step at a time. Ah, now you frown. Are you going to tell me that it is my duty to marry, as Drusilla does with such tedious frequency?"

"You need an heir," she said firmly. "A son to secure the succession, so that no one need worry about your Uncle Percival."

He sighed. "It is awkward, certainly, not knowing whether Percival is alive or dead. Giles is convinced he is alive somewhere, and surely Percival alone could have taken that money from the safe, so he must have survived the fire. But that is a problem for the future, for I am young and healthy and unlikely to die soon."

"That is what Miss Armiger thought, I daresay," Felicia said darkly. "She died in her bed one night, unaware of her own impending mortality. You could fall from your horse tomorrow and break your neck."

He sighed. "Very well. I will consider the matter, but do not expect me to rush into anything. You may remind me at monthly intervals."

"I shall not be here to remind you of anything."

He went very still. "Not here? You are leaving?" He looked at her fully, as if for the first time, taking in her travelling gown. *"Today?"*

"If I can obtain a seat on the mail tonight," she said calmly.

"The *mail!* I will not have you travel on the mail. If you must go — must you go?"

"I must," she said softly. "I only stayed to preserve you from Miss Claypole, remember? Lady Drusilla has located two governesses who meet her requirements, and my services are no longer needed."

"But you will not leave today," he said firmly, and this time he took her hand in his and did not relinquish it. "You will not leave until the new governesses are established and the girls are settled in their charge, and when you do, you will certainly not travel on the mail or the common stage. I shall provide a post-chaise and a maid to accompany you, and a footman to ensure you are treated well whenever you change horses or rest overnight."

"You are all goodness," she said, but she could not quite meet his eyes. She had never had any hope of his affection, but if she had nurtured any, his calm acceptance of her departure would have destroyed any vestige of it. She was no more to him than his wards' ill-educated governess, and an artist of little merit. He would have forgotten her within a month.

~~~~~

In two days everything changed. Miss Durward arrived from Nottingham and Miss Farrell from York, who between them encompassed every possible accomplishment to be taught to two young ladies. Then Mr Giles Warborough declared an urge to revisit his old haunts at Southampton, and announced that he would accompany Felicia on her journey.

"What could be more comfortable than to have a man to arrange every detail for you, Miss Oakes?" he said cheerfully. "You will have not the least thing to trouble you, and we shall travel together in the most pleasant and companionable manner."

She could hardly object to it. Fin provided both maid and footman, as he had promised, paid her salary for a full year and gave Mr Warborough a heavy purse to cover their expenses on the journey. So it was that far sooner than she had anticipated, Felicia found herself standing on the steps of Hawkewood Hall at an early hour, watching her boxes and portmanteau being strapped onto the back of the post-chaise. Juliana and Margarita wept and hugged her. Lady Drusilla, who had come to see her off and no doubt ensure that she actually left, wished her well and smiled in modest satisfaction. And Fin... Fin looked grief-stricken.

"Will you write to me?" he said plaintively.
~~~~~

"I cannot do that," she whispered. "It would be most improper."

"When have you ever cared about such things?" he cried, but he did not argue with her, for which she was grateful. Her heart was too full, and a single word or gesture or smile would bring on the tears that were so close to the surface.

"Will you see that Lord Arnwell receives my letter?" she said, although she had already extracted his promise to do so. "And will you visit him occasionally?"

"He will not want to see me."

"As to that, I cannot say, but he will want to see Hercules. Will you take him there? It is only necessary to let him off the lead and he will find his own way to the Sanctuary."

That raised a tentative smile. "You expect me to walk the dog now?"

She tried to return his smile, but it was too difficult. And then he handed her into the chaise, Mr Warborough and the maid climbed in too, and the door was slammed shut.

Her time at Hawkewood Hall was over.

# 19: Old Friends

The journey south was more comfortable than the mail, but that was all that could be said for it. Mr Warborough was a fussy traveller, so he regaled the hours in the chaise with anxious fretting over the horses, the postilions, the carriage, the next inn and his constant fear of impending disaster. The maid, a glum-faced housemaid of forty or so, said nothing and did nothing useful, for Felicia was perfectly used to dressing herself, but she was glad of her silent presence. Together with the footman, a young man of seventeen thrilled to be leaving Derbyshire for the first time, the servants imbued the travellers with an air of respectability, and ensured them efficient service whenever they stopped for horses, refreshments or accommodation.

It was fortunate that Mr Warborough liked nothing better than the sound of his own voice, requiring no response from Felicia. She was poor company, sunk in her own miserable thoughts and her spirits lowering with every mile further from Hawkewood Hall. Or rather, every mile further from Fin. She would never see him again, and no matter how many times she told herself bracingly that it was for the best and she would soon recover from her megrims, she could not rouse herself from her sorrow. During the day, she could just about maintain an air of composure, but at night, when the maid was snoring gently on her pallet, Felicia would pour hot tears into her pillow and wish with all her heart that she were back in Derbyshire, and could see him again.

On the fifth day, the chaise drew into the bustling streets of Southampton and rumbled under the arch at the Dolphin Hotel, where they were to stay. Felicia had written to Agnes on the journey, for there had been no time before leaving Derbyshire, and there was a note awaiting her at the hotel. *'Miss Oakes, How lovely to have you home! If convenient, Jimmy will be in town with the gig for the Tuesday market and will collect you from the Dolphin at 3. Agnes. PS I hope your journey was not too disagreeable.'*

"Tuesday! Four days away!" Mr Warborough exclaimed. "It is as if they do not want you. Shall I arrange transportation for you? It is not far from Southampton, I think. You could be there before dinner."

Felicia was more struck by the discovery that Jimmy Tucker had a gig at his disposal, and it sounded as if the Tuesday market was a regular outing. But she had no wish to descend upon the cottage unannounced.

"Not today!" she said, laughing. "They will want time to arrange everything for me. It is so unsettling to have a visitor arrive unexpectedly. They will have made themselves quite at home, no doubt, and spread into every corner of every room. They will wish to hide the mess, polish the furniture and obtain some decent mutton for the table. I do not wish to set them about the ears, especially in the kitchen. I am very fond of mutton."

He laughed but said, "You are hardly a visitor. It is your own house, after all."

"Tuesday will do very well. I shall have time to call upon my old acquaintances and do a little shopping before I am confined to the country."

And yet the confinement would not be so great with a gig. How pleasant that would be! Miss Armiger had always set her face against any means of conveyance. They went only where they could walk, and carried only what could be fitted into a basket or the small sledge they used to collect wood. Boscobel Cottage would not be so dire a prospect if she could but leave it occasionally, other than for church.

After settling into their rooms and changing out of their travel-stained clothing, Felicia and Mr Warborough met in their private parlour.

"It wants an hour — almost two — before dinner," Mr Warborough said. "I should write to Fin and Drusilla, I suppose, but I am minded for some air and a chance to stretch my legs after the confinement of the coach. Should you care to stroll about the town with me, Miss Oakes?"

She agreed to it readily, for surely the familiar sights would be a welcome distraction from her dismal thoughts. She fetched her spencer, bonnet and gloves and within a very few minutes they were stepping out of the front door.

Astonishingly, the very first person Felicia saw was an old friend. "Jane!" she cried. "Whatever are you doing here? Oh… and Mrs Pollard. Good day to you, ma'am."

She dropped into a respectful curtsy, just as she had in the days when she was a lowly drawing teacher and Mrs Pollard was the rich mother of one of her pupils. The habit of deference was hard to break, even though she was no longer a teacher, or even a governess. Felicia was a woman of modest but independent means now, and Mrs Pollard was just another wealthy woman, one who no longer had any power over her.

"Felicia!" Jane cried, her solemn face breaking into a wide smile. "Oh, Mama, you remember Miss Oakes from Miss Latimer's Academy?"

Mrs Pollard pursed her lips, clearly remembering Felicia all too well. She it was who had taken Jane to all the Southampton assemblies and permitted her to stand up with clerks and apprentices and other unsuitable young men, when her ambitious parent had intended her to marry the heir to a dukedom. That little scheme had not worked out terribly well, especially since the heir in question was now drowned off the Cornish coast. The sons of a viscount and a baronet had likewise evaded Mrs Pollard's traps, but she was ever optimistic, and Felicia wondered why she was in Southampton rather than one of the more fashionable watering-places such as Brighton or Bath, where there might be better pickings for a matchmaking mama.

Two minutes of conversation, and the news that the estate in Dorsetshire had been leased for the summer, enabled Felicia to hazard some guesses. Three expensive seasons in London for Jane without resulting in an eligible match no doubt necessitated some economies.

"Jane so enjoyed her time in Southampton," Mrs Pollard gushed, "so we thought to spend a few weeks here before beginning our round of visits to all the relations. So tedious, of course, but one must accept such invitations when offered, for a refusal would give offence. I shall take no pleasure in it myself, for the society my sisters move in is somewhat more confined than we are used to, but we shall make the best of it, shall we not, Jane? At least Mr Pollard will have a little sport to amuse him. I had hoped that my cousins at Valmont would have invited us, but naturally the new duke is not entertaining, not while the family is in deep mourning for his brother. I wrote to offer my condolences at once, you may be sure, and to suggest that Jane and I might comfort his grief, and he wrote me such an elegant letter of gratitude — expressed himself so well on the subject — but he felt he would be poor company for a young lady such as Jane just at present. So thoughtful! Perhaps next year, when he is out of mourning. Such a tragedy, to lose the eldest son so soon after the father! We wore black ribbons ourselves for some time in sympathy, but we had to leave off for the season, for how could Jane dance with black ribbons? Jane so loves to dance, and she shows to such advantage in the cotillion. Such gracefulness! She was greatly admired in London, as you may well imagine, but there was no gentleman who quite took her eye, so here we are, just on our way to subscribe to the summer balls at the Dolphin. Fancy meeting you here, Miss Oakes."

Her eye fell on Mr Warborough, patiently standing a little aside while they talked.

"That is a fine gentleman you are with. Jane, do you know that gentleman?"

"No, Mama."

"He is not from Southampton," Felicia said. "Mr Warborough is from Derbyshire."

She did not feel it necessary to say more, for the rector of Church Compton, of middle years and having neither title nor fortune, could hardly be of interest to Mrs Pollard, but in this she underestimated the lady. At the name, her eyes acquired a certain brightness.

"A relation of the earl?" she whispered.

"His uncle," Felicia whispered back. "Should you like me to introduce him to you?"

"Oh, indeed! How kind! Most obliging of you."

At a signal from Felicia, he willingly stepped forward with his ready smile, sweeping his hat from his head.

"Mrs Pollard, may I make known to you Mr Warborough, who is the brother of the Fourth Earl of Finlassan, and uncle to the present earl. Mr Warborough is rector of Church Compton parish in Derbyshire, and having happy memories of Southampton and wishing to refresh his acquaintance with the town has been so obliging as to accompany me on my journey from Derbyshire. Mr Warborough, this is Mrs William Pollard of High Farley in Dorsetshire, and her daughter Miss Pollard. I had the pleasure of sharing with Jane my small knowledge of drawing and painting when she was a scholar here in Southampton."

There was bowing and curtsying, and much polite exchange of pleasantries. Mr Warborough was an odd sort of man, Felicia reflected, but he had a thousand times the address of his nephew and could make himself agreeable in any company. He even succeeded where so many men had failed, and contrived to draw Jane a little out of her crippling shyness. Felicia delighted in her remarks, diffident though they were, and approved Mr Warborough's gentlemanly manners which led him to devote attention to her. Nor did he neglect Mrs Pollard, making himself so agreeable to her that she promptly invited him to dinner that very day.

"Oh, but you must come, and you too, *dear* Miss Oakes, for we had engaged for some friends to dine with us and they have cried off, I know not why, and it will be a great crime if we sit down just the three of us to a whole goose, you know."

Felicia thought it would be a great crime too, and was more than willing to assist them in disposing of the bird, so she was relieved when Mr Warborough agreed to it very readily. He was so willing, in fact, that he turned round at once to go back into the hotel and cancel the arrangements for dinner issued not ten minutes earlier, and when he emerged again with Mrs Pollard, it was to inform Felicia that he too had subscribed to the season of summer balls.

"Are you staying so long, sir?" she said, surprised.

"Ah, but it is five shillings for just one ball, you see, and fifteen for the whole season. I have only missed the first two or three, so even if I only stay for a month, it is still better value. And who knows but I might stay for longer. I am not at all decided, for I need not hasten back. The curate will perform the offices for me on Sundays, and will like very well to have the parish to himself. Yes, perhaps I will stay for the whole summer."

Felicia tried not to look too surprised at this, but upon reflection supposed that Mr Warborough was inclined to look favourably on anyone who was willing to feed him so freely on the slightest acquaintance. He seemed to eat often with Lady Drusilla, and perhaps he saw Mrs Pollard as a similar source of benevolence. Felicia fell in beside Jane as the party moved off up the High Street, and somehow, and she could not tell how it happened, they found themselves at Castle Square where the Pollards had leased a house, and were invited in. There they met Mr Pollard, ate cake and drank tea, with Madeira provided for the gentlemen, and this was such a pleasant diversion that there was scarcely time to return to the hotel to dress for dinner before they were required to present themselves once again at Castle Square.

There were two other guests that evening, a widow and her son, and it was quite obvious that the son was yet another of Mrs Pollard's efforts to secure a husband for Jane. It was equally obvious that such efforts were once again doomed to failure. The young man was handsome and fashionable, yet had not the courtesy to set Jane at her ease. His manners had too much of haughtiness to overcome her shyness. Where she had chatted freely to Mr Warborough only that afternoon, now she was tongue-tied and blushingly silent again. Felicia sincerely felt for her, and did her best to distract attention from Jane's difficulties by becoming excessively lively herself. For his part, Mr Warborough was so attentive to Mrs Pollard that she did no more than throw Jane a black look every two minutes or so.

When the ladies withdrew, Mrs Pollard swept the widow and her excessively fashionable turban to the sofa, immediately launching into some tale about *'my cousin at Valmont'*. This left Jane and Felicia to have a comfortable coze together beside the window.

"Are you sorry not to be at High Farley this summer?" Felicia said. "The town can be quite unpleasant in the hot weather."

"I shall miss it, of course," Jane said with a sigh. "Most of all I shall miss my lovely little mare. I like to ride every day, and that is not possible here. But we are all resigned to it, and we have some acquaintance near here."

"You mean Valmont," Felicia whispered. "How remiss of His Grace not to invite you all to stay with him."

Jane giggled. "Poor man! He is not His Grace yet, for he refuses to claim the title until it is quite certain that his brother has not married and left behind an heir. He has people scouring America to find out, although it is hard to imagine that a duke would marry without telling anyone. They do have a mail service there, after all. But I do not expect an invitation. Mama so loves to talk about him, yet the connection is very tenuous, and we barely know any of the Litherholms. Nodding acquaintance, that is all."

"So who else do you know here? Your friends from Miss Latimer's?"

"Yes, the Miss Narfields live a few miles from here, although I was never a particular friend of theirs. Their father is a baron, which Mama likes, and he has two brothers of marriageable age, which she likes even more, although we have never managed to meet any of them, despite Mama's efforts." She sighed. "We also know Sir James and Lady Godney, from Daveney Hall. Lady Godney is always pleased for us to make up the numbers at her evening parties in London, but I am not sure she will want to continue the acquaintance now." She lowered her voice. "We are not here from any nostalgia on my part, you may be sure. Your friendship was the only part of my time in Southampton that I look back on fondly. No, the real reason is that Papa has gone back into the ship owning business."

"Here in Southampton?" Felicia said.

"Yes. He had interests here many years ago, but when he married Mama, he sold everything and bought High Farley, for her family is rather grand and she expected to marry a gentleman. But you will remember the *Brig Minerva* which was lost earlier this year? It was owned by an old friend, a Mr Sherrard, and when it sank, he was cast into a great deal of trouble. There were those who said that a ship in calm seas and clear skies, and under an experienced captain, should not sink, and that there must have been mischief afoot. And then there was a duke aboard, too, and was it not an odd coincidence that the very ship bearing so important a personage should founder? There was an inquiry and it was agreed that nothing untoward had occurred, and the ship's maps… charts… whatever they are called, were wrong and the ship hit rocks that were not marked on the maps. The Second Mate, who had charge of the ship at the time, survived, and his testimony was crucial. But still, people talked, and Mr Sherrard's business declined abruptly. So Papa has taken a half share in Mr Sherrard's ships, and we are here to support the family in whatever way we can. Mama is not happy, as you may imagine, for she will be expected to entertain Mr Sherrard and his associates, and that does not quite suit her notions of our position in society. Still, Papa is adamant that it must be done."

"I think it is splendid of him to support his friend," Felicia said. "Not many men would do so, under such circumstances. Poor Mr Sherrard, thrust into difficulties by an accident that was not his fault. Yet I wonder… But it is of no consequence, I daresay."

Jane smiled. "Your wonderings are always intriguing, Felicia. What do you wonder?"

"I wonder why a ship sailing under clear skies should not have seen these rocks before hitting them, whether they were on the maps or not."

"The *Minerva* foundered at night."

"But a clear night, with stars and perhaps moonlight... and the ship should have been well out to sea, yet it hit the coast, did it not? And I wonder also about the Second Mate, who was in charge of the ship when it sank, yet swore that nothing untoward happened."

"That is exactly what Papa said after the inquiry," Jane said in a low voice. "If only there had been another witness, he said, to confirm what the Second Mate had said, but the deck boy was asleep and the passenger on deck at the time remembered nothing."

"There was a passenger on deck?" Felicia said. "Hmm. That is all terribly suspicious."

"So Papa thought, but then he said that the inquiry had exonerated everyone concerned and it did no good to ask such questions, and the matter was closed. But he wondered about it, too, just as you are doing. Oh, Felicia, how glad I am to see you again, for letters are not at all the same, are they? One never knows quite what is behind the words if one cannot see the face of the person writing them. And are you settled here for good? You will not return to Derbyshire?"

Felicia shook her head, a flood of grief washing through her. She would never return to Derbyshire, never walk through the Pillared Saloon or sit in the window in Fin's studio. She would never watch the girls' faces as they concentrated on their drawing, or run through the woods behind Hercules, or sit in the Sanctuary with Lord Arnwell. And she would never see Fin again… Tears rose unbidden.

"Oh, Felicia!" Jane patted her hand gently. "I am so sorry."

"So am I," she whispered. "So am I."

# 20: Boscobel Cottage (August)

Fin was fired with new born enthusiasm. He would set the past behind him once and for all, and then Felicia would have nothing with which to reproach him. He arranged to see Wistman every week to discuss estate matters. He told Bagnall to bring his letters to the sitting room, where he dutifully sat for an hour each day writing replies. He went out for dinner at Sir Geoffrey Barnet's house, and discovered that the experience was rather enjoyable. It would have been more fun had Felicia been there to tuck into the venison pasties and roast pigeons, and a dish of sugarplums sat forlornly untouched, but he could otherwise find nothing to complain about. There was a young lady there, a cousin or niece of some sort, but she was not thrust at his head — in fact he spoke no more than a dozen words to her — he had a pleasant hour with the gentlemen and the port, and then tested the limits of his rather rusty whist, before leaving at a respectably late hour well pleased with his own virtuous neighbourliness.

He even walked the dog. The creature was rather puzzled by him at first, but once he realised that there was a walk to be had, he entered into the enterprise with enthusiasm, bounding away with tongue lolling as soon as he was released. Felicia had been right about him knowing the way, too. On every occasion, Hercules rushed through the woods and straight to a fallen tree where a collapsed wall gave access to Shotterbourne. Over he went, with Fin following more slowly, arriving at a small temple with a view over the estate. Arnwell was there, petting the dog and chatting happily to him. He looked up in surprise as Fin approached.

"Finlassan? Are you short of footmen? Or has the Princess charged you with the task of exercising Hercules?"

"The latter. How are you, Arnwell?"

"Well enough. You?"

"The same."

Arnwell poured Madeira for him and they sat side by side in silence until Hercules indicated, with wagging tail, that it was time to leave.

"Come again, if you wish," Arnwell said.

"Thank you. Good day to you."

He went home and instantly sat down to write to Felicia, as he did rather often. Whenever he did something which he felt she must approve, he drew forth paper, prepared his pen, dipped it into the inkwell... and then stopped. She had said that she could not write to him, for it would be improper in an unmarried woman of only two and twenty to write to a man who was not a relation, but surely he, as her former employer, could write to her? That could not be improper, could it?

With a sigh, he wiped the pen and set it down again. He had no wish to bring trouble upon her head, and yet... how he longed to talk to her! Even a letter would be something. He wanted so badly to tell her of his successes, that he was doing as she had bidden him, that he was opening his eyes to the world at last. It meant nothing if he could not share it with her.

He rose from his desk, poured himself a glass of Madeira and went through to the studio. Her painting of the ballroom stood there on its easel, and he gazed at it, finding something new in it every time he looked. So much detail! So much movement and liveliness and *life*. Up on the balcony, two of the musicians were engaged in an altercation. A footman was in danger of spilling a tray of drinks — oh, it was Matthews, his valet, an excellent fellow with boot polish and starch, but an indifferent footman, pressed into service only when essential. And over by the doors to the terrace, two people were creeping away for a private assignation. Such delightful vignettes made him smile.

But always his eye was drawn back to the characters in the forefront of the painting. Fin himself was directly in the centre, dancing his turn in the set with such light-footed grace! A flattering portrait indeed. But now that he had examined the dancers closely, he could see that Felicia herself was his partner, making her steps on the other side of the formation, her skirts swirling elegantly. And behind them, Juliana standing waiting her turn, smiling at the man across from her, a handsome man of around forty. Kearney, he supposed. Felicia had met him, so she had drawn him from life, as he was just before he died, whereas Juliana was taken from her portrait in the library, perpetually nineteen years of age. And there was no Godfrey Buckley, he noticed. He was nowhere to be found in the picture.

Bagnall came in with his apologetic cough. "Matthews wishes to know if you will be dressing for dinner tonight, my lord, since the young ladies will be joining you."

That was an innovation, too. Thrice a week, on Tuesdays, Thursdays and Sundays, he ate with Juliana and Margarita and their two stiff-rumped governesses, and Drusilla joined them, too. He had begun the habit before Felicia had left, and then he had dressed for the occasion, for it had seemed right to mark her last few days at Hawkewood Hall with appropriate ceremony. Now that she had gone, he had lapsed rather. What was the point of donning knee breeches when the only audience was his sister, two children and two middle-aged women? In his mind, however, he heard Felicia's voice loud and clear, telling him that he *should* dress for dinner. So many things he *should* do, but had not.

"I suppose I had better make the effort, eh?"

"Very good, my lord. I shall inform Matthews. There are three letters on your desk that came in on this morning's London mail. Is there anything else, my lord?"

Fin waved him away, then, struck by a sudden thought, called out, "Bagnall!"

The butler turned, bowed again.

"The ball room... see that it is cleaned up."

"Very good, my lord."

"I might hold a ball next month... or September, perhaps. Yes, September. Tell Mrs Shayne, will you."

"A ball, my lord?"

"A ball," he said firmly. "What is the point of a ballroom if one never holds a ball? A ballroom *should* be used, after all. See to it, man, instead of standing there with your mouth open like a stuffed rabbit."

Bagnall bowed in offended dignity and withdrew.

Fin strode into the sitting room, sat down at his desk and wrote with swift strokes of the pen.

*'Dear Miss Oakes, I am to hold a ball in September. Please say you will come. Finlassan.'*

He folded it, wrote the direction, sealed and franked it, and put it on the letters tray to go to the post office tomorrow.

The three new letters met his eye. One was from the London lawyers, which he set aside for tomorrow. The second was from Aunt Geraldine, informing him that another of her multitude of indistinguishable daughters had produced a daughter of her own. The third was in a hand he did not recognise. He broke the seal and unfolded the letter, staring at it in bewilderment.

*'Kkboi yeceb orosc qyxop ybqyy ngsvv. Crolo ckpox yggbs docyy xgokb obokn ipqrs.'*

What the devil? It was no language he had ever seen, and every word precisely five letters long could only mean—

"A code!" he murmured to himself, with a frisson of interest. He looked again at the direction, but it read simply *'To The Rt Hon The Earl of Finlassan, Hawkewood Hall, nr Derby'*. It had come from London, but that told him nothing. Yet who would write to him in code? Something prickled at the back of his mind, but then slithered out of reach. Something to do with codes, but he could not recall it.

He tucked the letter in his waistcoat and went to change for dinner.

~~~~~
~~~~~

Felicia waited at the Dolphin at precisely three o'clock on Tuesday, her luggage in a neat pile in the yard. At half past three, she began to grow restless, and by the time Jimmy Temple drove into the yard, a few minutes before four o'clock, she was blazing with anger, not assuaged by observing that the gig was already laden with packages, and even two ducks in a cage.

"Well, this is a fine thing, Mr Temple, to keep me waiting all this time, and now you have no room for me," she said coldly. "I could have hired a chaise any time these last three days, but thought it best to wait for you. I now see that that was a mistake."

"G'day, Miss Oakes," he said, with a cheerful wave. "Plenty o'room for you, and your boxes may be sent on the cart, I dare say."

"My boxes travel with me, Mr Temple. You may leave all *your* boxes here, and *they* may be sent on the cart." She did not like to remind him that he lived at Boscobel Cottage on her benevolence, and although she paid him no wage, he was still in the position of a servant to her, and she was his mistress.

Perhaps he realised it, for he rubbed his nose thoughtfully, looking chastened. "Well... I canna leave the birds, but the rest may be sent on the cart, I suppose."

After no more than a half hour of negotiation with the Dolphin ostler, and some unloading and reloading, they eventually set forward, and Felicia tried not to mind having to carry a crate of ducks on her knee as they drove up the High Street. It was rather a salutary reminder of her newly reduced circumstances. She was no longer a governess in the household of an earl, with the ability to summon the carriage at will or ask the footmen to cart things about for her.

The remains of market day slowed their progress somewhat, but before long they were passing through the outskirts and then into open country. Felicia had passed that way but twice before, the first time at the age of ten when Mr Vickery and Mr Pierce, her guardians and trustees, had removed her to Miss Latimer's Academy, and the second time a year ago when she had come of age and been permitted to see Miss Armiger's effects. On both occasions it had rained. It was not raining today, but the sky was grey and threatening, and the country was flat and dreary. Felicia's spirits lowered with every mile post they passed.

"Is all well at the cottage, Mr Temple?"

"Oh aye, well enough." Long pause. "Pigs are doing well."

"Oh. Good."

After that, conversation lapsed, and Felicia supposed she would have to wait to find out the truth of the matter.

Eventually they came to the small hamlet of Delstone St Clements, where Mr Vickery was parson, but drove straight through, and then they were into the woods. Felicia had no very good memories of the woods surrounding Boscobel Cottage, which had always seemed vast and darkly threatening to her child self, but from the greater height of the gig she could see clearings and trees of great beauty tucked away in the gloom. She was struck by an urge to walk amongst the trees with her sketchbook. Fin would enjoy it too, for he had a way with trees, as his paintings of the temple on the hill showed.

Sooner than she expected, the gig drew to a halt outside a smart white fence surrounding a flower-filled garden. The neat house behind it boasted freshly painted window frames, cheerful yellow curtains at the open windows and roses growing in profusion all round the door. If it were not for the neat sign on the gate reading *'Boscobel Cottage'* she would not have recognised the place.

"That was never five miles from Delstone!" she said.

"Three, Miss Oakes," Mr Temple said. "'Tis three miles, and less through the woods. Daresay it seemed further when you were a girl."

"Miss Armiger told me five!" she said indignantly.

The door opened and the familiar faces came tumbling out, smiling and waving — Agnes Markham, the former housekeeper at Summer Cottage, Eliza Temple, the cook, and Lilian, the housemaid. And another man, whom Felicia had never seen before, slender to the point of emaciation, wringing his hands nervously and averting his eyes from hers.

"You remember Mr Trye?" Agnes said brightly.

Felicia dredged around in her memory. "The curate?" she said. "Gracious, I thought you had long since departed back to Delstone, Mr Trye. But thank you for caring for Boscobel Cottage for me while I was unable to live here myself."

"And a grand job he did, too," Agnes said briskly. "Come inside, dear, and let me show you to your room. Not that you need to be shown, naturally, for it's the same room you had as a child, but I'd like to assure myself that you have everything you need."

In they went, past the front door now a smart shade of blue, and up the stairs, the balusters also newly painted, and into her room. Felicia's stomach clenched in anticipation of the dreary walls of some indeterminate shade of dark green, the plain deal washstand and chair, the bed cover inexpertly crocheted by Miss

Armiger and the single shelf for her Bible, Prayer Book and candlestick.

Agnes threw open the door and Felicia cried out in delight. Gone was the gloom. The wainscoting was painted saffron with a delicately patterned wallpaper above it, and there was more yellow in the curtains and matching bed cover. Lacy cloths covered the several small tables now scattered about, three more shelves had appeared and beside the fire was a comfortable armchair.

"This is lovely!" Felicia cried, tossing aside her bonnet and giving the bed an experimental bounce. "You have even provided a new mattress. The old one was stuffed with lavender, and so lumpy you cannot imagine! I have had the greatest aversion to the scent of dried lavender ever since. You have done wonders, Agnes."

Agnes heaved a great breath. "Oh, thank goodness! We talked and talked about it, and wondered if perhaps you would be upset if we changed anything, but really, Miss Oakes, it needed livening up. The whole house was so *dark* when we first came here."

"Oh yes! Such a gloomy place! I was quite dreading it, but this is so cheerful that I hardly recognise it. I hope you have kept a good reckoning of all you have spent on my behalf."

"Oh, well… as to that… Mr Pierce told us to make the place ready for you and undertook to settle the cost from your account, which he still has in his management. I hope he did no wrong, Miss Oakes."

"Not at all. I am delighted, and shall tell him so. I saw him yesterday, and he assured me he will visit in a few days to go through the accounts and so forth, and discuss what I wish to do.

He suggested that I might sell the cottage and move into Southampton. Or there is Summer Cottage, which is still without a tenant."

Agnes's face fell, but she said stoutly, "That is as you wish, my dear, of course. We have been very happy here but we always expected our stay to end eventually." She sighed. "We shall have to find employment somewhere, and that will split us apart, I daresay. And poor Gerald — Mr Trye — will have to squeeze in at the parsonage. How he will miss this garden!"

"He enjoys the garden, does he?"

"Enjoys it? He spends every spare minute out there, and what we should have done without him, I can't think, for none of *us* know about the growing of parsnips or when to prune the pears. Now then, here's Lilian with hot water for you, so we'll leave you to clean off the dust of the road. Dinner in half an hour."

Felicia washed and then changed into a clean, if rather rumpled, gown. From her portmanteau, she gently withdrew one of her sketchbooks and settled in the armchair. Reverently, she turned the pages. Fin painting. Fin glowering at her. Fin sealing the letter she had written for him, a resigned expression on his face. Fin sternly reprimanding Bagnall for placing the sugarplums out of Felicia's reach. "Beside Miss Oakes, man!" he had said. "Such sweetmeats are of no interest to me." The memory warmed her inside. And then Fin smiling... ah, that smile! Even looking at her own representation of it, a faint echo of the real thing, made her melt into a puddle.

Angrily, she snapped the sketchbook shut before the tears could come, and went downstairs for dinner. It was a strange meal. They ate in the dining room, used by Miss Armiger only on Sundays and then only so that she could instruct Felicia on the correct manners for the table. Even now, with the distance of twelve years from those events, she felt the familiar nerves in her stomach as her mind recalled the stream of instructions to sit up straight... do not loll... eat small mouthfuls only... chew well and swallow... now a sip of water... lay down your knife and fork, and offer a topic of conversation.

This meal was nothing like that. Felicia took the place of honour at the head, and Mr Trye was persuaded to take what was clearly his usual place at the foot. "Such an expert carver, Miss Oakes," Agnes said. There was only one course and no removes, since the cook was seated at the table with everyone else, but there were eels, sole and crawfish as well as mutton, veal and partridge, and an array of vegetables, both dressed and plain, from their own garden. There was even a bottle of wine, bought by Jimmy Temple at the market to celebrate Felicia's return, although the two men had most of it. The conversation flowed freely, as between established friends, with much teasing and laughter. Felicia could not remember hearing laughter at the cottage before.

"This is a wonderful spread," Felicia said, when her hunger was finally sated. "When I was a child, we lived on boiled beef and potatoes."

"Potatoes are for the pigs," Eliza said, in shocked tones.

"For the pigs! How many do you have?"

"Five this year."

"Gracious! We never had more than one, and it was fed on whatever rinds and peelings and scraps we had."

"Potatoes are best," Mr Trye said, although he went bright red with embarrassment at his own temerity in speaking. "With meal and clover hay, boiled up. They do better with others of their kind. Sociable animals, pigs. Clever, too. Like people."

"How knowledgeable you are, Mr Trye," Felicia said. "I wish Miss Armiger and I had had the benefit of your advice. I had no idea half so many vegetables could be grown here. It always seemed to be cabbage, and not much else."

"Very reliable, cabbage," Mr Trye murmured. "Tasty, too."

"True but even the tastiest vegetable palls after a while, when there is nothing else. I should have loved to have asparagus once in a while."

"Seems to me your Miss Armiger was not used to growing her own food," he said.

"Very likely. She was more skilled in the schoolroom than in the garden, or the kitchen, for that matter. She could never cook like this. Poor Miss Armiger! Compelled to look after me when she would rather have been studying her Greek and Latin books. She insisted on teaching me Greek, to little avail. Well, that was such a long time ago. It is all ancient history, now."

They smiled, but not with understanding. Fin would have got her little joke. Or the marquess, perhaps. For a moment she was overwhelmed with grief. If she could only see them again!

Agnes patted her hand, and said how glad they were to have her home. Home! A dreadful thought. After the joy of Hawkewood Hall, a place so uplifting to her artistic soul, with beauty and elegance everywhere, could she ever be contented in the cramped environment of Boscobel Cottage? Even new paint and pretty curtains could not make it other than a remote and dismal place, nor wipe out the misery of her childhood years.

"We all hope you'll be as happy here as we've been," Eliza said, beaming with delight. "But you must tell us what changes you want. You're the mistress here, after all, and you needn't expect us to be always encroaching. We'll keep out of your way in future, but just for today we wanted to help you celebrate."

Silence fell, and although the Temples and Lilian looked at her expectantly, Agnes and Mr Trye exchanged glances. Of course they were nervous about their future. They had settled down here, living well, by the look of it, and would be happy to remain. Boscobel Cottage was not Felicia's home, but it was her friends' home and how could she turn them out of it?

"If this is an example of your encroaching ways," Felicia said brightly, "then I sincerely hope you will continue to encroach indefinitely. I do not know what the future may bring, but I shall make no changes at present. Let us all drink a toast to… to friendship, and fat pigs, and asparagus. Lots and lots of asparagus."

They laughed and raised their glasses and were merry for a long time, but Felicia could not shift the heavy lump of fear in her belly. This was her life now, her horizons shrunk to these four walls, and no amount of juicy ham or buttered asparagus could ease her grief at the life left behind.

# 21: A New Home

The third time Fin took the dog to Shotterbourne, the marquess was not there. The hamper of cakes and Madeira sat forlornly in the little pavilion, but it was otherwise empty, rain dripping steadily off the roof. Hercules snuffled about for a while, before settling under one of the marble benches, nose on muddy paws.

"Well, where is he, do you suppose?" Fin said, looking about him as if the marquess might spring out from behind a statue. "Surely a drop of rain would not put him off his daily walk."

A fluttering paper caught his eye, held between the upturned fingers of one of the marble nymphs lining the pavilion. Fin laughed, and retrieved the paper. *'Lungs bad today. A.'*

Fin grunted. "What do you think, old fellow?" Hercules sat up and wagged his tail. "A good idea. Come on, then."

Clicking his fingers to the dog, he strode away down the hill towards the house, Hercules bounding enthusiastically alongside. The surprised butler admitted them without demur, leaving them dripping in the pillared hall with two silent footmen, no doubt wondering how long it would take to clean the marble floor of the prints of muddy paws and boots. Eventually the butler returned.

"His lordship will see you now, my lord. He is in the Map Room."

Fin followed the butler up the imposing staircase to the saloon, through a drawing room, then an ante-room, along a corridor and then through another room, lined with books, and lit by a single lamp, since all the shutters were closed.

"Why so dark in here?" Fin said. "It would be a pleasant room with a little light."

"The windows have an unhappy prospect, my lord."

Fin was about to ask what he meant when he remembered — this room would overlook the remains of the burnt-out family wing.

Another short corridor led to the Map Room, where the marquess sat before a low-burning fire, swathed in a shawl.

"Well now, Finlassan," he said. Then, to the dog, who was bouncing energetically around the room, "Here, boy. Lord, you are muddy. Hillman, find a cloth, will you, and dry the poor fellow off. Madeira's over there, Finlassan. Help yourself."

Fin did so, gazing around him in wonder as he did so. The Map Room was indeed filled with framed maps, and a profusion of globes and devices. One in particular caught Fin's eye.

"What the devil is that?"

The marquess chuckled. "An orrery. A representation of the planets."

"So it is! Here is our own modest home in the heavens, with its moon, and here are Venus and… what is the innermost one?"

"Mercury."

"And Mars, Jupiter, Saturn and Herschel. How beautiful!"

"Out of date, of course," the marquess said. "There is a new one discovered lately — Ceres. Fits between Mars and Jupiter. I expect they will find more yet, as they make better telescopes."

"Fascinating! Has Felicia ever seen this? It would delight her."

"Would it? I thought you artistic types were all about the beauties of nature, not the mechanical."

"No one who sees such an exquisite work of art could fail to be moved by it," Fin protested. "I assume the gears mean that it does something?"

"Turn the handle on the side there."

And the planets moved, slowly spinning on their axes and revolving about the sun, and many of them with their own moons, too. Fin watched, mesmerised, as the delicate little balls executed their perpetual dance before his eyes.

A gentle tap on the door was followed immediately by Miss Buckley's face peering into the room.

"I beg your pardon if I intrude, my lord, but I wondered if you need anything? Some refreshments for your guest perhaps?"

"Hillman is perfectly capable of attending to such matters, Edith."

"Of course, of course, but a lady is always more attentive than a servant. Are you quite comfortable? Another cushion for your back? A footstool? Are you warm enough? Lady Lucia frets so over these little matters."

"Tell her I am perfectly at ease, and want for nothing," Arnwell said. "Thank you, Edith."

With a neat curtsy, she withdrew.

"Unpleasant woman, always sneaking here and there," Arnwell said. "I found her searching through my desk once. She said she was looking for wafers, but she could have asked the housekeeper if that was what she wanted. I would have her out of here in a minute if I could, but Lucia likes her and that is the end of it. No one else knows how to deal with Lucia when she gets into her little upsets. So you like my orrery, do you, Finlassan?"

"It is glorious!" he breathed. "I wish Felicia could see it."

"She wrote to me," the marquess said.

Fin's head shot up. "The devil she did! I wrote to her, but she has not replied. How is she? Is she well? Is she happy there? Is she working on a new painting?"

The marquess grunted. "Read it for yourself. Over there."

Jumping up, Fin followed the direction indicated to a small desk by the window, where a letter lay opened. He recognised her elegantly curved script at once.

*'Boscobel Cottage, Hants. Buongiorno Conte, thank you so much for your letter. Yes, I am settled in my little house at last, the mud is not so bad as I had feared, and I have not eaten boiled beef, potatoes or cabbage soup once. Even the sun is shining, which I swear it never did once when I was a girl. I miss my walks to the Sanctuary with Hercules, because although I can walk for miles in all directions here and the scenery is pleasant enough, there is no*

*reward of lemon cake and Madeira at the end of it, which as I am sure you are aware was almost as great an attraction as your company. I shall certainly <u>not</u> pass on your impertinent message to Mr Warborough, except to reassure him when next he visits me with his friends that his curate is ministering to his flock adequately, which will please him, since he plans to stay in the county for a few weeks. This conclusion is drawn from his having purchased a subscription to the Summer Balls at the Dolphin Hotel. Therefore you may enjoy Mr Cotham's entertaining sermons for a while longer. My good wishes to the Lady Lucia and Miss Buckley, and especially to you, mio caro Conte, from your affectionate friend, Felicia Oakes.'*

"Giles is staying in the south?" Fin said in bewilderment. "A few *weeks?* A subscription to balls? What the devil is he playing at? And who are these friends? He *has* no friends in Hampshire."

The marquess chuckled. "And now he has. How old is he?"

Fin performed some mental calculations. "Five or six and forty, I should guess."

"Well, then. A man in his prime, would you not say?"

"In his—? You cannot mean—? *No*, surely not!"

But the marquess only chuckled again, and Fin was left to wonder what precisely was the great attraction for Giles in Southampton, and, with a horrible gnawing feeling, whether it had anything to do with Felicia.

~~~~~

Felicia had managed to fill several days in ambling about the house and garden, reacquainting herself with Agnes, the Temples and Lilian and getting to know the timid Mr Trye and his garden,
~~~~~

bursting with produce. Then came Sunday, and church, and the astonishing revelation that the path she and Miss Armiger had habitually taken was indeed five miles long, but there was a shorter way which led past a farm and several cottages. Neighbours! They had had neighbours, and she had known nothing of it. How credulous she had been as a child, believing everything Miss Armiger had told her. She could have had friends of her own age, she discovered, for the farmer and his manager both had daughters near in age. She remembered them dimly from church, but Miss Armiger had never stopped to talk after the service, always hurrying home again.

"They tried to visit you," Agnes said, as they walked past the farm lane. "Tried several times, Mrs Wellings told me, but Miss Armiger sent them to the rightabout. Very reclusive, wasn't she?"

Mr Vickery, the Delstone St Clements parson, welcomed Felicia with great kindness.

"So happy to have you home," he said, his round face split by a wide smile.

"Look at you, all grown up, and quite the young lady," his wife said. "So pretty, you turned out, Miss Oakes."

Felicia was greeted by a number of people she recognised from years ago, but had to admit that she had forgotten their names, if she had ever known them.

"Ah well, Miss Armiger never liked to mingle with the likes of us," one affable yeoman told her. "Thought herself a touch above mere farming stock, I daresay."

Felicia protested at it, but during the sermon, she wondered if he might not be right. Her insistence that Felicia should learn to behave like a lady, and acquire the full range of accomplishments expected of the daughters of the gentry, was curious. No matter the needs of the garden, there had been two hours of lessons every morning, including not just reading, writing and arithmetic, but history, geography and a little of the sciences, music, drawing and painting, as well as French, Italian and Ancient Greek. Not Latin, however, which Miss Armiger had said was the language of men. In the last few months before her death, there had been deportment and the extension of Felicia's sewing skills, previously confined to hemming handkerchiefs and darning stockings, to include netting, tatting, embroidery and tapestry. The battered old harpsichord had been replaced with a new pianoforte and there had been talk of a harp for the future. And then, when lessons were over, they had grubbed in the dirt to feed themselves, or else boiled cauldrons of water for the laundry. It was eccentric in the extreme.

Mr Vickery had told her that he and Mr Pierce would call upon her on Tuesday morning at noon to discuss her financial situation and her plans for the future. As her former guardians and trustees, they had retained their management of her modest fortune while she was engaged at Summer Cottage, but now that she had been released from the care of her charges, they not unnaturally wished to know how she intended to proceed. She had no idea.

It had been in her mind to sell the cottage and move to Southampton, where she could obtain lodgings at little cost, and would perhaps only need one maid of all work to help with the cooking and cleaning. She could, if she wished, offer her services once more as a teacher of art at Miss Latimer's Academy.

Now that she had seen the cottage, however, and had understood how settled the others were there, it seemed cruel to uproot them. Nor was the place so isolated and dispiriting as she had found it as a child. With the gig, she could go into Southampton whenever she wished, Mr Trye and Jimmy Temple kept the table fully stocked, and Agnes and Lilian managed all the work of the house. Felicia would be free to paint all day, if she wished, and that was an attractive prospect.

Still, it would take her a long time to be happy at Boscobel Cottage herself, for the darkly lowering presence of Miss Armiger still hung over the house. Every room contained memories. The kitchen, of endless peeling, scraping and chopping. The outhouses, scene of boiling laundry and churning butter. The schoolroom, with the table at one end where they ate most meals and the desks at the other. The back parlour, where they had spent the long Sunday hours reading sermons or the Bible. Even though the fresh paint and cheerful presence of the new occupants had laid a happier veneer over the cottage, and Felicia was grateful for her own bright room, still she could not entirely shake off the old, bad memories.

Two rooms in particular were filled with Miss Armiger's shade, if that were not too fanciful a description. Felicia remembered her bedchamber as a dismal room, the narrow bed a twin to Felicia's own, the only furniture a washstand, press and bedside table. Every morning, it had been Felicia's task to bring her protector a cup of tea, placing it carefully on the little table beside the bed, next to the Bible and Prayer Book. Once a week, they had dusted the surfaces, changed the linen on the bed and swept the floor. Twice a year, the blankets and mattress stuffing had been changed, the curtains and rug beaten, and the window washed.

Felicia's strongest memory was of Miss Armiger's final days, lying with closed eyes in the bed, seemingly asleep. Three times Felicia had crept in with the morning cup of tea, but Miss Armiger did not wake. At the end of each day, she had crept in again and removed the stone cold tea from the morning, wondering when the sleeping woman would finally wake up, and yet shamefully glad that she did not, and Felicia was free from her hectoring. For a long time afterwards she had been guilty about that.

Then there was the front parlour… that had been Miss Armiger's sanctuary, where she retreated each evening after Felicia had gone to bed, there to do… who knew what? The door had been kept locked, and Felicia had never been in there, except once, after she came of age and Mr Vickery and Mr Pierce had at last permitted her to view Miss Armiger's papers.

Perhaps it was time to address the bad memories directly.

"Agnes, do you have the key to the front parlour?" she said one day at breakfast. "I shall speak to Mr Pierce and Mr Vickery in there when they come tomorrow."

"The front parlour? You mean Miss Armiger's study? I do, and the key to her bedroom, too. Lilian and I go in from time to time to clean, but we are very careful not to disturb her things."

"Has nothing been touched, even in her bedroom?"

"Nothing at all," Agnes said proudly. "Her clothes are still in the wardrobe, just as she left them. We replaced the charcoal she used against moths with camphor balls. Oh, and we put up new curtains, to match the rest of the front windows, and Jimmy did some repair work on the wainscoting in the study, but otherwise everything is just as it was. Mr Pierce was most insistent that it was for you to decide what to do with those rooms."

"Well, I had better look at the bedroom first, I suppose," Felicia said, although her stomach felt like lead at the prospect. She had rather hoped that the bedroom, at least, had been cleared out and refurbished, like her own room, but there was no point in postponing the inevitable.

Miss Armiger's bedroom was shockingly familiar. Nothing had been changed from those last dreadful days except that the body had been removed and the bed stripped. The folded blankets still sat at the foot of the bed, the press still held the neatly folded chemises, stays and petticoats, and a modest number of gowns.

"They are sadly out of date," Felicia said, pulling out a gown with full skirts and stomacher. "I suppose they are only good for burning."

"The materials are of excellent quality," Agnes said. "If you were to allow Mr Vickery to distribute them to the paupers in the village, they could still be of some use."

"Very well. Let it be so, but for Heaven's sake burn the mattress, and perhaps with some fresh paint the room could be put to use again."

Agnes laughed and agreed to it. Then they went down to the front parlour. This room was, if not exactly cosy, at least less sparsely furnished. There was a tall bookcase, quite full, and two more shelves of books. In a corner was a stack of copies of the *Gazette*, the London newspaper that Miss Armiger had read with religious fervour. The only time Felicia could remember her losing her temper was when the carter had failed to bring an expected issue, and no amount of pleading about flooding on the London road had appeased her.

In front of the window was a small desk, with nothing on it but a pen stand. She already knew that the drawers contained neat sheets of household accounts, translations of works in Greek or Latin, and plans for Felicia's education, but nothing else. Not a single letter, nor a journal. She had already gone through everything in her search for something — anything! — related to her own origins, but without avail.

"I shall bring you my account book, Miss Oakes," Agnes said. "I've noted every expense since we moved in, and Mr Pierce has approved it all, so I'm sure you will find everything in order."

Felicia smiled at her. "Agnes, you must stop treating me as the mistress of the house. At Summer Cottage, we worked together and ate together, did we not? We were all friends."

Agnes's face softened. "True, but even so, you were always above us. We were merely servants, but you were more than that, as the governess. Here, you're the mistress and we must respect that."

"I am somebody's illegitimate daughter," Felicia said softly.

"Makes no difference," Agnes said stoutly. "You own this place, and have money of your own besides. We're very grateful to you for allowing us to stay here free of rent while you were up north, and we'll be happy to stay on, either as your servants or as your lodgers, whatever suits you, but you will always be the mistress here."

"What do you wish to be — servants or lodgers?"

"That's up to you," Agnes said, a flicker of uncertainty crossing her face.

Felicia considered that. "It is awkward," she said, frowning. "I would feel uncomfortable treating you like servants, and yet — you ought to have an income. I should pay you for the work you do. That is only right."

Agnes's face cleared. "We'd be happier with a small salary, too. That way, we can save a bit, and if ever your circumstances change or you sell up here, you'd be able to give us all good references."

"So I would! Let it be so, then. I had better look at your accounts so I can talk knowledgeably to Mr Pierce and Mr Vickery tomorrow."

While Agnes went off to fetch her account book, Felicia went through the drawers looking for Miss Armiger's accounts for comparison. In one drawer, she found a leather-bound notebook, rather battered, that she had not seen before. Inside, the pages were covered with Miss Armiger's cramped handwriting, all in Ancient Greek.

"Agnes, where did this come from?" she said, when the housekeeper returned with her account book.

"Jimmy found that behind the wainscoting when he was fixing it. There was quite a big gap, and the book must have fallen over the back of the desk sometime and got stuck there. It's all that foreign writing, so I put it in the drawer with all the other foreign stuff."

"Hmm. But the others have a page of Greek and then a translation. This is all in Greek. I wonder what it means?"

"It can't be important, or she'd have noticed it was missing," Agnes said.

"Perhaps she hid it there deliberately!" Felicia said, excitement bursting over her. "Perhaps it is a journal! It might even tell me who I am!"

"Maybe it will, at that," Agnes said, but there was a sadness in her voice.

"You think I should not care," Felicia said slowly. "That I may never find out the truth of my origins."

"There's plenty never do," Agnes said. "The Vickerys had a foundling left on their doorstep, years and years ago. Never found out who left him there, but he's a fine young man now, making his way in the world. Apprenticed to a clockmaker in Portsmouth. Sometimes you just have to get on with life, and accept that there are some things only God knows."

"There *are* things only God knows, that is perfectly true, but my ancestry is not one of them," Felicia said firmly. "There are — or were — at least three people in the world who know who I am, namely my mother, my father and Miss Armiger. Miss Armiger is dead, but the other two may still be alive, and any one of them may have told others of me, or written something down. For I was not left on a parson's doorstep as a foundling, Agnes. Someone took great care to ensure I was raised safely and taught properly, or else why entrust me to someone like Miss Armiger?"

"That's a question I've asked myself many a time since we came here," Agnes said. "Why choose someone so miserly and reclusive as that? You make light of it, but it must have been a miserable childhood. You'd have been better off on the parson's doorstep, if you ask me. But fretting over it is no use, it eats away at your insides, something like that, so if that book really is a journal, or something about you, maybe it'll set your mind at rest."

"Yes!" Felicia said eagerly. "I just want to know! I shall fetch my old Greek primer and see if I can make anything of it. Just think, Agnes — perhaps at last I will know the truth!"

Agnes smiled sadly.

# 22: Mysteries

Fin grew increasingly impatient to receive a reply from Felicia to his letter. Each time Bagnall brought a fresh batch of letters and hers was not amongst them, he fretted a little more. He went every day to see Arnwell, rain or shine, but he had heard nothing further, either. And what was Giles up to? If he should be making up to Felicia—!

He was too distracted to paint, but there were one or two projects to occupy his hands, if not his mind. Juliana's paintings had arrived from Southampton, and he had placed them all in an unused bedroom, together with the three from his sitting room, so that he could properly catalogue them and decide how best to display them. He tried to suppress the slight feeling of disappointment as he looked through them initially. The originality and promise he had seen so clearly in her earlier work was muted in the later efforts. The subjects were trite — flowers or garden views, and a multitude of likenesses of her daughters — and the execution, while competent, showed no improvement over time. If anything, the later works were more sketchy, less satisfying, but perhaps her final illness was bearing down on her by then. He began a proper listing, but it was tedious work.

The removal of three paintings from his sitting room left an expanse of wall to be filled, and he knew at once what to place there. The larger space would be perfect for his twin paintings of the temple in tempest and calm, and Felicia's painting of the ballroom would fit neatly into the smaller space. The estate carpenter was engaged to construct the frames, and that was a pleasant way to pass an hour or two, gazing at the paintings and deciding on the most suitable shape and quantity of ornamentation.

For the ballroom scene, he had settled on an illusion of a pillared surround with an arched top. It would hide a small amount of the top corners, but it gave a magical sense of observing the ball from the outside. Such a glorious scene, and not just because he himself was in it. The movement and life she had captured always made him smile, and there was Arnwell, looking like any other genial old man. He should be invited to dinner, Fin decided, so that he could see how Felicia saw him. On the spot, he scratched a hasty note. *'Come for dinner on Sunday. I have something to show you. Finlassan.'*

His other project was less satisfactory. He had made several attempts to unravel the meaning behind the coded letter he had received, but to no avail. Sometimes the key to such a code was a passage from a book held by both parties, but more usually it depended upon a simple transposition of letters. Then he remembered that his father had possessed some kind of wheel as an aid to decoding letters from his cronies. Fin spent a frustrating day in the attics until he thought to ask Bagnall.

"His lordship kept his translating device in his desk in the library, my lord."

"I went through every drawer and shelf there not long ago, when I was looking for the wretched seal," Fin said. "It was not there."

"It is in the hidden drawer, my lord."

"The devil it is! Show me, man."

He strode off to the library, leaving Bagnall to follow at a pace commensurate with the dignity of a butler in the household of an earl. When Bagnall arrived, he reached behind the desk, something clicked, a small door shot open and there was the wheel.

"Why did my father show you how to open his secret drawer?" Fin said suspiciously.

"Oh, he did not, my lord, but housemaids who dust thoroughly discover such things and Mrs Shayne quite properly reported it to me. I have several times observed his late lordship using the device, so I understood its purpose. I do not know how the device works, however, my lord."

"Father told me how to use it, many years ago, but I never had his need for conveying government information secretly, nor brothers with whom I might have wished to communicate privately, so I never bothered with it."

Bagnall said nothing, but clearly he wondered why Fin had developed a sudden urge to find the wheel. His expression was such a comical mixture of rabid curiosity and professional dignity that Fin almost laughed. He was not about to explain himself to a butler, however.

Fin carried off the coding wheel in triumph to his sitting room and settled down to a sustained attempt to interpret the letter. Almost at once his head jerked up again. *Giles!* There had been a previous letter in code, but Giles had whisked it away. What had he said? Something to the effect that it was written very ill, or was a mistake. Then he had pushed it hastily into a pocket. He had been so flustered by it, so he must have known—

There was more to it, he realised. Until recently, Fin had never read his own letters, in fact he had not even seen them. They had been left to accumulate and every few weeks or months, Giles had gone through them. *The coded letter was for Giles!* Fin had never been meant to see it.

But who was it from? What did it mean? Was Giles, too, involved in secret government work? It seemed highly implausible that a reclusive country clergyman should be passing coded information about, and yet, here the letter was, and it was clearly not intended for Fin.

There was only one way to resolve the mystery and that was to read the message hidden in the letter.

~~~~~

Felicia's excitement at finding Miss Armiger's lost notebook evaporated very quickly. An hour of wrestling with her Greek primer extracted the words on the first page of the book: *'The History of Miss Margaret Pickering, being an account true in every particular of her humble birth, her education, her rise to a distinguished and responsible position, and her present circumstances, including many adventures and trials of her fortitude.'*

That was puzzling. Her first thought was that it must be a novel, and she was disgusted that Miss Armiger had wasted her time on such a pointless exercise, and yet never bothered to write a single word about Felicia's origins, or how she had come to have
~~~~~

charge of her. She had always been adamant that she was not Felicia's mother, and that seemed true enough. They were so unlike, and surely she could not be so unfeeling towards her own flesh and blood? Impossible! But then she remembered Lord Arnwell's suspicion that Fidelia Armiger was a false name — faithful esquire in Latin. Perhaps Margaret Pickering was her real name? Or the name of a good friend, perhaps, and there might still be something to be learnt from it. So she soldiered on with her Greek translation, but it was slow, difficult work.

She took to taking long walks. Sometimes she walked towards Delstone and its tiny shop selling a great profusion of goods. Often she met people she knew from church, who greeted her as a friend and invited her in for tea. Once she met Mrs Wellings and one of her daughters, and was invited back to the farm for buttermilk and plum cake. The following day, Mrs Wellings and two different daughters called at Boscobel Cottage. Felicia had friends!

Most of the time she walked far away from any houses, through the woods or onto the common beyond, and tried unsuccessfully not to think about Fin. She thought about Juliana and Margarita, too, and hoped they were getting on well with their new governesses, and that Fin was remembering to give them art lessons. She thought about the marquess, and hoped he was not sinking back into bitterness and loneliness. She even thought about Hercules, and wondered whether she should get a dog for herself.

Still, no matter how hard she tried not to, her thoughts were drawn mostly to Fin, and the letter he had written her. She had made a little case, painfully stitched over several days, to hold the several notes from him. The sorrowful *'Forgive me. Fabian.'* The more formal *'I should very much like to talk to you, if not inconvenient. Fabian.'* The pleading tone of *'Please come out.'*

And now, *'Dear Miss Oakes, I am to hold a ball in September. Please say you will come. Finlassan.'* More formal, since he had gone back to calling himself Finlassan. But a ball? Fin holding a ball? What on earth had got into him?

Always, when she thought about it, she wondered if she could bear it. To travel all that way, to see him again, perhaps even to dance with him... and then leave again as though nothing had happened. It was too much to expect of her, when she could hardly bear to be without him as it was.

So she walked, striding fiercely through the summer-green woods, head down, tears splashing unheeded down her face. There was a small pool buried deep within the woods that she remembered from her wood-gathering expeditions with Miss Armiger. Here she would sit and rest, weeping and rocking gently, aching to see Fin again and yet knowing that she must not. Each day she told herself that she was a little closer to peace of mind. She would never forget him, perhaps, but one day, sooner or later, she would be able to think of him with composure. And then she wept even harder.

It was on her return from one such walk that she first saw one of the Watchers, as she called them. She thought nothing of it, not then, for he was just a boy of perhaps sixteen or so, wearing the sort of rough clothes any of the farm labourers might wear. She heard a twig snap behind her, turned suddenly and there he was, not a hundred yards away. He froze and then, like a startled deer, ran off. The next day, she caught a glimpse of an older man, perhaps the boy's father. After that, she looked out for them and spotted one or other of them almost every time she left the house.

They were not local, for the parish was very small and she would have noticed them at church. If they had been carrying tools or bags, or had continued on their way like honest folk, she would have thought nothing of it, but they did not. Instead, when observed they ran away or melted into the woods. They seemed harmless, but how could she be sure?

One day, she decided to find out if they were truly following her or whether they were simply walking through the woods for reasons of their own. There was a path that curved around some dense bushes. Having discovered that the boy was following her, when she turned the corner, she stepped off the path and hid behind the bushes. In a very short time, the boy came round the corner and stopped with an exclamation, surprised by her disappearance.

Felicia scrambled out of her hiding place. "Looking for me?"

The boy jumped, then licked his lips. He swayed a little, as if poised for flight, but he did not run. Instead he held his hands up appeasingly. "We mean you no harm!"

"Who are you? What do you want?"

"We are friends, I assure you." His voice was cultured, educated. She saw now that his clothes, although plain, were of good quality, and the linen at his throat, even though it was carelessly knotted like a workman's, was freshly laundered. He was older than she had thought at first, perhaps twenty or so.

"Who *are* you? Why are you following me?" She took a step towards him and he turned and ran. Instantly, she gave chase, and at first she lost little ground to him, for he kept to the path. But then he plunged aside through a thicket of brambles, and she was not so incensed that she wanted to tear her skirts to shreds. "I will find out who you are!" she called after him.

But he was gone, and her threat was an idle one.

At dinner that night, she said, "Has anyone else seen two strangers wandering about, a young man of twenty or so and a man in his middle years?"

"Wandering about how?" Agnes said, eyes narrowed in suspicion.

"In the woods. I have seen them several times now, sometimes the younger man and sometimes the older."

"That will be the natura— um, nature… butterfly people," Jimmy Temple said. "They're staying over at the Nag's Head on the Fordingbridge road."

"Naturalists? I have seen no butterfly nets or any sort of equipment, and they are following me when I go on my walks."

"Following you?" Agnes said in horror. "*That* is not right!"

"Indeed not," Felicia said. "And they run away when challenged. At least, the boy does. His father is better at concealing himself, I think, so I am less aware of him, but when next I see him, I shall challenge him, too."

"You'll do no such thing!" Agnes said. "You'll stay right here at home while there are strange men wandering about, and you, too, Lilian. I'll mention it to Mrs Wellings, too. If you must go out, either of you, be sure to take Jimmy or Gerald with you."

"I shall certainly follow your advice," Felicia said. "In fact, if Jimmy will take me there in the gig, I shall visit the Nag's Head myself, I think."

But when they went there the next day, the strangers had decided there were insufficient butterflies to tempt them and had left. All they learnt was that they were father and son Mr Jameson and Mr Hubert Jameson, that they came from somewhere in the far north, Northumberland or perhaps Cumberland, they had paid their shot promptly and been very free with vails.

"They did not like being challenged, it seems," Felicia said. "Well, at least they have gone."

"For now," Jimmy said grimly. "You should still be very careful, Miss Oakes. It hasn't escaped anyone's notice that they only followed *you*. If they want something of you, they'll be back."

~~~~~

Fin wrestled with the translation wheel for days, making little progress. The letters of the alphabet were painted around the outer wheel, while the inner wheel showed three sets of letters — another alphabet, the alphabet in reverse and one with the letters jumbled up. The inner wheel revolved and could be held in position with a clip. If the correct position and which version of the inner alphabet to use were known, one might read the letter on the outer wheel and find the corresponding letter on the inner wheel and translate a coded message very quickly. Since Fin knew neither of these things, he floundered for some time, guessing at one combination or another without success, and almost gave it up altogether.

It was Saturday evening before he thought to tackle the problem systematically. He would start at 'A', try all three possible alphabets against the first ten letters of the code and see if he could make out any words. If not, he would move on to 'B'. Eventually, he would be bound to crack the code, assuming it had
~~~~~

been generated on just such a wheel, and if it had not… well, he would be stumped, and would have to wait until Giles returned. Giles! Still the real puzzle was why on earth he was receiving coded messages, and why they had to be directed to Hawkewood Hall and could not be sent to the parsonage. Very strange.

Fin worked methodically through the alphabet, until he came to the letter 'K', which yielded *'aareyousur'*. Almost he missed the significance, and was just about to move on when he realised.

"Are you sure!" he cried in triumph. "The next letter is 'E'." And so it was. When he had gone through the whole message, he read,

*'aareyousureheisgoneforgoodwillshebesafenowwritesoonwearerea dyfghi'.*

*"'Are you sure he is gone for good? Will she be safe now? Write soon. We are ready.'* What the devil does that mean? He? She? We?"

He reached for the decanter of brandy, and found it empty.

"Footman! *Footman!*" There was no response. With a tut of annoyance, he flung open the sitting room door. *"Footman!* Oh, there you are. What the devil do you mean by sleeping when you are on duty, man?"

"Beg pardon, my lord."

"I should think so. Fetch me more brandy, will you." Then, as the man smothered a yawn and turned to do his bidding, Fin had a sudden thought. "What time is it, Neil?"

"Wrong side of three, my lord."

Fin tutted in annoyance. "Then it is I who must beg your pardon. Forget the brandy and go to bed, man."

He sat down at his desk again, and stared at the paper before him. *'Are you sure he is gone for good? Will she be safe now? Write soon. We are ready.'* What could it mean? If it was intended for Giles, the people mentioned must be known to him. Only one 'he' had recently gone away — Godfrey Buckley. And if so, the 'she' could only be Felicia, the object of Buckley's attentions. Was she safe from him now? Who would ask such a question? And for what event were they ready?

Those questions could not be answered, but the more he thought about the matter, the more convinced he became that Felicia was involved somehow, and Giles too. Why else would he suddenly take an interest in her? And the Buckleys were surprisingly interested in a fatherless woman. But why should there be any question about her safety? She was certainly safe from Godfrey now, for either he had not spoken or she had refused him, and now he had gone, and she was far away from him. Yes, there was no risk from Buckley. Good, for she deserved better than that smooth-talking scoundrel.

*Was she safe?*

Should he write to Giles? It would be much easier to discuss it in person. He tucked the paper away in the desk. Whatever the solution to the mystery, it could not be resolved until Giles returned.

When Fin went to his room, he found Matthews fast asleep in the wing chair beside the fire. He sprang awake and with only one smothered yawn, helped Fin to undress.

"I am a great trial to you all, am I not?" Fin said. "I keep you up half the night without a thought for the inconvenience. I should run a more orderly household."

"That's what we're paid for, my lord," Matthews said equably. "An orderly household would be very dull, to my mind. Shotterbourne's an orderly household. That Miss Buckley keeps everything ticking over as regular as the church clock, so I hear. Meals at set hours, winter or summer, and menus planned a month in advance. Sounds dreadful boring to me."

"And to me," Fin said, with a wry smile, but he could not help wondering if Felicia — *was she safe?* — preferred to live in a world of regularity and calm, or one where anything might happen. The latter, he thought. Definitely the latter. But she would not abuse the servants as he had done. "Nevertheless, I must not take advantage of your good nature, Matthews. I do not need you to undress me at night, so you need not wait up for me in future, unless I ask you to do so."

"And then I'd find all your clothes tossed in a heap in the corner of the room, my lord, and the devil's own job to get them straight again. No, if it's all the same to you, I prefer to wait for you, so I can fold everything properly and put the trees in your boots."

Fin laughed. "Very well, Matthews, let it be so." He held his arms up so that Matthews could pull the nightgown over his head. "It is very agreeable to be ministered to with such keenness. Should you like it, do you suppose, if I were to travel occasionally? To London, say?"

Matthews' eyes glinted. "London! Are you planning to attend Parliament again, my lord?"

"It has been brought home to me that I *should* do so," he said, adjusting his nightcap. *Was she safe?* "I cannot say that the idea inspires me with any great enthusiasm, but it is my duty to do so," he added glumly. The thought flitted through his mind that Felicia would enjoy such a visit enormously. He sighed. "Is there any brandy up here, Matthews?"

"In the dressing room, my lord. In the cabinet just behind the door. I take it you won't be attending Morning Service at St Miriam's today, being as you're so late to your bed?"

"I must be a good Christian, must I not? Miss Oakes would insist upon it." *Was she safe?* "Wake me in good time, Matthews, and tell Padgett that we shall be going to London for the opening of Parliament. October… or whenever it is this year. He will need to have the travelling carriage in good order."

"Very good, my lord. Will there be anything else, my lord?"

"Nothing. Good night, Matthews. And thank you for being so patient with me."

Matthews' solemn countenance lightened into a smile. "My pleasure and privilege, my lord."

After Matthews had gone, Fin sat by the open window, knees pulled up to his chest, brandy in hand, thinking of London and all the sights in the metropolis to which he might take Felicia, and imagining her reactions to them all. She would  love it, of course! So much life to be observed in town, so many beautiful buildings, so many entertainments that she had never seen before… the theatre, the opera, Astley's, Hyde Park, Vauxhall Gardens, Almack's— no, not there. She would not be admitted. But the shops! Oh, how he longed to take her to every shop in Bond Street or Oxford Street and buy her whatever her heart desired. And jewels… how beautiful she would look adorned with proper jewels. Emeralds, perhaps, and diamonds, of course. Maybe some rubies… yes, rubies would be just the thing.

*Was she safe?*

Every once in a while, reality intervened to remind him that Felicia was no longer a part of his life, and he was conscious of a yearning emptiness inside him. What was she doing? Was she happy? Had she forgotten him altogether? Why had she not written? Surely she was not too busy to scribble a reply to his invitation!

He refilled his glass and ruthlessly suppressed such foolishness. Only when the brandy was gone did he crawl into bed and try very hard not to think about Felicia.

*But was she safe?*

# 23: Sermons And Lectures

Matthews shook Fin awake at some unearthly hour, setting a cup of chocolate beside the bed. Fin groaned, rolled over and closed his eyes again.

"You told me to wake you for church, my lord," Matthews said with what sounded suspiciously like glee in his voice.

"Uuurrgh. Time?"

"A quarter before nine, my lord."

"Oh, good God!" He hauled himself into a half-sitting position and groaned. He was not a man who habitually drank himself into a stupor, but it was fair to say that a certain quantity of brandy consumed the night before was not conducive to early morning health. His eyes were gritty from lack of sleep, his head was stuffy and his mouth was as dry as a sand dune. But he dutifully sipped the chocolate, while Matthews laid out his shaving gear and clothes, and after a while felt alive enough to allow himself to be prepared for the day.

*Was she safe?*

He would not think of that. The walk to church cleared his head somewhat, and he was able to snooze during the sermon, so he emerged from the church in rather better condition. Arnwell nodded at him.

"What time for dinner, Finlassan?"

"Five."

He grunted and turned towards his carriage. Fin was about to leave when he remembered that Giles was still away, and his absence had been greatly felt at the dinner table. Giles never said much to the point, but he could be depended upon to draw Drusilla's attention away so that Fin need not talk to her.

He turned back to find the curate. "Cotham! Excellent sermon, I am sure. Come for dinner tonight. We sit down at five."

Cotham's eyes gleamed with pleasure, and he bowed deeply. "Most obliged, my lord. How very kind." Another bow. "Too generous to a humble clergyman, who has no call at all upon your lordship's notice. So very obliging to—"

"No need to bob up and down like a turkeycock, man. Five, remember."

Drusilla caught up with him before he had reached the lych gate. "Mr Cotham? Dining with us?" she hissed. "What are you about, Fin? Do you know who his father is? A cooper in Derby! And you are inviting him to dine with *us!*"

"He is a clergyman, Drusilla. What does it matter who his father is? If he can eat his soup without dribbling he will be as welcome at my table as anyone else." And more than some, he almost added, but that was unfair. Drusilla was his sister and would always be welcome at his table, and he would try his best not to resent her censorious manner, if only for Felicia's sake.

*Was she safe?* He shivered.

"You realise that it will be only the two of you sitting over the port?"

"Not so, for Arnwell will be there."

"*Lord Arnwell?* You have invited Lord Arnwell for dinner?"

He turned away from her astonished face, and ignored her increasingly strident voice calling after him, telling him to talk to her and not to walk away from him in that high-handed manner. He cared nothing for Drusilla. Let her seethe. He beguiled the walk home with the pleasant glow that came from having done his duty for the day. Felicia would be proud of him, he was sure. He thought with pleasure of her pretty face smiling at him, her eyes glowing with approval. Such lovely eyes...although usually brimming with mischief, it was true. He smiled at the memory. What was she doing at that moment? Was she at church too? Was she wondering what he was doing? He hoped she was. For a moment he was overwhelmed with longing... to see her again, to hear her soft voice or the disdainful variant when he did something of which she disapproved. She was so beautiful when she upbraided him in that dignified way she had.

*Was she safe?* No... he would not drive himself mad with such thoughts. Buckley was gone and she was safe from him, at least, and Giles, whatever he was about in Southampton, had never shown the least interest in her. She was safe.

Drusilla arrived back at the Hall before him, her carriage rolling away just as Fin took the steps to the front door two at a time. His heart sank as he saw her face, and braced himself for the onslaught.

"How dared you ignore me in that insolent way, Fin! To treat your own sister with such abominable contempt is despicable. If I have something to say to you, then I shall certainly say it, you may be sure. Thank you, Neil, and here is my bonnet also. Ah, Mrs Shayne, help me with these buttons."

For a few moments, while she divested herself of her outer garments, there was a brief pause in hostilities. Fin tossed his hat, gloves and cane at Matthews and slunk out of the entrance hall. Naturally, Drusilla followed.

"Do not think you can escape me so easily, Fin."

Without breaking stride, he said, "I am going to my sitting room for brandy. A lot of brandy. Thus fortified, it is my earnest hope that my temper may survive whatever scolding you see fit to inflict upon me."

Padding alongside him, she continued her tirade unabated. "I wonder at you, Fin, truly I do. While it is gratifying that you are at last beginning to assume your responsibilities as a peer of the realm, you will do yourself no good if you choose to surround yourself with persons of a lower order like Cotham. He is a *curate*, for Heaven's sake. And to introduce such a man to Lord Arnwell is the outside of enough."

"Arnwell knows him. He sleeps through his sermons, just as we do."

"But he does not *dine* with him! No one of consequence would choose to dine with such a man."

"Why ever not? Cotham seems inoffensive to me, for a man of God. His manners are good enough, lacking only a little polish. His sermons show evidence of a certain quickness of mind, what I have heard of them, and he writes them himself, too. He is well-liked within the parish. There is nothing objectionable about inviting such a man to dine occasionally."

"What do his manners have to say to anything? He has no connections, no fortune or prospect of it, no patron to advance his career."

Fin stopped abruptly, so that Drusilla was obliged to skid to a halt too. She was breathing heavily from the fast walk. Fin's own breath was ragged. His temper hung by a thread. He reminded himself that Felicia would expect him to rise above such provocation, so when he spoke, his voice was measured. "You are far out there, for he has — or may well have — *my* patronage. If I like the man, I may give him the living at Eglington Hill when old Hawkins receives notice to quit. He must be ninety if he is a day, so it cannot be long."

"*Eglington Hill!* A living worth seven or eight hundred a year? For a man from nowhere? What madness is this? Eglington Hill is for Uncle Giles, you know that."

"Who has not the least need of it. He has two perfectly good livings already and an independent income as well. You want me to assume my responsibilities, Drusilla, so you must accept that I shall use my position to do a little good in the world, or my small corner of it, and help those worthy of help to advance themselves. If I deem Cotham worthy sof preferment, then I see no reason not to do something for him."

"What about family loyalties? To put a cooper's son above your own flesh and blood is—"

"Enough!" He strode forward into his sitting room and across to the sideboard where stood the brandy decanter, happily refilled after the depredations of the previous night. A little slopped over the side of the glass as he poured. Taking a long gulp, he turned to face the onslaught. There was no point in attempting to escape, for she was not a woman to be deterred from pressing her point.

"This is outrageous!" she said in a low voice. "You are so arrogant, Fin. You do what you want, always have done, with no regard for the wishes and feelings of other people and—"

"Not true," he said, stung. "Do you want to know why I attend St Miriam's? Why I take an interest in Arnwell? Why I want to help those who live in the shadow of Hawkewood? Not from any hectoring of yours, you may be sure!"

Drusilla's face darkened even more. How ugly she looked when she was angry, and she was almost always angry. "I know who you mean! That... that *nobody!* Oh yes, you listen to *her*, of course you do, but not to your own family! You would rather take the advice of that... that... *strumpet!*"

It was too much. The dam burst. He hurled the brandy glass past Drusilla's head so that it smashed against the wall in a cascade of sparkling glass slivers and amber spatters. Drusilla jumped away from the devastation with a squeak of fear, eyes wide.

"*Never, ever* speak of Felicia in those terms again," he growled. His fists were clenched impotently against his side. If any man had dared to speak so, he would have knocked him down and pounded him to pulp for his insolence. He might even have called him out. Yet women thought they could get away with anything, and Drusilla just never knew when to stop.

"Oh, Felicia, is it? Very cosy, I am sure. You have become obsessed with her, Fin, and who is she, truly? Some illegitimate nobody who fancies becoming a countess, no doubt. Just as well Giles and I got her away from you, because I doubt she would have left otherwise. You are an utter fool, and if ever you marry that insolent chit, that will be the day I wash my hands of you, and so I warn you."

He strode up to her, and, despite the defiant words, she backed hastily away from him until she could go no further and her back was to the wall.

"You know nothing at all about her," he hissed. "She has not the slightest ambition to become a countess, I assure you, and you wrong her greatly to speak so. Yes, I listen to her because she speaks with dignity, whereas you have never had an ounce of dignity in your life, Drusilla. You are a veritable Hell-cat, and lucky I still allow you over the threshold. I am not surprised you never married, but it would have done you a world of good to be taught a little conduct by a husband, and punished when you overstepped the mark, as you all too frequently do. I am utterly tired of your constant lectures, as if I were a child to be hounded into good behaviour. Such stratagems are not effective with children and they are certainly not effective with me. I am two and thirty years old, in possession of all my faculties and, as you continually remind me, a peer of the realm. I think I may order my life as I please, without reference to you or anyone else who accords me so little respect. Felicia points out all my weaknesses and failings, just as you do, but she does not harangue me or scream at me like a fishwife. She teaches by example. Since she herself is good and honourable and open-hearted, I wish — I very much wish — to be more like her. I try to model my behaviour on hers, and although there is still a long way to go, I believe there has been some progress. You have long wanted me to enter society once more, so you should be pleased that I am entertaining neighbours and holding a ball and—"

"A ball!"

"—going to London for the opening of Parliament."

"London!" she said, faintly.

"And yes, I shall consider marriage, in the fullness of time. Not yet, perhaps. Let me take just one step at a time."

"But not *her!*"

"Why the devil should I not, if I wished to?"

"You will ruin this family if you do, Fin. You will be beyond all hope of redemption. She is patently unworthy to be the wife of an earl."

"She is worth a thousand of *you,*" he spat. "Ten thousand. A hundred thousand. Get out of my sight, Drusilla. I am sick of your sanctimonious chattering. Footman! *Footman!* Clean up this mess."

~~~~~

Fin imagined he had seen the last of Drusilla for a while, but she was made of sterner stuff that took no offence, even at being called a Hell-cat, and compared unfavourably with a governess. She did not attend prayers in the chapel, but she arrived, attired in full evening dress, half an hour before dinner.
~~~~~

"We shall need another cover, Bagnall," Fin said. "We are in the Italian Room tonight, Drusilla."

"The Italian Room? Why, when you have a—? Well, as you please, naturally."

That was progress, that she had not questioned him endlessly about it. "I did not expect you to come tonight," he said, "and so I thought the round table would be more suitable for the small numbers." And the dining room was filled with memories of Felicia, but he did not mention that. Good memories, but still they weighed on him and reduced his spirits, and tonight he was determined to be a sociable host. Felicia would wish it so.

Drusilla nodded, although her lips were clamped shut in the effort not to protest. He knew what she would say — that the imposing dining room, with its gilded pillars and mirrors and the glorious painted ceiling, was a more fitting setting to entertain a marquess. But Arnwell was not likely to be impressed, and the Italian Room was altogether a more charmingly intimate room.

All afternoon, Fin had pondered how he would make his apology, but it had not occurred to him that he would be called upon to utter it quite so soon. But he knew how Felicia would do it — with simple words, and sincerity.

So he said quietly, "I am glad to see you here again, after the way I behaved this morning. I was an absolute bear, and I apologise unreservedly."

Her eyes widened in surprise, and she inclined her head slightly, but made no reply. By rights, she had some apologising to do too, but he had no expectation of it. Arnwell arrived just then, and the moment passed.

The evening was a success. Felicia's painting, so full of light and movement, was admired by all, even Drusilla, and Arnwell was touched to find himself depicted there, as well as Felicia herself, and Fin. Juliana and Margarita spotted their mother and father there, too, and although Margarita cried a little, the girls were happy to have such a charming remembrance of their parents.

At dinner, Drusilla sat between Arnwell and Cotham, and managed to be civil to both in equal degree. Fin had his two wards on either side of him, and Juliana, at least, was easy to talk to. The slightest of enquiries would induce a stream of information requiring little response. Margarita was less forthcoming, but she had her favourite topics which he was beginning to know. Her horse, the dog and anything to do with art were subjects on which she could speak with fervour. Miss Farrell and Miss Durward, the two governesses, were sensible, well-mannered women, although it grieved Fin to see them there when it should be Felicia.

"Have you heard from Miss Oakes?" he asked Margarita.

"Oh yes! She wrote when she first arrived in Southampton, and described the hotel where she was staying. Then she wrote again when she moved to her cottage. May we write to her? Miss Farrell said she has a new life now and might not be interested in what we are doing anymore, but I think she would."

"I should think that Miss Oakes must be wondering how you are getting on, and would be reassured to know that you are happy and progressing in your studies," he said. "It is my considered opinion that she would be pleased to receive a letter from you. She must miss you."

"We miss her too," Margarita said.

"Margie!" Juliana said, glaring at her. Then, turning to Fin, she said with rigid formality, "We are very content with our new governesses, my lord, and are grateful to you for providing them for us. And to Lady Drusilla, also," she added hastily, realising that Fin had had very little to do with it.

He smiled at them with understanding. "I am sure you are, Juliana, but you may be very happy with the present arrangement and yet still regret the loss of Miss Oakes. There is no disloyalty in that."

"No, indeed," said Miss Farrell. "Your feelings do you credit, girls, but do eat up, Margarita. It is most impolite to keep the rest of the table waiting. Juliana, sit up straight, dear."

When the table was being cleared ready for the second course, Fin leaned down to whisper in Margarita's ear. "Miss Oakes was very special, was she not? We all miss her."

She nodded and smiled conspiratorially at him.

When the ladies had withdrawn, Fin moved round the table to take Drusilla's seat between Arnwell and Cotham, Bagnall left the port on the table and he and the footmen withdrew. They talked at first on indifferent topics — the harvest, the new miller, Cotham's sermon, his scholarly treatise on the Ancient Greeks and their culture, an oak tree that had come down in the village blocking the Ashbourne road temporarily — but after a while, Cotham withdrew and Fin returned to the subject that was never very far from his mind.

"Have you heard from Felicia lately?"

The marquess shook his head. "Not a word, but Warborough must write, surely?"

"Not to me, and not much to Drusilla, either. There has been no word for weeks, and I should like to know that she is well and safe."

"Safe!" Arnwell said. "Is there any reason to suppose otherwise?"

Fin had not intended to mention it, but now that the word had slipped out, why not? Who better to discuss the matter than Arnwell, who knew both Felicia and Buckley. So he told him all about the coded letter that he had uncovered, and the translation of it.

"It can only refer to Buckley, would you not agree?" he said eagerly. "And therefore it must be Felicia whose safety is at issue, and surely she is safe, since she is gone to Hampshire and Buckley to Lincolnshire. Do you not think it must be so?"

Arnwell frowned, stroked his chin, tapped his disfigured hand on the table. He reached for the decanter, refilled his port glass and sipped.

"Who could have written this letter?" he said eventually. "A message in code, a means of communication used only by your father and a few close friends. Who?"

"There were six that I know of. Three are now dead, and one might as well be, one had to make a run for the continent and the sixth gambled away a good part of his fortune and has lived quietly in the country ever since. None of them have kept in touch since my father died twelve years ago."

"His friends, yes, but who else? Who within the family?"

"No one that I know of."

"You do not recognise the hand?"

"Not at all."

"Hmm. Yet there is one in the family, at least, who understands the coded system — Warborough. His brother. So who else do you suppose might know of it?"

"He was never close to anyone else in the family, besides his brothers, so—" Fin's blood ran cold. "*Percival?* No!"

"Why not? If that thieving, murdering Hell hound is still in the world somewhere, why might he not be still in communication with his brother? He cannot write directly to Warborough for some reason — perhaps someone might recognise the hand — so he directs the letters to you, knowing you will not open it, but if anyone else should, such as a secretary, the contents will be unreadable."

Fin reluctantly saw the logic in it. "But then why would he ask about Buckley and Felicia? It must be about them, for who else left here recently, who else might not be safe? Who else would Uncle Giles know about? Why would Percival care what happens here, if he even survives?"

"Oh, he survives," Arnwell said grimly. "That... that *devil* watched my house burn to the ground with my wife and all my children inside, and calmly opened my safe and stole twenty thousand pounds. Whether he started the fire or not, he left them to *die*, and then ran away. He is alive, I am sure of it, and I hope he is enjoying his life in this world for he will surely burn in the next. He will burn, just as my lovely Alexandria did."

He stopped, shaking, and covered his face with his good hand. Fin watched helplessly, not knowing what to say. What would Felicia do? He remembered her simple words at

Shotterbourne when the conversation had become awkward… always simple words.

"I am so sorry," Fin said.

Arnwell lifted his head, and looked straight at him, the tears in his eyes clear to see. "Finlassan, I do not know the answer to your mystery, and perhaps only your uncle can reveal it, but on the other matter that troubles you, there I can offer some advice."

"What other matter?"

"The question of Felicia Oakes. Do not delay, that is what I would say to you, for every day wasted in dithering is a day lost. If I had known that last year how little time remained to me with my beloved Alexandria, I would have savoured every moment. Follow your heart, Finlassan. I said as much to that oily upstart Buckley — marry where your heart is, I told him, and I tell you the same now."

Fin's world spun. Was that how the marquess saw it, that he was *in love* with Felicia? "*Marry* her?" he croaked. "You are mistaken if you see anything more than… more than…" Was it true? Could it possibly be true? "No…"

The marquess chuckled. "You are obsessed with her, Finlassan. How many times have you mentioned her this evening, and I would wager you thought of her a hundred times more. You are head over heels in love with the girl. Go and find her, talk to her and settle the matter once and for all. And while you are there, you can ask that devious uncle of yours why he is receiving coded messages from a lily-livered scoundrel like Percival Warborough."

# 24: In Pursuit

Amongst Felicia's earliest and most frequent visitors was Mr Giles Warborough. He always arrived bearing gifts — flowers, bottled apricots, brandy, a cheese knife and some sheet music, to all of which she smiled and thanked him effusively. He then sat in the back parlour, drinking Madeira and eating whatever Eliza had baked that day, or else walked about the garden admiring the beans and melons. He was endlessly fascinated by tales of Felicia's childhood, and insisted on sitting in the old schoolroom while she described its former arrangement and the lessons she was taught.

Sometimes he brought Mrs Pollard and Jane with him. He had rented a barouche from the Dolphin, and on fine days he took the ladies out for a drive in the countryside, which often ended at Boscobel Cottage. Then there was an impromptu picnic in the garden, or a walk through the woods where Mr Warborough gallantly escorted Jane and Mrs Pollard quizzed Felicia about her noble friends. Felicia was now a person to be cultivated, it seemed, despite her lowly origins.

"So grateful to you for introducing Mr Warborough into our humble circle," Mrs Pollard gushed. "So gentlemanly, but one would expect no less from the son of an earl. Do you make a long stay in Hampshire, Miss Oakes? You must be longing to return to Derbyshire."

"I am permanently settled here," she said.

"But your charges! The dear little girls! You will be needed, I make no doubt."

"Not at all, unfortunately. The Miss Kearneys have two governesses, both far more qualified than I."

"Kearney, eh. So they take their father's name rather than their mother's. A pity. Dulnain is a far more distinguished name. Who has ever heard of the Kearneys?" When Felicia made no reply, she went on, "But I am certain you will be returning to Hawkewood Hall in the fullness of time, Miss Oakes. The earl's wards may not need you as a governess, but perhaps you will be needed in some other capacity? You look innocent, but his lordship's attentions are most marked. Why else would he send you here in a post-chaise and four, accompanied by his own uncle, a footman and a maid?"

Felicia was too much astonished at the accuracy of her information to take umbrage at the assumption. Had Mrs Pollard been listening to the servants' gossip at the Dolphin Hotel? At least now her sudden friendliness was accounted for, if she believed that Felicia would shortly become a countess.

"I assure you, ma'am, you are entirely mistaken in supposing that Lord Finlassan's consideration arose from any motive other than kindness towards an employee."

Mrs Pollard smiled knowingly and smoothly changed to a less personal topic of conversation, leaving Felicia assailed by doubt. Fin had never been noted for his kindness, so perhaps there was more to it. Not marriage, clearly, for a bastard could hardly marry an earl, but something else, perhaps. Something less savoury? No, impossible. He had never shown the least hint of desire towards her, honourable or otherwise. His generosity was exactly as it seemed.

Once she had begun to use the front parlour again, Mr Warborough asked if he might look at it.

"I am fascinated by your Miss Armiger," he said. "Such a curious person to have charge of a young child, for she seemed most unsuited to such a position. I should like to see her private domain, that I might understand her better."

Felicia could not see the purpose to understanding a woman who had been dead for twelve years, but she willingly allowed him into the front parlour and watched as he thumbed through the books on the shelves and examined the pile of yellowed newspapers.

"Ah, the Gazette!" he cried. "Such dull books… sermons, history, more history, ancient history… a great reader of history. More sermons, a book about Greece, works by Homer, Plato, Euripedes, Aristotle…"

"No novels," Felicia said, much struck.

"Hmm? No, she cared nothing for novels. More Homer, Socrates, Anaximander… Who is Anaximander?"

*'She cared nothing for novels.'* What an odd thing to say, almost as if he had known her.

When the visit was over, Felicia returned to the front parlour and drew out the notebook she had found, reading over the inscription. *'The History of Miss Margaret Pickering, being an account true in every particular of her humble birth, her education, her rise to a distinguished and responsible position, and her present circumstances, including many adventures and trials of her fortitude.'*

She was now certain that notebook was no novel, for why should anyone write a novel who never read one? In which case, it must indeed be a true account of a real person, a friend of Miss Armiger's… or Miss Armiger herself? Yet it was so hard to read! With a sigh, she found her Greek primer, and settled down to work.

~~~~~

Fin's journey south was as fast as four horses and good roads could make it, but it still felt tediously slow. Now that he had made the decision to find Felicia, he was impelled to do so *at once*, immediately, without delay, and every change of horses, every toll-gate, every stop for food or a few hours' rest fretted him beyond endurance. They drove for every hour of daylight, stopping only when Padgett grumbled that it was too dark to see his own whip, let alone the horses, and then Fin merely paced about his room until the first lightening of the pre-dawn skies. He was so exhausted that he slept in the carriage, waking with aching head and a furious temper. If only he could fly there, like a bird, and not crawl on the earth like some accursed snail.

Eventually they reached Southampton and the Dolphin Hotel, but the news was not good. Yes, Miss Oakes had stayed there briefly but she had left and they had no knowledge of where she had gone.

"Boscobel Cottage, man. She lives at Boscobel Cottage."

"I regret, my lord, that I have no knowledge of such a place."
~~~~~

"Well then, what of Mr Giles Warborough, my uncle? He is here, is he not?"

"Unfortunately, he is not. He moved out shortly after Miss Oakes, I know not where."

"But I write to him here," Fin said. "What happens to those letters?"

"We take such missives back to the post office, my lord. Mr Warborough's man no doubt collects them from there."

"If my uncle is even in Southampton still."

"Oh, he remains in the town, my lord, for he has taken out a subscription to the summer balls here at the hotel. He always attends those."

"Well, that is something. When is the next ball?"

"Wednesday se'nnight, my lord. You may care to enquire at the post office, my lord, or perhaps at the circulating library. Either may have an address for Miss Oakes or Mr Warborough."

But they did not. The post office knew the names, but their letters were collected, not delivered. Nor did any of the likely shops have the direction of either, although they all knew Felicia. "Oh, Miss Oakes, yes, indeed, sir. She lives at Summer Cottage in Itchen. Charming lady." No one knew her new address.

On his second day in Southampton, Fin tracked down the office of Mr Pierce, Felicia's attorney, who had sent on Juliana's paintings. Pierce himself was not there and his clerk regretted that he could not on his own authority release the address of a client, not even for an earl. His superior would doubtless be happy to do it, but he could not himself take the liberty. His lordship would understand, he was sure. If his lordship would care to leave his card, he would see that Mr Pierce attended to his enquiry at the earliest opportunity.

Fin then made a systematic trawl through every single shop on the High Street, without success. He remembered the school where Felicia had taught, and after a couple of false starts, located Miss Latimer's Academy. The two Miss Latimers, one fat, one thin, cooed over him and entertained him to tea and macaroons and a very small glass of sherry, while regaling him with gushing tales of Felicia's many talents. She had called upon them three times, they revealed — so thoughtful of her, so gratifying that she remembered her old teachers — but they had no idea where she lived.

"Somewhere to the north of the town, I believe, was it not, sister? Or to the west. No, definitely the north. I think."

Since almost the entire Kingdom was to the north of Southampton, this was less than helpful. They showed him around the school, pointed out three of Felicia's works hanging on the walls, and hoped he would remember them if ever he decided to send his wards to school.

It was a hot day, and eventually, worn out and dispirited, he withdrew to his private parlour at the Dolphin, tossed aside his coat and waistcoat, ordered brandy and settled down to get seriously drunk, for what else was there to do? He had come all this way to find Felicia and she was nowhere to be found.

Tomorrow was Sunday, and a day of enforced idleness, but on Monday he would begin again. Perhaps Mr Pierce would be helpful, but if not, he would obtain a map and search for likely locations, and then he would hire a horse and ride to every village within a twenty mile radius. Boscobel Cottage might not be in a village, but Felicia would go to church somewhere, and once he found her parish, he would find the cottage.

He sat on the desk in front of the window, brandy glass in hand, looking down on the scurrying figures on the High Street, and thought about Felicia. Was it love, this shivering, all-consuming feeling? Arnwell had called it obsession, and that it was. Just as he was obsessed with his art, so he was obsessed with his muse, the fellow artist who inspired him. But was there more to it? Did he feel now the way he had felt about Juliana?

That was a surprisingly difficult question to answer. His memories of Juliana which he had once thought imperishable had become muted over time. He was aware that she had filled him with radiant joy, but he could not quite grasp the feeling itself. Somehow the warmth, the exquisite delight, the *rightness* he had felt when he was with her had thinned and almost blown away. All that remained was tenuous, like the last wisp of smoke when the candle is snuffed out.

With Felicia — he smiled as he thought of her, he could not help himself. He felt an affection for her that was more than mere friendship. Gratitude, perhaps. She had forced him out of his grief-induced solitude, forced him to face the world again. No, more than that, she had forced him to face himself, to understand his own weaknesses and try to improve himself. He was a better person because of her.

But was that love? He could not say. All he knew was that he wanted to see her again, hear her voice, see her smile... If only he—

There she was!

He cried out in joy, for there on the street below was the achingly familiar light step that made her skirts sway a little, the bonnet and pelisse he knew so well. She was scurrying along, head down, rushing somewhere… moving rapidly away from him. He jumped up and out of the room, taking the stairs two at a time, so that passers-by had to jump out of his way or flatten themselves against the walls. Someone called out to him but he could not stop. The least delay would be fatal! He must catch up with her, he must!

Out of the door and down the street he flew. Where was she… he had lost her! No, there she was, far ahead of him.

"Felicia! *Felicia!* Stop!"

She walked on unheeding, and he ran, ran, ran, long strides eating up the pavement. Someone crashed into him. He ran on.

*"Felicia!"*

She turned, saw him, stopped, waited, her face filled with amazement.

"Felicia…" Now that she was before him, almost within arm's reach, her head tipped to one side in amused puzzlement, he could not say a word. He had no idea what to say to her.

"Fin? Whatever are you doing?"

"I… I had to see you. To know if you are safe… well. Are you well?"

She giggled. "I am well, as you see, but why are you out in the street without a coat? You will take a chill in this rain."

It was raining, he discovered. His face was wet, and her bonnet dripped. His shirt was soaked. "I had not noticed. Why did you not write to me? You did not reply to my letter. Will you come? To the ball? It is for you."

Her face registered dismay. "Fin, you are insane. Where are you staying? The Dolphin?" She looked about her, considering. "Mr Pierce's office is just across the street. Let us go in there, and perhaps they will have a fire to warm you while someone goes to the Dolphin to fetch your coat."

"What does that matter?" he cried. "Felicia, tell me at once, are you happy?" A shadow crossed her face. Not happy, then. "Is it Uncle Giles? Is he pursuing you? He must be, or why else would he subscribe to the balls?"

Those expressive eyes displayed astonishment at that idea. "Mr Warborough? I assure you that any pursuit in which he is engaged is not directed at me. Will you not come inside out of this rain? I have no idea why you have come here, but I would not have you struck down with a fever because of it."

"I came to find you. I was worried about you."

She took his arm, and he allowed himself to be led meekly across the road, dodging between passing carts, and through a door. A young man came forward, the clerk he had spoken to earlier that day.

"Do you have a fire in your parlour?" Felicia said. "Lord Finlassan is very wet, and must warm himself at once."

Another door opened, and Fin followed them into the room. The fire was already lit, burning low, but the clerk fiddled about with coals and the poker until it blazed brightly. Felicia pulled Fin across the room to stand in front of it as the clerk withdrew.

"Now," she began, "you can tell me—"

"You are not happy," he burst out. "Why? Is it Buckley? Did he raise your hopes and—?" She was smiling and shaking her head. "Not Buckley? Then is it something *I* did? If I offended you—"

"No, no! You did nothing wrong."

"Why did you leave?" he said. "I did not want you to leave and there was no need."

"There was every need," she said firmly. "My position at Hawkewood was only ever intended to be temporary, remember? Just until a governess could be engaged. Now that that has been done—"

"What does that matter? The girls still need you. *I* need you. You must come back, Felicia."

Now her expression changed again, but he could not read it this time. "No," she said softly. "I have no place there."

"How can you say so? You will always have a place there, to set me straight and keep me in order, to inspire me, for I cannot manage without you."

Anger. She drew herself up straighter, moving away from him, and her eyes flashed contemptuously. "Of course you can! You know precisely what you ought to do and how you ought to behave. You are not a child, Fin. You will not do to me what you did to the Lady Juliana. I will not allow you to turn me into some kind of idol who dominates your life."

"But you are my muse."

"Your prisoner, you mean. Do you not see how cruel it is? All my life I have had to imagine the perfect life that reality denied me. A father who was rich or noble or heroic, a mother who loved me and wept when I was torn from her despairing arms, a family who discovered their lost daughter with cries of joy and swept me away to a world free of want and wrapped me in unwavering affection. Of course I knew it was all lies, but it comforted me when I was alone, and kept me from misery. But then you came along and gave me a tantalising glimpse of the life I had always envisaged. Your beautiful house, the estate, the glories of Derbyshire. When I was there the dreams and the truth merged until I could not tell one from another. I began to put down roots there, to feel as if I belonged and that was so dangerous, for the truth is that there is no place for me there. I am an interloper, I know that. I left because I had to and it was the hardest thing I have ever done. If I return, it would be ten times harder to leave again, and yet I must."

"Why? Why must you ever leave? Come back and stay for ever."

Her face was white. "I cannot. Do not ask it of me."

"Why not?"

"Because it cannot possibly be for ever. One day you will marry and your wife will certainly not want me there."

The door opened and a man peered round it. "Get out!" Fin said. The man scuttled away.

Felicia laughed suddenly. "Poor Mr Pierce!"

He stared at her, flummoxed. How could he persuade her? Why could she not see how much he needed her? No matter what she said, he could not see how he could go on with his life without her. She was indispensable to him, utterly essential to his happiness...

Then he knew the answer. He knew his own mind as certainly as he knew that the sun would rise tomorrow.

"Marry me," he said.

She became utterly still, her eyes wide with shock, her lips slightly apart.

"Please… marry me."

She put her hands in front of her mouth, so that all he could see of her face was the huge eyes staring at him. Such expressive eyes! The initial shock was giving way to something else… hope? Desire? Or was that his own wish imposing itself?

"Felicia? Will you marry me?"

She crossed her arms across her chest. "Yes. I will. I will marry you." She gave a little laugh. "I ought to be noble and self-sacrificing and protest that I am unworthy to be the wife of an earl — which is perfectly true — but I cannot do it. I want to marry you so badly… have wanted it almost since I first met you. I know I ought to refuse, but I love you far too well to contemplate it. I will marry you, yes."

Joy coursed through him, filling him with delicious warmth. He was giddy with happiness, and could feel a broad smile spreading across his face. She was his! She would never leave him, and the world was in perfect harmony. He laughed in delight.

# 25: Running Away

A discreet cough made Felicia jump.

"Oh! Oh, Mr Pierce."

"May I intrude for a moment? Is there anything your lordship requires? A towel, perhaps? Some brandy?"

Fin laughed again, and shook his head. "No brandy." He seemed… happy. Yes, happy. Perhaps he would regret his impulsive offer later but for the moment, Felicia could see that the tension had dropped away from him, and the intensity in his gaze had softened. There was a warmth in his eyes when he looked at her.

While Mr Pierce fussed around Fin, Felicia had a moment to wonder at her situation. She had gone in moments from despair and dark misery, through fear of her unknown pursuers to the astonishment of seeing Fin, dripping wet, barrelling down the High Street towards her. He had come to find her! He *cared* about her. And then the most shattering moment of all, those world-changing words — *'Marry me'*. In a haze of delirious selfishness, she had accepted him. They were, she supposed, betrothed, at least until some other impulse crossed his mind, and he thought better of it.

"I believe you wished to see me, my lord?"

"Did I? Oh… no, I have found what I was looking for." A quick glance at Felicia, and there was that warmth again.

"Then perhaps you are merely *sheltering* from the rain?" Mr Pierce said.

Felicia remembered her mission. "I wished to see you, but…" She glanced uncertainly at Fin. "Perhaps another day?"

"Now is as good a time as any, if Mr Pierce is free to attend to you." Then, hesitantly, he went on, "If you wish to consult him alone…"

She was gripped with a fear that if he went away he would have time to reflect on his rashness and change his mind, so she said quickly, "Not at all. It is nothing secret."

They went through to Mr Pierce's office, where chairs resistant to the effect of damp breeches and pelisses were found, and the fire was built up to satisfactory levels, warm enough to raise steam from their drying clothes. Felicia explained about the two men she had seen, who seemed to be following her, or perhaps watching her, for she had seen them only the day before as she left the shop in the village. Realising that they were observed, they had quickly vanished behind the church, and she had not felt it seemly to chase after them through the churchyard.

"They do not *approach* you, or accost you in any way?" Mr Pierce said, polishing his spectacles vigorously before replacing them carefully on his nose.

"Not at all, and I do not feel that they intend me harm, but what can they mean by it? Is there anything that may be done to deter them? Should I alert the constables, do you think?"

"As to the latter, it seems to me that you have no *need* for such *assistance*." He beamed at her, and then at Fin. "You have a powerful *protector* now, I believe."

"It is unsettling," Fin said, frowning. "I do not like it. We should return to Derbyshire at once."

"At once!" Felicia said. "I can hardly leave instantly, and it is Sunday tomorrow."

"Next week, then," Fin said. "Monday. Pack a few things, and I will make the arrangements. We can send for the rest of your belongings later. I will not have you hounded by these men."

There was no arguing with Fin in such a mood. Nor did she wish to, for a speedy return to Hawkewood Hall and the announcement of their betrothal exactly accorded with her wishes. Only when they had faced Lady Drusilla's outrage would she be certain whether this abrupt betrothal would stand, for she could not depend upon it. Somewhere inside her was a knot of fear. He had asked her to marry him, but he had spoken not one word of love. He had called her his muse, not his beloved, and perhaps he married her as the only way to keep his muse close. But if that was all this marriage should be, she would accept it gladly. At least she would be with him, would share his life, and that was enough.

She left the men to discuss details. One of the juniors returned from the Dolphin with Fin's coat and hat, although he had forgotten the gloves. Somewhat drier, and more respectably dressed, Fin offered his arm and they stepped out of the attorney's office onto a street already bathed in sunshine again, although the road still streamed with water, the puddles gently steaming in the afternoon heat.

They had not taken ten paces when Felicia stopped abruptly. It was the two men who were following her! They stood a little further up the street with their backs to Felicia, together with—!

She gave a squawk of outrage. Grabbing Fin's arm tightly, she dragged him into the nearest shop, a grocer's. "They are there!" she hissed. "The men of whom I spoke. They are right there on the street, and they are *talking to Mr Warborough!*"

She pointed them out to him, and he peered through the window. Within moments, the group broke up, the two unknown men disappearing down Broad Lane, while Mr Warborough walked on down the street and passed by the grocer's shop window. They quickly hid behind the sacks of rice and when they next dared to look, he was gone.

"He knows them!" Felicia cried. "Mr Warborough *knows* those men!"

"That settles it," Fin said firmly. "We leave at once. Whatever Uncle Giles is up to, it is nothing good, that much is certain. You will be safe at Hawkewood. Come, let us go back to the Dolphin and have the horses put to."

"Today?"

"Immediately, or as soon as Matthews has packed for me."

"What about my things? I need to go back to the cottage—"

"Too dangerous."

"But I shall have to tell Agnes, and Jimmy Temple is waiting for me at the Star with the gig. I must have some clothes, Fin."

He grunted. "Very well, but we will go in my carriage, not the gig. I will see that this Temple fellow gets word, but only after we have left. We must take no risks until we know what is going on."

She could not think that such urgency was called for, but as it showed a pleasing concern for her wellbeing she made no further protest. As they turned to leave, they found the grocer bowing and smiling at them.

"Good afternoon, madam. Good afternoon, sir. What may I offer you? We have an excellent range of teas, newly arrived direct from China."

"Nothing," Fin said, and would have turned directly for the door.

Felicia tugged on his sleeve. "We should buy something, since we have made use of the grocer's shop. Not tea, perhaps, but—"

"Something to please the young lady," the grocer said eagerly. "Some dried figs? Or something sweet? I have some delicious sugared almonds."

"We will take some of those," Fin said, smiling down at Felicia in the most heart-stopping way. "A pound… no, two pounds. You may eat them on the journey, my dear."

*My dear.* It was not quite the affectionate endearment she might have hoped for, but it reassured her that her future husband was not indifferent to her, and saw her as something more than an inspiration for his art.

<center>~~~~~</center>

It was astonishing what could be accomplished in a short time by an earl who was entirely certain that the world revolved around his wishes. He stormed around the Dolphin Hotel issuing orders

324

and he did not even need to raise his voice. His size, the windmilling arms and the peremptory tone were enough to have minions scuttling hither and thither as if he were the King himself. Within an hour, they were on the road, complete with the bemused sister of the head ostler, a stout matron hustled into her Sunday best to provide respectable chaperonage for Felicia.

With some difficulty, for she was still unfamiliar with the roads, Felicia directed the carriage to Boscobel Cottage, where she scooped a few clothes and other essentials into a portmanteau. Agnes followed her from room to room, wringing her hands.

"But why the haste? Why not wait until Monday, at least? Let us give you a proper farewell."

"Lord Finlassan insists."

"Is it about these men you have seen? Jimmy can protect you. This is too sudden a start, Felicia. What does he want of you, this Lord Finlassan, whisking you away so suddenly?"

Felicia smiled. "He wants to marry me, Agnes, and I have accepted him."

Agnes squealed with excitement, and there were no further objections. A man violently in love, as she supposed him to be, may be permitted whatever sudden starts his ardour demanded. With only a few tears and hugs, and many wishes for their future happiness, her friends waved Felicia away to her new life and she left Boscobel Cottage behind.

"I had barely grown accustomed to living there," Felicia said. "Who knows when I shall return?"

"Never, I trust," Fin said, but he made it a simple statement of fact, not an affectionate hope.

Was this marriage no more than a pragmatic acceptance? He was still in love with Juliana, and so he did not care whom he married. Felicia could be obtained without effort on his part, and he would have his muse and satisfy his need for an heir at one and the same time. It was a dispiriting thought.

Felicia leaned back against the squabs and watched the countryside go by. The harvest was in and the fields were bare, and even the trees were tinged with brown. Autumn was not far away. She tried very hard not to cry. It would be all right. She would make him happy and they would be content together. She had never expected love from him, after all, so she was not disappointed. She would *not* be disappointed.

~~~~~

Fin in haste was not a man to be deterred by trivial obstacles. At every stop, the clink of coins ensured that a fresh team was put to at once, or a hot meal presented, or rooms found, even in the busiest coaching inn. On Saturday he insisted that they push on even after it grew dark, and there was to be no delay even for the Sabbath. Only when Felicia protested did he reluctantly concede to an early stop so that she might read her Prayer Book for a while before dinner. While her chaperon, Mrs Cleat, took her temporary rôle as lady's maid to heart and unpacked a change of clothes for the evening, Felicia took the Prayer Book down to their private parlour.

When she opened it, a paper fluttered to the floor.

"A letter from one of your horde of admirers?" Fin said with a smile, handing it back to her.
~~~~~

"Sadly, not so. If I have ever had such a horde, they remained remarkably reticent. No, this is a copy I took of a strange letter someone sent to you. I thought it might be in code but—"

"You have a copy of it! Uncle Giles took the original and I had supposed that to be the end of the matter. Let me see," Fin said eagerly. "Good God, so it is. Look, look at this one that arrived more recently, and here is my translation of it." He pulled two papers from his waistcoat pocket.

"You can read the code!" she cried. "Oh, but... what does it mean? Who has gone away? Who is not safe? *'We are ready.'* This is all terribly ominous. Can you read this one, too?"

"I can try," he said grimly.

He fetched paper and writing equipment, and settled down at the table with the letter while Felicia read her Prayer Book. Even when Mrs Cleat crept in he did not stir, his concentration absolute. Felicia slipped out to bathe and change into a clean gown. When she returned to the parlour, he looked up at her with a grin and pushed a paper across the table to her.

*'K has been delivered of another fine son praise God. O is in good heart. We propose to return to S next year regardless. Be of good cheer. This will soon be over. P'*

The inn servants came in just then to prepare the table for dinner, and Mrs Cleat arrived too, so there was no further opportunity to discuss the letter, although Felicia was bursting with curiosity. Only when they had eaten and Mrs Cleat had fallen into a doze beside the fire, did she whisper, "What does it mean? Who is K or O or P? Where is S?"

He put his finger to his lips, then crossed the room. "Mrs Cleat? You are exhausted. We will not object if you go to bed."

She yawned copiously. "Oh, indeed, no, my lord. I'm not at all tired, and it's still early. It can't be much after six."

"Almost seven, and we shall be leaving at first light tomorrow. I would not have you deprived of your rest. Shall I ask for a supper tray to be sent up to your room? Some ham, perhaps, and a glass of something to settle you before bed. Will that not be agreeable?"

"Oh… well… if Miss Oakes will forgive me. I *am* rather tired. Not used to travelling at such speed."

"Of course you are not. We have imposed upon your good nature shockingly. There now, up you come. Waiter! *Waiter!* A supper tray for Mrs Cleat, if you please, with ham and a glass of wine. Yes, now, of course now. Go to it, man. Good night, Mrs Cleat."

Gleefully, he shut the door. "At last! I cannot imagine why she lingers when she must know she is not wanted."

"She is protecting my reputation," Felicia said, bubbling with laughter. "I daresay you are paying her a great deal of money to do so."

"I am not paying her to protect you from *me*," he said. "Besides, it was only a hundred pounds."

"Only—! I daresay she has never had so much money in her life. No wonder she is zealous. But tell me at once about this letter."

He poured himself another glass of claret and sat down beside her at the table, pulling his chair very close to hers. His nearness made her a little dizzy.

"I do not know what most of these letters mean, but P is Percival."

"*Percival!* Your uncle? The one who disappeared with all that money? But… why does he write to you in code?"

"That is a very good question," he said, smiling at her in a way that made her stomach flip-flop alarmingly. But she no longer needed to fear his smiles. He was her betrothed, and he could smile at her all he wished, and she at him.

But her smiles did not have the same devastating effect on him, for he continued calmly, "It is my belief that these coded letters are intended for Uncle Giles. Perhaps there is some reason why they could not be sent to the rectory — oh, Sayers, of course, my uncle's man. He haunts the tap room at the Shotter Arms, and is a regular blabbermouth, so that would account for it. Uncle Percival writes to me, therefore, since Uncle Giles would have told him that I never open my mail. In fact, now that I think about it, it was Uncle Giles who encouraged me to leave all that to him. But Uncle Percival wrote in code just in case I should decide to open the letters myself, or should ask a helpful governess to do so…" He smiled at Felicia so warmly that she grew hot with confusion. "How charming you are when you blush," he said conversationally. "However, my uncles are not aware that my father taught me a little of the skills required to interpret such codes. I am quite sure these letters are from Uncle Percival."

"Then he has been writing for some time," Felicia said. "He writes of people and places well known to your uncle. '*K has been delivered of another fine son...'* These letters have been coming for years, Fin."

His face hardened. "The conclusion is inescapable, is it not? Uncle Giles has known all this time where Uncle Percival is and everything he is doing. He is a *traitor*. But now that I know of his betrayal, I shall be sure to get it all out of him. It is unconscionable that he should be keeping such information secret."

They fell silent, and Felicia pondered the oddity of a situation where Fin's own uncle knew where Percival Warborough had gone to, and everything he had done. Had he married? Was the mysterious K, delivered of a son, his wife? Nineteen years since he left, with twenty thousand pounds in his pocket. He could have a whole new life somewhere.

Fin was staring at her with unnerving intensity.

"What is it?" she said apprehensively.

He licked his lips. "I..." A little cough. His hands were twitching repeatedly. "I should like to kiss you. If that would not be disagreeable to you."

Was he embarrassed? She laid one hand on his. "I should like that very much."

He stood, and she stood too. How should they position themselves? How awkward it was!

"I have never done this before," she said.

"Neither have I."

"Oh. Not even with—?"

"No. Should I...?"

He moved a little closer, and slid his arms around her. His nervousness was so sweet. She reached up one hand to stroke his face, and he closed his eyes and let out a gentle sigh. His cheeks were rough, in need of a shave.

"Fin. Look at me."

He opened his eyes, and smiled at her. Such warmth in his smile! Impulsively, she stood on her toes and turned her face up to him, and he leaned down and touched his lips to hers. Almost immediately he pulled away, with a little laugh. Was she doing it wrong? What was the matter? But then he pulled her tighter, and with one hand behind her head pulled her towards him and—

She was lost. He was kissing her! Or she was kissing him... or both, it was hard to tell. There was kissing on both sides, and a certain urgency that thrilled her to her very toes. He wanted her! *Desired* her, and she was more than a muse to him. Please God, let her be more than a muse to him.

When they broke apart, laughing, he said, "That was very pleasant."

"It was indeed, but you are such a great tall fellow that I have a dreadful crick in my neck."

"Ah. That can be mended, I believe."

Abruptly, he lifted her bodily off her feet, scooping her into his arms and then turning to survey the room. He chose the settle beside the fire, recently vacated by Mrs Cleat. Sitting down, he settled Felicia across his knees. "There! Is that more comfortable?"

It was, and his face was most conveniently placed for more kissing, which proximity they took advantage of for quite some time. It was the most restful thing in the world, she found, to sit so close, his strong arm around her back and his other hand resting on her waist. Whenever they paused and she opened her eyes, he was gazing at her with an intensity which turned her to jelly.

"I shall get a licence from the Bishop," he said softly. "Then we need not wait for the banns."

"No."

A little frown. "Why not?"

"I should like to take a little more time, so that… so that we both have a chance to think better of it."

He gave a sudden jerk, squeezing her tight. "*No!* I shall not… and I could not honourably withdraw, even if I wished to, which I do not."

"But I could, and would do so, if you ever change your mind. Fin, you must be aware that no one will consider me a suitable wife for you. An earl marrying a bastard? It is unconscionable. Lady Drusilla will certainly think so and—"

"I do not care what she thinks!"

"— society at large will think so too. You will be ostracised, and I should hate to be the cause of it. I want you to take your place in the world again, not to be permanently cast out."

"I care nothing for the opinion of the world," he said fiercely. "Anyone who objects to you because of your birth is no one I wish to know. All that matters to me is whether *you* truly want to marry me."

"I do, I do! More than anything in the world, but—"

"Then let me hear no more nonsense about withdrawal. You may set the date, but there will be a wedding, on that I am adamant."

Felicia could not argue against such determination. "I only hope you will not regret it."

He kissed her forehead gently. "I shall not," he said softly. "However, it would settle your mind, I believe, if we could uncover the story of your parentage. I shall write to Hadrian Dulnain, and see if we cannot get to the bottom of why you and Lady Olivia look so alike, and whether you might not be Sir Royston Lister's daughter. If you know exactly who you are, you may feel more comfortable about who you will become, my little countess."

# 26: An Unexpected Visit (September)

The rest of the journey north passed without any incident, but also without much rest. Mrs Cleat was not the only one exhausted by Fin's relentless pace. Felicia spent the days half dozing in the carriage, jolted into aching wakefulness at frequent intervals by rutted roads, delays at turnpikes or the yelling of ostlers. At night, her bed seemed to be still in motion, giving her strange, vivid dreams of men chasing after her and arms dragging her away from Fin.

Only one moment brought her some pleasure beyond the mere fact of being with Fin. They stopped to change horses at a nameless inn in a nameless town. Opposite the inn was a jeweller's shop and Fin strode across the road, returning not ten minutes later with two small packages for her.

"I could not decide which to buy, so I bought both," he said, frowning. "Do you like them?"

Unwrapped, the parcels contained velvet-lined boxes with a necklace in each, one of amber stones, the other blue. They were delicately beautiful, and she had never in her life held anything so fine.

"They are quite lovely," she said, fingering them in awe. "Thank you so much!"

He relaxed a little. "Mere trumpery, of course, but you must have something to wear besides that little cross. Is that your only piece of jewellery? Well, I shall buy you some real jewels when we go to London, and you may also look through Mama's things, although I daresay Drusilla has taken the best pieces. Mind you, her taste is terrible so she has probably taken all the hideous heirlooms and left the best behind."

He laughed, and Felicia laughed too, pleased to see him smile, for travelling seemed to throw him very much into a glowering mood. She had never been unduly unsettled by his moods, since they were never directed at her personally. It was the travel that wore him down, just as it did all of them, and it was his way to deal with the strains of the journey.

The advantage to travelling at Fin's breakneck speed was that it was soon over. They arrived at Hawkewood Hall at noon on the fourth day, and were immediately flung into another whirlwind of Fin's devising. Nothing would do but for Felicia to be assigned to the best rooms in the house, a bedroom, dressing room and a vast sitting room filled with elegantly feminine furniture with windows on three sides.

"These were your mother's apartments," Felicia said, looking out through the bay window. "This must be where she sat as she grew ill, and your father cut down the trees so that she could see the temple. But I should not be here."

"You have the same right to it as she did," Fin said, tucking her arm into his. "Come, let me show you around." The horde of servants rushing about with linens, ewers, holland covers and buckets of coal jumped aside as he passed through the rooms. From the bedroom, he opened another door and drew her through it. As he closed the door on the bustle of servants, silence fell. This room had heavier, more masculine fittings, and the furniture remained swathed in holland covers. "My father's bedroom. I shall move in here after we are married." He chuckled. "Now I have made you blush again." A hesitation. "Does the idea… distress you?"

"Oh no! Not at all, but… it is all so sudden."

"You are not… having second thoughts?" His voice was low and anxious.

"No."

"Ah." He drew her into his arms. "We will be happy, will we not, my little countess?"

But he sounded uncertain — so unlike himself! She lifted her face to his and he bent down to kiss her, but it was a hesitant kiss, little more than a quick touch of the lips. She wanted more, so much more!

Before she could hint as much, he pulled away from her with a frown. "I should send word to Arnwell. Let me leave you now to rest."

She had not the words to tell him how bitterly disappointed she was.

~~~~~
~~~~~

Fin's mind was in turmoil as the hours passed. Felicia had accepted him, but now his elation was giving way to a swirl of doubts. Did she truly want to be his wife, or was she simply dazzled by the prospect of being a countess? When she smiled at him, or kissed him — oh Lord, when she kissed him! — he had no doubt of her feelings, and she had told him that she loved him, after all. *'I want to marry you so badly… I ought to refuse, but I love you too well to contemplate it.'* He shivered as he recalled her words. *'I love you too well…'* Did she mean it? How could he bear it if she thought better of the whole thing?

But soon all opportunity for rational thought was lost, for Drusilla arrived. She had observed the carriage passing by and had come at once to welcome him home, only to discover from the servants that her worst fears had materialised. Fin was to marry the governess.

"Are you insane?" she said coldly, pacing back and forth across the sitting room carpet. "Have you completely lost all semblance of sanity? You will ruin this family, Fin, and it will be the death of me, I swear it."

He unstoppered the brandy decanter, then paused, the decanter hovering over the glass. Would Felicia say that he should not? But she was not there and he could not face Drusilla without recruiting his strength for the battle ahead. He poured himself a large measure, and then, recklessly, as much again.

He let Drusilla rant for a while, as he sipped his brandy and stared out of the window at the garden in its autumn decay. There were moments of glorious beauty in autumn, the trees a riot of extravagant golds and oranges and flame reds, but much of it was a dispiriting brown, the colour of mud. And then came winter, with no redeeming colours at all. Winter was all stark black and white.

But clear as a church bell he heard Felicia's voice in his head. *'No matter how desperate the winter, there is always a spring of warm sunshine and bluebells in the woods, and then high summer and poppies in the fields.'* He smiled. There would be difficulties, naturally, for no marriage was all plain sailing and smooth seas, but he loved her and she loved him, she said, so they would weather the storms together.

"—not listened to a word I have said!" Drusilla said indignantly.

He smiled even more widely as he turned to face her, biting back the acid riposte that spring effortlessly to his lips. He would be civil, if only for Felicia's sake. "I beg your pardon, but a man deep in love is surely permitted a degree of inattention, do you not think?"

Drusilla goggled at him. "You *are* insane. If you think this jumped-up—"

"No," he said quietly, holding up one hand. "You will not say one word of insult against Felicia. She is not from a great family but she is sensible and quick-minded and generous and well-mannered, and will not disgrace the family name in any company."

She looked at him thoughtfully, and for the first time, the pacing stopped, although she did not deign to sit down. "I say nothing against her person or her manners," she said, with a lift of one shoulder. "She is a little too impertinent, perhaps, and not nearly humble enough, but I say nothing to *that*. I will readily admit that her influence on you has been beneficial, and at least with a few new gowns and jewels she will look the part. But her birth and her lack of connections cannot be overlooked. You will both be cast out of all good society."

"Only the highest sticklers will object to the Countess of Finlassan, Drusilla, whatever her origins, and I care nothing for the good opinion of such people. Aunt Isabella and Aunt Geraldine will present her at court—"

"The Queen will not receive her!"

"Well, if she will not, so be it. I should like Felicia to be treated with the respect her position deserves when she is my wife, but it is of no consequence. We shall be content to live quietly here."

"You are determined to do this, then?" Drusilla said. "No residue of good sense remains to you?"

"Sister, whom would you have me marry?" he said. "Some grand lady of fashion with a noble family and a large dowry, or a woman who makes my heart sing with joy?"

Drusilla had no answer to that.

Dinner that evening promised to be lively. Fin's hastily scribbled note to Arnwell — *'Have brought Felicia back. We are to be married. Come for dinner tonight. Finlassan.'* — had borne fruit, for the marquess's carriage arrived precisely half an hour before the prescribed time for dinner. He greeted Felicia with affectionate pleasure, and congratulated the betrothed pair with many felicitations. Drusilla could not be excluded, naturally, and Juliana and Margarita were there with their governesses. The two girls were wildly excited to see Felicia again, then apologetic about the supposed insult to their new governesses, then even more excited to learn that Felicia and Fin were to marry.

One other attendee insisted on being present at dinner. Hercules was so excited to see Felicia again when she visited him in his quarters behind the stables that he howled piteously when she attempted to leave, and thereafter clung tenaciously to her side, even in the drawing room. He was so thrilled to see the marquess there as well, his two favourite people in the entire world, that Fin suspected the poor creature thought he had died and been transported to dog heaven.

"This is all the thanks I get for my efforts to walk him while you were away," he said to Felicia. "He cares nothing for me, I can see. "

She only laughed at him. "You are jealous, I declare," she said. "Just because he loves me best."

He tried to think of a suitable response to that — after all, he loved her best too, and there should be some riposte to be found there — but he always grew tongue-tied when she looked at him in that mischievous, teasing way, and the words would not form themselves.

There was one other guest. Shortly before the signal to dress for dinner, Fin had found Felicia at his desk in the sitting room, head down, industriously engaged in some book work.

"Why are you in here? You have a sitting room of your own, you know."

"There is no paper or ink there yet, and besides, in this room I am surrounded by your paintings. Do you mind?"

She smiled at him and he could only shake his head. So strange the effect she had on him, reducing him to quivering muteness. With an effort, he cleared his throat and said, "What are you doing?"

"Greek translation. This is a… well, I am not sure what it is, journal or fictional account or history, it is hard to say. It was written by Miss Armiger in Ancient Greek, and I am working on a translation in case it contains anything of relevance to me."

"Of your parents, you mean?" She nodded, and he picked up the notebook that lay on the desk. "This is the journal? You have not got very far."

"My Greek is very bad. I have to interpret every word with the primer, and half the words are not there or seem to mean something different. It is very hard."

"Cotham is something of a Greek scholar. Should you like him to translate it for you?"

She smiled with relief, and it occurred to him that she was remarkably easy to please. A note was dashed off to Cotham inviting him to dinner, and informing him of the task required of him. He arrived promptly, full of effusive gratitude. Another one who was easy to please.

"I hope you will not think the price too high when you begin work on the volume," Fin said to him. "It was written by the lady who raised Miss Oakes, and it may reveal some clues to her history, so you may appreciate her interest in the matter."

"I shall be most happy to do whatever I can to oblige Miss Oakes in the matter," Cotham said with one of his low bows.

Fin could not remember a pleasanter evening, not for years. Felicia sat beside him and he was allowed to pay her as much attention as he liked and no one could object, for they were betrothed now. Drusilla grumbled that the ladies outnumbered the gentlemen, but Fin could not care about such trivia. The girls and their governesses disappeared after the tea tray, but Fin, Arnwell, Drusilla and the curate made up a four for whist. Felicia sat distractingly close to Fin, saying little but watching the play and listening to the conversation with a tiny smile, as if everything pleased her.

It was gone midnight before Arnwell began to tire and the party broke up. As soon as the door had closed behind the departing guests, Bagnall coughed discreetly.

"Beg pardon, my lord, but there is a gentleman to see you in the library."

"At this hour? What sort of a gentleman?"

"One who wishes to speak to you most urgently, my lord. Alone," he added, with a significant glance at Felicia.

She took the hint, and bade Fin a shy good night. In a well-regulated world, she should not, of course, be living under the same roof as her betrothed, but Felicia's world had never been well-regulated, and where else could she go? He would not, under any circumstances, send her off to have her mind poisoned by Drusilla. Besides, they would be married very soon, as soon as he could obtain a licence, he hoped, and then it would hardly matter. He watched her disappearing with light feet up the stairs, and had a rush of longing to see her dance. She was made for dancing, his Felicia!

With reluctance, he tore his eyes from her retreating form and turned towards the library. When Bagnall threw open the door, he was astonished to see the familiar face of Godfrey Buckley. He was seated at a small table, enjoying what looked like a substantial supper, a decanter of wine to hand. He rose at once and came forward with a seriousness in his gaze that Fin had never seen before. Impossible to say what that portended.

"Buckley?"

"My lord, I abjectly beg your pardon for disturbing you at this unholy hour, but the matter is of some urgency, given your news. My felicitations on your betrothal, my lord, but it is of Miss Oakes that I must speak to you, for I believe she may be in the gravest danger."

Fin had reached for the brandy but now his hand stilled. "Immediate danger? Should I remove her from here at once? Post footmen outside her door?"

"She is on an upper floor? Then a footman would be sufficient."

Fin gave the orders to Bagnall, who loitered with dignified curiosity outside the door, and then poured himself a large brandy. "Finish your supper, Buckley, and then you may tell your tale. I am not minded for sleep yet, so you may take your time over it."

"You are very understanding, my lord." He neatly ate the rest of a pheasant, then pushed his plate away with a sigh. "You have an excellent cook, my lord."

"You had better stop this *'my lord'* business, since you will be a marquess one day. Call me Finlassan."

Buckley nodded an acknowledgement, although his eyes were wary, as if he expected Fin to withdraw that authority. He refilled his wine glass and turned back to Fin. "I have had the great good fortune to be invited to stay at Cottersmere Court this summer as a guest of the earl and the Dulnain family, and so I was present when Lord Cottersmere received your letter requesting his assistance regarding the ancestry of Miss Oakes. Her similarity of appearance to the Lady Olivia Dulnain is very striking, so an unorthodox connection to the family is a reasonable suggestion. The letter surmised that Miss Oakes might be connected to Sir Royston, who was also a guest. Sir Royston denied any responsibility and since he has a number of known by-blows, it seems unlikely that he would repudiate just this one."

"He does not like public reminders of his adventures, by all I have heard," Fin said, swirling the brandy around his glass.

"True enough, but he always takes care of them. No woman ever starved because she was got with child by him. A cottage somewhere, an annuity... he is not ungenerous, but once dealt with he dislikes to have the child flung back in his face, that is all. Everything tidied up neatly. If Miss Oakes were his child, he would have taken considerably better care of her, you may be sure."

"Very well, then. Not him. Could there be anyone else in the family who might have sired her? It does not matter two pennies to me who her father was, but it matters to her, and I would set her mind at rest if I could."

"Indeed, but Lord Cottersmere is also confident that no one on his side of the family is responsible. But I believe I may solve this seeming riddle. I cannot be sure, you understand... there is no proof, but it is my sincere belief that Miss Oakes is in truth the Lady Edwina Buckley."

"Who the devil is Lady Edwina Buckley?" And then he realised... "One of Arnwell's daughters? But... they all died in the fire!"

"No. The two youngest survived."

Fin jumped to his feet. "Impossible! You are insane, Buckley, and I will not have you telling Felicia such a story and raising her hopes. I have seen what remains of that part of the house and there is nothing but ashes. No one could have survived. Arnwell himself was dragged out half dead. I will not listen to any more of your lies!

"They did *not* all die, believe me, and may God strike me down if I lie! The two babes survived and were smuggled to safety. They did *not* all die!"

# 27: Revelations

Fin took a long draught of brandy, then refilled his glass and took another. Was it possible? Two events, equally implausible — that some of Arnwell's children had survived, and that Felicia was one of them. Either one stretched credibility, but for both to happen was akin to throwing a dozen double sixes in a row with the dice. Yet what could Buckley have to gain by such a story?

"Explain," he said.

"I can tell you little of the night of the fire," Buckley began. "I was but five years of age, and so my knowledge has come to me from two persons — my father and my aunt. Both were at Shotterbourne that night and—"

Fin frowned. "Both? Your aunt was there, of course, to attend Lady Lucia, but I understood that your father was barred from the estate after he tried to claim the title."

"True enough. He was forbidden ever to set foot in Shotterbourne again. Nevertheless, there are always ways of effecting entry. Unlocked gates, easily-climbed walls, bribeable lodge-keepers… He never revealed to me how he got in, but he told me he was there and that the fire was a terrible accident… that something went wrong."

"It started accidentally?" Fin said. "Or it was begun deliberately and got out of hand?"

"I never got a clear answer on that point. You must understand that Father told me nothing of this until I was almost an adult, and to be frank, in his later years he was seldom sober and grew increasingly muddled, so it was hard to make out the truth. But there was one other point— he said that, despite appearances, I should never inherit Shotterbourne or the marquessate, that the heir yet lived but was hidden away for safety. He never attempted to explain what the great risk was, or why it was such a secret that no one spoke of it, and perhaps it was no more than a figment of his disordered mind. Sometimes it seemed to me that he even thought that he had won his own claim to the title and was himself Lord Arnwell, so I took little notice of much that he said, but the idea lingered in my mind, naturally. The world believed me to be the heir presumptive, but it might not be so."

"You did not think to ask your aunt about the matter?"

"My father was not on good terms with her, and I did not care to go against his wishes. Besides, it would be resolved one way or another when Lord Arnwell should die. Either another heir would appear… or not. I was content to await events."

"While living in the style of a future marquess, no doubt," Fin growled.

Buckley laughed. "Oh, if only I could have done so! But I received not a penny from Lord Arnwell, and my father was almost destitute."

Fin grunted, not convinced, but said nothing, and Buckley continued his story.

"Two years ago, my father died and in sorting through his papers I discovered correspondence from my aunt which suggested that she knew something of the matter, and I felt compelled to make an approach to her to find out what she knew. At first she denied it, telling me that all the children had died, but then… Now I must come to Miss Oakes and yet another apology, for I have treated her abominably, I freely acknowledge it."

"You have indeed," Fin said coldly. "You thought her an heiress, and saw an opportunity."

Mr Buckley had the grace to look abashed. "You are aware of my circumstances, that my father all but ruined the estate with his foolish attempt to wrest the title away from Lord Arnwell, and took no steps to improve his position after, beyond drinking and gaming his way to an early grave. I have had to retrench greatly, and would have gone under had it not been for the tolerance of my banker."

"Who believed you to be heir to a fortune," Fin said.

"He did, and I was unable to disabuse him of the idea, for I was constrained by my own uncertainty as to the position. Even if it were true that the children had survived the fire, there was no guarantee that they still lived. Oswald was a mere babe at the time, and there are many perils in the world. But then Miss Oakes arrived, looking so like Lady Olivia, and all her circumstances consistent with the missing Edwina, even the day of her birth. At once my aunt suspected it, and confessed that she had known all along that the two youngest children had survived, by some unknown means. Thus she created her plot. I was to court and win Miss Oakes, who would then be revealed as the heiress to Lord Arnwell's unentailed fortune, which is considerably more than the entailed portion."

"A risky strategy," Fin said. "Arnwell hates the Buckleys so profoundly that he is perfectly capable of cutting his daughter out of his will."

"So I argued, too, but Aunt Edith had an answer to that. Presently the unentailed fortune is willed to a natural daughter the marquess has somewhere. There is not a judge in the land who would agree to overlook a legitimate daughter in favour of a illegitimate one, so Miss Oakes need only contest the will to have her fortune. If the son survives, he would have the small entailed properties, and I would have the larger part, and if he does not, I would have everything. That was the plan, but..."

"She would not have you," Fin cried. "She saw through you!"

"Not quite," Buckley said, smiling. "Naturally I was tempted, for who would not be? Lord Finlassan, you of all people must surely understand why I was drawn to Miss Oakes. I should explain, perhaps... but I should not mention— No, let me be honest, for it may make my actions more understandable, if not excusable. My affections and hopes have long lain with the Lady Olivia Dulnain. Since Miss Oakes is, in looks, so very similar to Olivia, it seemed to me that it would not be a difficulty to transfer my affections from one to the other. Miss Oakes is very easy to like, as you will surely agree, but there is something so open and artless about her that it smote my conscience powerfully to so deceive her."

"She does have that effect on people," Fin conceded, with a rueful smile.

Buckley smiled too. "Indeed. When it came to the point, I found that I could not propose marriage to her, and very likely she would not have accepted me anyway. I took myself out of her life, and made my hopes known openly to Lord Cottersmere, who invited me to Cottersmere Court to get to know Olivia better. Thus it was that I was there when your letter arrived two days ago, revealing that you were to marry Miss Oakes. That made it imperative to inform you of these suspicions at the earliest moment. I may be mistaken in this and Miss Oakes may have nothing to do with Lord Arnwell, but if there is any possibility of it, you must know of it."

"And Arnwell, too," Fin said. "But Felicia… it would be a cruelty to raise her hopes and tell her that she has a father, a home, a *family* and yet find out that there is nothing to it. How can it be proved, one way or another? To start with, how does your aunt know that two of the children survived yet Arnwell clearly believes them to be dead?"

"Aunt Edith heard strong rumours from the servants, but there was no evidence whatsoever, so she kept such tales from Lord Arnwell's ears. After the fire, his mind was dreadfully disturbed and Lady Lucia was not well, so my aunt was obliged to take over the running of the household in its entirety. I cannot imagine what would have become of them if she had not — an asylum, most likely. For both of them, familiar surroundings and a calm atmosphere enable them to function almost as normal, but the least disruption could be fatal. She has been most concerned about Lord Arnwell lately — attending church and attending dinner engagements! It could disrupt his mind totally."

"He seems sane enough to me," Fin said thoughtfully. "Eccentric, of course… reclusive… and bitter, naturally, but I should have said he is no more insane than I am. His actions, bizarre as it may seem to ruin one's own estate, are yet directed by a clear purpose — to deprive you of as much of your inheritance as he can. It is vengeful, but not at all insane."

Buckley frowned. "That is a good point. Perhaps time has enabled a recovery of sorts, but I should not like the responsibility of telling him that two of his children may or may not be alive, that we cannot prove it and we do not even know where the son may be hidden."

"The responsibility would be mine, for I shall tell him myself," Fin said absently. "But why were they hidden in the first place?"

"My father said they needed to be kept safe," Mr Buckley said. "Although safe from what — or whom — is a difficult question."

"From whoever started the fire," Fin said. "That is the logical conclusion, is it not? And forgive me, Buckley, but I have always wondered if your father started the fire himself in vengeance for losing the title."

"To deliberately murder an entire family? My father was not the most honourable of men, my lord, and he was lucky he was never called out by the many he cheated at the card tables, but he would never stoop so low as that. If he was responsible for the fire at all, the deaths were a mistake, the consequence of a small blaze that got out of hand."

"And yet, your father thought they were not safe…"

*Is she safe?*

"Percival!" Fin said, abruptly sitting forward as he remembered the coded letters. "Percival thought they were not safe, too. He is *still* worried if Felicia is safe, and not from your romantic snares... there is some other risk."

"Percival?" Buckley said, shaking his head in bewilderment. "Your uncle? The one who stole all that money on the night of the fire?"

"Yes! He has been writing secretly to Giles from wherever he is hidden — with the boy! What was his name? Oswald... he is keeping Oswald safe, and Miss Armiger, whoever she was, kept Felicia safe. Percival must have realised that the fire was a deliberate attempt to kill the whole family, so he got the two youngest children out, stole the money to live on and sent them somewhere safe. And Giles knows... has known all these years. Perhaps not where they were, but that they had survived and were hidden away."

"That... seems to be a reasonable assessment," Buckley acknowledged.

"But Buckley, do you not see? It *must* have been your father who started that fire, because he was the only one who stood to benefit. He tried to kill Arnwell and his whole family, but he failed. The children were hidden away to protect them from him."

"My father was a broken man, Finlassan, who was incapable of harming anyone. Besides, he died two years ago. If he were the threat, the heir could have reappeared then."

"Perhaps he does not know that, or perhaps... perhaps he thinks *you* are the threat now?"

Buckley swore. "How in God's name am I to prove my innocence?"

Fin chuckled. "I have no idea, but one thing is very clear — we must lay the whole story before Arnwell tomorrow. It is for him to decide how to proceed."

~~~~~

Fin, Felicia and Buckley waited for the carriage in the entrance hall. Felicia was white-faced and silent, having been woken early to the astonishing news that she might be the Lady Edwina Buckley, daughter of the Marquess of Arnwell. Buckley was subdued, too, for his own father was surely implicated in the disastrous fire.

Fin was not quite sure what to think. If Felicia was indeed Arnwell's daughter and a great heiress, then perhaps she would want to see something of the world before settling down to marriage. Perhaps she would not want to marry a grumpy, reclusive earl after all.

The carriage arrived, and silently they entered it, the doors were closed and they moved off. They rattled down the drive and crept through the village behind a shepherd herding some sheep along the main street. They had reached the village square and were about to turn through the Shotterbourne gates when Felicia gave a cry.

"There he is! The green coat... by the inn... the man who followed me... he is here! *He is here!*"

Fin yelled, "Stop!", Buckley banged on the roof of the carriage with his cane, and they lurched to a halt. Fin had the door open and leapt to the ground in an instant. He tore across the road, heedless of an oncoming cart, and over the village green, his long legs striding. The man in the green coat watched unmoving at first,
~~~~~

perhaps puzzled by the sight of a gentleman tearing towards the inn, but then alarm set in as he realised his danger. He turned and fled into the inn.

Fin barrelled through the door after him, through the tap room to a chorus of cries of "Hey there!" and "Watch out!", into the smoky back room and through the open door to the kitchen. The green coat was half way across it, to outraged shrieks from the cook and her helpers, and a clatter of falling pans. Fin did not break stride, racing through the mêlée, pushing aside a man entering through the far door, and out into the yard, a whirlwind of feathers and squawking chickens.

The green coat had vanished. Where had he gone?

"Over the wall, my lord," a maid called out, pointing.

With a cry of thanks, Fin set off again and leapt the low wall, only to find himself in a neat garden. Where was he? There! Off again, and in the open Fin's long legs had the advantage. He was gaining… gaining… but the green coat dashed into a small orchard. He was heading for a wrought iron gate leading into the woods, and there perhaps he would be able to evade capture.

Except that the gate was locked.

The man pulled frantically, then pushed, then jiggled the handle in desperation. It was useless. With no way out, he turned to face Fin, who, without hesitation, thumped him hard on the jaw. It was only as his fist connected with flesh that he saw his quarry clearly. He was naught but a boy! Younger than Felicia, pale-faced and plainly terrified. And now he lay, half unconscious, in a crumpled heap at Fin's feet.

"My lord! My lord!" Buckley jogged across the manicured lawn. "Well done indeed! A famous capture. That was splendid right hook. But who is he?"

"That is what I intend to find out," Fin said grimly, hauling the boy to his feet. He groaned slightly and swayed a little, but otherwise seemed able to stand. Blood poured from his nose, but he raised his eyes to Fin's with an assessing expression.

"He seems harmless enough," Buckley said, blandly. "To what did you take exception? His coat is not quite the latest fashion, but perfectly respectable for country wear, I should say, or would be without the mud. Oh, I rather fear there is a tear about the shoulder, too. What a pity."

Fin managed a small smile, but was still too angry to view the occasion with amusement. "He and his father hounded Felicia when she was in Hampshire, following her about in the most threatening manner."

"We meant her no harm," the boy said. "We would never hurt her. Quite the reverse, for we were watching over her to ensure no harm came to her."

His accent was good, like his clothes, and if he had met him in other circumstances, Fin would have stated without hesitation that he was a gentleman. Now... he was merely puzzled.

Several men from the inn arrived, and one had rope with which to bind the boy's hands and feet.

"Throw 'im in the cellar, shall we?" one of them said. "Just till someone fetches the constable, like."

"No, he will stay within my sight at all times," Fin said.

"Aye, 'e might scarper, sure enough."

"Indeed he might. Leave his feet untied, if you will, but make sure the binding on his hands is secure. Buckley, will you help me lead him up to the house? I will not take him in the carriage with Felicia."

"Where are you taking me?" the boy said, not at all fearful. "Which house? Yours?"

"Later," Fin said. "For now, I hope it will not inconvenience you too greatly if I require you to accompany us to Shotterbourne."

"Excellent," the boy said, grinning. Buckley laughed at such insouciance.

They made their way out of the garden, past two elderly ladies hovering anxiously on a small terrace.

"Good day, Miss Trimm, Miss Mary!" Buckley called cheerfully. "No cause for alarm, and no damage to your pear trees."

They made an odd procession up the long drive to Shotterbourne, Buckley and Fin walking ahead with the boy held by a long rope. Behind, the carriage followed slowly. As they arrived, a troop of footmen emerged. They were expected, for Fin had sent a note to Lord Arnwell.

The boy was gazing around him, wide-eyed and unafraid, until his eye caught the burnt-out shell of the family wing and his expression clouded. Fin took hold of his rope and tugged on it, forcing the boy into the pillared entrance hall. His jaw dropped and he gazed around him in unabashed amazement. At the top of the stairs, Arnwell appeared, with Miss Buckley at his side. He descended the stairs slowly.

"What is all this?" he said, frowning at the boy, an unexpected addition to the party.

"Pray forgive me for bringing such a peep-o-day boy into your house, Arnwell," Fin said. "I hope he may not bleed all over your floors. He has been harassing Felicia and I dare not let him out of my sight."

"Has he indeed?" Arnwell said, frowning.

But the boy smiled at him. "Lord Arnwell?"

"I am. And who may you be, ruffian?"

The boy lifted his chin, and with an unexpectedly haughty demeanour said, "I am the Earl of Shotterbourne."

The marquess made a strangled sound deep in his throat.

"The *devil* you are," Fin murmured.

"Wait…" Felicia sounded confused, as well she might be. "You went by the name of Hubert Jameson in Hampshire."

"That has been the name I have taken for many years," the boy said. "My true name, however, is Oswald Buckley. I am the only son and heir of Lord Arnwell, and therefore take the courtesy title of Earl of Shotterbourne."

Fin laughed. "What an interesting day this is, for here is another of your children, Arnwell. We believe Felicia to be the Lady Edwina Buckley."

"Nonsense." It was Edith Buckley who spoke. "It is all a sham. I knew this would happen! It is always so when there is no body to be buried… just like the poor Princes in the Tower, impostors appear and the credulous fall for their tall tales. I have been a victim myself, but now I know better. There were no survivors that night. All the children died along with their mother, and anyone who says different is lying."

And in that moment, Fin understood everything.

# 28: Reunions

All the air whooshed out of Felicia's lungs. Was it all about to be snatched away from her, this dream of a family and a true name and a history? But Fin smiled at her and shook his head very gently at Miss Buckley's words, and Felicia was reassured. Whatever happened, whether Felicia was Lady Edwina Buckley or a bastard of no account, she still had Fin. That must not be forgotten.

"There is much to be talked over, I think," Lord Arnwell said calmly. "Let us all go into the saloon, yes, this ragamuffin boy too, Finlassan. Hillman, bring some tea, and something to eat. Macaroons… cake… something sweet. Come now, all of you. Princess, will you take my arm, since Finlassan has his hands full."

Gently he shepherded them up the marble staircase. Felicia was glad of Lord Arnwell's arm as she trod with care up the polished steps. The boy gazed about him in wonder, craning his neck to gaze at the magnificent arched ceiling high above and twisting to see the lines of marble pillars.

"It is beautiful, is it not?" Felicia said.

"Awe-inspiring! I never imagined— I have heard so much about it, and seen pictures, but nothing quite prepares one for the reality."

"I am glad you approve, ruffian," Lord Arnwell said, with a chuckle.

"Look your fill, for you will not be here long," Miss Buckley said.

"Enough, Edith," the marquess said gently.

The saloon was another sight to impress the boy. With an amused expression, Fin cut him free of his bonds, and allowed him to walk around the perimeter while the others settled on sofas and chairs around one of the fires. Felicia watched Lord Arnwell anxiously. He seemed calm, but it must be agonising for him to have the prospect of a living heir dangled before him, and then perhaps to have it snatched away again immediately. For her, it made no material difference, for she would marry Fin and be happy… she had a future. But if Miss Buckley was right, then for the marquess there was no future. One shining moment of hope, that was all, instantly dissolved into the same dreary prospect of an empty life and a slow decline of failing health.

The servants moved about silently, opening some of the shutters to let in sunshine, lighting fires, laying out cakes and pastries and bowls of hothouse grapes, handing round glasses of Madeira, just as if this were any normal morning call. Only the dishevelled Mr Jameson struck a discordant note, with his torn, muddy coat and the blood staining his neckcloth, and the usual conversation of such occasions was lacking. Eventually the servants were satisfied that the requisite level of hospitality had been attained and withdrew.

"Now, Edith," the marquess said. "You will tell us all that you know, and we shall listen respectfully, shall we not, ruffian?"

"Yes, my lord."

For some reason, Lord Arnwell found the composed answer amusing.

Fin found the boy a footstool to sit upon, one that would not be too stained by his mud and drips of blood, and they all turned to Miss Buckley expectantly.

"There were rumours right from the start," she said. "One or other of the children had somehow survived... smuggled out and hidden away somewhere, although no one had a reason as to why. The stories differed so wildly that I took no notice, and there was no point in raising false hopes. Gradually it all died away, until *she* came here." She cast a supercilious look at Felicia. "Yes, you look so innocent now, miss, but I saw what you were about with your insinuating ways, and I know Lady Drusilla did, too. We both saw how you ingratiated yourself, first with Lord Finlassan and then with Lord Arnwell."

"Now, just a minute—" Fin began, but Lord Arnwell shushed him with a frown and a little shake of his head. He subsided, but Felicia loved him for leaping to her defence.

"I thought at first it was just the usual — a pretty young woman flattering the men to see what she might achieve. A title, perhaps, from Lord Finlassan. But with Lord Arnwell, she conceived a bolder plan. I hoped to catch her in a lie, and to my regret I used Godfrey as a decoy, to see if she could be ensnared, but she was too clever for us."

"No, he drew back from any deceit in the end," Felicia said. "However he might have begun, he ended honourably, upholding his principles."

"How very touching," Miss Buckley said sourly. "Nevertheless, she is not Lady Edwina, and now we have another impostor!" She looked at Mr Jameson with such disgust that Felicia was shocked. "I suppose she set you onto her little scheme, did she?"

"You are mistaken, ma'am," Mr Jameson said politely. "I have had almost no conversation with the lady." He seemed entirely at his ease in the company, and despite the blood stains and mud and the bruises on his face, he comported himself with a graceful dignity, as if he were truly an earl.

"So you say, and I say you are a liar and a charlatan and a rogue. You are not the Earl of Shotterbourne and you cannot prove that you are."

"Now that is where you are wrong," came a deep male voice from the opposite side of the room, where the still-closed shutters cast a deep gloom.

Miss Buckley squealed in alarm, and Buckley leapt to his feet, but the others were smiling, Felicia noticed, even Lord Arnwell.

"Who are you?" Miss Buckley cried, although there was a hint of fear in her voice. "How did you get in here without the servants seeing you? Come out of the shadows and show your face like an honest man."

"Yes, come forward, Uncle Percival," Fin said calmly.

Miss Buckley's intake of breath was audible.

Felicia recognised the newcomer the instant he moved towards them. There before her was the older man who had followed her in Hampshire, although, like the boy, he looked rather more the gentleman in appearance than when she had seen him last.

"You are Percival Warborough?" she said, bewildered. "Then why did you give me such a fright in Hampshire? I do not understand what is going on here."

"Forgive me for that, my dear, and for sneaking in upon Edith's farrago of nonsense in this way. I worked here for long enough to know all the concealed doors and servants' stairs."

Fin rose to his feet. "I am glad to see you again at last, Uncle, and to have the answers to some of my questions, but there is one I cannot make out. Who is 'K' who recently gave birth to a fine boy?"

Percival Warborough burst out laughing, and strode across the room to shake Fin's hand. "Lord, how you have grown, nephew. Katherine is my wife, as I am sure you have guessed. So my correspondence with Giles has been intercepted. Ah, no, Edith. No sneaking away, if you please."

Miss Buckley had quietly made her way to one of the side doors of the saloon, but Mr Percival Warborough ushered her back to the group clustered around the fire and loomed over her as, with pursed lips, she seated herself in a chair, while Fin poured Madeira for the newcomer.

Felicia quietly pulled a plate of macaroons nearer, and chewed absently. Fin was clearly convinced that the boy was legitimate — was he truly the heir? And her brother! Astonishing thought. Nor did Fin show any fear of what Mr Percival might say. He seemed to know that he was not the wicked man he had been painted.

She tried to remember the letters he had written, the coded missives intended for Mr Giles. What had they said? After the part about 'K' and her son, there was *'O is in good heart.'* Oswald! Of course. And something about *'returning to S'*. Was that Shotterbourne? And the other letter, with its words about *'Will she be safe now?'* Felicia herself… they knew of her, and were trying to protect her, just as the boy had said. Oswald. Her brother. The thought made her shiver. It was true, then. She had a family. She *belonged.*

Fin drew his chair near to hers, and took her hand in his. "Now we shall know the truth," he whispered. "At last."

Mr Percival sipped his Madeira, and then set his glass down carefully on a low table. "Let me tell you of the night of the fire," he began. The others were silent, all watching, waiting expectantly, but Miss Buckley turned her head away from him with a disbelieving expression on her face. "Lord Arnwell was at the card table, and losing heavily. He sent me to fetch another purse of money from his room, for I had a key to the drawer where he kept such items. You all know what I found — smoke, fire, disaster. I raised the alarm, but within minutes the whole family wing was ablaze. The central staircase acted as a great chimney, drawing the flames upwards. I could see there was nothing to be done there. But there was still hope for the nursery, which was close to the upper walkway to the main part of the building."

The marquess made a low noise in his throat, but he said nothing.

"I ran to the service stairs and along the gallery," Mr Percival continued. "In the ante-room at the corner of the house, I met the escaping nursery party. The wet-nurse had been awake to feed the baby, and there had been time to wake the nursery maid and the governess, Miss Pickering."

"Pickering!" Felicia cried. "That was the name on the journal I found! *'The History of Miss Margaret Pickering, being an account of her birth, education, her rise to a distinguished position, and her present circumstances.'* There was something about trials of her fortitude as well, which was how she felt about looking after me, I daresay. It was all written in ancient Greek and I could not read it, but Mr Cotham, the curate, is translating it for me."

"Ah! Interesting," Mr Percival said. "So only those three survived, with the two babies, Edwina and Oswald. I sent them to the chapel to await help, for that was the furthest point from the fire, and the safest. I myself went back to do what I could to help, although the whole family wing was ablaze by then, so it seemed hopeless. Downstairs, all was in chaos, people rushing here and there, but the men had organised chains of buckets, so I was not needed for the rescue efforts. I could not find Lord Arnwell, so I decided to make my way to the chapel. As I passed through the ante-room to the chapel wing, I heard voices outside the window, two voices, a man and a woman. I will tell you exactly what they said, for the words are seared into my mind indelibly. *'We have killed them all. They will all die, and it is our fault. You sent me to the wrong place. It was meant to be the library.'* And the other said, *'So much the better for us. We should have done it long ago.'*"

The marquess hissed. "So it *was* intentional, the fire?"

"So it would seem. I realised at that moment that those children were in terrible danger. A person who would plan to murder an entire family would not hesitate over two infants. The boy was the heir to the title and entailed estates, but Edwina would also have a great fortune, so she was not safe either. I knew

I had to get them far away from Shotterbourne, and keep them from harm. So I went to the safe and took the money I knew was there — twenty thousand pounds. I collected the party from the chapel and told them what we had to do. We all went to the rectory and woke Giles, so that he knew his part. I gave him a letter to give to you, my lord, so that you would know that the children were safe."

"I received no such letter," the marquess growled.

"Giles was instructed how to place it in the secret drawer in your desk, but we had no idea how gravely ill you were, such that you would not be at your desk for many weeks or months. Perhaps the letter was found in that time. We agreed that Giles would place a notice in the *Gazette* if ever it were safe to return, or if it were rendered necessary by your demise. Had I known at that time how close you came to death that night, my lord, perhaps I would not have taken your son so far away, but at the time it seemed the only way."

The marquess nodded, but said nothing.

Mr Percival continued, "I entrusted Edwina to Miss Pickering and the nursery maid, with ten thousand pounds to enable them to establish themselves, and instructions not to tell a soul where they were or who Edwina was. I myself took Oswald with his wet-nurse and the remaining money. We went to Scotland, to the Earl of Strathmorran, an old friend of mine, who agreed to aid our exile. Oswald was to be raised as a gentleman at Glenbrindle Castle with James's own sons, and I offered to earn my bread tutoring the boys. I did not know until recently where Miss Pickering went, but it seems she went to Giles's old haunt of Southampton. And there we all stayed, waiting for a message that never came. I communicated irregularly with Giles, not often, for I did not dare, and when his man intercepted one of the letters we devised a more devious way to correspond, such that my letters were directed to Hawkewood Hall. This arrangement you have breached, nephew, I understand."

"Devious indeed, to write in code," Fin said, with a smile. "But perhaps you were not aware that my father taught me how to understand such codes?"

Mr Percival laughed. It was astonishing to Felicia, overwhelmed as she was with one revelation after another, how much at ease they all were, even the marquess, who gazed at the boy — his son! — avidly. How different their lives had been. Oswald had grown up in a castle with the sons of an earl, with people around him, with *friends.* She had scraped carrots from the mud with her bare hands under Miss Pickering's heartless gaze. Even the nursery maid had left. Fin perhaps saw something of her grief, for he picked up the hand he held and stroked it gently.

"It was Giles who alerted us to the possibility that Edwina had been found, and in the most fortuitous fashion," Mr Percival said. "There was an evening you all dined here, and Lord Arnwell said something about Edwina, and how Miss Oakes was very like her in manner, and… and it made sense to him. He remembered a conversation about her birthday, and realised then that the Buckleys had the same suspicion, and that she might be a target for them — in marriage, perhaps, for the fortune, but perhaps for some worse fate. When she left Derbyshire, Giles accompanied her in the hope of finding out whether that suspicion was correct. Oswald and I joined him in Southampton while he tried to find out if the Miss Armiger who had raised Miss Oakes was in fact Miss Pickering, the governess. Meanwhile, Oswald and I watched over Edwina," Mr Percival went on, with a smile towards Felicia. How strange to be addressed by such a name! "It was not our intention to frighten you, but we could not be certain of your safety once your identity had been suspected."

"You could have told me who you were," she said mildly.

"We felt the time was not ripe to reveal ourselves. We needed to be sure that you were indeed Edwina, but Finlassan forestalled us by whisking you back here. So here we are, and now you know the truth."

"A fine story," Miss Buckley sneered. "Yet you cannot prove any of it. These impostors will not convince any impartial judge. Why, they could be any street urchins, taught a degree of etiquette and dressed suitably. You have not the slightest proof."

"So you have already said, and you would be quite wrong," Mr Percival said equably. "The Earl of Strathmorran and his entire household will vouch for the identity of Oswald, having known him from the moment of his arrival. His former wet-nurse, Molly, is part of the household to this day, and will testify that the babe she nursed is indeed the Earl of Shotterbourne."

"I can vouch for him, too," the marquess said unexpectedly. "He has his mother's eyes. I have not the least doubt that he is my son."

Mr Percival smiled, but said, "Edwina is more difficult to prove, since Miss Pickering is dead, but fortunately we have her testimony in the journal she wrote, which the curate is translating, and no doubt it will confirm everything."

"There is no doubt in my mind," the marquess said, "and I see that Finlassan also is convinced. What about you, Buckley? Do you acknowledge the truth of it?"

Mr Buckley chewed his lip anxiously. "I do... I do acknowledge it, but there is one point which is not yet clear to me. Mr Percival Warborough spoke of two voices whom he overheard speaking about the fire, yet he did not name them."

"You can guess, I believe," Lord Arnwell said gently. "I see it in your eyes."

Buckley nodded. "Yet it must be spoken aloud, I believe. Mr Warborough must say the names."

"Let me do it for him, for it is all terribly clear to me at last," the marquess said. "The man who set the fire as directed and discovered too late that he had burned the family wing instead of the library — that was your father, Lambert Buckley, a weak man, easily led by a stronger mind, but not evil, I think. The other, who told him where to start the fire with the intention of eliminating my entire family at one stroke — you all know the name, I am sure. Who else knew the house well enough to misdirect Lambert? Who else had a desire to see my branch of the family wiped out in favour of Lambert's? Who else hated me for winning the title and almost bankrupting Lambert? Who else must be kept away from my surviving children at all costs? Who?"

He raised one implacable finger and pointed directly at Edith Buckley.

She laughed weakly. "Such nonsense! As if anyone would believe such a story. It is ridiculous. She is a fraud, and the boy too."

"And you knew," the marquess said in a low voice. "You knew that Oswald and Edwina survived. You found the hidden letter from Percy, and you kept it from me, hoping, no doubt, that grief and despair would see me into my grave. I am very sorry to disappoint you, but it seems that I will outlast you, unless by some miracle you evade the hangman's rope. Percy, Oswald, Finlassan… might I trouble you to secure her? There is a cellar where she may be held until the magistrates can be got here. The courts will settle it."

Miss Buckley jumped to her feet, and the men rose and stepped towards her. "Never!" she shrieked, and turned and ran for the door, the men in pursuit. Wrenching open the heavy door, she disappeared onto the gallery above the hall, with a thunder of booted feet behind her. And then…

A long wailing scream. A series of crashing thumps. Then silence.

Felicia raced out onto the gallery, the marquess just behind her. Fin, Mr Percival and Mr Buckley stood at the top of the marble stairs. At the bottom, a crumpled, motionless heap, her head at an odd angle, lay Miss Buckley.

"No one touched her," Mr Buckley said, his voice high with distress. "She tripped on her gown, I think. She just fell."

From a side door at the furthest end of the gallery emerged a figure in white muslin. Lady Lucia peered over the balustrade at the figure below.

"Edith?" she said, in a high, quavering voice. "Are you all right, Edith, dear?"

She looked across at the group at the top of the stairs, then back to the still, silent body. One embroidered slipper had come to rest halfway down the stairs, an incongruous and chilling sight.

"Edith? Edith?"

The gentlemen took charge of the situation. Felicia found herself being hustled back into the drawing room. Beyond the closed door could be heard the occasional low murmur of voices. Once there was a high, keening wail, soon hushed. After that, silence. Felicia sat down, placed the macaroon plate on her knee and began to eat.

After a while, the door opened, and the marquess entered with Mr Jameson… no, he was the Earl of Shotterbourne, Felicia remembered, Lord Arnwell's son and heir. Oswald. *Her brother!* The two seemed on good terms, the marquess resting one hand on his son's shoulder.

"Well, that is not the ending any of us would have wished," Lord Arnwell said sombrely, "but perhaps it is better so. Edith will still face justice from the One who judges us all, but she escapes earthly justice and we can begin a new life, free from her suppurating evil. I have never liked her, with her sneaking ways, but I never thought she was responsible for the fire. I had never imagined her to be so wicked."

"How is Lady Lucia?" Felicia said.

"She is in the care of her maids, and the physician is sent for. I do not know how she will go on, truly I do not."

His voice was so bleak that Felicia ran to him and wrapped her arms around his waist. "We must all help her."

"Indeed we must, Princess."

She pulled away from him. "You need not call me that any longer, for I have a *name* now. I have a family at last."

"So you have, little one. You are not the *Prinzessin von Nichts,* and I am no longer *il Conte di Niente.* May I call you Edwina?"

She nodded. "And I... I shall call you Papa."

And she buried her face in his chest and wept for joy.

# Epilogue (October)

'Castle Square, Southampton. 9th October. My very dear friend, for so I may always call you, I trust, and I know not how else to address you. Miss Oakes you were to me at first, and then Felicia, and briefly Lady Edwina, and soon you will be Lady Finlassan, and it is fortunate that the last will be of some duration so that I may have time to grow accustomed. I need not add that you will wear your new name with grace, as you have all your previous titles. Your many letters have been avidly read, as you may imagine, and you will excuse my lack of response for you have had all the news and I have had none. But now at last I have something to impart to you of a nature most exciting for me, and such as I know will make you happy, dear friend. You know, of course, that Mr Giles Warborough returned to our sleepy town a little over a week ago, and at first we were all astonished at his speedy return and the alacrity with which he accepted every invitation, no matter how trivial. But no longer! Within three days, his attentions became so marked that even I, scarcely daring to hope, could not be deceived. Yesterday, he spoke to Papa and asked permission to pay his addresses and — we are *engaged! I cannot tell you how happy it makes me to have attached so amiable a man, who is everything I could have wished for in a husband. Papa was concerned that he is so much older than I am, but I do not regard it — he is six and forty, although one would never guess it from his appearance or the vigorous manner in which he engages in the country dances, and he is vastly more interesting than the callow young men who courted me previously. Mama is disappointed, naturally, for she had such hopes of a title for me, but Giles is the son of an earl and therefore an Honourable, and that will be enough for her to boast of. He had some thought of leaving his curate to manage at Church Compton and buying Summer Cottage for us to live in, but Mama has persuaded him that living near Hawkewood Hall and Shotterbourne would suit me much better, and so it would, for then I shall see my very dear friend as often as I wish, and just think how charming that will be. Mama and I will be in London later this month, so we will no doubt see you there. Wish me joy, my best of friends, as I wish for you also. Your deliriously happy friend, Jane Pollard (soon to be Jane Warborough).'*

~~~~~

The curricle bounced down the Shotterbourne drive so rapidly that Felicia was obliged to cling tightly to the rail.

"Is it necessary to travel quite so fast?" she said.

Fin merely laughed. "My dear, when a gentleman acquires a sporting vehicle and a fine set of matched greys, he cannot crawl about like a curate in a gig, looking like a slow-top."

"Better a slow-top than overturned in a ditch," she murmured, but he laughed heartily at her and urged the greys
~~~~~

even faster. He laughed so much these days that she hardly knew him.

Between them, Hercules sat, tongue lolling, his ears blown back, looking as if he were enjoying the ride hugely. He had insisted on following her when she had moved to Shotterbourne, to Lord Arnwell's delight, although what would become of him when she married Fin and returned to Hawkewood she could not guess. Probably he would divide his time between the two houses and be fed twice as often and be thoroughly spoilt.

At the far end of the drive, the new troop of gardeners paused their scything to doff their hats as the curricle bowled past them. Then the greys swept through the open gates and into the village. Felicia waved to the Miss Trimms peering interestedly from the window of their cottage. A few men loitering outside the inn removed their hats, and two maids from Hawkewood curtsied as they drove through the village. Then they turned into the gates of Hawkewood Hall and immediately turned aside onto a narrower road.

"Oh, are we not going to the house?" Felicia said. "I told Juliana and Margarita I would see them today."

"And so you shall," Fin said with a broad grin. Ah, a surprise! How he loved to surprise her, and such moments were a sign of his affection, but if only… No, she must not be churlish and wish for more. He cared about her and exerted himself to please her, and that must be enough. She could not expect him to love her, for his heart belonged to Juliana, she understood that. There was no point in yearning for more from him, or else she might grow bitter and discontented. She would be happy with what she had, as she always had been.

They drove swiftly through the shrubbery, dank and gloomy at this time of the year. Then an open area with a small lake and a neat stone pavilion that she had never seen before. Beyond that was a wild, rock-strewn landscape, untamed by man, before they plunged into a ragged woodland of birches and scrubby saplings, their leaves strewn across the track.

"I have never been in this part of the estate before," Felicia said, wonderingly. How astonishing to own so much land that it would take an hour or more to traverse the perimeter! But Fin just smiled.

After a few minutes, they entered a more solid woodland of oak and beech and elm, their leaves a myriad of autumn colours. Before long, they reached a clearing where a wagon sat, the horses picketed nearby with two grooms in attendance. Fin pulled up the greys, and one of the grooms rushed to hold their heads. Hercules, with a bark, scrambled past Felicia and jumped down, and Fin descended a little more cautiously.

"Down you come," he said to Felicia, holding up his arms to lift her to the ground. His hands at her waist made her blush, and almost she wished that the grooms were elsewhere so that the gesture would seem more intimate and less practical.

There was a smooth, dry path leading away from the carriage drive, and Fin pointed. "This way."

Within moments, they had left the little clearing behind, and the trees closed in around them. Above their heads was a ceiling of reds and golds and oranges and yellows and browns — a thousand tints of autumn. Around their feet were the fallen colours like tiny flags, piled up in great, crackling heaps, still crisp and dry. Hercules snuffled happily and Felicia spun round in delight, her boots kicking up clouds of leaves.

"You always look as if you are dancing," Fin said with a smile.

She twirled lightly through a few steps, arms out. "Autumn inspires me. So beautiful! I must bring my pastels here, although I doubt I could capture the scene. Where are we going?"

"You will see."

Soon the path began to rise, up and up, steeper and steeper, winding back and forth across the hillside. Hercules had galloped on ahead, but Fin progressed more steadily and Felicia tucked her arm in his and walked by his side. Such a simple activity, walking through the autumn woods, but there was so much happiness to be enjoyed in it. Her heart was full of love for her betrothed, and yet she had not the words to express such feelings. And perhaps he would be embarrassed by them, who could say?

Abruptly, they emerged from the trees, although the stumps of those that had once grown there were clear to see. Work on the replanting had begun, however, for there was bare earth where scrub and brambles had been torn up. And there before them was the temple that she had seen so many times from the house. She stared about her, fascinated.

"Did you guess where I was leading you?" Fin said with a smile.

"I had begun to suspect," she said. "How much I wanted to come here, but it was too far for Margarita's legs, and Hercules always wanted to go to Shotterbourne. How beautiful it is!"

The temple was built in the same style as the house, with identical marble pillars, and the same elegant yet restrained decoration, all delicate curves and subtle details. It was larger than Lord Arnwell's Sanctuary, and although not fully enclosed, had sufficient surrounding walls to provide some shelter from the elements. Inside, there were marble benches around the perimeter walls and, incongruously, a giant sculpture of Neptune rising from the waves.

"The First Earl made his fortune in sea trade," Fin said. "He raised this monument in honour of his origins."

"Sea trade? Slavery?"

"Probably, for a great many fortunes were made thus, although the official tale is spices and silks. Ah, I hear voices."

They passed through the temple and down the steps on the far side, and there on the greensward beyond were Juliana and Margarita, twin easels set up side by side as they painted the temple, while their governesses sat primly on folding chairs nearby.

"Miss Farrell, Miss Durward, well met," Fin said genially, as the four all curtsied. "Juliana, Margarita, what have you to show us?"

While Fin discussed art with the girls, Felicia walked forward to the point where the land dropped away. From here, the vista stretched out in all directions — to the wild moors, over the tree-shrouded River Shotter, and almost directly below to the eastern face of Shotterbourne. The Sanctuary was tucked away out of sight behind a lower hill, but much of the formal gardens were visible, their shape at last beginning to emerge from almost twenty years of neglect. It would take a great deal of work to restore them, but the marquess had hope for the future now, and was determined to erase the years of bitterness.

There was one task he had determined upon of a more sorrowful nature. He had finally agreed to let the ruins of the family wing be cleared, and already numerous bones had been uncovered and laid tenderly to rest in the family mausoleum. The original plans of the house had been brought out and an architect engaged, and the destroyed wing would be rebuilt just as it was. The past could never be left behind entirely, but it could perhaps be laid to rest honourably.

After the discussion of the girls' artistry, the party all settled in the temple with a hamper of delights — cold meat, tiny pastries, quails' eggs, and three kinds of cake, with flasks of lemonade for the young ladies and Madeira for the adults. Just when they had all eaten their fill, as if by magic a line of footmen arrived to remove the hamper, easels and chairs, the girls and their governesses set off down the hill to the wagon, and Fin and Felicia were left alone. Fin led her a little way around the hill, where a marble bench looked towards Hawkewood Hall, his home and soon to be hers, too.

"Where is Hercules, do you suppose?" she said.

"He has probably gone over the wall into Shotterbourne. How is everyone there?"

"Very well. Lady Lucia is quite herself again."

"No recurrence of the violent rages?"

"None. It is astonishing that for all these years it was believed that only Miss Buckley had the power to manage her lapses, when in fact it was due to medication. Mostly laudanum, I believe. It was fortunate that her lady's maid discovered the bottles hidden away." She hesitated, then went on, "My own lady's maid arrived yesterday, and it seems I am to be fashionable whether I wish it or not. Or at the very least, suitably attired. Within two hours of her arrival she had trimmed my hair, thrown out half my wardrobe as unfit to be worn and miraculously removed a stain from my velvet pelisse that had been there for four years at least. She is a treasure, I suppose," she added glumly.

He laughed, and said, "Never mind, my dear. If you dislike her, you may send her away any time you like and we shall find you another. When we go to London, Aunts Isabella and Geraldine will take charge of your wardrobe, and you may take their advice without the least fear. Just do not take any advice from Drusilla, for she has abominable taste. She even dislikes the new epergne I gave her."

"But it is so beautiful!" Felicia said. "She will grow to like it in time, I am sure."

"I hope so. She may even grow to like you a little better, one day."

"Now, let us not expect miracles."

That made Fin laugh. "Oh, I almost forgot. There was a letter for you."

Felicia recognised the handwriting at once. "It is from Agnes Markham, to thank me for the lease I had Mr Pierce draw up. They may stay at Boscobel Cottage all their lives now, if they wish. Although I still feel guilty about the business, for the cottage should belong to Lord Arnwell by rights... I mean, to Papa. It was his money, after all. Miss Armiger had no business to use it to buy property in her own name. Do you know, I think Hercules has abandoned us altogether. He prefers Shotterbourne to Hawkewood, I believe."

"What about you?" Fin said. "Do you prefer Shotterbourne, too?"

There was a certain anxiety in his eyes that made her heart beat faster. He cared! "You must know that I prefer Hawkewood," she said breathlessly.

"Because it is more elegant?" he suggested tentatively.

"Because it has *you* in it," she said. "I do not dislike Shotterbourne, and I shall be very happy to stay there until I marry, but Hawkewood is where my heart is."

He smiled then, and curled one arm around her waist. For a hopeful moment, she thought he might be about to kiss her, but instead his head drooped and he said, "I... I want you to know that... I will do everything possible to make you happy, but..."

All her pleasure in the day evaporated. "Fin, have you changed your mind?"

His head shot up. "*No!* Not one iota, but... Felicia, I am *terrified* of making a mull of this. With Juliana, it never occurred to me that we might not be happy together. We were so deep in love, how could it be otherwise? But now I know that she never loved me and it would have been impossible for me to make her happy and—"

"But *I* love you!" Felicia cried. "You cannot fail to make me happy because I love you with all my heart!"

"Do you? Truly?"

"You must know I do."

"But how can anyone love an ill-tempered, selfish imbecile like me?"

"Oh, Fin! What an idiotic man you are! Do you remember that time you painted all night — the stormy painting, remember? — and I crept up on you just as you were finishing the work. I had never seen anyone so absorbed in an endeavour, so intense, so focused that the world ceased to exist. You were only half-dressed, your hair was a tangled mess and there was paint on your cheek. You looked magnificent."

"Oh," he said in astonished tones.

"You were — you *are* — a painter, Fin, a creator of magic in oil and canvas and coloured powder, and I could see the energy pouring out of you to make something that had existed only in your mind before. I adored you from that moment onwards. I tried to fight it, but you are just irresistible to me. When you asked me to marry you, it was impossible to refuse, however unequal the match. I wanted to be with you so badly I could not bear to give you up. I understand that you will always be driven by the urge to paint and will forget everything for a while, even me. But when you have finished, you will remember again that you have a wife and there I shall be, waiting for you, loving you."

"Oh," he said again. "But I hope you will be painting alongside me, dear one. I want us to paint *together*, to inspire each other."

"I hope that too," she said, suddenly shy.

"It was not so instant with me," he said. "I was so *cross* with you at first for disrupting my secluded life and forcing me out into the world again that I did not realise what was happening to me… what you were doing to me. When you were invited to dine at Compton House, I felt compelled to be there also, to protect you from Buckley, or so I told myself. And then there was the day at

Ashbourne… and all the time, although I would not admit it to myself, I was drawn to you."

She was holding her breath, she realised. Would he say the words? Would he?

"It was not until Lord Arnwell pointed it out to me that I understood my own feelings," he went on. "Even then, I thought perhaps he was mistaken, that I was simply overjoyed to meet another painter. All the way down to Southampton, I told myself that all I needed was your friendship. But then, when we stood in the attorney's parlour, I saw it so clearly, that you were — you *are* — indispensable to my happiness, and I had been in love with you for an age without realising it. At that point, I— Felicia? What is it?"

"You said it," she whispered. "That you love me."

"Well, of *course* I do. You must have known that."

"But you never said the words."

"Did I not?" He frowned. "But… why else would I want to marry you?"

"I need to hear you say it!"

"I…" He gulped, took a deep breath, then the words came out in a rush. "I love you. I. Love. You. I love you. Dearest Felicia, I love you with all my heart and soul. I love you with every breath I take, with every beat of my heart, with every drop of blood in my body. I love—"

With a great sob, Felicia drew his face towards her and pressed her lips against his, and for a long, long time there was no sound at all. As soon as they broke apart, he murmured, "I love you, I love you, I love you, I love you." He laughed, and then, with a great howl so loud that even the trees seemed to shiver, he roared, "I LOVE YOU!"

Felicia laughed in delight.


THE END

# Thanks for reading!

If you have enjoyed reading this book, please consider writing a short review on Amazon. You can find out the latest news and sign up for the mailing list at marykingswood.co.uk.

**Family trees**: Hi-res version available at marykingswood.co.uk.

**A note on historical accuracy:** I have endeavoured to stay true to the spirit of Regency times, and have avoided taking too many liberties or imposing modern sensibilities on my characters. The book is not one of historical record, but I've tried to make it reasonably accurate. However, I'm not perfect! If you spot a historical error, I'd very much appreciate knowing about it so that I can correct it and learn from it. Thank you!

**Pastels: painting or drawing?** My heroine, Felicia, paints and draws in many media, but her favourite method is the use of pastels. These are sticks of pure colour, and can be used in outline form, like pencils, or to fill the paper, much like watercolours. Because of the versatility of pastels, there is great debate as to whether it qualifies as drawing or painting. In my research, most exponents of the art that I encountered described it as painting, so that is what I have chosen to do, too, but either is acceptable.

**The great houses:** Mostly the houses I give my characters to live in are generic, or an amalgam of styles from the era. However, in this book I based the houses on real buildings. Shotterbourne, home to the Marquess of Arnwell, is based on Holkham Hall in Norfolk, designed by William Kent. This is still open to the public, and you can find pictures online of the magnificent pillared entrance hall with its staircase and galleried landing. Hawkewood Hall, home to the Earl of Finlassan, is based on Suton Park House, London, designed by Robert Adam (which may not still exist).

***Isn't that what's-his-name?*** Regular readers will know that characters from previous books occasionally pop up. None actually appear in this one, but there are mentions of Sir James and Lady Godney, from *The Widow*, and the Narfields, from *The Apothecary*. There is also a mention of one who dates right back to *The Daughters of Allamont Hall.* The Earl of Strathmorran lives in Scotland, at Glenbrindle Castle in the mythical county of Morranshire. His heir, Lord Kilbraith, a cousin to the Allamont sisters, made a romantic appearance in *Dulcie*, and turned up again in *Lord Humphrey.* Congratulations to anyone who spotted this reference.

**About the Silver Linings Mysteries series:** John Milton coined the phrase *'silver lining'* in *Comus: A Mask Presented at Ludlow Castle*, 1634

> *Was I deceived, or did a sable cloud*
>
> *Turn forth her silver lining on the night?*
>
> *I did not err; there does a sable cloud*
>
> *Turn forth her silver lining on the night,*
>
> *And casts a gleam over this tufted grove.*

Ever since then, the term *'silver lining'* has become synonymous with the unexpected benefits arising from disaster. The sinking of the *Brig Minerva* results in many deaths, but for others, the future is suddenly brighter. But it's not always easy to leave the past behind...

**Book 0: The Clerk:** the sinking of the *Minerva* offers a young man a new life *(a novella, free to mailing list subscribers)*.

**Book 1: The Widow:** the wife of the *Minerva's* captain is free from his cruelty, but can she learn to trust again?

**Book 2: The Lacemaker:** three sisters inherit a country cottage, but the locals are surprisingly interested in them.

**Book 3: The Apothecary:** a long-forgotten suitor returns, now a rich man, but is he all he seems?

**Book 4: The Painter:** two children are left to the care of a reclusive man.

**Book 5: The Orphan:** a wilful heiress is determined to choose a notorious rake as her guardian.

**Book 6: The Duke:** the heir to the dukedom is reluctant to step into his dead brother's shoes and accept his arranged marriage.

Any questions about the series? Email me at mary@marykingswood.co.uk I'd love to hear from you!

# *About the author*

I write traditional Regency romances under the pen name Mary Kingswood, and epic fantasy as Pauline M Ross. I live in the beautiful Highlands of Scotland with my husband. I like chocolate, whisky, my Kindle, massed pipe bands, long leisurely lunches, chocolate, going places in my campervan, eating pizza in Italy, summer nights that never get dark, wood fires in winter, chocolate, the view from the study window looking out over the Moray Firth and the Black Isle to the mountains beyond. And chocolate. I dislike driving on motorways, cooking, shopping, hospitals.

# Acknowledgements

Thanks go to:

All those fine people in Albany, Australia who restored the *Brig Amity* and gave me the germ of an idea.

Allison Lane, whose course on English Architecture inspired me.

Shayne Rutherford of Darkmoon Graphics for the cover design.

My beta readers: Barbara Daniels Dena, Amy DeWitt, Megan Jacobson, Melanie Savage, Quilting Danielle, Rosemary Paton, the readers of Rachel Daven Skinner at Romance Refined

Last, but definitely not least, my first reader: Amy Ross.

# Sneak preview of The Orphan: Chapter 1: In Want Of A Guardian (March)

Miss Evelina Parfitt smoothed the soft kid of her gloves, and settled herself on the carved wooden bench in the hall to wait. The carriage was ordered for half an hour before noon, but it would not arrive until ten minutes after that time. Violet would arrive no earlier than ten minutes later. There would be a further delay as she changed her bonnet twice. When the horses had been walked twice down to Berkeley Square and back, and the clock had struck the hour, Violet would be ready to depart. Perhaps.

Green, the butler, and Mrs Bowdler, the housekeeper, hovered anxiously. They knew better than most the price to be paid if the young mistress should find some fault with their management of the household. Heaven forfend that she should deign to be ready and the carriage not waiting for her outside the door.

Evie was of more robust constitution, even though her employment prospects were just as subject to the whims of Miss Violet Barantine. She had been engaged to impart the polished manners of the *beau monde* to the daughter of a jewel merchant, and escort her into those fringes of society which would accept her. Despite the large salary, complete with a generous dress allowance, she would be rather relieved if her young charge should take a pet and dispense with her services, for there was little pleasure to be had as companion and chaperon to a flighty girl like Violet. At eighteen years of age, with a mother long dead and an over-indulgent father, Violet had been for so long the sun around whom the household revolved that she knew no other way.

The carriage arrived, waited, departed. Violet appeared at the top of the stairs waving two bonnets.

"Evie? The chip straw or the velvet? What do you think?"

"When you asked me at breakfast, I suggested the silk as being the most appropriate, and I see no reason to change my opinion."

"But black silk is so lowering, Evie. It makes me look so sallow and ill."

"Black is a depressing colour, it is true, but you would not wish to appear disrespectful of your papa, not so soon after his death. The chip straw is a little too frivolous for town wear, dear, and the velvet makes you look far older than your years, whereas the silk bonnet is perfectly styled to enhance the shape of your face."

"So it is! I look very well in it, do I not? Mrs Carrington said so too, and she knows about such matters, for her bonnets are worn by all the most fashionable ladies of the *ton*. The silk, then."

She whisked away to her room, and the hall lapsed into silence. The carriage returned, waited again, departed. Green checked his pocket watch for the fourteenth time. Mrs Bowdler paced. Evie sat motionless, hands resting in her lap. The carriage returned, waited. Violet appeared at the top of the stairs.

"Evie? I am not sure about this pelisse. What do you think?"

Evie rose to her feet. "We have an appointment, Violet, and it would be very bad form to keep the gentlemen waiting. You may go and change if you wish, and I will see Mr Camberwell and Mr Baxter on your behalf."

She walked steadily towards the door, but Violet flew down the stairs and reached it before her. "Just button my gloves, will you?"

"You have two lady's maids for the purpose, Violet, who would be most offended if I should usurp such a task from them."

Miss Lidderdale and Miss Coleman had followed their mistress down the stairs, albeit at a more decorous pace. After a politely worded dispute as to which of them should have the honour of buttoning the gloves, they settled on one apiece, so that Violet was soon perfectly attired to venture forth. With a final adjustment of the curls artfully framing her face, a last tug at the sleeves of the expertly constructed pelisse, and the lace veil set in place, the two maids stepped back, satisfied. Green sprang forward to open the door and Violet passed through without a glance.

As she followed her charge, Evie murmured, "Thank you, Green."

"Oh yes, thank you, Green," Violet said, turning to him with her most entrancing smile.

"My privilege to serve so charming a mistress," Green murmured.

She dimpled even more. Henry, her personal footman, held open the carriage door. She entered it, Evie followed, Henry jumped up behind and they rolled off, almost exactly on the hour. Evie breathed a sigh of relief. Another effort to cajole Violet into rational behaviour successfully accomplished, and without undue delay. A good morning's work.

"Will young Mr Baxter be there today?" Violet said plaintively. Tedious business meetings were lightened considerably for her by the presence of a personable young man to admire her. They all *did* admire her, naturally. Even in mourning, with her father barely a month dead, Miss Violet Barantine was a sight to gladden the heart of any man, and Violet was young enough to enjoy her fledgling power over gentlemen.

"I cannot say," Evie said. "I know only of Mr Camberwell and Mr Baxter, your trustees."

"Will there be ratafia cakes? Last time there were ratafia cakes."

"Too many cakes are ruinous for a lady's complexion," Evie said.

"But I might have just one? That would not be ruinous, would it?"

Evie conceded that a single cake might not be sufficient to destroy Violet's looks entirely.

But when they were shown into the sumptuously appointed office of Mr Camberwell, attorney at law, they found themselves facing a larger group than expected. Mr Baxter, Violet's financial adviser and a joint trustee of her fortune with Mr Camberwell, was well known to them, and the eager face of the young Mr Baxter was there too. But who were the other two gentlemen?

"Miss Parfitt, Miss Barantine, allow me to present to you another colleague from the legal profession, Mr Willerton-Forbes, and this is Captain Edgerton, formerly of the East India Company."

Mr Willerton-Forbes was a dapper man, too fashionable for a lawyer. Captain Edgerton was a more flamboyant dresser, who took one look at Violet and immediately executed a flourishing bow, before stepping forward to hold a seat for her. She responded in her usual manner, with a tinkling laugh, a slight blush and a smile in acknowledgement of his admiration. It was very cleverly done, Evie could not deny, and must be convincingly innocent in those who did not know Violet well.

"There is good news, Miss Barantine," Mr Camberwell said, beaming at her with as much paternal fervour as if she were his own daughter. "I shall leave Mr Willerton-Forbes to tell you of it."

The lawyer cleared his throat. "Indeed, indeed! Good news of a most unexpected nature, Miss Barantine. The tragedy of the sinking of the *Brig Minerva* off the Cornish coast, which has so painfully deprived you of your sole remaining parent, has attracted sympathy from many people. One of them has been greatly affected by the great loss of life, and has set aside a sum of money — a rather large sum of money — to compensate all those who survived the disaster, and the next of kin of those who were so unfortunately lost to the world."

Violet blinked at him.

"The sum allotted," Mr Willerton-Forbes said, "is one thousand pounds to each person so affected, to be dispensed in whatever manner is most convenient."

"Is that not good news, Miss Barantine?" Mr Camberwell said. "Is it not splendid news? Not such as to recompense you for the sad loss of your dear father, but is it not a splendid gesture by this unknown person?"

"A thousand pounds? That is not very much. I am worth a hundred thousand pounds," Violet said robustly. "At least!"

"Oh, true, it is but a drop in the ocean," Mr Camberwell said hastily. "But still, an extra thousand pounds will be—"

"What about my guardian?" Violet said. "When you read Papa's will to me, it said that Mr Newbold was to be my guardian, but he drowned too. So what is to happen now? Am I not to have a guardian?"

"You must have a guardian, Miss Barantine. There must be someone set over you to determine where you live and — should you wish to marry — to give approval, for otherwise you would have to wait until you are of age, you know."

"Oh no, I intend to be married long before then. What a shocking thing to be still unmarried at one and twenty."

Evie smiled, well aware that she herself was regarded as an old maid by her young charge, and therefore much to be pitied, being still unmarried at the advanced age of nine and twenty.

Captain Edgerton put in smoothly, "I am sure that will not be your fate, Miss Barantine."

Violet dimpled at him, with the delicate blush and lowered eyes with which she received every compliment. "Mr Camberwell, you could be my guardian, could you not? Or Mr Baxter?"

"That would not be wise, Miss Barantine. We are the trustees of your fortune, and it is frowned upon rather for the guardianship of your fortune and your person to reside in the same gentleman."

"Then what is to be done? What happens when the lease of the house ends? Must I move? Evie tells me that my guardian would determine such matters, but if I have no guardian—"

Mr Camberwell and Mr Baxter exchanged glances. "You need not worry about that, Miss Barantine," Mr Camberwell said soothingly. "Everything will be arranged, in time, and you may leave everything to us."

"But who will it be? I should not like to be in the hands of someone I dislike, or some dreadfully stuffy person. How will he be chosen? May I have no say in it?" Violet pouted prettily. "That does not seem fair!"

"Such matters are not for young ladies to determine. Since you have no living relations, a guardian will be appointed for you by the Court of Chancery. Naturally, Mr Baxter and I, as your trustees, will make a recommendation, but the court will decide what is best for you."

Mr Willerton-Forbes coughed. "If I may elaborate a little, for the benefit of Miss Barantine, gentlemen?" Mr Camberwell nodded, unable to refuse such an eminent lawyer, although he was clearly not happy about it. "In law, as you are above the age of fourteen, you may choose a guardian for yourself. The court may not agree with you, but generally if a respectable and suitable person should apply to the court to be appointed as your guardian, there will not be any dissent."

Violet's face lit up. "I may choose for myself?"

"In law, you may."

"Then I choose Mr Eliot Armitage."

There was a stunned silence. Evie could not think of a less suitable guardian for a flighty girl of eighteen, but she trusted the gentlemen to scotch the idea. However, her faith in them was misplaced.

"I do not know the gentleman," Mr Baxter said plaintively. "Is he a previously unknown relation, Miss Barantine?"

"No, but is that important? Respectable and suitable, *that* gentleman said, and Mr Armitage is certainly that, is he not, Evie? Why, we met him at Lady Frampton's, who is of the first stare of fashion, so he must be so."

"And that is the only occasion upon which we have met him," Evie said crisply. "He is a single man of some fortune, I was told, who is invited everywhere, but as to whether he is a suitable person to be your guardian, it is difficult to say."

Certainly difficult to say with Violet in the room, but Evie was almost thirty and need not be protected from the realities of masculine life. When she had enquired of the other chaperons about Mr Armitage, they had whispered words that needed no explanation. Lady Frampton herself had added bracingly, "He is rich enough not to prey on heiresses, so you need not be concerned for your charge's fortune. Only for her heart. Eliot is..." She sighed nostalgically. "...quite devastating to female sensibilities. You should permit him one set of dances, no more."

And so Evie had, and Violet had made no demur, but ever since that evening she had talked of nothing but Mr Armitage, and at every evening engagement she had wondered hopefully if he would be there, before her father's death had brought such outings to a halt temporarily. He was not the first charming young man for whom she had developed a *tendre*, and Evie had hoped that this infatuation would go the way of the rest and be rapidly replaced by a new interest, but if he were to become her guardian, who knew how it would end?

"Shall I make some enquiries around the clubs?" Captain Edgerton said. "See what is known about him… his… erm, family circumstances, that sort of thing?"

"That would be most helpful," Mr Camberwell said with obvious relief. "Mr Baxter and I… it is more difficult…"

"Of course, of course! Two gentlemen of your standing in society asking about a man wholly unknown to you would attract some most unwelcome comment, whereas I have some acquaintances of whom the most discreet enquiries may be made. This is just the sort of delicate little undertaking I enjoy."

"That is settled, then," Evie said briskly, rather hoping that Violet's fancy would have shifted before the idea could come to fruition. "Have you made any progress in locating the title to the late Mr Barantine's business, Mr Camberwell?"

"Not as yet, Miss Parfitt, but we are optimistic. Our splendid Royal Navy is currently engaged in retrieving everything that may be retrieved from the wreck of the *Brig Minerva*, and once Mr Barantine's… ah, *effects* are returned to us, we hope to find the title amongst them."

"He carried the title to his business on his person?" Mr Willerton-Forbes said. "That is rather singular."

"Indeed, but Mr Barantine had little faith in the conventional means of security for documents, such as safes," Mr Camberwell said. "He liked to carry all his most important documents with him at all times, in a specially constructed waterproof container."

"What about my diamonds?" Violet said. "Papa was bringing home a fortune in diamonds, and I was to have the largest of them. He promised me."

"They will be found amongst his effects, I make no doubt," Mr Camberwell said. "As soon as everything arrives from Cornwall, you may choose your diamond, Miss Barantine."

Violet smiled, satisfied.

~~~~~

Several days after this meeting, Evie was in the study at Bruton Street writing to her aunt, when Green informed her that Mr Willerton-Forbes and Captain Edgerton wished to speak with her. She laid aside her pen, and stood to receive the two gentlemen.

"How very kind in you to see us at such short notice," Mr Willerton-Forbes said. "Miss Barantine is not at home today?"

"She is busy upstairs with fittings for some additions to her wardrobe," Evie said with a smile. "If, as I suspect, you wish to talk to me about Mr Armitage, then that is a matter best accomplished without Violet's presence, I feel."

"Indeed it is," Mr Willerton-Forbes said. "Captain Edgerton has been pursuing his enquiries with some success. Captain?"
~~~~~

"Miss Parfitt, you said that Mr Armitage is a single man of fortune who is invited everywhere, and I have heard nothing to contradict that. He is thirty years old, he lives in Grosvenor Square and there is an estate in Essex, where his parents still live. His father is very elderly now and never leaves the house. He has four sisters, all older than he is and all very well married, one to a baron, and one to a baronet. All perfectly respectable and sober."

"But?" Evie said with a smile. "I feel sure that you are about to reveal a flaw."

Captain Edgerton rubbed his chin thoughtfully. "Mr Armitage is a gentleman who holds the female sex in great admiration, Miss Parfitt."

"You mean that he is a libertine?" she said. Mr Willerton-Forbes started, and the captain began to protest, but Evie laughed. "Gentlemen, I am not some green girl fresh from the schoolroom. I am nine and twenty years old, and know something of the world. Mr Armitage is a known rake, and I was warned to keep Violet protected against his wiles, as best I could. He is hardly a suitable person to have guardianship of a girl of eighteen."

"As to that, the court would perhaps see only a man of fortune from a respectable family," Mr Willerton-Forbes said cautiously. "He is of an age to be a responsible guardian. No, the question is whether he would accept such a charge. He is a man who... hmm, likes to enjoy himself, let us say. It is by no means certain that he would wish to undertake such a responsibility."

"It might hinder his pursuit of pleasure, you mean?" Evie said, amused. "Indeed. He sounds like a frivolous sort of man, although when I met him, he appeared to be the model of propriety."

"In public, I believe it is so," Captain Edgerton said. "However, my informants tell me that his house at Grosvenor Square is the scene of parties of a certain type. Of interest to young gentlemen, if you understand me, Miss Parfitt."

"Will you speak plainly, Captain? I should not like to put Violet into the hands of a man who regularly drinks to excess, or who might introduce her into unsavoury society. That would be very dangerous."

"I have heard nothing of that nature. His bachelor parties are very discreet, the gentlemen drawn from the cream of society — the sons of the best families in England. He keeps that side of his life entirely separate from his other activities. He is, as you have already been advised, invited everywhere. Almack's, Carlton House, all the most notable occasions of the season. Miss Barantine could hardly have chosen better, for as her guardian, Mr Armitage will be able to introduce her into a most superior level of society."

Evie chewed her lip thoughtfully. "Even so…"

"Miss Parfitt," Mr Willerton-Forbes said, "May I enquire as to the reason Miss Barantine wishes Mr Armitage to become her guardian?"

"Oh, she wishes to marry him, of course. She is besotted with him at this moment. Next month, there will be someone else, and the month after that… but at present, he is the object of her marital ambitions, and I should not wish the poor man to be forced into marriage against his will. Violet is… quite ruthless in her pursuits, I regret to say."

"Then guardianship would offer him the greatest protection," Mr Willerton-Forbes said, eyes twinkling. "For a guardian to marry his underage ward would be most improper, and the courts would take a dim view of the matter, too. However, this may all be moot, for the very idea may horrify him. Shall I suggest that Mr Camberwell to make an approach to the gentleman?"

"Yes, please do," Evie said. "The sooner the matter is settled one way or the other, the better."

But a few days later, Mr Camberwell visited with surprising news. Mr Armitage would be delighted and honoured to become Miss Barantine's guardian.

The other news was less welcome. Violet's father's remains had been returned to London for burial, together with his personal effects recovered from the *Brig Minerva*. Neither the title documents for his business, nor the hoard of diamonds, were amongst them.

END OF SAMPLE CHAPTER of *The Orphan*

For more information or to buy, go to marykingswood.co.uk.

Made in the USA
Coppell, TX
04 May 2020

24003074R00233